MATERNAL

BODY *and* VOICE

in TONI MORRISON,

BOBBIE ANN MASON,

and LEE SMITH

Maternal Body and Voice

in Toni Morrison,
Bobbie Ann Mason,
and Lee Smith

Paula Gallant Eckard

UNIVERSITY OF MISSOURI PRESS
COLUMBIA AND LONDON

Library of Congress Cataloging-in-Publication Data

Eckard, Paula Gallant.
    Maternal body and voice in Toni Morrison, Bobbie Ann Mason, and Lee
Smith / Paula Gallant Eckard.
        p.   cm.
    Includes bibliographical references and index.
    ISBN 0-8262-1402-9 (alk. paper)
    1. American fiction—Women authors—History and criticism.
2. Mothers in literature.   3. Women and literature—United States—
History—20th century.   4. American fiction—20th century—History and
criticism.   5. Smith, Lee, 1944—Characters—Mothers.   6. Mason, Bobbie
Ann—Characters—Mothers.   7. Morrison, Toni—Characters—Mothers.
8. Mother and child in literature.   9. Body, Human, in literature.
10. Motherhood in literature.   11. Voice in literature.   I. Title.

PS374.M547 E29   2002
813′.54093520431—dc21

                                                                    2002024562

⊗™ This paper meets the requirements of the
American National Standard for Permanence of Paper
for Printed Library Materials, Z39.48, 1984.

Designer: Stephanie Foley
Typesetter: The Composing Room of Michigan, Inc.
Printer and binder: The Maple-Vail Book Manufacturing Group
Typeface: Goudy

To my children, from whom I have learned so much

And to my granddaughter, Julianna Grace,
from whom I hope to learn even more

CONTENTS

This study of maternal experience in selected novels by Toni Morrison, Bobbie Ann Mason, and Lee Smith has been a lifetime in the making. Multiple experiences, both personal and professional, have led to this study. Spanning many years of my life, they have shaped my attitudes towards childbearing and motherhood in profound, often contradictory ways.

For the most part, I grew up associating maternity with blood, anger, and silence. My mother was pregnant several times during my childhood and adolescence, but she rarely spoke of the pregnancies, childbirths, or the many miscarriages she had. Expressing little emotion, she said few words about the losses she endured. I nonetheless sensed within her a raw mixture of grief and anger. One experience more than any other reveals the disturbing elements I came to associate with motherhood. Late one night when I was about fifteen, I got out of bed to check on my pregnant mother, who had been cramping and bleeding hours before, only to find her missing and my aunt on her knees washing bloody sheets in the bathtub. Standing in the doorway, I asked what happened, but my aunt gave me no response. She continued her work and I watched as a ring of blood formed on the white enamel walls of the tub, the water deepening in color. Her silence confused and angered me, but thankfully I was old enough to discern what had taken place. As I crept back to bed, I figured out that my mother had been taken to the hospital to be treated for yet another miscarriage. But, given the copious amount of blood I had seen, I was not sure if she would be all right this time. A few days later, my mother returned home pale and silent. I searched her face for the sorrow I knew had to be there, but I could not locate any. Her tense, contracted body resonated with fury instead. Without any words spoken, I knew that she was angry with herself, my father, and a world that expected pain and sacrifice from women. I felt guilty for being one of the children that had lived.

The images and emotions of that night have stayed with me through the years. My mother's wasted blood still pulses through my thoughts, my life, and perhaps my writing as well. I experience wrenching dreams of childbirth in which I sometimes give birth to a beautiful, perfect daughter. But always, with overwhelming sadness, I realize she is not mine, and I have to give her back. In other dreams, I rock grotesque babies, born without eyes, mouths, or even bodies, as they sleep in cradles of blood. Despite the nightmarish nature of these reminders, the silences surrounding my mother's losses have disturbed me more. Like the lost children, these silences have created voids that contain greater anguish than my dreams. Throughout my life, I have struggled with these empty spaces, seeking ways to understand them, to fill them, to eradicate them.

For quite different reasons, I associate the maternal experiences of my grandmothers with silence as well. Although my grandmothers bore twenty children, five girls and five boys each, their maternal stories have eluded me. My paternal grandmother died before I was three; my maternal grandmother lived three thousand miles away in Canada and I rarely saw her. I know, however, that both grandmothers gave voice to their thoughts, feelings, and experiences through writing. My father's mother, Anna Lee Pennigar Gallant, wrote poetry; my mother's mother, Hulda Elizabeth Wicklund Humbke, maintained a diary almost daily throughout her life. As a child, my maternal grandmother emigrated from Sweden with her family in the late 1800s to settle in western Canada. Marrying at sixteen, she and my German grandfather carved out a long life together on the wild, expansive prairies of Alberta, surviving blizzards, exhausting farmwork, and other hardships that our modern sensibilities cannot comprehend. When my grandmother died twenty-five years ago at the age of eighty-seven, she left behind over 130 direct descendants—children, grandchildren, great-grandchildren, and great-great-grandchildren.

I regret never hearing my grandmothers' stories for myself. What little I know about them has come to me second- and thirdhand from other family members. Sometimes, in my imaginings, I try to visualize their lives and experiences as mothers. I strain to hear their voices, misplaced somewhere in memory. However, if I listen carefully in dreams or during quiet moments of the day, I can recall my Grandmother Gallant's slurred speech as she fussed over me from her wheelchair, cruelly confined by a paralyzing stroke and a leg amputation. Or, when I talk to my mother on the telephone, I can hear traces of my Grandma Humbke's warm Swedish laughter in her voice, reaching through time and space much as it did when I was young. Before modern telecommunication and inexpensive long distance, my mother and I would call my grandmother in Canada every few months, three female voices traveling back and forth along the thousands of miles of wire between us to be briefly linked together. Later, my younger sisters, Candice and Diana, joined in these conversations, but their voices drowned out the sound of my grandmother's voice, pushing it farther away and eventually into memory.

While personal associations involving the maternal body and voice have fueled this literary study, more recent professional experiences have contributed to its development. Before I began teaching English and pursuing graduate work in that area, I spent many years working as a registered nurse and certified childbirth educator, careers that no doubt stem from the experiences described earlier. In these capacities, I came into an intense, firsthand understanding of maternal experience. I taught more than a thousand expectant mothers and attended many births, including those experienced by my sisters, close friends, and the women in my classes. During this time, I gave birth to three children and lost another child through miscarriage. Each of these experiences left me with an increased knowledge of the maternal body, a renewed sense of awe concerning the power it contains, and a sharper awareness of the challenges imposed by pregnancy, childbirth, and motherhood. I also acquired a richer understanding of the diverse nature of women's experiences and the many complex factors affecting maternity. I observed the importance that family, culture, economics, and personal attitudes assume in shaping women's experiences of their bodies and their maternal roles. I saw the damage that fear and ignorance wreaked and the difference that support and education could make. No two women, I discovered, go through pregnancy, childbirth, breast-feeding, and motherhood in quite the same ways. Each woman effectively creates her own "herstory," a maternal history and set of stories that are uniquely hers.

Perhaps it is their concern for "herstory" that draws me most to the works of Toni Morrison, Bobbie Ann Mason, and Lee Smith and has led me to include them in this study. These writers powerfully foreground maternal experience in their novels and give serious, focused attention to the body and voice of the mother. They create female characters of different ages, cultural backgrounds, and life situations, thus depicting an unusual variety of maternal experiences. Morrison, Mason, and Smith also portray the impact of patriarchal history and thought on the mother's body and voice. They show that while silence is often imposed upon the maternal, a rich consciousness nonetheless exists within many of the mothers they create. Moreover, all three writers pull together elements of realism, metaphor, language, and culture that give voice and complex meaning to motherhood. For these reasons, their novels help me to understand maternal experience in ways my previous experiences did not allow. These writers not only remove the silences surrounding the maternal in a literary sense, but also speak with truth about the experiences of many women, including my own. Their works have prompted me to reexamine my own experiences of pregnancy, childbirth, and motherhood. I have realized that, unlike my mother, I suffered little fear, pain, or loss of blood during the births of my three sons. Even the miscarriage I had was a simple, uncomplicated event. Overall, my experiences in childbearing have proven to be quite different from my mother's. Hers contained enough blood and pain for the both of us.

To conclude my discussion of the foundation for this study, I wish to describe a recent incident that revealed much to me about maternity and the development of the female voice. A year or so ago, my mother gave me a small black notebook in which she had recorded the events of my first year of life. She detailed every new food, new tooth, and new accomplishment. She described every rash and fever. She wrote about all the friends and gushing relatives who came to visit me. Strangely, she did not write about these things from her perspective, but from mine. She discarded her own voice and imagined her daughter's instead. She gave me words when language was still beyond my grasp, empowering me to speak. I hope this study will prove that her efforts were not in vain and that I have successfully given voice to the mother's experience in return.

ACKNOWLEDGMENTS

I would like to extend my sincere appreciation to Dr. Mary Ann Wimsatt and Dr. Julian Mason for their guidance, support, and encouragement. Their exemplary scholarship and dedication to southern literary studies have inspired me while their friendships have sustained me. To Wilma Asrael and Barbara Huberman, modern pioneers in childbirth education and women's healthcare, I owe an equal thanks for starting me on what has been a long and satisfying study of motherhood.

I offer my gratitude also to director and editor-in-chief Beverly Jarrett, managing editor Jane Lago, and editor Gary Kass, all of the University of Missouri Press, for their enthusiasm and expertise in getting this manuscript published. I appreciate their patience and persistence more than they likely know.

A loving thanks to Kirby Maram and Greg, David, Justin, and William Eckard for their help and unfailing confidence. Finally, I wish to acknowledge the very special mothers in my family, my mother Dorothy Humbke Gallant, my sisters Candice Gallant Cooper and Diana Gallant Carter, and my daughter-in-law Whitney Eckard, whose lives and stories have enriched mine beyond measure.

I gratefully acknowledge the permissions granted to me by the editors of the following journals that published earlier and different versions of my material.

Chapter 4 contains material published in "Maternal Mythologies and Southern Literature: An Essay in Honor of Julian Mason," *Postscript* 10 (1993): 25–34.

Chapter 8 contains material published in "The Prismatic Past in *Oral History* and *Mama Day*," MELUS 20:3 (1995): 121–35.

Chapter 9 contains material published in "*Fair and Tender Ladies*: The Taste of Literature," *Pembroke Magazine* 33 (2001): 98–106.

Thanks also to friend, former colleague, and outstanding fiction writer Nanci Kincaid for allowing me to include her comments from interviews, lectures, and readings she has given.

ABBREVIATIONS

I have adopted the following abbreviations to identify the literary works quoted from in this study:

Toni Morrison

BEL   *Beloved*
BLU   *The Bluest Eye*
SUL   *Sula*

Bobbie Ann Mason

CS   *Clear Springs*
FC   *Feather Crowns*
IC   *In Country*
SHI   *Shiloh and Other Stories*
SL   *Spence + Lila*

Lee Smith

FTL   *Fair and Tender Ladies*
OH   *Oral History*
SG   *Saving Grace*

MATERNAL
BODY *and* VOICE
in TONI MORRISON,
BOBBIE ANN MASON,
and LEE SMITH

Introduction

"Mothers don't write, they are written." As these words suggest, motherhood and maternal experience have been largely defined and "written" by other forces. Religion, art, medicine, psychoanalysis, and other bastions of patriarchal power have objectified the maternal and disregarded female subjectivity. Indeed, throughout the history of western culture and literature, maternal perspectives have been ignored and the mother's voice silenced. Even early feminist theorists sorely neglected maternal subjectivity, for, as Maureen Reddy points out, "feminism was largely a daughter's critique," which viewed mothers and motherhood with suspicion.[1]

Generally speaking, maternal subjectivity—the presentation of pregnancy, childbirth, and the experience of motherhood from the mother's perspective—has not been well represented in written culture. Reddy and Brenda Daly assert that "in women's accounts of motherhood, maternal perspectives are strangely absent," with daughters' voices being the ones usually heard "in both literary and theoretical texts about mothers, mothering, and motherhood, even in those written by feminists who are mothers." Moreover, they remind us that childbirth has often been depicted in fiction "as metaphor, not as narrated experience" told by the mother.[2] This has led to a further de-

1. Susan Rubin Suleiman, "Writing and Motherhood," 356; Maureen Reddy, "Motherhood, Knowledge, and Power," 81.
2. Brenda Daly and Maureen Reddy, introduction to *Narrating Mothers: Theorizing Maternal Subjectivities*, 1, 4.

valuing of maternal experience and has diminished maternal subjectivity within the culture.

In recent literary and theoretical texts, however, more substantial attention has been given to motherhood and to the physical, psychological, social, and cultural dynamics affecting the maternal experience. Important late-twentieth-century writers of fiction such as Toni Morrison, Bobbie Ann Mason, and Lee Smith scrutinize these dynamics closely, emphasizing particularly how they affect the body and the voice of the mother. By employing such a focus, these writers lessen the objectification the maternal has received and restore a rich subjectivity that foregrounds the mother's perspective and experience. Moreover, their fiction reflects a deep concern for history and culture and a woman's experience of these forces. They challenge the traditional representations of black and white motherhood that have appeared in southern literature and society and instead render complex portrayals of motherhood that defy cultural stereotypes.

In this study I will examine how maternal experience and the body and voice of the mother are depicted in selected works by these writers: Morrison's *The Bluest Eye* (1970), *Sula* (1973), and *Beloved* (1987); Mason's *In Country* (1985), *Spence + Lila* (1988), and *Feather Crowns* (1993); and Smith's *Oral History* (1983), *Fair and Tender Ladies* (1988), and *Saving Grace* (1995). Female experiences in these works, which are highly individualized, take place in different cultural and geographic settings. Although their experiences of life and motherhood may differ significantly, African American and white southern women have an intertwined historical legacy and share a common ground in the transforming experience of maternity. The novels of Morrison, Mason, and Smith reflect this shared history and experience, as well as ambivalent connections to the South. Even when the novels move outside the South, as in Morrison's case, the region continues to exert a strong influence in the creation of the maternal. Time, place, and motherhood come together in compelling ways, seriously affecting the body and voice of the mother in the process.

The extraordinary sense of place that all three writers create in their works no doubt stems from the personal connections each has to a specific geographic region. Born in 1931, Toni Morrison grew up in Lorain, Ohio, leaving there at age seventeen to attend Howard University in Washington, D.C. Although she claims never to have "felt like an

American or an Ohioan or even a Lorainite," she nonetheless evokes a strong sense of place in her novels, one that is suggestive of the small-town life she experienced while growing up. The Ohio communities that Morrison depicts in such novels as *The Bluest Eye*, *Sula*, and *Beloved* have autobiographical origins that contribute substantially to "the details, the feeling, the mood" of the places she creates in her fiction. She admits to a tendency to focus on neighborhoods and communities, which in her own life provided "life-giving, very, very strong sustenance."

According to Morrison, black neighborhoods emphasized cohesiveness and responsibility. She describes how they took care of people in need and generally "meddled in your lives a lot." The Ohio towns and communities she portrays in her fiction assume these functions; however, they are significant for other reasons, primarily their proximity to the South. Morrison points out that Ohio is "an interesting state from the point of view of black people": it borders the southern state of Kentucky, and "at its northern tip is Canada."[3] Certainly, the South and its slaveholding past cast troubling shadows over the lives of Morrison's characters in the fictional Ohio towns she creates. As her novels show, geography and history impose terrific burdens that span multiple generations. For many of Morrison's characters, particularly mothers, the weight is crushing.

Born in 1940, Bobbie Ann Mason hails from western Kentucky, whose small towns and rural landscapes provide the settings for her short stories and novels. Rather than examining the South's troubled past, she explores the cultural changes at work in the contemporary South of the late twentieth century. The Kentucky towns and farms in her novels are in a state of flux, dramatically altered by the rise of suburban neighborhoods, shopping malls, and fast-food restaurants. Virginia Smith sees Mason's use of her home region in her fiction "as a metaphor for profound shifts in the contemporary social terrain and for a transient American culture."[4] Unlike Morrison's characters, who must bear the burdens of the past, Mason's have difficulty contending with the present. They experience tumultuous changes in their person-

3. Quoted in Robert Stepto, "Intimate Things in Place: A Conversation with Toni Morrison," 10–12.

4. Virginia Smith, "Between the Lines: Contemporary Southern Women Writers Gail Godwin, Bobbie Ann Mason, Lisa Alther, and Lee Smith," 134.

al lives—dysfunctional families, divorce, unemployment, illness—as their once-rural society gives way to mass culture. In many instances, the traditional moorings of family and community are lost, while the past seems irrelevant and largely unknown.

For Mason's female characters, these changes strike at the core of their identity as wives and mothers. Some are left perplexed and confused, unsure how to respond to the changes imposed upon them. Others adapt and survive. Whatever the case, Mason believes that her characters communicate "the familiarity of common experience" and that "their language grows out of cohesive culture."[5] Despite the personal upheavals endured by her characters and the social and economic changes affecting their communities, Mason's fiction suggests that an inherent cultural stability exists. Paradoxically, this furnishes a foundation for her characters, enabling them to adapt to change and new cultural elements more easily than one might suppose.

Like Morrison and Mason, Lee Smith draws upon her roots to create a sense of place in her fiction and to undergird the lives and experiences of her characters. Born in 1944, Smith grew up in the mountains of western Virginia in the mining town of Grundy. The Appalachian region provides the setting for several of her novels, including *Oral History*, *Fair and Tender Ladies*, and *Saving Grace*. Harriet Buchanan observes that Smith, like Mason, writes about "people, times, and places with warmth, humor, and ironic detachment."[6] At the same time, Smith is deeply concerned with cultural change and its effect on individuals and communities. Her female characters, immersed in mountain traditions and culture, find themselves in confrontation with harsh Appalachian realities that make survival difficult at best. Change is often thrust upon them, leaving them with divided loyalties, a pervasive restlessness, an ambivalence towards the past, and a discomfort with the present.

Patriarchal expectations also define the existence of Smith's mountain women. Burdened by responsibility and guilt, they live out hard lives taking care of others, often subjugating their own needs, desires, and ambitions in the process. Smith herself sees such roles and expec-

---

5. Quoted in Dorothy Combs Hill, "An Interview with Bobbie Ann Mason," 105.
6. Harriet Buchanan, "Lee Smith: The Storyteller's Voice," 324.

tations as "very limiting and very rigid." She declares: "Guilt is the great disease of Southern women. Just free-floating guilt that will attach to anything."[7] The expectations imposed by patriarchal culture and the guilt internalized by her female characters form complex layers of oppression that silence the maternal and limit self-actualization for women.

Given the cultural concerns inherent in the novels of Morrison, Mason, and Smith and the importance each writer places on time and place in defining female experience, an examination of historical perspectives affecting both black and white mothers is crucial. Elizabeth Fox-Genovese, Jacqueline Jones, Deborah White, Sally McMillen, Judith Leavitt, and others provide the historical and cultural grounding of motherhood vital to this study. Their investigations into social, medical, and historical areas demonstrate how deeply interwoven motherhood is with the cultural fabric of the United States. The work of these scholars moreover reveals the crushing impact of patriarchal thought on the lives of both black and white mothers in the Old South. Their research validates and illuminates the realities of maternal experience depicted in the novels discussed here.

Certain theoretical perspectives are equally imperative in discussing motherhood in the works of Morrison, Mason, and Smith. I will use both a cultural model of feminist criticism and a "maternalist" approach to examine maternal experience and the body and voice of the mother in the novels selected for this study. According to feminist theorist Elaine Showalter, a cultural model of feminist criticism "incorporates ideas about woman's body, language, and psyche, but interprets them in relation to the social contexts in which they occur." As Showalter makes clear, a woman's conceptualization of her body and reproductive function is "intricately linked" to the cultural environment. Moreover, a feminist theory of culture acknowledges differences among women as writers and insists that factors of race, class, history, and nationality are as important literary determinants as gender. Showalter asserts that women's culture forms a collective experience within the cultural whole "that binds women writers to each other over time and space."[8] Her

7. Quoted in Dannye Romine Powell, *Parting the Curtains: Interviews with Southern Writers*, 294.
8. Elaine Showalter, "Feminist Criticism in the Wilderness," 27.

ideas about the unifying effects of women's experiences hold special import for this study.

Similarly, Sara Ruddick, in her essay "Maternal Thinking," stresses the intersections and divergences in women's experiences of motherhood. Recognizing that such factors as class, ethnicity, and geographical and historical settings affect maternity, she states: "Maternal practice responds to the historical reality of a biological child in a particular social world." Ruddick acknowledges that some aspects of mothering are "invariant and nearly unchangeable," while others, "though changeable, are nearly universal."[9] Morrison, Mason, and Smith illustrate the very realities that Ruddick describes. Their novels show significant divergences in the construction of motherhood and maternal experience—divergences that are profoundly shaped by differences in race, class, culture, and geographic region. However, enough intersections exist that I can "bind" these writers together to show how maternity serves as a vital substructure in their works and thus contributes to a collective female literary experience.

The "maternalist" approach that I wish to include is a mode of feminist criticism that, according to Naomi Schor, is "concerned with identifying the productions of the female imagination, charting female psychosexual development, psychoanalyzing feminine desire, making once again audible a muffled or silenced maternal voice."[10] In order to examine these areas in the novels of Morrison, Mason, and Smith, I will use certain facets of the linguistic and psychoanalytic theories of Julia Kristeva, Hélène Cixous, and Luce Irigaray as they pertain to the maternal body and language. Specifically, Kristeva's ideas concerning the fluidity of "women's time"; maternal sexual pleasure or *jouissance* of the female body; and the importance of the womblike semiotic chora, the prelinguistic realm underlying symbolic discourse, aptly pertain to the fiction of all three writers. Similarly, Cixous's and Irigaray's emphasis on the female morphology of language and the primacy of the mother in the development and use of language has considerable relevance in my study. The theories of Kristeva, Cixous, and Irigaray richly illuminate the connections that Morrison, Mason, and Smith make among lan-

---

9. Sara Ruddick, "Maternal Thinking," 214–15.
10. Naomi Schor, "Feminist and Gender Studies," 270.

guage, creativity, and the maternal body in their fiction. Moreover, the concern that Kristeva, Cixous, and Irigaray express about the impact of a masculine, paternal order of culture on female identity is explored in the fictional works chosen for this study. Indeed, Morrison, Mason, and Smith share a common concern about the impact of patriarchal culture on the body and voice of the mother, something their novels powerfully reflect.

I believe it will also be helpful to incorporate the ideas of other feminist theorists into the examination of individual novels. For example, the writings of Barbara Christian and Karla F. C. Holloway, particularly their discussions of the mythic and spiritual dimensions contained in the works of black women writers, have considerable bearing on Morrison's novels and may have applicability to the works of Mason and Smith—both white writers—as well. The thoughts of Tillie Olsen and Elaine Orr on the demanding realities of women's lives and the impact of sex roles on women's creativity and expression help illuminate the lives of some of the fictional mothers studied here. In another example, the theories of Adrienne Rich and Jane Gallop on the vital connections between the female body and the development of feminine thought will prove useful in examining Mason's *Spence + Lila*. Similarly, Sandra Gilbert and Susan Gubar's discussion of women, madness, and writing in their important work *The Madwoman in the Attic* has implications for Ivy Rowe in Smith's *Fair and Tender Ladies* regarding her sexual maturation and the development of her writerly voice. Ideas posited by feminist theologians Carol Ochs and Mary Daly about the impact of patriarchal religion on female identity will enhance my study of Smith's *Saving Grace*, a novel that creates disturbing connections between maternal experience and Christianity. Annis Pratt's discussion of female spiritual quests in *Archetypal Patterns in Women's Fiction* further illuminates the spiritual journey that Smith's protagonist takes in *Saving Grace* to resolve conflicts between the matriarchal and patriarchal elements undergirding her life.

I wish to reiterate that my primary objective is to examine closely how Morrison, Mason, and Smith portray maternal experience and depict the body and voice of the mother in selected novels. I will, however, address the cross-cultural connections that exist among their works. Despite racial and cultural differences, striking similarities can

be found in the renderings of the maternal in the fiction of these writers. While all three closely examine the myths and realities of motherhood and the impact of these on the maternal body and voice, their
works reflect other commonalities as well. For example, Morrison's
Beloved and Mason's *Feather Crowns,* both of which are historically
grounded, emphasize the commodification of motherhood and the female body. Additionally, in both *Beloved* and Mason's *Spence + Lila,*
the female breast and breast-feeding serve as powerful symbols of maternal experience. Smith, like Morrison, blends realism and magic to
construct events, settings, and elements of the maternal. Both inter-
twine ghostly presences and other phenomena with the maternal experiences of their characters. And, like Mason, Smith is concerned
with the rapidly changing southern landscape in the modern world and
the impact of cultural change on women's lives and their experiences
of motherhood.

Given my thematic focus, I think it is important to also acknowledge that Morrison, Mason, and Smith effectively engage in a kind of
"maternal thinking," or what Ruddick terms "the *thought* that has developed from mothering." Ruddick describes the basis of this thinking
as something that extends quite beyond the maternal passions of the
heart and envelops instead "the intellectual capacities [the mother] develops, the judgments she makes, the metaphysical attitudes she assumes, the values she affirms." It is an intellectual engagement that involves "a unity of reflection, judgment, and emotion."[11] Morrison,
Mason, and Smith achieve this kind of unity in their portrayal of maternity and the mother's experience. In so doing, they correct the neglect and ambivalence that has been associated with the subject of maternity in literature. In their novels, they conduct honest, intense, and
direct assessments of the maternal experience, something that many
women writers have avoided or failed to do. This is no minor accomplishment, as the difficulty in rendering the mother's experience is
complex and daunting.

According to Marianne Hirsch, the difficulty associated with the depiction of maternal experience in women's literature is rooted in four
major areas. First, since motherhood is largely a patriarchal construc-

11. Ruddick, "Maternal Thinking," 213–14.

tion, women identify their mothers with victimization and martyrdom. Second, feminist writings, which place a high value on women's control of their bodies and lives, reflect a discomfort with the vulnerability and lack of control associated with motherhood. In feminist views, maternity often forces a state of dependency on women—a dependency on the medical establishment, on men who "are involved in the production and rearing of children," on society and other women, and "on the children themselves." The creative image of giving birth to oneself pervades feminist writing, but Hirsch questions what happens to "actual" mothers and children when "women figuratively become their own 'mothers.'" She argues that it is easier to exclude the rendering of maternal consciousness and experience because so much of it is beyond reason and control. A third reason Hirsch advances for the neglect of maternal experience in literature is the pervasive fear and discomfort with the female body that both feminist and nonfeminist women experience. Hirsch notes that most areas of feminist analysis have resisted using biology to address female experience, but, as she ironically observes, "Nothing entangles women more firmly in their bodies than pregnancy, birth, lactation, miscarriage, or the inability to conceive."

Lastly, in Hirsch's estimation, feminist ambivalence about power, authority, and anger cause a separation between feminist and maternal discourse. Much feminist theoretical writing in the United States "is permeated with fears of maternal power and with anger at maternal powerlessness." To eradicate these fears and projections, Hirsch calls for feminist theorists to begin "listening to the stories that mothers have to tell, and . . . creating the space in which mothers might articulate those stories."[12] Certainly Morrison, Mason, and Smith have created that space within their texts. In doing so, these writers have done much to confront the discomfort and fear connected with maternity. They challenge patriarchal structures and attitudes and establish a discourse in which the mother's body, language, and experiences are fundamental. In depicting maternal experience, each writer also honors the integrity of individual experiences and the cultures from which they emanate.

12. Marianne Hirsch, *The Mother/Daughter Plot: Narrative, Psychoanalysis, Feminism,* 165–67.

Morrison, Mason, and Smith reveal that the maternal is a powerful force that shapes human lives and communities and is a critical determinant in the development of female voice and identity. By centering maternal experience so strongly in their novels, these writers establish the primacy of the mother and obviate the neglect to which motherhood and the maternal perspective have been subjected.

1

~

Historical and Theoretical Perspectives on Motherhood

Throughout human history, motherhood has been fraught with contradictions, confusing dualities, and power struggles. Patriarchal constructions of women have fueled the development of conflicting ideas about mothers and maternal experience. The body and voice of the mother have suffered particular oppression. In *Of Woman Born*, feminist writer Adrienne Rich explains how on one hand the female body has been seen as "impure, corrupt, the site of discharges, bleedings, dangerous to masculinity, a source of moral and physical contamination; 'the devil's gateway.'" At the same time, the woman as mother is deemed "beneficent, sacred, pure, asexual, nourishing." Indeed, the female body is "a field of contradictions," a space that Rich considers to be "invested with both power, and an acute vulnerability." She contends that the female body "is the terrain on which patriarchy is erected" and that motherhood is "'sacred' so long as its offspring are 'legitimate'—that is, as long as the child bears the name of a father who legally controls the mother."[1]

Rich's observations have particular relevance for the study of southern motherhood and for the fictional works of Toni Morrison, Bobbie Ann Mason, and Lee Smith considered in this study. Rich's description of the patriarchal construction of women in *Of Woman Born* is also an apt description of the patriarchal structures that undergirded the Old South and that contributed significantly to the suffering and anguish experienced by black and white southern mothers of the era. Childbearing

1. Adrienne Rich, *Of Woman Born*, 13, 73, 31, 20.

11

was a critical event in the lives of many of these women. Their experiences had considerable impact on shaping the attitudes, beliefs, and practices that affect maternal roles today. Unquestionably, the realities of antebellum motherhood figure significantly in the cultural psyche of the South. They help to explain why maternity functions as such a powerful force in the fiction of Morrison, Mason, and Smith. All three writers infuse the maternal experiences of their characters with compelling realities that are deeply rooted in time and place. Despite their racial differences, their works reveal the enormous impact that southern history and culture have had on women's lives. With the exception of Morrison's *Beloved* and Mason's *Feather Crowns*, the fictional works discussed in this study are largely grounded in the twentieth century. However, given the tremendous impact of the past within all of the texts, a historical examination of nineteenth-century southern motherhood is necessary in order to fully understand each writer's treatment of motherhood and the importance ascribed to the maternal body and voice.

Historically speaking, both black and white women were very much "written" by the patriarchal forces of the Old South. Their lives and roles were clearly defined for them in the plantation system, and it was in the realm of sexuality and motherhood that the patriarchy delivered the most oppression. Women's bodies were the terrain upon which the southern patriarchy was erected. Black and white women endured repeated childbearing expressly for the benefit and support of the patriarchy. Their progeny renewed white southern families on one hand and the system of slavery on the other. Slavery, as Elizabeth Fox-Genovese has noted, shaped the experiences of all women in the Old South, affecting the domestic and childbearing roles of both black and white women. The relationship between mistress and slave was often a complex and strained one. Fox-Genovese asserts that, despite the "shared experience of life in rural households under the domination of men," black and white southern women were "deeply divided" by race and class. Ironically, though their lives intersected intimately and daily within the plantation household, no genuine sisterhood resulted. They were bound together primarily "by their specific and different relations" to the household's master.[2]

2. Elizabeth Fox-Genovese, *Within the Plantation Household: Black and White Women of the Old South,* 38, 43, 101.

In her literary study of black and white women of the Old South, Minrose Gwin observes that white women, "fictional or actual, writers or subjects," failed to recognize the humanity of their black counterparts, seeing them only "as a color, as servants, as children, as adjuncts, as sexual competition, as dark sides of their own sexual selves—as black Other." White women resented the forced sexuality of black women, who were "to be used as vessels of sexual pleasure or to breed new property." Gwin believes that the virgin–whore dichotomy imposed on white and black women greatly affected their images of themselves and of each other. In particular, white southern women internalized the prevailing attitudes about themselves as women on pedestals, "emblem[s] of chastity and powerlessness," and proceeded to function as "faithful standard-bearers of the patriarchy and its racial constructs."[3]

In her nineteenth-century diary depicting antebellum life and politics, Mary Boykin Chesnut, a noted antebellum author, links sexuality, slavery, and the southern patriarchy. Her observations support Gwin's theory that white southern women reinforced the racial and gender attitudes of their fathers and husbands. Disturbed by the frequent sexual relationships between white men and female slaves and by white women's passive complicity in the matter, Chesnut laments: "God forgive us, but ours is a *monstrous* system. . . . Like the patriarchs of old our men live all in one house with their wives and their concubines, and the mulattoes one sees in every family exactly resemble the white children—and every lady tells you who is the father of all the mulatto children in everybody's household, but those in her own she seems to think drop from the clouds, or pretends so to think."[4] Chesnut's words illustrate the self-serving attitude of denial that permeated southern thought about the complicated familial relationships that emerged under slavery. Moreover, her writing reveals the peculiar and strained relationship that resulted between black and white women because of the sexual proclivities of the southern patriarchy.

Despite the divisiveness that existed between black and white women of the Old South, they nonetheless shared some common ground in their experience of motherhood. In *Motherhood in the Old South*, a

---

3. Minrose Gwin, *Black and White Women of the Old South: The Peculiar Sisterhood in American Literature*, 4–5.

4. Mary Boykin Chesnut, *Mary Chesnut's Civil War*, 29.

historical study of antebellum motherhood, Sally McMillen shows how the rituals of childbirth "united black and white women, dissolving for a moment racial barriers."[5] This is evident in Morrison's *Beloved* when Amy Denver, a white indentured servant, assists the slave Sethe in childbirth when their paths intersect during their respective flights to freedom. Similarly, Mittens Dowdy, a black mother with a nursing baby of her own, serves as a wet nurse to help Christie Wheeler feed her newborn quintuplets in Mason's *Feather Crowns*. In both novels, racial barriers are removed as black and white women work together in the cooperative experience of childbearing and infant feeding.

Citing numerous antebellum letters and diaries by white southern women of privileged status, McMillen provides an effective argument against Gwin's assertion that white women did not recognize the humanity of their black counterparts. McMillen's study indicates that some white southern mothers felt a clear appreciation for the black midwives who assisted them in childbirth. They were also grateful to the black wet nurses who fed their infants when they were unable to breastfeed due to illness or an inadequate milk supply.[6] McMillen's study reaffirms the common ground between black and white women. She points out that, although their stations in life and their individual experiences differed greatly, black and white women shared many of the same dangers and threats to their lives as well as the potential loss of children. Fear, anguish, and powerlessness pervaded the maternal experience for many mothers. Motherhood was a central and compelling experience in the lives of both black and white women of the South, one that was profoundly shaped by the patriarchy in which they lived.

The antebellum patriarchy wielded a great deal of power over women's lives. Its construction of motherhood further enmeshed maternity into the fabric of southern culture. As McMillen makes clear, the Old South prided itself on well-defined gender roles, with white southern men of privileged class holding "the upper hand in both the public and the domestic spheres." Such patriarchal structure "was essential to maintaining order in a rural, slave-owning society." Southern men glorified the maternal role and believed that childbearing and childrear-

5. Sally McMillen, *Motherhood in the Old South: Pregnancy, Childbirth, and Infant Rearing,* 57.
6. See McMillen, *Motherhood in the Old South,* 70–72, 111–12, and 124–29, for a discussion of the role of slave women as midwives and wet nurses.

ing were central to a woman's existence. Motherhood was deemed a "sacred occupation," one that the South celebrated and exalted. Women embraced these beliefs as strongly as their husbands did, often treating childless women with scorn and pity. Chesnut, herself childless, describes in her diary how she came to the defense of a woman without children. She tells a group of reproachful women that Mrs. Browne "was childless now, but that she had lost three children." Having elicited the women's sympathy for Mrs. Browne, Chesnut shrewdly observes, "Women have such a contempt for a childless wife." Later in her diary, however, Chesnut more wistfully comments, "Women need maternity to bring out their best and true loveliness." She condemns the scorn directed at childless women and at the same time acknowledges how important maternity is to female identity, an importance vigorously reinforced by the southern patriarchy.[7]

Nineteenth-century white southern families were larger than the national norm, since there were few social or economic constraints to limit fertility. Nationally, family size fell from 7.04 children per woman of childbearing age in 1800 to 5.4 in 1850, but southern families remained large throughout much of the period, with eight to twelve children not unusual. Pregnancy rates were actually higher than official statistics indicated, since census figures did not reflect miscarriages, stillbirths, or early infant deaths. The figures also did not account for the fact that some women did not marry or bear children. One explanation for the large size of southern families may lie in the fact that privileged white southern women often married relatively young, thus increasing their childbearing years and possibly their number of pregnancies. Moreover, a large family was considered a reflection of the husband's masculinity, as well as "the vigor of the patriarchy, the importance of the southern family, and the prosperity of the region."[8]

For whatever reasons, antebellum southern women experienced frequent childbearing. Women often were either pregnant or nursing a baby every year of their marriage until their mid-forties, and devoted "thirty or more years" to the bearing and raising of children. Such fecundity prompted one southern physician of the period to conclude that "all women should be considered pregnant until proved other-

7. Ibid., 35, 24; Chesnut, *Civil War*, 28, 105.
8. McMillen, *Motherhood in the Old South*, 32, 33.

wise." With the repeated occurrence of pregnancy and childbirth, motherhood in the Old South came at a great price. It seriously compromised the health and well-being of many women. Pregnancy was often complicated by exhaustion, as well as by assorted physical ailments and communicable diseases. Pregnant women were "particularly vulnerable" to malaria, and while it was not usually fatal to adults, attacks of the disease were often severe, leaving sufferers weakened and susceptible to other infections. Childbirth itself brought a great risk of death and permanent, debilitating injuries. Indeed, pregnancy was often viewed as a state in which women had nine months to get ready to die.[9]

Maternal deaths in childbirth were all too common in the South; they were "well acknowledged in cemeteries, newspapers, census figures, and letters." According to McMillen, "one out of twenty-five white women in the South who died in 1850 died in childbirth." Southern women were twice as likely to die because of childbirth than northern women. McMillen points out the numerous reasons for this discrepancy. The South was more unhealthy, as malaria, dysentery, and other fevers were endemic to the region. Moreover, the mild winters of the South were less likely to kill organisms that carried disease. Also, since nineteenth-century southern women bore more children than their northern counterparts, their lives were put in jeopardy more frequently. McMillen further suggests that, although most southern doctors trained in the North, they approached childbirth with a "continuing commitment . . . to heroics." In other words, they may have been more likely than northern doctors to intervene during childbirth with drastic procedures that were intended to "save" both mother and child but instead subjected them to increased danger.[10]

Even experienced women approached childbirth with fear. For example, southern mother Mary Ann Gwynn, who had borne several children already, wrote in 1843, "This business of having children is an awful thing." Judith Leavitt points out that if a woman did not die from such problems as hemorrhage, infection, toxemia, or convulsions, she was often left with a prolapsed uterus or with tears in the vaginal or rectal walls that made sexual intercourse painful and resulted in a contin-

9. Ibid., 3, 32, 30, 49.
10. Ibid., 84, 81.

uous leakage of urine or feces. As a result, a woman could be rendered a permanent invalid isolated from almost all social contact.[11]

Besides risking death or injury in childbirth, women also suffered the frequent loss of children at birth, during infancy, or in early childhood. In 1850, more than 38 percent of all deaths in the United States involved children under the age of five; by 1860 that figure had increased to 43 percent. Children succumbed to such diseases as cholera, pneumonia, whooping cough, croup, tuberculosis, dysentery, measles, and scarlet fever. Southern mothers spent an inordinate amount of time nursing sick children, particularly children suffering from diarrhea and dysentery. Despite their efforts, death was a frequent visitor, rendering motherhood a sorrowful experience. Given these statistics, one can easily understand Christie Wheeler's grave concern for her infants in *Feather Crowns*. Another southern mother, Mary Henderson, makes clear the reality of her maternal losses in an 1855 diary entry: "In four years I have known little else but the most heartrendering affliction, having buried four bright, lovely, beautiful children."[12]

Despite the deadly risks associated with childbearing and constant threats to their children's health, antebellum women appeared to accept their domestic roles. McMillen reminds us that southern women were "raised to align themselves with male perceptions" and that childbearing "brought tangible rewards in a society that offered few alternatives." Their letters and diaries reflect the great time, energy, and concern they gave their children and families. For the most part, southern women did not appear to openly question or challenge their roles within a patriarchal household and society: "[A]part from complaining in letters or describing their loneliness and sorrow in journals," they were fairly silent about their lots in life. McMillen expresses doubt that southern women "were content with their situation," but also believes that women were so indoctrinated to accept male views and superiority that they could not defy patriarchal expectations. To have done so would have seriously "torn the social fabric," or, more precisely: "If women became independent, might not slaves seek some of the same freedoms? It was far easier to control all levels of southern society than

11. Mary Ann Gwynn quoted, ibid., 56; Judith Leavitt, *Brought to Bed: Childbearing in America 1750–1950*, 29.

12. McMillen, *Motherhood in the Old South*, 167, 143; Mary Henderson quoted, ibid., 167.

to allow selective liberties. Most southern women had been properly brought up to accept their position and to veil their protests. They generally accepted their rigidly defined role and devoted their time and energy to maternal and domestic duties, making the best of their hardships."[13]

For slave women, the experience of motherhood was qualitatively worse than that experienced by white women of privileged status. Although they suffered from similar physical ailments and diseases and often lacked adequate medical care as well, slave mothers' experience of maternity proved to be more wrenching. Their sexuality and their ability to bear children rendered them particularly vulnerable within the system of slavery. In her famous autobiography, *Incidents in the Life of a Slave Girl*, Harriet Jacobs makes the sexual vulnerability of slave women poignantly clear. Relentlessly pursued by her master, Jacobs must maintain constant vigilance to repel his advances. She envies the protection given white women, stating, "But, O, ye happy women, whose purity has been sheltered from childhood, who have been free to choose the objects of your affection, whose homes are protected by law, do not judge the poor desolate slave girl too severely!"[14] Most female slaves did not enjoy such privileges or protection. They were routinely forced to endure the sexual advances of white males of the plantation or were paired with male slaves to increase the master's holdings by bearing children who could be worked on the plantation or sold for profit. In any event, female slaves could claim neither their bodies nor their children as their own.

In the system of slavery, according to Jacqueline Jones, motherhood had great economic significance, as "each new birth represented a financial gain for the slaveholder." Ironically, these births were also important in preserving the integrity of the slave family because young women who demonstrated their fecundity early were less likely to be sold. Deborah White tells us that mothers and small children were sometimes sold as a family unit, which helped preserve some continuity within slave families. Social activist Angela Davis confirms that the slave woman had both a biological and social destiny related to motherhood: "As her biological destiny, the woman bore the fruits of pro-

13. Ibid., 6, 182, 183.
14. Harriet Jacobs, *Incidents in the Life of a Slave Girl*, 54.

creation; as her social destiny, she cooked, sewed, washed, cleaned house, raised the children." Paradoxically, however, Davis sees the "drudgery" of this domestic labor as "survival-oriented activities" and thus "a form of resistance." It helped female slaves achieve some autonomy for themselves and their men. Moreover, domestic labor thrust the black woman "into the center of the slave community," making her "essential to the *survival* of the community."[15]

Deborah White's investigations into the lives of female slaves provide further evidence that motherhood was an integral component in their existence, identity, and economic value. While male slavery centered around work, much of female slavery was connected with "bearing, nourishing, and rearing children whom slaveholders needed for the continual replenishment of their labor force." Often forced into procreative sexual relations, slave women began childbearing at approximately 20 years of age and had children every 2.5 years until the age of 35. According to White, slave owners often accorded special treatment to pregnant and nursing mothers, as well as to women who were "exceptionally prolific." Such mothers would be given less demanding work and were classified as "half hands" or "three-quarter hands." Jones reports, however, that many pregnant slaves were overworked, something that slave owners failed to connect with the high miscarriage and infant mortality rates. In 1850, the infant mortality rate was twice as high for slave women as for white women. Fewer than two out of three children born to slave mothers survived to the age of ten.[16]

Diets "dangerously low" in protein and other nutrients and diseases such as pneumonia, cholera, smallpox, and diarrhea also compromised the health of slave women. The vitamin-deficiency diseases of scurvy, rickets, pellagra, and beriberi (due to daily meals of rice, fatback, cornmeal, and salt pork) were not uncommon among the slave population. Although slave women were "slightly less likely" than white women to die from complications in pregnancy and childbirth, they also suffered from premature labor, breech presentations, convulsions, puerperal

15. Jacqueline Jones, *Labor of Love, Labor of Sorrow: Black Women, Work, and the Family from Slavery to the Present*, 35; Deborah White, "Female Slaves: Sex Roles and Status in the Antebellum Plantation South," 67; Angela Davis, "Reflections on the Black Woman's Role in the Community of Slaves," 7.

16. Deborah White, *Ar'n't I a Woman?*, 69; White, "Female Slaves," 60, 67; Jacqueline Jones, *Labor of Love*, 35.

fever, placental retention, ectopic pregnancy, and prolapsed uterus—
conditions that seriously threatened their health and the lives of their
infants.[17]

Despite the many difficulties and indignities surrounding maternity,
motherhood in the slave community held much significance because it
brought status to women. According to White, motherhood was considered far more important than marriage in terms of a young woman's
identity and her coming of age. Much mystery surrounded conception
and childbirth, and the mother-child bond was regarded as the most important and sacred relationship within a slave family. Prenuptial intercourse was not deemed "evil," nor were out-of-wedlock births con-
demned.[18]

The ascendancy of motherhood over marriage perhaps lay in the fact
that slave marriages were fragile institutions. They were not recognized
as legal, and any vows spoken were not binding. In slave marriage cer-
emonies, preachers changed the vows to "Until death or distance do you
part." Having children bought some security for a married couple, but
if her husband was sold off, a female slave was expected to begin an im-
mediate "search for another spouse with whom to have more children
for her owner."[19]

Reasons for the supremacy of the mother-child dyad can also be
traced to the African heritage of the slaves. In West Africa, according
to White, having children was traditionally "the most important responsibility of each individual," and often a marriage was not thought
to be consummated until after the birth of the first child. Since mothers
and children lived together in huts separate from men, "the mother-
child relationship usually had more depth and emotional content than
either the father-child or husband-wife relationship." White also emphasizes that in many West African tribes, "the mother-child relationship is and always has been the most important of all human relationships."[20]

Other scholars have noted the reverence that motherhood has been
accorded in African societies. In discussing women's novels of the

17. White, *Ar'n't I a Woman?* 83.
18. White, "Female Slaves," 68; White, *Ar'n't I a Woman?* 106.
19. Geoffrey Ward, Ric Burns, and Ken Burns, *The Civil War: An Illustrated History*,
9; White, *Ar'n't I a Woman?* 103.
20. White, *Ar'n't I a Woman?* 107; White, "Female Slaves," 69.

African diaspora, Abena Busia describes the centrality of the mother in matrilineal societies: "[She] is the key to the political, spiritual, and even economic foundations of the society—a fact which has implications beyond the individual or even the family, and extends itself to the cohesion and survival of the group." In patrilineal societies, Busia further notes, women are still able to "retain a strong degree of autonomy" because of the respect given to motherhood and "female/fertility gods."[21]

Obododimma Oha also emphasizes the importance of the mother in African societies: "The idealization of the mother figure is psychologically and culturally ingrained, permeating literature and music at all levels." Oha describes how the Nigerian writer Flora Nwapa celebrates food and the female labor connected with it in maternal terms. In Nwapa's poetry, collected in *Cassava Song and Rice Song* (1986), the lowly cassava, a starchy food staple cultivated by Igbo women that can be processed into many forms, is personified as the "Great Mother Cassava." Nwapa elevates the status of the women who toil and the cassava plant itself, which Igbo men deem inferior to their yam crop. She praises the mother-cassava for the enduring sustenance it has provided, giving it a revered maternal identity and establishing a powerful mother-earth connection. The centrality of the Great Mother Cassava in Nwapa's poetry reflects the African view noted by Barbara Christian that "every woman is a symbol of the marvelous creativity of the earth." The mother, in turn, serves as "the symbol of Africa itself." Not surprisingly, should an African woman prove barren, her childlessness is seen as a terrible misfortune. She is viewed as "an incomplete woman."[22]

The veneration of the African mother evolved along different lines as slavery developed. Christian points out that "the sanctification" of the slave mother occurred through the stereotype of the mammy, who was "mythologized in America as the perfect worker/mother, content in her caring, diligent in her protection of her master's house and

---

21. Abena Busia, "Words Whispered over Voids: A Context for Black Women's Rebellious Voices in the Novel of the African Diaspora," 9.

22. Obododimma Oha, "Culture and Gender Semantics in Flora Nwapa's Poetry," 113, 108; Barbara Christian, *Black Feminist Criticism: Perspectives on Black Women Writers*, 5, 218, 216. "The symbol of Africa itself" is Christian's paraphrase of a point made by Wilfred Cartey in *Whispers from a Continent* (New York: Vintage Books, 1969), 3.

children against any who might injure them, whose descendent is the 'perfect domestic.'" In reality, the slave woman's mothering activities assumed "tremendous importance" in protecting her *own* children's physical and spiritual well-being. Christian points out that slave narratives, historical accounts, and folklore reaffirm the critical role that mothers "played, through sacrifice, will, and wisdom, to ensure the survival of their children," who in turn became symbols of hope and freedom. American slavery, however, subverted black motherhood and "revealed one of its most significant elements—that women are valued not for themselves, but for the capacity to breed, that is, to 'produce' workers, and for their ability to nurture them until they are equipped to become 'producers' for the society." Or, as Harriet Jacobs expressed it in her narrative: "Women are considered of no value, unless they continually increase their owner's stock. They are put on a par with animals."[23]

While historians have collected considerable information about the external lives of female slaves, less is known about the actual feelings of slave mothers. Deborah White asserts that "they left few narratives, diaries, or letters," thus making it difficult to draw conclusions about their emotions.[24] The extant writings of white southern women, however, provide much information about their feelings about motherhood and family. Although the wives, daughters, sisters, and mothers of white plantation owners lived constrained lives within the southern patriarchy and did little to protest their subjugation, they were still able to write and record their thoughts, emotions, and life experiences. The hopes, fears, joys, and sorrows expressed through the writings of white southern mothers stand in contrast with the silences surrounding the experiences of slave women, whose feelings remain largely unknown. Only through narratives such as Jacobs's, which makes clear the special and poignant burdens of female slavery, or through the reconstruction of the maternal experience in such novels as *Beloved*, is the maternal subjectivity of slave mothers realized.

Although slave narratives such as Jacobs's and the diaries and letters of white southern women convey much about the experience of motherhood in antebellum times, the maternal subjectivity contained within these documents is limited regarding pregnancy and childbirth.

23. Christian, *Black Feminist Criticism*, 220, 219; Jacobs, *Life of a Slave Girl*, 49.
24. White, "Female Slaves," 59.

McMillen points out that nineteenth-century southern women rarely described their confinements in their letters or diaries. She attributes this silence about childbirth to a desire to forget the experience and to "move ahead to the joys and demands of caring for the newborn." Some mothers were "too ill or exhausted" to write following childbirth or found writing about the experience "embarrassing to feminine sensibilities." McMillen also realistically acknowledges that "maternal responsibilities left mothers little time or energy for writing." Or, as southern mother Ella Clanton Thomas makes clear in her 1858 diary, "housekeeping and married life are not compatible with keeping journals."[25] Marriage, motherhood, domestic responsibilities, and cultural attitudes about the female body all worked to diminish the maternal voice.

In general, maternal subjectivity, which presents the experiences of pregnancy, childbirth, breast-feeding, and motherhood from the mother's perspective, has not had a visible place in the history of written culture. In *Women Writing Childbirth*, Tess Cosslett describes how childbirth, perhaps the most pivotal event in the maternal experience, "has long been marginalized as a subject for public representation." Prior to the twentieth century, childbirth rarely appeared in fiction, and if it did, it was presented from an audience's point of view. Readers were given the perspective of the father, the doctor, or others in attendance, but never the mother's. Moreover, male critics responded with "distaste," finding childbirth scenes repugnant. Thus, for the most part, accounts of childbirth were found only in women's private writings or in anonymous letters to magazines. The pain and grave risks associated with nineteenth-century childbirth, however, made it a difficult subject for women to write about. In regard to southern mothers, McMillen indicates that the few accounts of childbirth that were detailed in letters, diaries, and doctor's records provide compelling evidence "of the sorrowful and painful aspects of the experience."[26]

Although more accounts of pregnancy and childbirth, both fictional and nonfictional, have emerged in the twentieth century, maternal subjectivity has still been marginalized. Cosslett asserts that in literature of the past few decades mothers are often objectified, depicted as

25. McMillen, *Motherhood in the Old South*, 80, including the quotation from Ella Clanton Thomas.
26. Tess Cosslett, *Women Writing Childbirth: Modern Discourses of Motherhood*, 1; McMillen, *Motherhood in the Old South*, 80.

"machines for producing babies." She notes that birth has evolved into a highly technologized event, with official discourses, such as medical discourse and the discourse of natural childbirth, being used to define the mother's experience. Similarly, feminist writer Alice Adams believes women's experiences of their bodies are "*mediated* by their interactions with institutions and discourses." Female experiences such as menstruation, pregnancy, childbirth, and menopause are "filtered through a screen of social influences," and often the negotiated reality is different and unrelated to the actual physical experience.[27] Not only does this serve to mute the mother, it also invalidates her experience of her own body.

The silences surrounding maternal experience are complicated ones since so many psychological, social, political, and economic factors figure into their construction. In her essay "One Out of Twelve," Tillie Olsen describes the various silences that have occurred throughout human and literary history. She speaks with anguished intimacy about the silence of maternal voices, noting that until recent times most "distinguished achievement" in literature by women came from childless women. Throughout her stories and essays, Olsen has chronicled her own struggle for voice and literary achievement while coping with the demands of motherhood, work, poverty, and emotional and physical hardship. Writing with clear-eyed realism in her essay "Silences," Olsen describes the incompatibility of maternity and the writer's life, given the urgency of children's and families' needs: "More than in any other human relationship, overwhelmingly more, motherhood means being instantly interruptable, responsive, responsible. . . . It is distraction, not meditation, that becomes habitual; interruption, not continuity; spasmodic, not constant toil. . . . Work interrupted, deferred, relinquished, makes blockage—at best, lesser accomplishment. Unused capacities atrophy, cease to be." The myriad, relentless responsibilities of women's lives often limit their opportunities for expression, for creativity, for achievement.

More seriously, perhaps, patriarchal dictums reinforce the idea that motherhood and creative expression cannot coexist within the individual woman, further silencing the maternal voice. Olsen describes

27. Cosslett, *Women Writing Childbirth*, 1–2; Alice Adams, *Reproducing the Womb: Images of Childbirth in Science, Feminist Theory, and Literature*, 5.

how Elizabeth Mann Borghese, accomplished musician and daughter of Thomas Mann, was instructed by her analyst, "You must choose between your art and fulfillment as a woman," a choice which Olsen decries as "a coercive working of sexist oppression."[28] As this example aptly illustrates, modern psychoanalysis has assumed a powerful role in the construction and limitation of women. Freudian psychoanalysis in particular has negated the mother's voice. In traditional psychoanalytic practice, as Shirley Nelson Garner, Claire Kahane, and Madelon Sprengnether explain, narratives are usually rendered from the child's perspective, and the mother as "speaking subject" in the drama is missing. Women are also effectively silenced in the Lacanian model, which views women as the "unconscious" of language. In this model, Western discourse is viewed as following "a male morphology, analogous in its linearity, unity, and visible form to the phallus"; since women do not possess a language capable of articulating their experiences, they are "left mutes or mimics."[29] According to Patricia Bizzell and Bruce Herzberg, both the Freudian and Lacanian theories derive meanings from language using "psychosexual allusions that many scholars see as sexist and politically repressive."

In contrast with proponents of male psychoanalytic models, French feminist theorists Julia Kristeva, Hélène Cixous, and Luce Irigaray privilege the mother's body and voice in their theories of language development and sexual identity. They offer an alternative model that restores subjectivity to maternal experience. Their theories provide intellectual insight and illuminating metaphors for analyzing the maternal dynamics that Morrison, Mason, and Smith incorporate within their fiction.

In her linguistic theories, according to Bizzell and Herzberg, Kristeva "seeks to correct" the phallocentrism and biological determinism inherent in the models developed by Freud and Lacan. She asserts instead that the multiple meanings contained within language result from multiple influences that are "less biologically determined and more dependent on cultural and literary traditions."[30]

In Kristeva's theorization, as Toril Moi explains, women have been

28. Tillie Olsen, *Silences*, 31, 18–19, 31.

29. Shirley Nelson Garner, Claire Kahane, and Madelon Sprengnether, introduction to *The (M)other Tongue: Essays in Feminist Psychoanalytic Interpretation*, 25, 23.

30. Patricia Bizzell and Bruce Herzberg, eds., *The Rhetorical Tradition*, 1228–29.

"reduced to the role of the silent Other of the symbolic order" in patriarchal culture. Moreover, motherhood is perceived as "a conspicuous
sign of the *jouissance* of the female (or maternal) body, a pleasure that
must at all costs be repressed." Moi notes Kristeva's assertion that procreation within patriarchal culture must be "strictly subordinated to the
rule of the Father's Name." Kristeva believes that women have been
"excluded from knowledge and power" and that woman's only access to
the symbolic order is through the father, "who is both sign and time."
She thus calls for a "masculine, paternal identification" for women "because it supports symbol and time, [and] is necessary in order to have a
voice in the chapter of politics and history."[31]

According to Moi, Kristeva believes that we lack "a satisfactory discourse on motherhood." Any belief in the mother, Kristeva states, is
"rooted in fear, fascinated with a weakness—the weakness of language."
Whereas the paternal is the highly symbolic Word, the maternal is associated with the more fluid realm of the semiotic chora. Adams remarks that the word "chora," which is derived from the Greek word for
"womb," denotes "a receptacle or maternal space that underlies the symbolic." This space contains the pre-oedipal, prelinguistic, presymbolic
forces that undergird symbolic discourse. Its only order is created by
"pulsions," patterns of nonspecific drives. Analogous to the maternal
womb that is also organized around rhythms, the semiotic chora seemingly "create[s] something . . . from nothing"; its prelinguistic characteristics suggest "the intimate, nonsymbolic contact between mother
and child." A life-infusing, creative force, the semiotic chora is also a
deeply disturbing and troubling realm. For the speaking subject, Adams
says, the chora is a place of both "generation and negation, birth and
death." She explains: "To . . . remain within the chora means the destruction of the subject, a descent into psychosis," because symbolic language is impossible within the chora. The maternal and the semiotic
chora pose problems in a larger sense as well. According to Mary Caputi, Kristeva sees that "there is always something primal, maternal, and
'abject' which threatens the Law of the Father." While the chora is creative and life-affirming, it is also "disruptive, overwhelming, even ter-

31. Toril Moi, ed., *The Kristeva Reader*, 138; Julia Kristeva, *About Chinese Women*,
143, 153, 156.

rifying in its ability to recall the archaic and unmediated in the face of cultural law and order."[32]

Like Kristeva, Cixous and Irigaray reject the phallocentrism of male psychoanalytic thought. In particular, they question Freudian and Lacanian definitions of the female as "one who lacks, first, a penis, and, second, the power of language the penis represents."[33] Instead, Cixous and Irigaray stress the maternal and its influence in the development of language and the self. The female body, with its shifting rhythms, diffuse experience of sexual pleasure, and ability to bring forth new life, serves as a vital linguistic source.

Cixous posits an *écriture féminine*—feminine writing—and suggests that women's sexuality and history will alter the prevailing masculine order through such writing—creating, according to Susan Sellers, "alternative forms of relation, perception, and expression." Sellers notes that Cixous also emphasizes the "inscription of the rhythms and articulations of the mother's body which continue to influence the adult self." In "The Laugh of the Medusa," Cixous describes how women "have been driven away" from writing just as they have from their own bodies. She says she believes that it is "[b]y writing her self [that] woman will return to the body which has been more than confiscated from her." She insists, therefore, that "[w]omen must write through their bodies," that their bodies "must be heard." To censor the body, Cixous further asserts, is to "censor breath and speech at the same time." In discussing feminine writing in *The Newly Born Woman*, Cixous strongly invokes the maternal body, using it as a powerful metaphor for the source of female voice and language: "[W]oman is never far from the 'mother.' . . . There is always at least a little good mother milk left in her. She writes with white ink." She reiterates the importance of this source, stating that the "Dark Continent" of the female body, the mother's body, is "*neither dark nor unexplorable:* It is still unexplored only because we have been made to believe that it was too dark to be explored."[34]

32. Moi, ed., *Kristeva Reader*, 160; Kristeva, "Stabat Mater," 175; Adams, *Reproducing the Womb*, 21–22; Mary Caputi, "The Abject Maternal: Kristeva's Theoretical Consistency," 35.

33. Bizzell and Herzberg, eds., *Rhetorical Tradition*, 1225.

34. Susan Sellers, introduction to *The Hélène Cixous Reader*, xxix; Hélène Cixous, "The Laugh of the Medusa," 1232, 1236, 1239, 1236; Hélène Cixous and Catherine Clément, *The Newly Born Woman*, 94, 68.

Irigaray similarly connects the maternal body to language and creativity. She asserts that women bring many things into the world besides children, that women give birth to "love, desire, language, art, social things, political things, religious things." However, Irigaray also believes that this creativity has long been forbidden to women and that women must reclaim "this maternal creative dimension that is our birthright as women." Recognizing the precarious situation of the mother, Irigaray warns that we must not again "kill the mother who was immolated at the birth of our culture" or allow her "to be swallowed up in the law of the father." According to Garner, Kahane, and Sprengnether, in contrast with the male morphologic structures found in Western discourse, Irigaray seeks to open language using "a female morphologic figured by the female genitals—the two-lipped vulva 'in touch . . . joined in an embrace' and the diffuse multiple structure of female pleasure." Like the female body and its sexual functioning, women's language then is "fluid, autoerotic, diffuse."[35]

I would like to add my own observations at this point in order to suggest that the connection that Irigaray draws between the female genitals (the vulval lips) and language is exquisitely related to the maternal body and the physiology of childbirth. During the first stage of labor, quite often a rim or "lip" of the uterine cervix remains as a final impediment to the full dilation and effacement of the cervix. This lip is poised gently, holding back the baby and delaying its birth much as the lips of the mouth hold back words waiting to be spoken. Usually a few more contractions, some cautious bearing down by the mother, or assistance from the accoucheur removes the lip of the cervix so that the delivery of the baby may proceed. A similar connection can be found between the lips of the mouth, which give utterance to words, and the lips of the vulva, which must part during birth. This oral-genital connection is acknowledged by some childbirth instructors in their directions to parturient women. During the second stage of childbirth, mothers are told to not clench their teeth but to relax the mouth and lips while they push or bear down. This seems to relax the musculature of the lower body, including the birth canal, and facilitates the delivery of the baby. Thus, by linking the mouth with the vagina, voice and birth are symbolically connected.

35. Luce Irigaray, *Sexes and Genealogies*, 18; Garner, Kahane, and Sprengnether, introduction to *(M)other Tongue*, 23.

Intricate connections between the mother's body, her sexuality, and her voice and language indeed exist. The *jouissance* to which Kristeva refers, the *écriture féminine* of Cixous, and the female morphology of language postulated by Irigaray all find their origins in the maternal body and in the full range of woman's sexual and reproductive functions. These functions are complexly intertwined and reveal that the maternal is anything but passive. Psychologist Niles Newton has identified startling connections between female sexual excitement and "uninhibited, undrugged" childbirth. According to Newton, a woman's breathing, facial expressions, sensory perceptions, and responses of the musculature and central nervous system, as well as the sounds she makes, are remarkably similar in childbirth and sexual orgasm.

Newton's study reveals that as labor and sexual excitement intensify, a woman's breathing becomes faster and deeper, leading eventually to breath holding in the final stages. Facial expressions also intensify, with a strained, "tortured expression" apparent in the latter stages of each event. Like an athlete "undergoing great physical strain," the woman's mouth is open, her eyes glassy, and her muscles tense. In both labor and sexual orgasm, the upper muscles of the uterus contract rhythmically and the mucus plug in the mouth of the cervix loosens. In childbirth, as delivery nears, a woman experiences a strong urge to bear down using her abdominal muscles; similarly, as orgasm approaches these muscles forcefully contract. Sensory perception is also altered during labor and sexual excitement, with the woman becoming "increasingly insensitive" to her surroundings. The actual delivery of the infant and the experience of orgasm involve unusual bodily strength on the part of the woman. Childbirth and orgasm are often quite vocal events and are usually followed by enormous relief, a sense of well-being, and a rush of emotions. These comparisons make clear that a woman's full and active participation in childbirth and sexual pleasure stands in stark contrast with the silence and passivity demanded of the mother in a patriarchal culture. As Irigaray admonishes, we must give the mother "the right to pleasure, to sexual experience, to passion, give her back the right to speak, or even to shriek and rage aloud." Certainly, as Newton has shown, the mother already has the capability to exercise these rights.[36]

While the theories of Kristeva, Cixous, and Irigaray have been wide-

36. Niles Newton, *Maternal Emotions*, 87–88; Irigaray, *Sexes and Genealogies*, 18.

ly applied to discussions of female experience in Western literature, they do not completely illuminate the experience of African or African American motherhood. In fact, some critics have noted that they are at odds with the reality of black women's experience or at least insufficient in explaining that reality.[37] I believe they have the same applicability in the examination of the maternal body and voice in Morrison's novels as they do in Mason's and Smith's. However, acknowledgment must also be given to the womanist theories that explain black female experience, identity, and voice within multicultural contexts.

Alice Walker is credited with coining the term "womanist," as distinct from "feminist," which in many circles has been regarded as referring to "radical *white* women." Walker uses the term, according to Joy James and T. Denean Sharpley-Whiting, to "render the adjective 'black' superfluous for gender-progressive 'women of color' . . . positing a culturally specific womanism that extends beyond women of African descent but is identifiably different from the dominant feminism of white (bourgeois) women." In her 1983 book *In Search of Our Mothers' Gardens*, Walker defines "womanist" as being "[c]ommitted to survival and wholeness of entire people, male *and* female," a definition that Sherley Anne Williams extends to include the "valorization of women's works in all their varieties and multitudes."[38]

Along similar lines of thought, Hortense Spillers, in "Interstices: A Small Drama of Words," calls for a discourse that is more pluralistic in meaning to better accommodate the "actual realities" of women in America. Busia states that in this essay, Spillers "raises the issues of sex, of power, and, critically, of *words.*" Walker's and Spillers's emphasis on the primacy of words, language, and discourse has far-reaching implications for the articulation of the diverse experiences of women of color. Their emphasis also underscores the powerful connection between orality and the expression of maternal experience within African, African American, and other diaspora communities. This connection assumes a critical role in preserving not only women's voices and stories, but en-

37. See Karla F. C. Holloway, *Moorings and Metaphors: Figures of Culture and Gender in Black Women's Literature*; Sylvia Wynter, "Beyond Miranda's Meanings: Un/silencing the 'Demonic Ground' of Caliban's 'Woman'"; and Oha, "Flora Nwapa's Poetry."

38. Busia, "Words Whispered over Voids," 5; Joy James and T. Denean Sharpley-Whiting, introduction to *The Black Feminist Reader*, 5; Alice Walker, *In Search of Our Mothers' Gardens*, 1; Sherley Anne Williams, "Some Implications of Womanist Theory," 304.

tire communities as well. As Busia observes: "Black women's stories teach and celebrate the role of women in communal survival. They teach how women have survived to become mistresses of their private, and, increasingly, their public worlds." The orality inherent in African and African American traditions contrasts with the silencing that Kris- teva, Cixous, and Irigaray see as afflicting women in Western culture. For black women, language and voice are thus essential instruments of power. Busia further explains: "Language can also *shape* our realities, and either enslave, by concealing what it might truly express, or liberate, by exposing what might otherwise remain concealed."[39]

Karla F. C. Holloway has also noted African American culture's em- phasis on the orality of women's lives, as well as that culture's impor- tance in preserving memory and myth through songs and stories, which in turn serve as the "oral archives of their culture." Given this empha- sis on female oral traditions, Holloway posits an Afrocentric model for interpreting black women's literature that "acknowledges both a spiri- tual *and* a physical mother at its center" and that foregrounds the orac- ular nature of women's culture. This maternal core contains an ances- tral mother, who exists as a "spiritual presence," and a goddess figure, who further extends the mythic dimensions within the texts of black women writers. The combination of oral traditions and important mother/goddess figures aid in the recovery of myth, something that Holloway sees as connected to "the emergence of textual complexity." Holloway asserts: "Both myth and memory acknowledge a linguistic/ cultural community as the source of the imaginative text of recovered meaning." In addition, she views myth as a "vehicle for aligning real and imaginative events in both the present and the past and for dissolving the temporal and spatial bridges between them." In contrast with writ- ten history, myth emphasizes orality. It becomes "a dynamic entity that (re)members community, connects it to the voices from which it has been severed, and forces it out of the silence prescribed by a scripto- centric historicism."

Holloway's model for understanding the "literary revision of the myth- ic principle" in the texts of black women writers has applicability not only to Morrison's works, but also to those of Mason and Smith. All

---

39. Hortense Spillers, "Interstices: A Small Drama of Words," 80; Busia, "Words Whispered over Voids," 6, 7, 29, 7.

three writers are concerned with the recovery of memory, the mythic underpinnings of female experience, and the powerful connections between language and culture. They also emphasize the importance of community and link its survival to the maternal. Through these elements, they are able to achieve what Holloway terms a "critical recovery of cultural organization and patterns of memory and telling" within their respective cultural settings. Morrison, Mason, and Smith each contribute to a growing discourse that articulates the diverse realities of women's lives. Through their examination of maternal experience and women's voice and language in their novels, they help preserve cultural memory. They seamlessly fuse past and present and reveal, to quote Busia, "what might otherwise remain concealed."[40] In doing so, Morrison, Mason, and Smith restore the mother's lost voice and her diminished subjectivity and give us new ways of thinking about maternal experience.

40. Holloway, *Moorings and Metaphors*, 22–25, 30; Busia, "Words Whispered over Voids," 7.

Toni Morrison

Toni Morrison's works are fantastic earthy realism. Deeply
rooted in history and mythology, her work resonates with
mixtures of pleasure and pain, wonder and horror. Primal in
their essence, her characters come at you with the force and
beauty of gushing water, seemingly fantastic, but as basic as
the earth they stand on. They erupt, out of the world, sometimes gently, often with force and terror. Her work is sensuality combined with an intrigue that only a piercing intel-
lect could create.

—Barbara Christian,
"The Contemporary Fables of Toni Morrison"

Barbara Christian's observations regarding Toni Morrison's extraordinary depictions of the real and the fantastic were written in 1980, at
which point Morrison had published only three works—*The Bluest Eye*
(1970), *Sula* (1973), and *Song of Solomon* (1977). Time has proven that
Christian's assessment holds true for the rest of Morrison's oeuvre as
well. From *The Bluest Eye* to *Paradise* (1998), Morrison has indeed in-
fused her works with a "fantastic earthy realism" that grounds her characters in time and culture and connects them to larger, more mythic
realms of experience.

This blending of myth and reality is an important element in Morrison's efforts in "evolving a mythology of black culture." Morrison says
she sees this mythology already existing in the music, folklore, and spiritual life of the African American community and in the human rela-

tionships there. Cynthia Davis points out that Morrison "immerses the reader in the black community" and reveals the realities of black lives that are shaped and defined by "the surrounding white society that violates and denies their blackness." Davis asserts that Morrison is "concerned with the sources of myth" and with distinguishing between "false 'myths' that simply reduce, misinterpret, and distort reality . . . and true myths that spring from and illuminate reality."[1]

In her rendering of maternal experience, Morrison shows an identical concern for differentiating the various myths upon which motherhood is constructed and for illuminating the diverse realities of female experience. Not surprisingly, she imbues the maternal with the same "fantastic earthy realism" given to her works as a whole. Deftly fusing shocking realities with myths, Morrison depicts motherhood as a complex state that is influenced by powerful biological, psychological, and cultural forces. She reveals the all-encompassing, elemental force of the Great Mother inherent in the maternal and at the same time demonstrates the individual vulnerability of the African American mother who bears the crushing weight of history and the destructive, self-negating attitudes of the dominant culture on her body and psyche. Morrison expertly shows that maternal experience centered in African American culture is not monolithic, but rather reflective of diverse and complex realities.

The primacy of the maternal in Morrison's fiction is manifested through the numerous "mothers" that populate her texts. It is not unusual for a single novel to contain twelve or more women who assume maternal roles or identities of some kind. Intensely interested in female relationships, Morrison creates triadic structures of grandmothers, mothers, and daughters to illustrate the importance of matrilineal heritage, as well as to reveal the difficulties associated with such bonds. She depicts communities of women—aunts, cousins, neighbors, midwives—who function tangentially in the background of her characters' lives. She also pairs black and white mothers to demonstrate how issues of race, culture, and class affect maternity. Altogether these women represent the myriad realities the maternal can assume.

The mothers that Morrison depicts in her fiction are given mythic

1. Charles Ruas, "Toni Morrison," 112; Toni Morrison quoted, ibid., 112; Cynthia Davis, "Self, Society, and Myth in Toni Morrison's Fiction," 7, 19.

dimensions that elevate them above ordinary realities and that rein-force Morrison's efforts to evolve a mythology of black culture. These women embody the Great Mother, a maternal archetype arising from mother-goddess figures of ancient religions. Woman's extraordinary ability to conceive, bear, and nourish human offspring lies at the heart of the Great Mother archetype. Or, as Joseph Campbell has observed, "There can be no doubt that in the very earliest ages of human history the magical force and wonder of the female was no less a marvel than the universe itself; and this gave to woman a prodigious power." Shari Thurer, in her study of the history and myths of motherhood, describes the Great Mother as "the original deity" who inspired worship; she was "immanent, not transcendent" and was "located within each individual and all things in nature, not above them."[2] Intimately connected with the earth, the all-powerful Great Mother was associated with birth, transformation, death, and rebirth. The mothers in Morrison's fiction mirror the Great Mother's propensities for life and death, for procre-ation and destruction. Her maternal figures are complex, often possess-ing negative qualities that disturb and confound the reader. They have the potential to be loving, nurturing, judgmental, punishing, and even murderous. They are not romanticized or glorified in any traditional sense. They are flesh-and-blood, sexual women who erupt with passion, incite fear and terror, inspire adoration, and provoke sorrow. Collec-tively, they represent the Great Mother in all of her incarnations.

On an individual level, the mothers that Morrison creates are ex-ceedingly diverse. They exist in the flesh or only in fragile memories. They are named and unnamed, some occupying center stage while oth-ers are relegated to the periphery of the text. Maternity comes to the very young, such as eleven-year-old Pecola Breedlove in *The Bluest Eye*. At the other end of the age spectrum, the Great Mother figures of Eva Peace in *Sula* and Pilate Dead in *Song of Solomon* dominate our imagi-nations. Such mothers as Sethe and Baby Suggs in *Beloved* are equally unforgettable; the terrible anguish of motherhood that they experience is almost beyond comprehension. Other mothers are less visible, how-ever, and are given such marginal reference as "Somebody's grand-mother" or "Teapot's Mamma" (SUL 16, 172). Sethe knows her moth-

---

2. Joseph Campbell, *The Masks of God: Primitive Mythology*, 315; Shari Thurer, *The Myths of Motherhood: How Culture Reinvents the Good Mother*, 1, 9.

er only by a mark under her breast, a circled cross "burnt right in the skin" (BEL 61). Sethe's mother remains unnamed in the novel, and for the most part she exists only in fragmented memories. Sethe's "Ma'am," as she is called, was hanged early in Sethe's life and her body burned and mutilated beyond recognition. This attempt at erasure or annihilation of the maternal fails, however, for "Ma'am" still functions as a vital link in the matrilineal heritage of Sethe and her daughters.

Other mothers in Morrison's texts are similarly defined by their absence, leaving behind orphaned and abandoned children scarred for a lifetime. Generally speaking, children who suffer the loss of a parent find that grief resurfaces periodically throughout their lives. In describing this process, a *Newsweek* reporter explained: "Children mourn piecemeal; they must return to it at each stage of maturity and conquer grief anew. Over the years, the sharp pang of loss turns to a dull ache, a melancholy that sets in at a certain time of year, a certain hour of the night. But every child who has lost a parent remains, in some secret part of his or her soul, a child forever frozen at a moment in time, crying out to the heedless heavens."[3] Morrison's characters who suffer a maternal loss early in life seem similarly plagued by a pervasive melancholy and restlessness. The absent mother continues to affect characters, events, and entire texts from the recesses of the past. Moreover, the repercussions of the loss of the mother are horribly visited upon succeeding generations, particularly the young and unborn. Losing the mother often represents the loss of childhood, and in Morrison's fiction, "orphans" not only lose their own childhoods but deny those of the next generation as well. In *The Bluest Eye*, for instance, a drunken and delusional Cholly Breedlove, who was abandoned at the age of four days upon a junk heap, rapes his eleven-year-old daughter Pecola. Joe Trace, similarly rejected at birth in *Jazz* (1992), kills his young lover in a Harlem nightclub. *Song of Solomon*'s Macon Dead, whose mother dies in childbirth, tries to force the abortion of his own son. And in *Beloved*, Sethe attempts to kill her four children rather than send them back to slavery, the institution that had murdered her mother.

While all of Morrison's novels depict complex manifestations of the maternal, *The Bluest Eye*, *Sula*, and *Beloved* foreground maternity to the greatest extent. In these three novels, Morrison presents motherhood

3. Jerry Adler, "How Kids Mourn," *Newsweek*, September 22, 1997, 61.

with compelling and brutal honesty. She juxtaposes silence and voice in each novel and uses the maternal body as a source of myth and metaphor to undergird the realities of female experience. Indeed, the "fantastic earthy realism" that characterizes her novels as a whole gives the maternal in these works a richer, more terrifying expression. Morrison's adroit blending of myth and reality, horror and beauty, body and voice results in a complex portrait of the maternal that reveals devastating and confounding truths most readers would prefer to deny.

2

~

The Bluest Eye

THE INVERTED MATERNAL

In *The Bluest Eye*, Morrison subjects the maternal to grotesque inversion through the pregnancy of eleven-year-old Pecola Breedlove. Pecola's tragedy reveals a cultural and personal devastation of astounding proportions. Moreover, her eventual descent into madness and silence comes to symbolize the split between body and voice that permeates the maternal throughout the novel. Rejected by her mother and raped by her father, Pecola gives birth prematurely to an infant whose death symbolizes her own failure to thrive. Her fervent desire for blue eyes adds yet another layer of complexity to her experience because it reveals that she is as much a victim of her culture as she is of familial abuse. The blue eyes, which in Pecola's mind would grant her beauty and acceptability, symbolize the blond-hair, fair-skin standard of beauty revered in Western culture. To aid in this transformation, she drinks white milk from a Shirley Temple cup and delights in eating Mary Jane candies. Pecola's quest for beauty and acceptance bizarrely escalate after her father drunkenly rapes her. After visiting Soaphead Church, "a self-styled conjure man," Pecola loses final touch with reality.[1] Believing that he has granted her wish for blue eyes, she spends the remainder of her childhood locked in a pitiful insanity, "walking up and down, up and down, her head jerking to the beat of a drummer so distant only she could hear" (BLU 158).

Altogether, the rape, the ensuing pregnancy, and the quest for blue eyes fuel Pecola's descent into madness and chilling isolation. To a great

1. Keith Byerman, "Beyond Realism," 101.

extent, these things represent a complex, volatile mixing of cultural dynamics and family dysfunction. The conflicting societal values that Pecola internalizes are rooted in her parents' lives and experiences as well. Although their actions as parents are reprehensible, Pauline and Cholly Breedlove have been unwittingly manipulated and warped by white culture. In depicting their experiences, Morrison demonstrates the destructive impact of white culture on African American identity. Pauline, who feels "uncomfortable" with other black women, prefers the perfect beauty and perfect lives depicted in the false realm of Hollywood movies (BLU 94). She admires how white men in the movies take "such good care of they women" (BLU 97). She emulates Jean Harlow by styling her hair in a similar fashion. However, while watching a Harlow film and enjoying her identification with the white starlet, the five-months-pregnant Pauline breaks a tooth eating candy. The broken tooth and the pregnancy destroy the effect of the movie and serve as a reminder of her imperfect beauty and her violent, unhappy life with Cholly.

Pauline later finds beauty, perfection, and power in the kitchen of her white employer. Here, she is "queen of canned vegetables." Pauline reigns over creditors and service people imperiously and ingratiates herself with the Fishers, who lavish her with praise and the nickname "Polly." Regarding her as an ideal servant and valuable possession, they declare, "We'll never let her go." The more entrenched Pauline becomes in the white household, the more neglectful she becomes of her own. Her dingy house stands in humiliating contrast with the perfect beauty of the Fishers' home, while her husband and children become mere "afterthoughts . . . dark edges that made the daily life with the Fishers lighter, more delicate, more lovely" (BLU 101).

Cholly's sense of self, particularly his manhood, has been similarly warped through white influence. He endures excruciating humiliation during his first sexual encounter as an adolescent when two white men find him having sex in a vineyard with friend Darlene. The men goad Cholly into completing the act: "[G]et on wid it. An' make it good, nigger, make it good" (BLU 117). Terrified, Cholly is unable to finish. He directs his hatred and anger not at the white men whose standards he fails to meet, but at his female partner, "the one who had created the situation, the one who bore witness to his failure" (BLU 119). The impotence he experiences with Darlene fuels the sexual confusion and self-loathing that drunkenly coalesce in his daughter's rape years later.

The first pages of *The Bluest Eye* belie the horror that unfolds in Pecola's life. The novel opens innocently enough with the idealized world of the Dick and Jane schoolbook primers, replete with happy children and smiling parents. The familiar, wooden language of the primer appears: "Here is the house. It is green and white. It has a red door. It is very pretty. . . . Who will play with Jane?" (BLU 7). However, the false-myth realm of Dick and Jane cannot mask or alter the realities of poverty, dysfunctional families, or racial difference and prejudice. Like Pecola's world, the world of Dick and Jane soon spins out of control, and becomes a perverse mirror of the Breedlove family. With machine-gun rapidity, the text becomes more and more compressed. Words, sentences, and images run together so that the original innocence and idealized unreality of the primer world are lost forever. Certain words and phrases leap obscenely and ironically off the page: "fatherdick" and "smilefathersmile" grotesquely foreshadow Pecola's rape, while "verynicemother" can be parsed as "ice mother" (BLU 8).

Using images of infertility, loss of innocence, grief, and despair, Morrison establishes a sense of maternal failure early in the novel and makes it clear that children will not thrive in this inverted world. The novel's primary narrator, Claudia MacTeer, looking back on her childhood, tells us that "there were no marigolds in the fall of 1941" because the seeds had "shriveled and died." Despite the best efforts of Claudia and her sister to nurture the marigolds and despite their deep concern for Pecola's baby, in their youth and innocence they fail at ensuring the survival of either. Like the marigolds planted in the "unyielding" earth, Pecola's baby fails to thrive (BLU 9). Its death represents the death of innocence, which Pecola has already endured; however, for Claudia and her sister, Frieda, the baby's death diminishes the sense of hopeful possibility that childhood should engender. Bearing guilt over the failed marigolds and, by symbolic extension, the dead baby, Claudia assumes responsibility for narrating Pecola's tragic story.

The failure of maternity finds further expression in the disruptions of the natural world in *The Bluest Eye*. Morrison structures the novel around the four seasons. The seasons correspond to the changing, cyclical rhythms of the maternal body. Thus, inversions in the natural world find representation in Pecola's maternal experience. In keeping with the

Dick and Jane school-year orientation to time, autumn is the first season in the novel. Barbara Christian, in exploring the fablelike qualities and mythic inversions in *The Bluest Eye*, notes, "Appropriately, the year does not begin in January or in the spring, but in the fall when school starts according to the rhythms of a child's life." More compellingly, Christian reminds us that since the novel begins with fall, "Pecola's story will not be the usual mythic one of birth, death, and rebirth, from planting to harvest to planting. Hers will proceed from pathos to tragedy and finally to madness, as the earth will not accept her seeds."[2]

Besides fall, other seasons are inverted as well, and their inversions symbolize serious disruptions of nature and of the maternal. The rhythms of childhood and maternity are corrupted to an extreme in *The Bluest Eye*. Morrison inverts the Greek myth in which a grieving Demeter, the goddess of corn, ravages the earth in her attempts to retrieve her daughter Persephone, who has been raped and abducted to the underworld by Hades. Eventually, Persephone is restored to her mother for nine months out of each year; similarly, vegetation is present on the earth during the seasons of spring, summer, and fall. In *The Bluest Eye*, Morrison disrupts these mythic cycles of fertility and regeneration. Pecola's rape takes place in spring, while summer becomes a season not of growth and fruition but of death and descent into harrowing insanity. Pecola's baby comes too soon and dies, while Pecola herself, thinking she has at last acquired blue eyes, lives out her "tendril, sap green days" locked in madness (BLU 158).[3]

Pecola represents the ultimate and most tragic inversion of the maternal—barren, mad, silent, and, despite her sexualization and subsequent maternity, just a child. Her experience, in fact, constitutes a grim inversion of Christian's formulation of the Africanist view—that "every woman is a symbol of the marvelous creativity of the earth"— and represents instead an American tragedy. Through a terrible coalescing of forces, Pecola's story embodies a failure of family, community, and the larger culture to nourish, protect, and celebrate its children, regardless of color or circumstance.

Although Pecola's experience commands our attention, Morrison

2. Barbara Christian, "The Contemporary Fables of Toni Morrison," 62.

3. Madonne M. Miner, in "Lady No Longer Sings the Blues: Rape, Madness, and Silence in *The Bluest Eye*," explores Morrison's treatment of the Persephone myth more fully, using both traditional and feminist interpretations of the myth in her analysis.

foregrounds the maternity of other women as well. Pecola's coldly rejecting mother, Pauline Breedlove, is juxtaposed with Claudia's practical and caring mother, Mrs. MacTeer. The two women contrast in numerous ways. Unlike Pauline, whom Pecola formally calls "Mrs. Breedlove," Mrs. MacTeer is referred to as "Mama" throughout Claudia's narration. Because she is introduced in the text before Pauline Breedlove, Mrs. MacTeer serves as a moral compass, a standard of maternal decency and protection. Both Mr. and Mrs. MacTeer present secure models of parents, who, despite their modest means and difficult lives, provide love, protection, and stability for their daughters. They stand in sharp contrast with the dissolute Breedloves and with the flat, lifeless family of the schoolbook primer as well.

Morrison does not idealize Mrs. MacTeer. Unlike the placid, unreal mother of the primer, Mrs. MacTeer is blunt, bossy, and impatient. While she is very much a real and embodied mother, a strong physical and emotional presence in the lives of her children, she is powerfully associated with voice. Her scolding words leap off the page. When Claudia contracts bronchitis, Mrs. MacTeer chastises her unmercifully: "Great Jesus. Get on in that bed. How many times do I have to tell you to wear something on your head? You must be the biggest fool in this town." Her administration of Vicks salve is rough, but loving and necessary. When Claudia vomits in the bed, her mother continues the tirade: "You think I got time for nothing but washing up your puke?" Claudia rationalizes her mother's anger, noting: "She is not talking to me. She is talking to the puke, but she is calling it my name" (BLU 13). In Mrs. MacTeer, Morrison gives the maternal voice full range of expression. Mrs. MacTeer speaks her mind freely and often, expresses her anger without hesitation, scolds, berates, comforts, laughs, and sings. More than by any other attribute, she is defined by her words. Her "fussing soliloquies," as Claudia calls them, allow Mrs. MacTeer to give voice to her grievances. While they are "interminable" and "insulting," her tirades are indirect and are aimed at "folks and *some* people" (BLU 23).

Keenly aware of her mother's voice, Claudia refers to it often throughout her narration. She is perceptively attuned to the words, sounds, meanings, and even the musicality of her mother's voice. She describes Saturdays with her mother as "lonesome, fussy, soapy days," while Sundays are full of "don'ts" and "set'cha self downs" (BLU 24). She notes her mother's adeptness at "connecting one offense to another until all of the things that chagrined her were spewed out." After her mother's words and anger are finally spent, Claudia reveals that Mrs. MacTeer "would burst into song and sing the rest of the day" (BLU 23). For Claudia, it is the singing voice of the maternal that resonates most deeply. Her mother's bluesy singing about "hard times, bad times, and somebody-done-gone-and-left-me times" creates longing and desire (BLU 24). It makes Claudia wish for the same life difficulties in order to experience the love and loss that come with being grown up.

Claudia also links her mother's voice to other aspects of growing up. When Pecola gets her first menstrual period while in the MacTeers' care, Mrs. MacTeer takes motherly control and ushers "the-little-girl-gone-to-woman" into the bathroom to clean her up. As she helps Pecola through this female rite of passage, the maternal voice celebrates the experience. While Mrs. MacTeer rinses out Pecola's underwear in the tub, Claudia, excluded from the experience, listens outside of the bathroom: "The water gushed, and over its gushing we could hear the music of my mother's laughter" (BLU 28). As if to underscore the womanly significance of the event, Claudia's description creates an image that brings together the female mysteries of reproduction, the gushing waters of the maternal womb, and the mother's voice resounding in laughter above it all.

The scene evokes the image of the laughing Medusa, Hélène Cixous's transformation of the terrifying monster of Greek mythology into a positive source of female beauty, language, and power. According to myth, after Medusa dallied with Poseidon in Athena's temple, the angry goddess changed her hair into deadly serpents and set her beautiful face into a grimace so horrible it turned all who looked upon her to stone. Patricia Bizzell and Bruce Herzberg assert that the Medusa evolved into a negative and destructive symbol of consuming female sexuality in Freudian psychoanalytic thought. Cixous attempts to dispel this image by transforming Medusa's "grimacing lips into a laugh" and filling her mouth with "beautiful language." In calling for a new and powerful female use of language, Cixous invokes this revised image of Medusa, noting, "She's beautiful and she's laughing."[4]

In some respects, Medusa, a female symbol derived from classical mythology, may seem an odd association to make with Morrison's text

4. Bizzell and Herzberg, eds., *Rhetorical Tradition*, 1227; Cixous, "Laugh of the Medusa," 1239.

and the African American mother Mrs. MacTeer. However, Mrs. Mac-
Teer's powerful associations with language and voice and the fact that
her laughter emanates during a very female sexual rite of passage show
Morrison's shrewd awareness of the power of female voice as Cixous delineates. Truly, Mrs. MacTeer represents Cixous's speaking woman, who
Toril Moi states "*is* entirely her voice." Mrs. MacTeer's full repertoire of
lectures, soliloquies, laughter, and songs confirm this alignment. In addition, Claudia's attentiveness to her mother's voice corroborates the
importance Cixous places on the primeval source of female voice: "In
women's speech, as in their writing, that element which never stops res-
onating, which, once we've been permeated by it, profoundly and im-
perceptibly touched by it, retains the power of moving us—that element is the song: first music from the first voice of love which is alive
in every woman."[5]

Claire Kahane notes that this maternal song, which emanates from
an imaginary realm, is "ubiquitously heard in all feminine texts." Under different circumstances, the maternal voice in *The Bluest Eye* might
resemble Janie's "flute song forgotten in another existence and remembered again" in Zora Neale Hurston's *Their Eyes Were Watching God*.
However, there are no blossoming pear trees for Claudia and Pecola as
there are for Janie; in Claudia and Pecola's world, the soil fails to nourish even marigold seeds. Nonetheless, the maternal voice of Mrs.
MacTeer permeates Claudia's sense of self and gives her the ability to
narrate Pecola's story. In contrast with Pecola, who succumbs to madness and silence, Claudia develops a voice and will of her own. These
insulate her from the damaging, destructive myths of beauty that im-
peril Pecola. Claudia refuses to accept the blue-eye, blond-hair standards of beauty thrust upon her. She treats the white dolls and Shirley
Temple mug she is given with a perceptive contempt. She violently rejects the "yellow-haired, pink-skinned doll," an offensive contradiction
to her developing sense of self (BLU 20). Claudia's anger and outrage
over "the universal love of white baby dolls" suggest a reactionary ambivalence and the possibility that she too has internalized white standards of beauty to some degree (BLU 148). According to Barbara Christian, the dolls serve as "measures of her own lack of desirability."[6]

5. Toril Moi, *Feminist Literary Theory*, 114; Cixous, "Laugh of the Medusa," 1236.
6. Claire Kahane, "Questioning the Maternal Voice," 83; Zora Neale Hurston, *Their Eyes Were Watching God*, 23; Christian, "Contemporary Fables," 62.

However, Claudia's prayers for Pecola's unborn baby to live indicate a rejection of the artificiality of the dolls and the standards of beauty they represent. In contrast with the dolls' synthetic falseness, she conjures up a stunning, real-life image of the baby in Pecola's womb, one which celebrates the beauty of the baby's blackness and, in a sense, her own: "It was in a dark, wet place, its head covered with great O's of wool, the black face holding, like nickels, two clean black eyes, the flared nose, kissing-thick lips, and the living, breathing silk of black skin" (BLU 148).

Claudia's words reveal her racial pride and self-love; their exquisiteness underscores her facility with language. Like her mother, Claudia possesses a flexibility of voice that is manifested in multiple ways. For example, in reconstructing Pecola's story, Claudia incorporates the points of view of Pecola, Pauline, Cholly, Soaphead Church, and other characters in her own first-person narrative. Speaking in both past and present tense, Claudia frames the novel using an adult perspective but recounts Pecola's story from the "inside" of childhood. Sometimes her adult voice slips into her child narration, making boundaries of time difficult to delineate. In any event, Claudia the child speaker is shrewd and perceptive. As a child, she speaks with her mother's wit and sauciness, while her adult voice seems to be informed by the blues her mother sings. Looking back in time, a mature Claudia speaks in a wiser, mellower voice that resonates with sadness, loss, and remorse over Pecola's tragedy. Similarly, the diverse voices and points of view within the text also reflect the blues elements in Claudia's voice. These shifts in time, voice, and perspective effectively blend the immediacy of childhood with the weight of memory and regret. Altogether, they represent the "amalgam" that Houston Baker sees as constituting the blues matrix, mirroring the multiplicity of sounds and rhythms in a jazz performance.[7] These musical elements, which Morrison includes throughout her fiction, are critical to her efforts in evolving a mythology of black culture. They also give the female voice full expression. Given the variations of voice and perspective in her reconstruction of Pecola's story, Claudia is indeed her mother's daughter. Not only has she achieved the voice of the mother, she has surpassed it in skill and virtuosity as well.

7. Houston Baker, *Blues, Ideology, and Afro-American Literature: A Vernacular Theory*, 5.

While Mrs. MacTeer represents the maternal voice that empowers Claudia, Pecola's mother is more closely aligned with the body of the mother and with the silent maternal that denies and destroys the daughter. Pauline is given some voice in the novel, chiefly in the form of brief monologues that reflect her interiority rather than her speech. For the most part, her speaking voice is fragmented, angry, and inarticulate. When Pecola upsets a berry cobbler in the Fishers' kitchen, Pauline viciously and incoherently turns on her: "Crazy fool . . . my floor, mess . . . look what you . . . work . . . get on out." In contrast with the indirect and articulate "fussing soliloquies" of Mrs. MacTeer, Pauline's words are fractured and spit out "like rotten pieces of apple" (BLU 87). Pecola receives the full brunt of her mother's anger and words. Only when Pauline turns to soothe the white Fisher child, who embodies the "absolute beauty" that she cherishes, does her speech become fluid and sweet: "[T]he honey in her words complemented the sundown spilling on the lake" (BLU 97, 87).

Unlike Claudia, who experiences her mother's voice in a multiplicity of words and sounds, Pecola's experience of her mother is associated with silence. Even when her parents brutally assault each other, they do so without talking or cursing. They fight with "a darkly brutal formalism," and their assaults are virtually silent except for the "muted sound of falling things, and flesh on unsurprised flesh" (BLU 37–38). When Pecola overhears their lovemaking, she once again links her mother with silence. Pauline's silent experience of sex is confusing and frightening to Pecola: "It was as though [her mother] was not even there. Maybe that was love. Choking sounds and silence" (BLU 49).

Although Pauline's experience of her body seems locked in silence, her monologues reveal a significant degree of maternal subjectivity. Paradoxically, as Pauline describes her experiences of sex and maternity, we see that her silence is not absolute. She clarifies her silence during sex: "I don't make no noise, because the chil'ren might hear" (BLU 103). She experiences sexual orgasm as "little bits of color floating up into me" and coalescing into a rainbow inside her body. Pauline remains silent as she climaxes, but links her body with sound: "I'm laughing between my legs, and the laughing gets all mixed up with the colors" (BLU 104). The fusion of color, laughter, and orgasm suggest Julia Kristeva's *jouissance*, the sexual pleasure experienced by the female body that in Christian ideology must be repressed. According to Kristeva, motherhood is proof of maternal *jouissance,* of the mother's pleasure taken in the act of coitus, "a primal scene." Since it threatens to disrupt the symbolic order of patriarchal society, maternal *jouissance* is censured and procreation subordinated "in the name of the father."[8] For Pauline, maternal *jouissance* is similarly short-lived, as her sexual experiences with Cholly become hurried, detached, and repugnant. She admits to missing "that rainbow," but has largely repressed the experience of it: "I don't recollect it much anymore" (BLU 104). Ironically, given Cholly's adolescent sexual humiliation by the two white men, he is denied the possibility of full, mature sexual expression as well.

Pregnancy and childbirth for Pauline also reflect an ironic mixture of sound and silence, of love and rejection. In contrast with Claudia and her mother, who are connected through words and voice, Pecola and Pauline are linked through the body and silence. Pauline's maternal feelings are initially positive. When she becomes pregnant with Pecola, her second baby, she does so on purpose. She talks to her unborn child during her pregnancy, and, when the baby is born, declares she would "love it no matter what it looked like." However, the "friendly talk" and positive maternal feelings disintegrate into cold, rejecting silence (BLU 98). This process begins with Pauline's dehumanizing experience of childbirth, which robs her of voice and power and short-circuits her maternal feelings. Attended by an assortment of doctors in a large hospital ward, Pauline's experience is marred by racism, paternalism, and gross depersonalization. She receives a pelvic examination that is brutal and violating: The doctor, she says, "gloved his hand and put some kind of jelly on it and rammed it up between my legs." To some extent, this mirrors her rough, impersonal sex with Cholly and foreshadows the rape of the daughter she is about to deliver. Adding to the depersonalization of the examination, the doctor absurdly generalizes about her labor and refers to black women as if they were nonhuman: "[N]ow these here women you don't have any trouble with. They deliver right away and with no pain. Just like horses" (BLU 99).

In contrast with the solicitous talk and concern they give to the white mothers in labor, the doctors attending Pauline do not speak to her directly. Looking only at her stomach and between her legs, their actions

8. Kristeva, *About Chinese Women,* 146.

further dehumanize her experience of childbirth. The metaphor of a foaling mare laboring in silence is applied to Pauline and sets her apart from the other women in labor. However, she refuses to retreat into absolute silence and purposefully moans louder to validate her pain. She wants "to let them people know that having a baby was more than a bowel movement. I hurt just like them white women" (BLU 99). Although her moans are wordless, they reassert her right to pain, to maternity, and to a human identity. Sadly, the dehumanization she resists is nevertheless internalized and passed on to her infant daughter. The seeds of rejection too deeply planted, Pauline fails to see Pecola's newborn beauty and humanity and likens her to "[a] cross between a puppy and a dying man. . . . Lord she was ugly" (BLU 100).

Given the emotional and physical detachment that develops in their relationship, Morrison's use of the female body to bring mother and daughter together is ironic. With recurrent blood images, Morrison creates a circularity that perversely fuses mother and daughter. Blood, like the milk Pecola so greedily drinks, serves as a unifying symbol of the maternal, but its meaning also suffers inversion. The onset of Pecola's menstruation marks the first appearance of the image. With blood running down her legs and a brownish-red stain discoloring her dress, Pecola "ke[eps] whinnying, standing with her legs far apart." Claudia and Frieda inform the terrified Pecola that "ministratin'" means she can now have a baby (BLU 25). While menstruation signals Pecola's new capacity to bear children, her "whinnying" also links her with the maternal, as it suggests the mare metaphor used to define Pauline's experience of childbirth.

Morrison gives the imagery of blood further development when Pecola knocks over Pauline's freshly baked blueberry cobbler in the Fishers' kitchen. Not unlike the menstrual fluids of the earlier image, the hot purple juice splatters on Pecola's legs. Indeed, in each case Pecola's discomfort and confusion are similar. When an angry Pauline knocks Pecola to the floor, however, causing her to slide in the dark juice, the implications of the image become more disturbing. Phillip Page, in his analysis of the fragmented, split-apart world of The Bluest Eye, sees the incident as marking "the emotional death of Pecola through her abandonment by her mother in favor of a blond, blue-eyed, white girl into whom Pecola immerses her identity." He views it as evidence of

Pauline's own "fractured life" and identity.[9] Perhaps worse, Pauline's violent reaction thrusts her daughter into fuller contact with the berry juice/menstrual blood image and foreshadows the complete and brutal immersion in the realities of womanhood that Pecola is to suffer.

The next berry/blood image, which is more recursive, appears in Pauline's recollection of berry-picking as a child. The smashed berries in her dress pocket stain her dress and are similar to the stains of Pecola's first menstruation. The image also circles back to the purple juice of the cobbler "bursting here and there through crust" in the kitchen scene (BLU 86). Whereas Pecola's menstruation means being able to have a baby, Pauline's experience has overtly sexual and orgasmic meaning. She tells how the berry stains from childhood never washed out of the dress or herself: "I could feel that purple deep inside me" (BLU 92). The purple, along with other colors drawn from her childhood world, gives rise to sexual feelings, which Cholly elicits from Pauline upon their first meeting and which are later manifested through her "rainbow" orgasms. These provide another point of bodily connection between mother and daughter, as the "nine lovely orgasms" Pecola experiences while eating the Mary Jane candies (BLU 43) reflect the same "sensory pleasure her mother enjoyed."[10]

The berry stains on Pauline's dress and the blood on Pecola's are recalled by the muscadine stains on the white cotton dress Darlene wears during Cholly's humiliating sexual initiation in adolescence. This draws the father into the circle formed by these images and eventually into contact with the fused bodies of mother and daughter. When Cholly spies Pecola standing at the sink washing dishes, her repetition of her mother's "simple gesture" of scratching the back of her calf with a toe fills Cholly with "a wondering softness" and tenderness that draws him to the merged mother/daughter body. Memories of Pauline fused with the desire of doing "a wild and forbidden thing" lead Cholly to rape his daughter, or, as he sees it, "to fuck her—tenderly." For Pecola, however, the pain and confusion embedded in the earlier blood and ruptured-berry images are given their most horrible manifestation. Her father's

9. Phillip Page, *Dangerous Freedom: Fusion and Fragmentation in Toni Morrison's Novels*, 39.
10. Ibid., 40.

penetration is violent: "The tightness of her vagina was more than he could bear. His soul seemed to slip down to his guts and fly out into her, and the gigantic thrust he made into her then provoked the only sound she made—a hollow suck of air in the back of her throat. Like the rapid loss of air from a circus balloon" (BLU 128).

Pecola's voiceless response to the rape becomes a point of connection between mother and daughter, as her silence mirrors Pauline's own silent experience of sex with Cholly. This connection with the mother is further entrenched when, after regaining consciousness on the kitchen floor, Pecola associates "the pain between her legs with the face of her mother looming over her" (BLU 129). The image not only merges the maternal and paternal violations Pecola suffers, but also reverses the association a mother not infrequently makes between her newly born child and the genital-splitting pain of childbirth. Perhaps in the worst inversion of all, with the pregnancy that follows the rape Pecola's fusion with the maternal body is complete. And with her madness, she becomes the living embodiment of her mother's silence, relegated forever to the realm of the silent Other.

3

~

Sula

FINDING THE PEACE
OF THE MOTHER'S BODY

In *Sula* (1973), Toni Morrison subjects maternal experience and the body of the mother to further inversions. Depicted as a negative, destructive force, the maternal functions more as the antimaternal. As in *The Bluest Eye*, maternal experience is associated with silence and psychological disconnection that affects not only individuals but family and community as well. For the most part, the novel focuses on the female friendship between Sula Peace and Nel Wright as they move from adolescence to adulthood in the small, fictional town of Medallion, Ohio. The two characters seem markedly different. Sula grows up willful and rebellious, while Nel remains the quieter and more cautious of the two. However, despite their disparate natures, they find an intimacy together, as both are the "[d]aughters of distant mothers and incomprehensible fathers (Sula's because he was dead; Nel's because he wasn't)" (SUL 52). They form what Barbara Christian terms the "ultimate bond, the responsibility for unintentionally causing the death of another."[1] When the two girls, both twelve years old, play by the river one spring afternoon, they become caught up in the passions and pain of adolescence. An emotionally wounded Sula, who has just overheard her mother's declaration that she does not like her, connects with Nel more intensely than before. Playing together in the grass, both are vaguely aware of sensual stirrings within their bodies. Shortly thereafter, the two girls begin to tease Chicken Little, a small boy who has wandered up from the riverbank. Sula playfully swings him over the river's

1. Christian, "Contemporary Fables," 82.

edge and lets him fall from her grasp into the water. As Sula and Nel watch the child drown, their complicity in his death does not go unnoticed. Shadrack, a psychologically scarred World War I veteran who institutes National Suicide Day in order to get death out of the way and to avoid its terrifying "unexpectedness," also witnesses the event (SUL 14). According to Christian, he assures Sula "of her own permanency" and reminds her that she need not fear death. Thus, enmeshed within the rhythms of life and death, Sula and Nel form an even tighter bond, one that will paradoxically pull them apart and send them on divergent paths when they reach adulthood. The impassive Nel will remain in Medallion, choosing the traditional route of marriage and motherhood. The more adventuresome Sula will escape to college and city life, later returning to her hometown as a seductress, rebel, and virtual outcast.

While the conflicted friendship between Nel and Sula serves as the work's focal center, other female relationships are equally important because they provide the maternal underpinnings of the novel. The maternal, which functions as a powerful presence, is particularly evident in the multigenerational connections shared by Sula, her mother, Hannah, and her grandmother Eva. Their relationships are not easy ones; indeed, the triad ultimately proves to be consuming and deadly. While Hannah occupies a middle and more vulnerable position, Eva and Sula mirror each other to a frightening degree. Both are strong-willed, independent women who ignore social conventions and act with godlike impunity in the lives of others. In a milder sense, Nel is similarly linked to her mother, grandmother, and great-grandmother. Nel grows up possessing only fragmentary connections to her Creole foremothers. When she accompanies her mother, Helene, to see Helene's dying grandmother in New Orleans, they arrive too late. Nel never meets her great-grandmother Cecile, who rescued Helene from the brothel where she was born. She is similarly distanced from her grandmother Rochelle, Helene's mother. A New Orleans prostitute, Rochelle is so vain and childlike that any meaningful relationship with her is impossible. Helene and Nel's inability to communicate with Rochelle also stems from their ignorance of the mother tongue. Since neither can speak or understand Creole, both mother and daughter are denied connection with their maternal heritage. This disunity transfers itself into Helene and Nel's emotionally sterile relationship.

In *Sula*, Morrison emphasizes the silences surrounding the maternal.

In doing this, she privileges body over voice; as Marianne Hirsch observes, "Maternal speech is sparse in this novel."[2] Indeed, the voice of the mother is severely limited in *Sula*, while communication between mothers and daughters is difficult and inadequate at best. Morrison gives the maternal body primacy in *Sula* instead. The body of the mother serves not only as a potent source of myth and metaphor in the novel but also as a perversely unifying symbol.

Eva Peace is the dominant maternal figure in *Sula*, and her body serves as the primary maternal symbol in the novel. Eva contains the Great Mother's propensities for procreation and destruction. Her name suggests the first mother, Eve, but "Peace" seems at first an ironic misnomer, given her imperious and demanding nature. In her later years, townspeople describe her as "mean," and daughter Hannah accuses her of "hating colored people" (SUL 171, 37). Nonetheless, Eva generously opens her large house to the homeless: cousins "passing through," "stray folks," and children in need of a home (SUL 37). She takes in three unrelated boys and, with regal dispensation, names them all Dewey. She coaxes them out of their "cocoon" and sees that they go to school (SUL 38). However, as myth and reality violently come together during the course of the novel, the full meaning and implication of Eva's name is realized. One by one, her own offspring find the "peace" of the mother's body.

Eva's body provides the central metaphor of love and sacrifice in *Sula*, adding both mythic and inverted dimensions to the maternal. The past reveals the terrifying and disturbing extent of Eva's maternal sacrifices. As a young mother, Eva has to maintain constant vigilance over her children's fragile existence after her husband deserts the family. She sees playfulness and affection as absurdly superfluous luxuries she can ill afford to give daughters Hannah and Pearl and son Plum. The three beets she hoards to feed her starving children are in her estimation more ample proof of maternal love. "Don't that count? Ain't that love?" she angrily declares to Hannah years later (SUL 69). Eva's maternal acts, although they keep her children alive, are not enough for them to flourish. Like Pecola and the marigolds that do not grow in *The Bluest Eye*, Eva's children fail to thrive. Instead, they grow up "stealthily" with an emptiness at the core. Both Pearl and Hannah marry, but Pearl

2. Hirsch, *Mother/Daughter Plot*, 179.

moves away and exists only in "frail" letters (SUL 41). A poorly nurtured Hannah visits the same insufficient affection upon her daughter,
Sula, who grows up with an unconscionable lack of human sympathy.
Plum, who perhaps receives the most maternal affection during childhood, returns home from World War I addicted to heroin, rapidly re-
gressing into infantile dependency.

The dynamics present in Eva's relationships with her children coin-
cide with Phyllis Chesler's observations about mother-child relationships in a patriarchal society. In *Women and Madness*, Chesler states,
"Female children are quite literally starved . . . for physical nurturance
and a legacy of power and humanity from adults of their own sex
('mothers')." Chesler also notes that "[m]ost mothers prefer sons" and
are more nurturant of them.[3] Certainly, these dynamics seem to be present in Eva's relationships with her children. Hannah and Pearl are denied maternal warmth, while Plum is bathed "in a constant swaddle of
love and affection" (SUL 45). This, however, pales in comparison to
Eva's ultimate sacrifice made during their childhood. She substitutes
her body for what she cannot give emotionally to her children, particularly her daughters. Desperate to feed and provide for her children, Eva
sacrifices her leg for ten thousand dollars. Her leg, then, becomes the
primary symbol of maternal love and sacrifice in the novel.

Stories abound about Eva's leg—she sold it to a hospital or "stuck it
under a train and made them pay off." Eva herself adds to the mythmaking about her leg, telling the children bizarre tales about how she
lost it. Her remaining leg is equally mythologized: It is described as
"magnificent," "glamorous," and beautifully "stockinged and shod" with
a felt slipper or black lace-up shoe (SUL 31). Eva entertains a host of
gentleman callers who admire "her lovely calf, that neat shoe" (SUL
41). Carolyn Denard observes that Eva "is not preoccupied with alien
standards of physical beauty or measurements of self-worth." Thus, the
sacrifice of one leg and the adornment of the other are intense acts of
self on Eva's part. Unlike Pauline and Pecola Breedlove, who embrace
white societal standards, Eva refuses to subscribe to conventional notions about female beauty and sexuality. She incorporates her disabili-
ty into her sexual appeal, creating what Keith Byerman calls "an ersatz
throne" from a rocking chair and wagon from which she entertains her

3. Phyllis Chesler, *Women and Madness*, 41.

callers. The sacrifice that Eva makes in order to provide for her children casts her as "the victim of a white- and male-dominated society."[4] Eva's missing leg, the ten thousand dollars given in restitution, and the glamorously shod remaining leg symbolize the perverse relationship between the maternal body and the societal and economic forces that demand both its glorification and its sacrifice. Eva's mutilation of her body serves as an indictment of these forces and suggests that there is a cultural responsibility to set maternal limits and to prevent such sacrifices.

To a significant extent, Eva also represents the sexualized maternal. Eva's sexuality connects her with her female descendants, creating the triadic structure that binds Eva, Hannah, and Sula together: "It was man love that Eva bequeathed to her daughters. . . . The Peace women simply loved maleness, for its own sake" (SUL 41). Although Eva, Hannah, and Sula center their passions on men, the experience and enjoyment of their own bodies is equally important. Without regard to social proprieties, they take various lovers and exuberantly engage in sex. Thus, in a sense, Morrison gives the Peace women "the right to pleasure, to sexual experience, to passion" that Luce Irigaray demands for the mother. Irigaray links these acts to maternal speech and insists that women must find or invent "words that do not erase the body but speak the body" and that link them with the bodies of their mothers and daughters. Paradoxically, while Morrison limits maternal discourse in the novel, she does not "erase" the female body. Granted, much about the maternal body is inverted in *Sula,* and certainly Eva's missing leg could be seen as an erasure of sorts. In this connection, Hirsch views the missing leg as a mark of the sparse maternal discourse and the ambivalent treatment given to voice in the novel.[5] But the sexual pleasure and independence that Eva, Hannah, and Sula enjoy demonstrate Morrison's ability to "speak the body" in other ways. Moreover, the sexuality of mother, daughter, and granddaughter serves as a unifying agent within the Peace women's genealogical lineage.

Eva, Hannah, and Sula all live apart from men, resisting marriage and the limitations it imposes. Each possesses the independent, sexual temperament of the ancient mother-goddess that Adrienne Rich describes in *Of Woman Born.* The Great Mother represented a primal female

4. Carolyn Denard, "The Convergence of Feminism and Ethnicity in the Fiction of Toni Morrison," 176; Byerman, "Beyond Realism," 108, 107.

5. Irigaray, *Sexes and Genealogies,* 18, 19; Hirsch, *Mother/Daughter Plot,* 179.

power that functioned autonomously in a pre-patriarchal world. According to Rich, the Great Mother "acknowledged no individual husband" and existed "not to cajole or reassure man, but to assert herself." Although Eva and Hannah experience brief marriages, all three Peace women define themselves and their sexuality outside the boundaries of matrimony. Deborah McDowell asserts that Morrison, like other female writers, "equates marriage with the death of the female self and imagination."[6]

Hannah, widowed at an early age, never remarries but still concerns herself with men and their attentions. She "would fuck practically anything," but refuses to sleep with her lovers at night for it "implied for her a measure of trust and a definite commitment." She becomes a "daylight lover" and engages in sex quickly and generously. Sula, in turn, shares her mother's attitude towards sex. Having learned from Hannah's casual couplings "that sex was pleasant and frequent, but otherwise unremarkable," she is equally promiscuous (SUL 43–44).

For Sula, sex becomes a means to assert herself and to defy social convention. She seduces her best friend's husband and is accused of the worst degradation of all: sleeping with white men. However, sex also enables Sula to experience a range of emotions not easily accessible to her: joy, sorrow, misery, loneliness, and "her own abiding strength and limitless power" (SUL 123). McDowell views Sula's sexuality as "an act of self-exploration" that is linked to creativity and freedom from the "social definitions of female sexuality and conventions of duty." In this regard, Sula is particularly like Eva, who rejects the constraints of marriage and limited definitions of female identity. Eva nonetheless tries to foist marriage and motherhood on Sula, telling her: "When you gone to get married? You need to have some babies. It'll settle you" (SUL 92). Sula rebels against these conventional female roles, which, says McDowell, "restrict if not preclude imaginative expression."[7]

In her refusal to limit her sexual and creative expression, Sula inverts the maternity that Eva suggests. Like the female artist who desires to give birth to herself, Sula retorts: "I don't want to make somebody else. I want to make myself" (SUL 92). Sula's words reflect the absence of maternal love she perceives herself to have experienced. After over-

6. Rich, *Of Woman Born*, 71, 65; Deborah McDowell, "'The Self and the Other': Reading Toni Morrison's *Sula* and the Black Female Text," 82.
7. McDowell, "'The Self and the Other,'" 83, 84.

hearing her mother's words "I just don't like her" (SUL 57), Sula grows up to be, as Roberta Rubenstein points out, an "emotional orphan." Hannah, poorly nurtured herself, thus passes on a perverse maternal legacy. As a result of Hannah's rejection, Rubenstein says, Sula fails to develop an ego and instead becomes "a center of negative energy, withheld emotion, and absence of guilt."[8] Hannah's hurtful words leave Sula devoid of empathy and conscience. A wounded, egocentric adolescent, she sends Chicken Little to a watery death, making no attempt to rescue the child after he slips from her grasp into the river. Later, as an adult, Sula watches her mother burn to death in Eva's front yard with the same lack of conscience. Thus, Sula's desire "to make myself," rather than the babies that Eva suggests, is a compensatory act. It is an ironic, futile attempt to replicate the maternal nurturance missing in her life. And with her complicity in the deaths of Chicken Little and Hannah, Sula embodies the antimaternal spirit that is so pervasive in the novel.

Maternal love and the mother's body find their worst inversions in Eva's relationships with Hannah and with her son, Plum. Unlike Hannah, Plum grows up bathed in too much maternal affection. When he returns home from the war addicted to heroin, he rapidly regresses into infantile dependency. Eva, believing Plum is trying to crawl back into her womb, douses him with kerosene and sets his bed afire so he can "die like a man" (SUL 72). The imagery associated with Eva's sacrificial act depicts the maternal body with both horror and beauty and, paradoxically, itself heralds a return to the womb. With the kerosene seeping into his skin, Plum perceives "some kind of wet light traveling over his legs and stomach with a deeply attractive smell." The kerosene recreates the warmth and wetness of amniotic fluid and the dank, musky odors of birth and the mother's body. To Plum, the "wet lightness" of the kerosene is a "baptism" of sorts. Comforting and seductive, it lures him "into the bright hole of sleep." Like an unborn infant in the womb, he lies "in snug delight" as Eva lights the kerosene and gives him a fiery rebirth (SUL 47). She later confesses to Hannah, "I birthed him once. . . . Godhavemercy, I couldn't birth him twice," but symbolically that is what she has done (SUL 71).

Hannah suffers a similar immolation, and her death also constitutes a tragic inversion of the maternal where fire and water come together.

8. Roberta Rubenstein, "Pariahs and Community," 132.

Trying to light a fire in the yard, her clothes ignite and transform her into a "flaming, dancing figure." Morrison creates a return-to-the-womb reenactment similar to Plum's, save that this one is instigated by the maternal instead. Eva throws herself from the window in hopes of covering her burning daughter with her body. But she fails to reach Hannah, and the leg that had been her children's salvation years before now by its absence prevents her from saving her eldest child. A neighbor couple introduces the element of water when they douse Hannah, "the smoke-and-flame-bound woman," with a tub of water. They succeed in extinguishing the flames, but the water fails to renew life. An inadequate substitute for the maternal fluids, it creates steam that "seared to sealing all that was left of the beautiful Hannah Peace" (SUL 76). The horribly burned and blistered Hannah is reduced to hot, bubbling flesh not unlike the primordial mass from which human life began.

Maternal blood is also spilt in this reverse birthing. Following her abortive attempt to save Hannah, an injured Eva nearly hemorrhages to death after arriving at the hospital. Bleeding profusely, she is left unattended on the floor. The blood that seeps beneath her stretcher recalls the copious amount of maternal blood lost following a traumatic birth or miscarriage. Eva's pain, her spilt blood, and her injured body evoke Old Testament injunctions against the female body and are suggestive of Eve's punishment through childbirth. Byerman, however, sees Hannah's death as Eva's punishment for her hubris in killing Plum. He also notes the irony of the missing leg: "[T]he very sign of Eva's power comes to be the negation of that power." Lying in the hospital ward, Eva realizes her maternal failure and "the perfection of the judgment against her" (SUL 78). Thus, Eva embodies the mother who is, according to Christian, "both sacrificer and sacrifice, [a] woman who learns to accommodate to life's meanness but only with a vengeance." Christian wryly concludes, "If the warm, all-nourishing mama stereotype were alive and well, the creation of Eva has done away it."[9]

Morrison incorporates other inverted birth images in *Sula* that are similarly linked to death and the destructive mythos of the maternal. Water, a significant component in these images, suggests the inherent duality contained within the fluid realm of the maternal: the ability to take life as well as give it. Chicken Little's death in the river suggests a

9. Byerman, "Beyond Realism," 108; Christian, *Black Feminist Criticism*, 28.

paradoxical comingling of birth and womb-regression images. As Sula swings him over the river's edge, the child's "frightened joy" and "bubbly laughter" reveal his innocence and vulnerability. His sudden release over the water is a kind of expulsion from that innocence—a birth of sorts into evil and death. When the water has "darkened and closed quickly" over the place where Chicken Little sinks, he is restored to the womb and to darkness (SUL 60, 61). Perversely, he is transformed not into an infant or fetus but into a bloated corpse that is "unrecognizable" to everyone, including his own mother (SUL 64).

Sula's death at age thirty also symbolizes a return to the womb and a reunification with the maternal body. Through recursive imagery involving fire and water, her death is linked with Hannah's and Plum's. As Sula is dying in Eva's bed from an undisclosed but painful illness, she dreams of the "Clabber Girl Baking Powder lady" (SUL 147). The smiling figure, a familiar one emblazoned on cans of baking powder, beckons Sula in the dream. As Sula approaches her, the baking-powder lady disintegrates into a pile of powder, which Sula desperately tries to scoop into the pockets of her blue-flannel housecoat. The "white dust" of the disintegrating woman could be the heroin of Plum's addiction and is similarly seductive (SUL 147). Indeed, the phrase "Clabber Girl Baking Powder lady" suggests the street terms "white girl" and "white lady," which were contemporaneous slang terms for cocaine and heroin. Just as Plum succumbs to his addiction, Sula feels equally overcome: "The more she scooped, the more it billowed. At last, it covered her, filled her eyes, her nose, her throat, and she woke gagging and overwhelmed with the smell of smoke" (SUL 148).

Besides the smoke and fire imagery, Sula's panic and the blue housecoat in her dream connect her to Hannah's frantic actions when her blue cotton dress goes up in flames. On her deathbed, Sula admits that she was "thrilled" watching her mother burn: "I wanted to watch her keep on jerking like that, to keep on dancing" (SUL 147). The physical pain Sula experiences in dying becomes retribution for watching her mother die, and it parallels the pain suffered by Hannah and Plum during their immolations. Sula's burning, spreading pain is much like Hannah's agony of "cooked flesh" (SUL 77). As intractable pain grips Sula, she perceives it as "a kind of burning, followed by a spread of thin wires to other parts of her body." The pain manifests itself in horrifically sensate ways, evolving into "waves, hammer strokes, razor edges, or small explosions" (SUL 148). Like Pecola and her fusion with the maternal, Sula comes into intimate knowledge of the mother through pain and achieves a fleeting identification with Hannah. As severe as the pain of childbirth, Sula's fiery pain represents a terrible maternal legacy visited upon a childless daughter who would otherwise have never known the primal pain of the mother.

As the process of dying continues for Sula, she regresses, making the retreat into the womb more complete. Like the addicted, helpless Plum who dreams "baby dreams," Sula imagines a fetal state of existence: "[S]he might draw her legs up to her chest, close her eyes, put her thumb in her mouth, and float over and down the tunnels" (SUL 71, 149). Rubenstein sees Sula's longing for a "sleep of water" (SUL 149) as "an image of merging into the embracing womb, the mother from whom she has felt radically separated." Rubenstein asserts that this image links Sula with Chicken Little's death and with the townspeople who suffocate in "a chamber of water" (SUL 162) on the National Suicide Day celebration when they attempt to destroy the unfinished, abandoned tunnel that was to link their town to a town across the river.[10] However, Sula's desire to return to the enveloping waters of the womb most profoundly matches Plum's wish to reenter Eva's womb. The fact that Sula dies in Eva's bed confirms this parallel and demonstrates a symbolic achievement of what Plum tried to accomplish—unity with both the literal mother and the Mother of all mothers.

In another sense, Sula reenters not only the womb but also a version of Julia Kristeva's semiotic chora, which for the speaking subject is a place of "generation and negation," in Alice Adams's words. In Sula's case, as in Plum's and Hannah's, a return to the womb through death means destruction of the self and of symbolic language. Like Hannah, who loses her senses and is reduced to "gesturing and bobbing like a sprung jack-in-the box," Sula is silenced (SUL 76). Morrison emphasizes the voicelessness that accompanies her dying: "Several times she tried to cry out, but the fatigue barely let her open her lips, let alone take the deep breath necessary to scream" (SUL 148). Sula's corpse is found in Eva's bed "gazing at the ceiling trying to complete a yawn" (SUL 172). This final image of Sula suggests not only a last and futile attempt for breath, but also for voice and meaning.

10. Rubenstein, "Pariahs and Community," 135.

As in *The Bluest Eye*, Morrison's rendering of the maternal in *Sula* demonstrates the complex intersections of cultural, psychological, and biological factors in shaping female experience. More specifically, she shows how the silencing of the female voice and the maiming of the mother's body can create deadly reverberations that impact not only individuals but also families and communities. Certainly this is the case in *Sula*, beginning with the desperate impoverishment that Eva and her children suffer early in their lives. Their emotional and physical deprivation, along with the sacrifice of Eva's leg, reflects to a great extent how economic divisions in American culture devalue mothers and children and how racial divisions reinforce such devaluation. The ten thousand dollars Eva receives for her leg demonstrates that the maternal body is a commodity of sorts, one that Eva gladly sells to save her children from starvation. Sadly, her sacrifice is not enough to prevent her children from internalizing negative attitudes about the self or to circumvent the emotional disconnections within the family that result despite her selfless act. Morrison clearly shows that without a psychic rootedness and a secure place within one's family, one's place within society is equally fragile and uncertain. Eva's offspring experience a significant amount of social displacement—Hannah through indiscriminate sex, Plum through heroin addiction, and Sula through a variety of amoral actions that progressively distance her from community and personal conscience. Cut off from self, each other, and the community, all three characters experience the maternal body as an ironic final haven. However, given the searing, voiceless deaths that Hannah, Plum, and Sula each suffer, the peace they find hardly seems restorative, thus making Morrison's use of the maternal body as a metaphor for love and sacrifice a disturbing and complicated one.

4

~

Beloved

HISTORICAL REALITIES /
MATERNAL MYTHOLOGIES

Toni Morrison's use of what Barbara Christian calls her "fantastic earthy realism" finds its fullest expression in her depiction of motherhood in *Beloved* (1987). The maternal in *Beloved* exists on several levels and is subjected to multiple inversions. Rooted in both reality and myth, it is manifested through imagery, language, and individual experiences. As in *The Bluest Eye* and *Sula*, Morrison foregrounds the mother's body and examines issues of silence and voice surrounding the maternal. In *Beloved*, Morrison reveals the wrenching impact of slavery on motherhood, but at the same time she sustains the maternal by constructing a new and mythic model built on generations of female experience. She also successfully bridges the dichotomies of body and voice. Thus, despite the horrors it depicts, *Beloved* emerges as a more hopeful work than her previous books.

The novel, which is set in rural Ohio following the Civil War, contains multiple stories, voices, and shifts in time. The narrative swings back and forth in time to reveal the disturbing and complicated maternal experiences of Sethe, a former slave living with her mother-in-law, Baby Suggs, and daughter Denver in a farmhouse on the outskirts of Cincinnati. While much of the novel takes place in this 1873 postwar setting, the past lies at the devastating core of the novel and impacts the present with vicious intensity. Indeed, as Valerie Smith points out, "The characters have been so profoundly affected by the experience of slavery that time cannot separate them from its horrors or undo its effects."[1] Certainly, this is the case for Sethe and Paul D, another former

---

1. Valerie Smith, "'Circling the Subject': History and Narrative in *Beloved*," 345.

slave from the Sweet Home plantation in Kentucky, who comes to live with Sethe and Denver in Ohio after the war. Having endured unspeakable horrors during slavery, both find the past a constant, threatening presence in their lives.

For the most part, the novel presents itself as a mystery. Morrison reveals the past in bits and pieces, as the whole truth revealed at once would be more than characters or readers could bear. While Paul D's story centers around the physical and psychological assaults that he and other male slaves, including Sethe's husband, endured at Sweet Home, the violations that Sethe suffered there are deeply rooted in female experience. The essential mystery concerning Sethe's past grows out of her Sweet Home experiences of having her breast milk stolen and being beaten by the overseer's nephews. A pregnant Sethe flees the plantation in order to escape further brutality and to join the children she has already sent to Cincinnati to live with their grandmother. After giving birth to Denver during the journey, she successfully rejoins her family, only to be tracked down by the same men who had brutalized her at Sweet Home. Cornered in her mother-in-law's woodshed, a desperate Sethe tries to kill her children rather than see them returned to slavery. Before she is caught, Sethe is able to murder one child, a baby daughter known only as "Beloved" and whose name comes from the incomplete engraving of "Dearly Beloved" on her tombstone. The angry baby ghost that haunts Sethe's house in the opening pages of the novel is the murdered Beloved herself. Later, she is transformed once again into the well-dressed young woman who mysteriously emerges from a nearby stream. To a significant extent, Beloved embodies the past and serves as a disrupting force in the present. Moreover, with her multiple incarnations, Beloved also represents the complex, multilayered treatment given to maternal experience in the novel.

The first and most obvious level of the maternal in *Beloved* consists of the social and historical realities that lie beneath the text. Morrison acknowledges that the actual story of Margaret Garner of Ohio provided the historical substance of *Beloved*. According to various accounts, Garner, like Sethe, attempted to kill her children rather than return them to slavery. She succeeded in killing one child, whom Morrison transforms into the figure of Beloved. According to Morrison, "I just imagined the life of a dead girl which was the girl that Margaret Garner killed, the baby girl that she killed." With Garner's story becoming

Sethe's, Morrison depicts both the cruel realities of motherhood under slavery and the interiority of such maternal experience. Gurleen Grewal explains this portrayal further, stating that Morrison's novel "reveal[s] the silences in the generic, first-person slave narratives and cross[es] the boundaries between fiction and history."[2]

The Sweet Home experiences of Sethe and her mother-in-law reflect the slave mother's social and biological "destiny" to bear children that Angela Davis describes and the fragile family units that result. Neither Sethe nor Baby Suggs can legally marry the fathers of their children, and their respective experiences of motherhood demonstrate how futile maternal attachment can be. Baby Suggs bears eight children by six different fathers, including one child "she could not love" and others "she would not" (BEL 23). Two daughters are sold off in childhood and a son is traded in exchange for lumber. She manages to keep her son Halle the longest—twenty years. Sethe, on the other hand, has six years of "marriage" with Halle, who fathers all of her children. However, her own childhood is emblematic of the harsh familial realities of slave life. Like other slave children whose mothers return to work in the fields shortly after childbirth, Sethe is deprived of her biological mother, whom she knows only as "Ma'am." As a result, she is nursed by another woman and raised by Nan, who gives Sethe not only nurturance but links to her maternal history as well. Nan's description of the rapes she and Sethe's mother endured on their passage from Africa confirms Deborah White's historical account of how female slaves were not imprisoned in the holds of the slave ships but were kept unshackled on the quarterdeck to accommodate the sexual advances of the crew.[3] Of the pregnancies Ma'am experienced during her journey to Sweet Home, Sethe was the only offspring that she did not destroy. Nan tells Sethe: "She threw them all away but you. The one from the crew she threw away on the island. The others from more whites she also threw away. Without names she threw them" (BEL 62). Sethe is allowed to live because her father was black and the only man that her mother allowed herself to embrace.

2. The story of Margaret Garner can be found in Gerda Lerner, ed., *Black Women in White America: A Documentary History*, 60–63; Morrison quoted in Gloria Naylor, "A Conversation: Gloria Naylor and Toni Morrison," 206, 208; Gurleen Grewal, "Memory and the Matrix of History: The Poetics of Loss and Recovery in Joy Kogawa's *Obasan* and Toni Morrison's *Beloved*," 156.

3. Davis, "Reflections on the Black Woman's Role," 7; White, *Ar'n't I a Woman?* 63.

Ma'am's refusal to put her arms around her white rapists, the infanticide she commits, and her unwillingness to bestow names on any of her offspring except Sethe, who is given her father's name, are symbolic gestures of defiance. Her actions also demonstrate the few methods slave women had for resisting or retaliating against their white owners. As White asserts, slave women likely had some means, probably natural or herbal remedies or perhaps the assistance of midwives, to prevent or abort unwanted pregnancies. Research shows that slave mothers were often accused of accidentally or deliberately smothering their infants. Michael Johnson estimates that smothering was responsible for the deaths of more than sixty thousand slave infants between 1790 and 1860. However, White points out new studies indicating that many of these deaths may have been due to crib death, or Sudden Infant Death Syndrome. Linking prenatal care and nutrition to SIDS, she holds slave owners accountable for these deaths since they controlled the medical care, the food allotment, and the work loads that slave women received. According to White, "[I]t was the planters who fed pregnant women too little and worked them too hard who were more responsible for 'smothered infants' than the women who subsequently bore the guilt and blame" for the deaths.[4] When infanticide did occur, Elizabeth Fox-Genovese explains, it could be considered "a crime against [the] master's property."[5] Certainly this is the opinion of Schoolteacher, the plantation manager who tracks Sethe down, when she attempts to murder her children rather than see them sent back into slavery. To him, Sethe and her children are nothing more than ruined livestock, creatures that have been mishandled and rendered useless for serviceable work.

Without question, *Beloved* is a powerful chronicle of the social and historical elements of motherhood under slavery. At the same time, it also reaches into deeper, more mythic levels of maternal experience. *Beloved* is very much a novel of transformation, one that is closely linked

4. White, *Ar'n't I a Woman?* 84; Michael Johnson, "Smothered Slave Infants: Were Slave Mothers at Fault?" 495; White, *Ar'n't I a Woman?* 89. Ironically, recent research suggests that many cases of SIDS today are in fact due to smothering, and law enforcement agencies have stepped up efforts to investigate infant deaths said to be due to SIDS. See "N.C. to Look at More Crib Deaths," *Charlotte (N.C.) Observer*, December 2, 1997, C4, and "Cot Death Diagnosis May Hide Suffocation," BBC Online Network, August 17, 1999, http://news.bbc.co.uk/hi/english/health/newsid_422000/422012. stm.

5. Fox-Genovese, *Within the Plantation Household*, 324.

with the female blood-transformation mysteries found in ancient and primitive cultures. These mysteries are thought to lead a woman into the experience of her own creativity and to produce what Jungian scholar Erich Neumann calls "a numinous impression" on men.[6] Blood, a vigorous symbol in Beloved, forms the mythic core around which the text develops. Its uses in the novel correspond with the three blood-transformation mysteries once associated with the female body.

Menstruation is the first mystery, and its onset is universally regarded as a fateful moment in the life of a woman, a sign of her entry into adulthood and into the procreative processes of life. Indeed, in The Bluest Eye, an awed Claudia and Frieda regard Pecola's menstruation as "sacred" (BLU 28). Pregnancy is the second blood mystery, in which the embryo, according to primitive beliefs, develops from the menstrual blood that no longer flows out of the body during pregnancy. While pregnancy marks a period of profound transformation, birth, says Neumann, heralds a "new archetypal constellation that reshapes the woman's life down to its very depths." After childbirth, a mother is charged to "nourish and protect, to keep warm and hold fast" the child who is extraordinarily dependent upon her. The third blood mystery occurs after childbirth with the transformation of blood into milk. Belief in this process served as the basis for the primordial mysteries of food transformation.[7]

The blood-transformation mysteries in Beloved are not manifested in biological order. Time is not linear in the novel, so the functions of menstruation, pregnancy, birth, and lactation are not always preserved in their natural sequence. At times they even appear fused. This disruption of the natural rhythms of the female body parallels Morrison's portrayal of the confusion and disruption that slavery imposes on human lives. Furthermore, to cogently describe the novel's blood-transformation mysteries requires that events, which are not linear to begin with, be subjected to more disordering. The first blood mystery of menstruation is found in Beloved in the twenty-eight days of unslaved life that Sethe has with her children at the house on Bluestone Road. The twenty-eight days correspond to the lunar cycle, but they are also representative of the menstrual cycle. This period marks a

---

6. Erich Neumann, "Transformation Mysteries of the Woman," 83.
7. Ibid., 83–84.

menarche, suggesting a new beginning for Sethe. She is integrated into the community in much the same way a young woman in primitive society would be assimilated after the onset of menstruation. During the time before the arrival of Schoolteacher to reclaim Sethe, she is fully immersed in the free black community. She enjoys the stories and camaraderie of both men and women and learns about freedom from them, how to claim herself, "how it felt to wake up at dawn and *decide* what to do with the day" (BEL 95). This stage of Sethe's psychosocial integration into the community is short-lived, as she becomes an outcast when she kills her daughter at the end of these twenty-eight days.

Pregnancy and childbirth play a pivotal role in *Beloved* and constitute the second blood-transformation mystery. A pregnant Sethe flees Sweet Home, and Denver's birth during her flight to freedom is full of myth and mystery. Instead of the customary community of women present at such births, Sethe is attended by an unlikely midwife in the Kentucky wilds. Amy Denver, a scrappy young white woman fleeing her own "master," stands in stark contrast to the black women who would normally be present. She is not a mother or an experienced midwife, and she has only "been bleeding for four years" (BEL 83). By rights, Sethe should distrust and fear Amy Denver, but there is no difference of power between the two young women since both are runaways. Moreover, the universality of female experience and the urgency of childbirth help to unite them.

Amy serves in the traditional role of a *doula*, a woman who supports and nurtures the mother through the difficulties of childbirth, postpartum, and lactation. Before labor fully commences, Amy "mothers" Sethe, massaging her swollen, battered feet and singing a lullaby learned from her own mother. Amy also tenderly ministers to Sethe's excoriated back, which has been etched by Nephew's whip into the image of a chokecherry tree containing a wild tangle of branches, leaves, and putrid blossoms. The tree, formed by pus, blood, and raised welts of flesh, is a perverse symbol of life and female experience, with pain, suffering, and fertility mixed together. Sethe's wounds also represent an inscription of sorts and demonstrate how the slave mother's body painfully served as a text written upon by the white patriarchal culture. The wild and bloody image of the tree graphically symbolizes the tangled, violent relationships that slavery often fostered between black women and white men. The tree serves as a branding which declares that Sethe's body, like her children, is not hers to claim.

While the pregnant maternal body is inscribed with symbol and meaning, the onset of labor proves to be equally significant. Sethe's labor begins as she and Amy reach the river that will carry her to freedom. In a life-affirming fusion of reality and myth, Sethe's water breaks at the river's edge, and the amniotic fluid mixes with the waters of the river. As Sethe struggles to give birth in a leaking boat, the baby's head appears in a face-up position. The baby, unable to maneuver through the birth canal, becomes stuck and appears to be drowning in its mother's blood. In a duel between life and death, as blood and river water threaten, Amy screams "Push!" while Sethe whispers "Pull" (BEL 84). Thus, two women—midwife and mother, white and black—work together to deliver the baby and, symbolically, the next generation of women.

While Denver's birth is given both realistic and mythic treatment, Morrison gives Beloved an ironic rebirth of sorts. Beloved's first appearance in the novel as a grown woman is rendered through birth imagery. She mysteriously emerges out of a stream, fully dressed, exhausted, and unknown. Like a newborn who has undergone the long, rhythmical forces of labor in the maternal womb and is then forced through the narrow confines of bone and tissue, Beloved emerges from water and collapses on the bank of the stream. She is "sopping wet," painfully tired, and her shallow breathing and hurting lungs suggest a newborn who has just experienced the trauma of birth and sucked in the first blasts of air outside the womb. Although she is fully grown and finely dressed in black with "good lace at the throat and a rich woman's hat," Beloved's appearance suggests a new being: Her skin is "lineless and smooth" except for three tiny scratches on her forehead that look like "baby hair." Childbirth imagery that parallels Denver's birth can be seen in Sethe's reaction to the strange newcomer. When Sethe first glimpses Beloved, she is struck by a sudden, overwhelming desire to urinate. Failing to reach the outhouse, she lifts her skirts outside its door and voids an "endless" amount of water in the dirt. Sethe herself links the urgency and the amount of her urination with the copious amniotic fluid that flooded the boat when Denver was born: "But there was no stopping water breaking from a breaking womb and there was no stopping now" (BEL 50–51).

Beloved's behavior following her "birth" resembles an infant's. She gazes at Sethe with "sleepy eyes," and when she is offered water to drink, she lets it dribble down her chin without wiping it away (BEL 51). During the days following her "birth" she is incontinent, unable to walk, and constantly sleeps. Ironically, Beloved has to relearn everything and progress through the stages of infant development. This experience continues throughout the novel as Beloved rapidly passes through infancy into egocentric toddlerhood, childhood, and tumultuous adolescence. During each stage, Beloved is obsessed with her "mother" to a degree that surpasses normal mother-child bonds. She and Sethe engage in a bizarre dance of testing and exploring their relationship, of expressing and acting out the anger, guilt, and ambivalence that rage between them. Beloved seems bent on consuming her mother out of both love and hate. Sethe is "licked, tasted, eaten by Beloved's eyes" during her infantile state (BEL 57). As an angry child, Beloved tries to choke Sethe. Eventually she seduces her mother's lover. All of these acts symbolically culminate when Beloved takes the shape of a pregnant woman. In this state, she is the embodiment of the second blood-transformation mystery of blood forming into life.

Beloved's association with blood and the second transformation mystery is evident during other stages of her existence as well. In Beloved's first incarnation, as a real child, her mother murders her rather than see her returned to slavery. To prevent her recapture by Schoolteacher, Sethe takes a handsaw to Beloved's throat, and her near-decapitation spills rivers of blood onto the floor of the shack. This desperate act represents a subversion of the second blood-transformation mystery. Blood that would normally form life is instead associated with death. However, death is not the final stage, as the murdered child is transformed in ways that parallel female blood transformations. The pulsing red pool that appears at the beginning of the novel is the incarnation of the blood spilt in the shack. It also represents the primordial mass of blood and menstrual fluids waiting to form into life again, which it does when the fully grown Beloved emerges out of the stream. Through this imagery, Morrison, as in *The Bluest Eye*, enacts a harsh revision of the African view noted by Christian which links maternity with "the marvelous creativity of the earth." Morrison shows how slavery subverts the most essential myths and basic truths of motherhood.

The pulsing red pool also suggests the nonspecific drives and pulsions of Kristeva's semiotic chora, the maternal space underlying the symbolic. With the maternal body "as the gateway between the semiotic and the symbolic," according to Alice Adams, both the womb and chora attempt "to create something (body or meaning) from nothing." Until Beloved's story is fully articulated and meaning is made of Sethe's maternal experience, Morrison keeps both contained within the "nonexpressive," nonlanguage realm of the chora, manifested through the mysterious pulsing red light that haunts Sethe's house. Grewal identifies the house at 124 Bluestone Road as a metaphor for female interiority and sees Beloved as a "ghostly figure who haunts her mother's matrix, the matrix of black history."[8] As Beloved grows and develops within Sethe's house/womb, so does the reader's awareness of history and the horrors of slavery, particularly a woman's experience of it.

Beloved's transformation into an obviously pregnant woman also associates her with the maternal womb and further inverts the second blood-transformation mystery. Her pregnant state is not seen as a positive, life-giving condition and instead parallels the negativity ascribed to the maternal womb (and to women's role in general) in symbolic discourse. According to Lorraine Gauthier, Kristeva sees women's role in society as "a negative one, in which women constantly expose the gaps in masculinist symbolic discourse."[9] Beloved is a most threatening presence. To the community, she is a "devil-child," clever and beautiful, and represents what the community would rather deny and forget (BEL 261). As the embodiment of the past, Beloved is a living womb, a repository of stories from the horrifying annals of slavery. As such, she not only challenges patriarchal discourse and its writing of history but also threatens to disrupt the new, unslaved lives that individuals in the community have managed to build for themselves. Sethe's perception of Beloved, however, is quite different. Beloved is her restored daughter whom she is willing to protect and kill for if necessary. Indeed, the entire cycle threatens to begin again when Sethe imagines that another white man, Edward Bodwin, is coming for her children. Instead of killing the adult Beloved, Sethe attacks Bodwin. This time the community successfully intervenes to prevent further bloodletting. Mean-

8. Adams, *Reproducing the Womb*, 22; Grewal, "Memory and the Matrix of History," 155.

9. Lorraine Gauthier, "Desire for Origin/Original Desire: Luce Irigaray on Maternity, Sexuality, and Language," 46.

while, Beloved is transformed again. She vanishes into the woods, a mythic, naked woman with fish for hair. Although Beloved disappears in this novel, she will be reincarnated as Joe Trace's primitive mother, Wild, who haunts the woods in *Jazz*.

Lactation and breast milk constitute the third and final blood-transformation mystery evident in *Beloved*. Like blood, milk is a powerful and pervasive symbol in the novel. A "privileged" sign of the maternal, it is a metaphor for nonspeech in Kristeva's theorization and serves as a precursor to language in *Beloved*. A unifying element that links mother and daughters, milk is also a symbolic reminder of the mother tongue that has been silenced and that Sethe, Denver, and Beloved later reclaim. Milk is central to the text in other ways as well. The stealing of Sethe's breast milk provides the critical juncture that sets events in motion and eventually propels Sethe to flight. When Schoolteacher's nephews attack the pregnant and lactating Sethe, they engage in an act of sexual, racial, and maternal defilement that represents a complete perversion of the third female blood-transformation mystery. Sethe's maternity offers her no protection from violence, just as it failed to exempt other slave women. Jacqueline Jones tells how blood and milk often flowed together during the whippings of nursing mothers. She describes how trenches were dug to accommodate the bellies of pregnant women during whippings and afford their unborn children, the master's valuable property, some protection. As "graves for the living," these trenches served as a symbol of how women's roles as workers and childbearers ironically and violently came together.[10] Quite literally, their bodies served as the terrain upon which the patriarchy was erected.

With a hole dug to protect the unborn Denver, Sethe is whipped and silenced; she bites off a piece of her tongue during the ordeal. This image mirrors the silencing of Sethe's mother, who wore "the bit" clamped upon her tongue so often that her lips were forced into a permanent smile: "When she wasn't smiling she smiled" (BEL 203). Unlike Ma'am, who was hanged, Sethe regains her will and voice following the attack by Schoolteacher's nephews. The theft of her milk makes Sethe all the more determined to get milk to her infant daughter in Ohio, even "if she ha[s] to swim" (BEL 83). Later, when she recounts the attack to Paul D, her repeated, outraged cries of "they took my milk" demonstrates

10. Kristeva, "Stabat Mater," 173–74; Jacqueline Jones, *Labor of Love*, 20.

that she is able to give voice to the unspeakable violation she endured (BEL 17). Her words also suggest the lamentation of slave mothers who were forced to serve as wet nurses and provide care and attention to the master's children at the expense of their own.

After giving birth to Denver following her escape from Sweet Home, Sethe has two children to nurse. Milk thus continues as a powerful symbol of the maternal throughout the novel. It represents life, sustenance, and maternal nurturance while everything in the culture and environment conspires to destroy such forces. Breast-feeding maintains the symbiosis begun during pregnancy and strengthens the mother-infant bonds necessary for healthy growth and development. However, in *Beloved* this process is interrupted and subverted when Sethe and her children are tracked down. In the horrifying killing scene in the shack, the symbols of blood and milk fuse together in a perverse mixture of life and death. Holding both a dead child and a living one, Sethe forces a bloody nipple into her live baby's mouth. Thus, Denver takes her mother's milk and the blood of her sister at the same time. This act brings together the primary roles of women as mother, daughter, and sister. Later, in an image that reinforces the paradoxical fusion of life, death, and motherhood, the hot sun dries Sethe's blood-and-milk-soaked dress "stiff, like rigor mortis" (BEL 153). The dried blood and milk thus create a scarlet emblem upon Sethe's dress, symbolizing her maternity and her sin of daring to claim her children as her own.

As in *The Bluest Eye* and *Sula*, the maternal body serves as a vital source of myth and metaphor in *Beloved*. However, *Beloved* does not reflect the same dichotomizing of body and voice shown in the earlier novels. Body and voice are effectively split in *The Bluest Eye*, and voice is all but absent in *Sula*. In *Beloved*, Morrison seems intent on unifying these two aspects of the maternal in order to depict a more holistic and collective rendering of female experience. The fact that Morrison so sharply foregrounds the mother's body and her experience of childbirth and lactation essentially gives voice to the maternal experience. Ultimately, however, voice evolves through the female experiences connecting generations of women in *Beloved*. These connections are forged primarily through language and storytelling, even when the mother tongue has been silenced and forgotten. This is evident in the character of Nan, who spoke the language and is the repository of women's stories from the past extending back to Africa, and in Sethe, who heard the language of Nan and her "Ma'am" as a child and attempted to pick "meaning out of a code she no longer understood" (BEL 62). These connections are further entrenched in Denver, the keeper of her mother's stories. Denver in turn uses these stories as a net to hold Beloved. Like the blood and milk that fuses the two sisters together in the shack, Sethe's stories bind the characters together. The female connections also lead to Baby Suggs, the Great Mother who is the spiritual voice of her community.

While Sethe is powerfully aligned with the maternal body, Baby Suggs epitomizes voice. Like that of Claudia's mother in *The Bluest Eye*, her voice is given full range of expression. Before Sethe's arrival at 124 Bluestone Road, the house mirrors Baby Suggs's spirit and voice: It is "a cheerful buzzing house where Baby Suggs, holy, loved, cautioned, fed, chastised, and soothed" (BEL 86–87). In her sermons, her voice achieves even greater virtuosity: Baby Suggs preaches, prays, advises, sings, and shouts. She exhorts the people of her community to give voice to their own spirits—to laugh, cry, and sing. However, when she commands them to dance, to touch one another, and to love every part of their flesh—"Love it hard. . . . *You* got to love it"—Baby Suggs celebrates the physical body as well (BEL 88). Rather than dichotomizing body and voice, Baby Suggs integrates them. Her exhortations reveal an instinctive knowing that a fully integrated self is critical to both individual and community identities, as well as to the physical and spiritual survival of all. Baby Suggs embodies Abena Busia's idea that the orality of black women's traditions in African and diaspora cultures plays a critical role in communal survival. In addition, she "nurture[s] the spoken word" in the same manner that Karla F. C. Holloway ascribes to black women writers.[11] Through her songs, stories, and sermons, Baby Suggs celebrates language, serves as the oral archive of her community, and preserves culture and memory.

Such holistic integration of body and voice, self and community becomes Baby Suggs's legacy to Sethe, Denver, and Beloved. In separate chapters, the three achieve voice through first-person interior monologues that articulate their individual experiences, with Beloved reaching into the past to voice even Ma'am's experience of the Middle Pas-

11. Busia, "Words Whispered over Voids," 29; Holloway, *Moorings and Metaphors*, 26.

sage. In the poetic "rememory" passage, all of the voices are unified, blending mother, daughter, and sister into one. With astounding intimacy, Sethe, Denver, and Beloved engage in what Morrison deems "a kind of threnody in which they exchange thoughts like a dialogue, or a three-way conversation, but unspoken . . . unuttered."[12]

> Beloved
> You are my sister
> You are my daughter
> You are my face; you are me
> I have found you again; you have come back to me
> You are my Beloved
> You are mine
> You are mine
> You are mine
>
> (BEL 216)

These lines reflect a kind of female interiority and internal voice arising from a maternal source. The fluid boundaries within the passage suggest the fluidity of women's bodies and language that Hélène Cixous posits. Given the emphasis on milk throughout the novel, the passage also mirrors the associations Cixous makes between milk and the reclamation of the maternal voice. In *The Newly Born Woman*, Cixous writes: "Voice: milk that could go on forever. Found again. The lost mother/ bitter-lost. Eternity: is voice mixed with milk."[13] Morrison achieves the same sense of reunification in the rememory passage and in the breast-milk imagery she uses throughout the novel, particularly the scene where Denver takes the blood of her sister along with Sethe's milk. The fused voices in the rememory passage, like the blended blood and milk, reflect women's multiple roles and delineate the intricate nature of female relationships. "I have found you again . . . You are mine" could refer to mother, daughter, or sister quite interchangeably, but the words also comprise a reclamation of memory, identity, and the mother tongue long denied by the slaveholding patriarchy. The passage effectively integrates female and racial experiences into one voice. It also fore-

12. Quoted in Marsha Darling, "In the Realm of Responsibility: A Conversation with Toni Morrison," 249.
13. Cixous and Clément, *Newly Born Woman*, 93.

shadows Sethe's discovery of self at the end of the novel, her startled realization that *she* is her own "best thing" (BEL 273). This establishment of both individual and collective identities is perhaps the ultimate procreative experience. Thus, in *Beloved* the maternal becomes something more than blood and milk, extending beyond exclusively female functions into a more universal realm. It is a spirit that infuses, undergirds, and transforms human experience. Most importantly, the maternal in *Beloved* emerges as a force that celebrates both the individual and a people and gives voice to their experiences. Although its final chapter insists "This is not a story to pass on," the novel is a powerful testament to the importance of memory, remembrance, and the maternal (BEL 275). *Beloved* is a story that must be passed on.

Bobbie Ann Mason

For the most part, maternal experience in Bobbie Ann Mason's fiction assumes less mythic proportions than in Toni Morrison's work. While Morrison's treatment of motherhood has deep Africanist roots that transcend space and time and while she unites myth and reality into a powerful substructure within her fiction, Mason gives maternity a quieter, minimalist role in keeping with the blue-collar, everyday lives she depicts. The contemporary lives of many of her characters seem worlds apart from Morrison's, who suffer the devastating impact of history and white patriarchal culture. In much of Mason's fiction, her characters are ostensibly ordinary, their lives unassuming. They eke out difficult, gritty existences on farms and in small towns in western Kentucky without any real connection to the past or sense of the future.

Immersed in the chaos of modern life where Kmarts, fast-food restaurants, television, and pop music define and shape their lives, Mason's characters cope with pernicious and unrelenting change. They are caught in the turmoil of a traditional rural society giving way to mass culture, and their lives are plagued by unhappy marriages, divorce, difficult children, unemployment, illness, and aging. Their family and community relationships are often fragile and do not provide an enduring sense of continuity and stability. Television sitcoms, soap operas, and rock lyrics provide substitute connections and further homogenize their existence. According to Edwin Arnold, Mason's characters are "beset by a change that is too rapid and all-encompassing." Caught between the past and present, they find that their cultural heritage "no longer holds except in memory and guilt." In Mason's works, the culture of the present has "effectively displaced, transformed, and cheapened the traditional."[1]

1. Edwin Arnold, "Falling Apart and Staying Together: Bobbie Ann Mason and Leon Driskell Explore the State of the Modern Family," 136.

With skill and insight, Mason casts motherhood against this back-drop of cultural change, showing how change affects not only the body and voice of the mother but also women's roles in all their dimensions. She suggests that marriage and motherhood have not been entirely grat-ifying experiences for many of her female characters, particularly for those in Shiloh and Other Stories (1982). The women in Mason's short stories grapple with the changes that time and modern life have brought to their lives. They seem plagued by a restless, unidentifiable unease, a condition that Betty Friedan labeled "the problem that has no name" in her groundbreaking 1963 book, The Feminine Mystique. Friedan's work focused on the problems of white middle-class housewives in the 1950s and early 1960s who were experiencing excessive feelings of bore-dom, isolation, emptiness, and uselessness. Friedan, explains Carol Hy-mowitz and Michaele Weissman, asserted that both "women and men shared a basic human need to grow" but that the feminine-mystique cul-ture of the time thwarted women's growth and kept them in passive, de-pendent roles throughout their lives.[2] Although Friedan's work was aimed at educated, upper-middle-class women of a different era, Ma-son's small-town, working-class characters seem to share the same dis-quieting restlessness that Friedan chronicled. A few even embark on courses of self-improvement to develop their own potential, something Friedan strongly advocated. However, their journeys to new lives and selves are not easy ones.

In some respects, the women in Mason's stories are literary descen-dants of Tillie Olsen's working-class mothers, who also live difficult lives, endure troubled relationships, and must reconcile the tensions be-tween past and present, memory and consciousness. Mason's mothers seem plagued by the same dilemma associated with Olsen's mothers, who represent the "microcosm of the larger human riddle of the con-flicting demands of self and others."[3] Mary Lou Skaggs in "The Rook-ers," from Mason's Shiloh collection, is saddled with an agoraphobic husband who will not go anywhere and a college student daughter who has returned to the nest but maintains an emotional separateness from her mother. Mary Lou's only satisfying outlet is playing cards with the "Rookers," a group of elderly widows whose vitality, eccentricity, and

2. Betty Friedan, The Feminine Mystique, 15; Carol Hymowitz and Michaele Weiss-man, A History of Women in America, 342.
3. Mickey Pearlman and Abby H. P. Werlock, Tillie Olsen, 96.

sense of humor renew her. However, for the most part she remains locked in a frozen pose, torn between stagnation and growth, permanence and change, staying and leaving, and only vaguely aware of these conflicts at work within her. Similarly, Cleo Watkins in "Old Things" suffers a sense of displacement. She is caught in a generational struggle between her daughter and grandchildren, who have moved in with her because of changes in their own lives. Cleo has difficulty comprehending her daughter's divorce and new lifestyle, her granddaughter's telephone patter, and "a new kind of arithmetic" that her grandson is learning and that is completely unknown to her (SHI 80). In a futile attempt to regain control of the past and present, Cleo rearranges loose photos in a family album, while knowing that the pictures, like her family, will not stay in their proper places. She is like Mary Lou, who endlessly shuffles her playing cards. For both characters, time has drastically altered their roles as wives and mothers, leaving them without familiar moorings.

Norma Jean Moffitt, in the title story "Shiloh," presents a striking example of a Mason character who more actively seeks a path of redefinition and change. Much to the confusion of Leroy, her disabled trucker husband, Norma Jean has moved beyond the domestic sphere of marriage. She embarks on a frenetic course of self-improvement by working out with weights, eating Body Buddy cereal, and taking writing courses at the community college. Leroy meanwhile stays home watching television, smoking marijuana, and busying himself with string art and macramé. When Norma Jean leaves the house each day, however, she closes the door not only on a stagnant marriage but also on a painful past involving the crib death of an infant son. The loss of the couple's only child irrevocably mars their relationship and creates a silent chasm of grief and guilt between them. The child is never mentioned aloud, but its wasted, unfulfilled potential mirrors what has become of the marriage. Without question, Norma Jean's maternal experience is brief and sad, her voice practically nonexistent. At the end of the story, when the couple visits the Shiloh battlefield, the site of one of the bloodiest battles in the Civil War, Norma Jean tells Leroy of her decision to leave the marriage. As she walks away, skillfully negotiating the serpentine path through the Shiloh cemetery, she appears to be charting a new and separate life of her own. Leroy watches her walk toward the bluff of the Tennessee River, waving her arms, "doing an exercise for her chest muscles," but he remains uncomprehending (SHI 16). Mason leaves their fates open-ended, but given the sorrowful burdens of the past, so powerfully symbolized by the historical battlefield and cemetery, it seems unlikely that future happiness for either spouse will be easily won.

As "Shiloh" indicates, Mason's emphasis on contemporary culture and the changes it brings to women's lives does not mean she disregards history or its complexity, meaning, and irony. She adroitly blends popular and historical elements while showing how their intersections shape the lives of her characters. Mason in fact adopts a revisionist approach in her treatment of history and culture. Robert Brinkmeyer asserts that she "is charting a new direction for Southern fiction, a rebirth of sorts adapting patterns from the past to enrich and comprehend the disorder of contemporary experience." He argues that Mason establishes "a tension between a traditional past and a modernist present" but contends that she does so to reveal "how this tension no longer carries any significant weight and authority."[4]

Harriet Pollack, on the other hand, argues that Mason, like other contemporary southern women writers, vigorously challenges official history throughout her oeuvre. She explains that for Mason and others, "history is not the chronicle of great deeds and greater battles, borders, treaties, and territories, but an account of lives lived on the margins of official history and culture—of lives silent in history because, by race, class, or gender, they lacked access to official power and event." According to Pollack, Mason's emphasis on cultural/historical changes is a way of depicting "transitional periods not only in the lives of her characters, but in the landscape and values of twentieth-century America." Such changes have significant implications for Mason's female characters, who must "redefine what it means to be a woman, a daughter, a wife, a mother." Through her examination of the processes of redefinition and change, Mason carefully locates "the intersections between 'herstory' and 'history.'"[5]

In rendering maternal experience in her novels, then, Mason reveals how women's lives excruciatingly intersect with "official" history and patriarchal institutions. She also demonstrates how such forces often

4. Robert Brinkmeyer, "Finding One's History: Bobbie Ann Mason and Contemporary Southern Literature," 21, 26.

5. Harriet Pollack, "From Shiloh to In Country to Feather Crowns: Bobbie Ann Mason, Women's History, and Southern Fiction," 96–98.

wield power over the mother's body and define her experience of it. In this regard, she is much like Morrison, who also depicts the impact of history and patriarchal forces on motherhood. Such intersections are poignantly evident in Mason's first novel, In Country (1985). For teenaged Sam Hughes, the Vietnam War and its impact on the different generations of her family profoundly shapes her life and evolving identity. Not only must she come to terms with her father's war experiences, but in the post-Vietnam era of changing gender roles she also struggles to understand her mother's maternity and that of her best friend Dawn. Their maternity is juxtaposed with the sorrowful maternal losses that Sam's paternal grandmother and other mothers have endured because of the Vietnam War.

In Spence + Lila (1988), farmwife Lila Culpepper contends with the ravages of disease and old age and their effects upon her maternal identity. When she is hospitalized for breast cancer, Lila enters the intimidating realm of modern medicine, where she endures patronizing doctors, confusing medical terminology, and painful procedures in order to save her life. In rendering Lila's experiences, Mason shows how her memories as a wife and mother intersect with these hospital realities and lessen the depersonalization they cause. Similarly, Mason links Christie Wheeler's unusual experience of motherhood in Feather Crowns (1993) to technological developments emerging at the turn of the last century. When Christie gives birth in 1900 to the country's first known set of quintuplets, her life is enormously impacted by patriarchal forces that Pollack identifies as "the quartet of medicine, science, money, and male authority."[6] Because of these forces, Christie and her five infants become products that are shamelessly exploited.

As Mason's novels clearly show, history and culture are powerful determinants in women's lives, regardless of age or life circumstances. She depicts how these external forces shape female experience, identity, and consciousness. Mason suggests that the biological experiences of sexual maturation, pregnancy, childbirth, breast-feeding, and aging are culturally mediated events. Moreover, she illustrates how the mother's body develops into a field of contention that pits female experience and women's ways against patriarchal societal forces. In doing this, Mason unflinchingly demonstrates the realities of maternal experience in a

6. Ibid., 102.

changing American culture. At the same time, she portrays the maternal body as a rich source of memory and metaphor involving strong connections to both geographic and cultural landscapes. In addition, Mason's multidimensional rendering of the mother's body is paralleled by her treatment of female consciousness. While the maternal voice is muted or limited at best in her novels, Mason nonetheless gives her principal female characters an interiority that articulates the depth and complexity of their experiences. Such subjectivity stands in contrast with the objectification that history and culture have imposed upon the mother's body. It also remedies the mind-body split that generations of women have endured because of such objectification. Thus, in depicting maternity and motherhood in her novels, Mason recenters female experience within twentieth-century American culture and gives "herstory" new expression and meaning.

5

~

In Country

MOTHERS, DEAD BABIES, AND WAR

Perhaps more than other wars of the twentieth century, the Vietnam War strongly evokes images of a nation's youth sacrificed on the altar of an obscure political agenda. Many young men who fought and died in Vietnam were there not of their own volition but because they had been drafted into a cause they did not understand or support. Even for those who served voluntarily, the war proffered radical changes in the concepts of soldiering, honor, and duty. Meanwhile, back home, a deeply divided America subjected the concept of patriotism to violent scrutiny. The political and moral discord that resulted, along with the war's lack of clear objectives, served to further marginalize the men who fought in Vietnam and who returned to a fractured, unappreciative nation. June Dwyer asserts: "The Vietnam War decentered the American soldier; instead of heroically inhabiting the conflict, he became the Other, an individual far removed from the true meaning of the event. At best, he was misunderstood, at worst, ignored."[1]

Seventeen-year-old Sam Hughes in Bobbie Ann Mason's 1985 novel, *In Country*, attempts to rectify this decentering and to discover the truth of her father's experience in Vietnam. A coming-of-age tale set in 1984, the novel chronicles Sam's quest for her dead father, a Kentucky farmboy who was killed in a Vietnam jungle. It thoughtfully depicts her efforts to explore the "inside" of history forged on both national and personal levels. For Sam, who is on the threshold of adulthood, nearly the

1. June Dwyer, "New Roles, New History, and New Patriotism: Bobbie Ann Mason's *In Country*," 72.

83

same age as her father Dwayne when he died, the search proves critical to the development of her identity, her moral consciousness, and her future in a changed America. The title of the novel hints at the complex grappling that Sam must undergo to fully understand what going "in country" meant for her father, her uncle, and other Vietnam veterans. For them, the term refers to time spent in Vietnam, particularly in jungle and wilderness combat. For Sam, who struggles to grasp the male experience of war, "in country" takes on new meaning as she undergoes her own initiation involving both physical and psychological challenges. On yet another level, "in country" has ramifications that are more nationalistic. The term could well apply to Sam's attempts to understand her country, its role in Vietnam, and ultimately what it means to be a citizen of the United States of America.

Sam's journey to the Vietnam Veterans Memorial in Washington, D.C., with her grandmother and uncle frames the novel and establishes the quest motif that is central to the work. Here at "The Wall," as the memorial is known, past and present collide, while boundaries between public and private realms of experience dissolve. Rendered in the present tense, these opening and closing scenes reveal the immediacy of emotion that the memorial inspires and remind the reader of the continuing impact of the Vietnam War on the daily lives of its survivors, including Mason's characters. The chapters in between these framing sections recount the past and document Sam's struggles to understand not only her father's role in Vietnam and his death there but also the war's effects on her family and country.

With mimetic realism, the inner sections of the novel depict Sam's constricted life in the small town of Hopewell, Kentucky, where she looks after her mother's brother Emmett, an emotionally scarred Vietnam veteran who suffers from the effects of Agent Orange. Her mother, Irene, has remarried and moved to Lexington to start a new life, leaving Sam with responsibility for Emmett and with unanswered questions about Vietnam. In her steadfast refusal to discuss the war, Irene dissuades Sam from exploring it as well, telling her: "It had nothing to do with you" (IC 57). Hurt and angry, Sam accuses her mother of wanting to forget both Vietnam and her father. Emmett, on the other hand, cannot let go of his memories of the war. Plagued by nightmares, headaches, and skin problems, Emmett exists on the fringes of society, unable to hold a job or maintain a love relationship. Although he had at one time entertained a young Sam with wildly adventurous stories acted out with toy helicopters and jet fighters, Emmett is now also reluctant to discuss the realities of Vietnam. When Sam begins to probe for more information, Emmett's friend, Tom, another veteran, tells her: "You don't want to know how real it was" (IC 95).

Not easily deterred, Sam persists in her search for the truth about her father and the Vietnam War. Consequently, politics, history, and the paternal become closely aligned, making Sam's quest an unusual one for a daughter to assume. Ostensibly, her search for her father dominates the text; indeed, all of Sam's actions lead towards this goal. However, Mason also creates a maternal subtext that provides critical underpinnings for her protagonist's quest. She incorporates the maternal into different facets of language, imagery, and plot within the novel. The mother's body and voice are often rendered indirectly and metaphorically, but are no less vital in Sam's efforts to unearth familial history and to learn about her father. In addition, Mason juxtaposes various maternal and paternal elements throughout the novel to create a sexual dualism that adds balance and perspective to Sam's development. In order to locate the father successfully, Sam must come to terms with the mother and with the maternal elements that infuse her life. Perversely, Mason employs a dead-baby motif in Sam's quest that reflects a moral questioning about war and a marked ambivalence about gender roles. Sam's exploration of these subjects enhances her understanding of her family and country as well as the sacrifices both have made. Most important, it enables her to achieve a more complete vision of herself and her place within the confines of history.

The sexual dualism in the novel is given its most intense representation through Sam's examination of the social constructions of gender and what it means to be male or female in post-Vietnam America. This is a fairly solitary endeavor that sets her apart from other young women and men in her community. Ellen Blais points out that, except for Sam and Emmett, most characters in the novel continue to accept "conventional, pre-sixties notions" about gender: "The women marry early, bear children in their late teens, and fuss over their homes while the men go off to work in the local factories or, in the sixties and seventies, wage war in Vietnam." Blais notes how both Sam and her uncle reject these roles. The dysfunctional Emmett putters around the house wearing a skirt, evoking images of Sergeant Klinger from the film and television series M*A*S*H about the Korean War. Sam, unlike her mother and her best friend Dawn, rejects early marriage and motherhood. Instead, she focuses on trying to understand the war experiences of her uncle, his friends, and ultimately her father. This endeavor is essential to Sam's exploration of gender and to her own evolving identity. Blais explains the importance of Sam's focus: "[T]o understand her father is, in a sense, to understand the masculine part of herself."[2]

Other critics have pointed out Mason's inversion of gender roles and her revisionist approach to history as well. As in her *Shiloh* stories, Mason shows the quiet dismantling of established structures that traditionally have defined individuals, families, communities, and entire nations. Dwyer believes that Sam's attempts to understand her heritage constitute a search for both parents, as well as for her country. To a great extent, Sam "plays the historian," reading diaries and letters, interviewing her uncle and his friends, and following similar trails to better understand the war, and hence the male experience. Dwyer argues that Sam initially possesses "old historical expectations [involving] heroes and villains, strong leaders, clear causes." With these elements noticeably absent in the Vietnam conflict, Sam's quest leads to a radically different discovery. Dwyer asserts that she finds a "new history," one devoid of traditional structures and comprising instead "a web of connections, not a patriarchy, but an extended family without a father figure at its head." Along similar lines of thought, Virginia Smith also considers the historicity inherent in Sam's quest. Smith claims that Sam's examination of Vietnam stands as a metaphor for America's search for values following the war, particularly the nation's "quest for historical knowledge that might prevent future Vietnams."[3] Both character and country must conduct painful examinations of history and culture. In Sam's case, the process is deeply felt and extends into intense questioning of gender roles and experiences.

To locate her father and the paternal aspects of her being, Sam consults many sources. Given that patriarchal culture historically has "written" both men and women, Sam begins with the standard, patriarchal approach to discovering identity: She turns to "dull history books," which tell her little about the realities of war or Vietnam (IC 48). She

2. Ellen Blais, "Gender Issues in Bobbie Ann Mason's *In Country*," 107.
3. Dwyer, "New Roles," 72; Virginia Smith, "Between the Lines," 168.

reads her father's diary and his letters to her mother in order to learn what Dwayne was like as a young man and about his experiences in Vietnam. She is also searching for information about her parents' relationship and her own origins. By reading these written texts, Sam is in effect consulting paternal authority for an explanation of history, her family, and her connections to both. Her initial reliance on official, patriarchal representation of both personal and public histories demonstrates the deeply ingrained power of paternal authority within a culture and upon the individual.

Barbara Ryan views Sam's search for her father as "a symbol representation of modern man's desire for the Logos—origin of meaning and authoritative discourse." She sees Sam's desire to know her biological father as "an expression of modernity's deep sense of loss, caused by the sensed fragmentation of the social and even personal self." Ryan also argues that the television sitcoms and music videos that Sam watches during the course of the novel are nonauthoritative texts that "fail to satisfy her." Even Bruce Springsteen's rock lyrics, which so appeal to Sam, "are not the Logos, the paternal word" for which she is searching. Thus, given Sam's reliance on authority at this stage of her quest, it is understandable that she would turn to Dwayne's letters and diary and view them as official, patriarchal discourse. They represent the father, what Ryan defines as "the idealized paternal, the Word that was her beginning, that encompasses her, that will give her both significance and coherence."[4]

When Sam reads her father's letters, she finds that they provide her with a limited and confusing perspective on the war. The language he uses is hardly authoritative. Dwayne's letters to Irene are light and breezy; they do not give the "official" history of the war at all. In the manner of typical American soldiers' communiqués from Vietnam, he talks of the inconveniences of barracks life, night inspections, and pesky mosquitoes. Invoking the slang of popular culture, Dwayne describes his company's operation as "a snap" and optimistically states, "We'll be out of here by fall" (IC 180). Sam responds with disappointment because the letters do not reveal much about Vietnam or her father's experience of it. In trying to discern her father's humanity, she wonders what emo-

4. Barbara Ryan, "Decentered Authority in Bobbie Ann Mason's *In Country*," 199– 202.

tions lie hidden behind the words. She observes: "He didn't say whether he felt lonely or if he was having a good time or if he was miserable" (IC 181). Sam concludes that her father's letters are "strangely frivolous, as if he were on a vacation, writing back wish-you-were-here postcards" (IC 182).

In reading one of her father's last letters to Irene, Sam comes close to locating her origins. Dwayne tells Irene that the biblical name Samuel is his favorite name for the child they are expecting. His next statement—"If it's a girl, name it Samantha. . . . I think it's a name in Chronicles"—gives Sam a glimpse of her unborn self in her father's consciousness. Conversely, it also indicates to Sam that her father "was counting on a boy," that her female name was a paternal afterthought (IC 182). Sam's failure to find her name in the Bible leaves her feeling insignificant; it also makes connection with the paternal and the Word more difficult.

Her father's diary entries that Sam later reads move her closer to the truth of Vietnam. Like his letters, Dwayne's diary writing seems very different from the authoritative Word, the Logos. Written in pencil and with words that "staggered off the lined paper," his entries about weapons and troop movements are "perplexing gibberish" to Sam. His handwriting is "small and squinched," his notations brief (IC 201). Eventually, Dwayne's diary entries lead Sam "in country," into a fuller understanding of his combat experiences in Vietnam. She glimpses the actual war as her father experienced it: cutting trees and wading through a swamp while suffering from depression, diarrhea, cracked and bleeding hands, and feet "like boiled chicken's feet" (IC 204). In his diary, Dwayne likens his platoon's search for enemy camps to the rabbit hunting he had once done at home. The reality of the war intensifies when Sam reads how the men stumble upon the body of a dead Vietnamese soldier "rotting under some leaves, sunk into a little swamp-like place." Dwayne emotionally disconnects himself from the body, comparing it to what he had studied in high school biology. A platoon buddy takes a tooth for good luck, believing that the "special gook stink" of the corpse will offer him protection. Dwayne connects this action with his uncle's practice of "deer hunting with deer piss on him" (IC 203). His diary notations link the rituals of war and hunting, both traditional realms of the paternal. They also bridge the time and space of the killing fields of Vietnam and the hunting fields of Kentucky.

Given the patriarchal construction of history, the diary depicts an ironic diminishment of the paternal at both the individual and national levels. The graphic, unheroic reality of Vietnam as depicted in Dwayne's diary stands in stark contrast with the traditional heroism ascribed to veterans of previous wars. The diary does not present the official, authoritative version of Vietnam but instead presents a more intimate, often horrific account of one soldier's experience. The odd blend of physical privation and emotional indifference that permeates Dwayne's experience reflects both the national and individual impotence associated with what proved to be an interminable, unwinnable war.

Sam is mortified by what she finds in her father's diary. As she reads it, shame and anger overwhelm her. She realizes that her idealized father, the historical father of patriarchal-myth construction, was in reality "a frightened and vindictive country boy." Sam later tells her Uncle Emmett: "I hate him. He was awful, the way he talked about gooks and killing" (IC 221). Ryan notes that Sam does not find a father who is "heroic, congenial, paternal, or authoritative," but rather one who is "a very fragmented and disturbed authority figure . . . and yet a very human, precariously mortal man-child." Thus, within the text and within Sam's mind, the paternal loses much of its power and authority. Sam has been seeking access to the "official order" through the father as Julia Kristeva advocates. Such a masculine, paternal identification, according to Kristeva, is necessary because it enables women "to have a voice in the chapter of politics and history."[5] However, at this point in Sam's quest, such identification is impossible. In her search for the father, Sam has effectively deconstructed the paternal, revealing instability within the patriarchal order.

Sam's exploration of the maternal provides the balance she needs in order to complete her quest. It proves to be a richer medium for her growth and developing consciousness than is the paternal. The maternal courses throughout the novel and manifests itself thematically as well as through language, imagery, and symbols. Mason, like Toni Morrison, inscribes the maternal body with meaning and delineates complex connections between women. In contrast with male war experiences, the distinctly female experiences of pregnancy, birth, and breast-feeding

---

5. Ryan, "Decentered Authority," 208; Kristeva, *About Chinese Women*, 156.

appear often as metaphor and reality in the novel. These events create a sense of women's time, cyclical time that stands in juxtaposition to the linearity of patriarchal history that so concerns Sam. Although their voices and stories are not fully developed, many "mothers" populate the text. These include Sam's mother, Irene; Sam's best friend, Dawn, who becomes pregnant; and Dawn's mother, who died in childbirth and functions as a maternal counterpart to Sam's dead father. Other examples include Sam's paternal grandmother, Mamaw, whose experience of losing her son parallels that of the Vietnamese mother on the cover of *Newsweek* carrying her own dead child. The image of the latter is so disturbing that Irene rips the magazine away from a young Sam, who is nevertheless left with an indelible image of maternal grief and loss. Other Vietnamese mothers are mentioned often throughout the novel, perhaps to confirm the universality of sorrow associated with motherhood and war.

Sam's relationship with her mother is an uneasy and ambivalent one. She resents her mother's remarriage after Dwayne's death and she resents her new baby sister, Heather. In moving to Lexington with a new husband and baby in tow, Irene essentially divorces herself from the past and any connections to Sam's father. Sam bitterly complains that her mother will not tell her anything about Dwayne—"what he was like or what his favorite foods were or anything." Moreover, because her mother is also silent about Vietnam, consigning it to the past, Sam observes, "My mother acts like the Vietnam War was back in the Dark Ages" (IC 64). Whereas Morrison's mothers are deeply connected to history and memory, Irene struggles to be free of them both. She tells Sam: "But I can't live in the past. It was all such a stupid waste. There's nothing to remember" (IC 168). In her struggle to disassociate herself from the past, she is clearly reacting to its power and hold. However, in contrast with the paternal—which more fully embodies the past, history, and stasis in the novel—Mason succeeds in linking the maternal with the present and with change.

Although Irene chooses marriage when she becomes pregnant out of wedlock with Heather, she encourages Sam to pursue a less traditional route. At the news of her pregnancy with Heather, Irene rushes Sam to the doctor for birth control pills to spare her a similar fate. Irene also insists that Sam go to college in order to get away from Hopewell and from taking care of Emmett, telling her: "You *have* to go to college, Sam.

Women can do anything they want to now, just about" (IC 167). She buys Sam a car, a gift of great significance given the gender-role restrictions in Hopewell. Or, as Sam observes: "Boys got cars for graduation, but girls usually had to buy their own cars because they were expected to get married—to guys with cars" (IC 58). The Volkswagen, an anti-establishment symbol of the turbulent 1960s and 1970s, represents a gift of mobility, freedom, and opportunity for Sam. The car gives her "a strange exhilaration, as if she were free to do anything she wanted to" (IC 178).

Despite her reluctance to discuss Sam's father and Vietnam, Irene does not represent the silent maternal. Her voice, though not one of official authority, is nonetheless an insistent one that encourages Sam to make choices that would defy patriarchal expectations. Ironically, Irene's own life contains the conventional trappings of marriage and motherhood, and she usually appears in the novel feeding or nursing baby Heather. Indeed, Irene's identification with breast-feeding and milk, one of Kristeva's "privileged" signs of the maternal, might relegate her to the realm of the semiotic, but Mason gives her a voice that speaks in opposition to the paternal. In certain respects, Mason privileges the maternal over the paternal. After all, she juxtaposes a live mother with a dead father, and although the father speaks to Sam through the more "official" written words of his diary and letters, it is the mother's voice that Sam ultimately heeds. Irene subverts the patriarchy by encouraging Sam to make nontraditional choices. The birth control pills, the car, and college are powerful counterforces to conventional gender-role expectations. Through the simple act of providing birth control pills for her daughter, Irene radically undermines the procreative dictates of the patriarchy and encourages the expression of female *jouissance*.

Irene also serves as a bridge between the past and the future. For the most part, she represents the "here and now," but by helping Sam locate Dwayne's letters, Irene enables her to connect with the past and with her father. Most important, Irene's actions in the present grant Sam the possibility of a future unencumbered by traditional roles and limited choices. In order to find the father, Sam must go through the mother. Irene tells her the letters "might still be in my room somewhere" (IC 169). When Sam searches her mother's old bedroom for them, she also finds pieces of her mother's past, including various mementos, knick-knacks, pictures, and old clothes and undergarments. The room and its contents are symbolic of maternal space. Through her exploration of the room, Sam comes into brief but intimate knowledge of the mother. Similarly, Sam's grandmother Mamaw also serves as a vehicle for locating the paternal. She finds Dwayne's diary and gives it to Sam, thus providing her with the most critical and revelatory source of information about her young dead father.

While Sam's mother is an important embodiment of the maternal, Mason moves beyond characters and into language, imagery, and cultural meaning to reinforce the maternal underpinnings of her text. As Hélène Cixous and Luce Irigaray have theorized, the maternal provides a vital source of language and exerts a powerful influence on the development of the self. In Mason's novel, this is no less true. Sam's development, language, and consciousness are profoundly informed by the maternal. Her use of simile to interpret people and events around her particularly reflects this. Mothers and babies appear frequently in figurative language, demonstrating that although Sam's search appears focused on the father, the maternal permeates her language and thinking. Sam notes how her mother is said to have "babied" Emmett (IC 23). Emmett, in his long Indian-print skirt, looks "tall and broad, like a middle-aged woman who had had several children" (IC 32). Later, when he leads Sam home from Cawood's Pond, Emmett retains this maternal identity: From the back, to Sam, "he look[s] like an old peasant woman hugging a baby" (IC 226). Sam, during her own "in country" experience at the pond, recalls Coleridge's "Rime of the Ancient Mariner" and links the speaker of the poem with the maternal: "The man in the poem was sorry he had shot the albatross, and he went around telling everybody at a wedding about it, like a pregnant woman thrusting her condition on everyone" (IC 215).

The maternal also shapes Sam's thoughts and behavior throughout the novel, sometimes in a paradoxical manner. For example, Sam assumes a mothering role with her uncle, even though she has not been fully parented herself. With her mother's remarriage and subsequent move to Lexington, Sam insists on taking over the job of caring for Emmett. Sam also responds to her older, Vietnam vet lover's impotence in a maternal manner. Psychological scars from the war leave Tom unable to function sexually. Although she is amused by his talk of penile implants and imagines his penis "expanding and growing, like Pinocchio's nose," Sam stifles a giggle and instead puts her arms around him in a comforting fashion: "Since he couldn't get inside her, she wanted to enclose him with her arms." Whatever sexual impulses Sam might have felt are transformed into maternal ones. Indeed, Sam and Tom become Madonna and child, for when Sam wakes a couple of hours later, she finds that Tom, like a child, is "still clinging to her in his sleep" (IC 128, 129). In other respects, Sam embodies the antimaternal; like Morrison's Sula, she rejects marriage and motherhood, and she encourages her friend Dawn to terminate her pregnancy.

The maternal body itself is a source of rich metaphor and symbol in the novel. As in *Beloved*, breasts and breast-feeding serve as important symbols of the maternal. Whereas Morrison powerfully connects Sethe's breasts to African American maternal identity under slavery, Mason links Irene's breasts and American popular culture. Irene, who had bottle-fed Sam in infancy, now follows a new trend and enthusiastically breast-feeds Sam's baby sister. When Sam observes her mother nursing the baby, she carefully notes the details of her mother's breast and views it in junk-food terms: "Her breast was pale and oval, and the nipple looked like the end of a Tootsie Roll. Sam wondered if that was where Tootsie Rolls got their name" (IC 167). Mason incorporates other examples that connect the maternal breast and breast-feeding to consumer products. Sam views her mother as "holding on to the baby as if it were a piece of baggage fastened to her person with Velcro" (IC 169). Sam even likens the baby's burp after she finishes nursing to the "Tupperware joke about the walrus"—possibly a reference to the "burping" sound made when a Tupperware bowl and lid are sealed (IC 168). In an association that links breast-feeding and cigarettes, Sam notes how her boyfriend sits in his van "tugging on his cigarette, like Irene's little nursing baby" (IC 187). Irene also relates her breasts to popular culture; when Sam observes how large her mother's breasts are, Irene exclaims: "Yeah, while I'm nursing. I feel like Jayne Mansfield" (IC 172). Irene's identification with Mansfield, the movie star icon of the 1950s whose celebrated breasts fueled many a sexual fantasy and left subsequent generations of women feeling inadequate, sexualizes the maternal and connects Irene with popular culture.

These examples demonstrate how the maternal body is a text written upon and defined by the larger culture. Meaning and value are inscribed by a Hollywood-crazed, consumeristic world that is ignorant of the mythos and function of the mother's body. Although her characters interpret the maternal breast in terms of contemporary culture, Mason, with humor and irony, recognizes the possibility that it may be the maternal breast, with its elongated Tootsie Roll nipple, that is defining both the culture and its products. Candy bars and cigarettes are nothing more than pop-culture substitutes for the oral gratification provided by the maternal breast. Similarly, the well-endowed Mansfield's breasts are not unlike the large, engorged breasts of a lactating mother, which suggests that the sexual fervor and envy associated with Mansfield really represent a desire for the maternal. At any rate, Mason's depiction of breasts and breast-feeding reflects the bizarre cultural warping to which the most sacred feature of the maternal anatomy has been subjected.

While the maternal breast is associated with such popular-culture elements as Tootsie Rolls, cigarettes, Tupperware, and Jayne Mansfield in the novel, pregnancy and childbirth are linked with other aspects of culture. In her rendering of these experiences, Mason establishes a metaphorical connection between childbearing and going to war. Katherine Kinney, in her study of the relationship between sex and war in Mason's novel, explains that the events of childbirth and going to war traditionally constitute "rite[s] of passage in which children become adults by conforming to culturally prescribed roles, be it as soldier or wife and mother." However, by so closely associating motherhood, death, and war, Mason blurs the distinctions between male and female experiences. Kinney argues that Mason, in her treatment of "the metaphorical relationship" between childbirth and going to war, presents "the ambiguities and ambivalence of gender difference as a series of collapsing and reforming social constructions." For characters such as Dawn and Mamaw, "having babies and going to war remain natural facts beyond question." In contrast, Sam questions traditional gender roles and possesses a distinct and wary ambivalence about motherhood. To Sam, pregnancy represents the death of possibilities and a reinforcement of traditional roles and their restrictions. Sam sees Dawn's pregnancy as "tragic" and is sickened by what it will mean for her friend. Sam reflects: "[I]t used to be that getting pregnant when you weren't married ruined your life because of the disgrace; now it just ruined your life, and nobody cared enough for it to be a disgrace" (IC 103). She suggests that Dawn get an abortion, which Kinney sees as indicative of Sam's rejection of both "compulsory motherhood" and the "heritage of gender roles" that limits female experience.[6] Later, when Sam contemplates the significance of teenage relationships and the "miracle" of her own beginnings, she rejects traditional, romanticized notions of love, marriage, and motherhood even further. Cynically, she observes: "Making a baby had nothing to do with love, or anything mystical, or what they said in church. It was just fucking" (IC 192).

Mason employs the dead-baby motif throughout the novel to demonstrate Sam's ambivalence about pregnancy, war, and conventional gender roles. After she finds out about Dawn's pregnancy, Sam experiences a grotesque dream in which a baby she has had with Tom is pureed in a food processor and kept in the freezer. Every morning this horrific mixture, which is "the color of candied sweet potatoes," is thawed into a baby again (IC 83). The pureed baby suggests aborted fetal tissue, which Sallie Tisdale so chillingly describes in her essay about working in an abortion clinic: "[I]n the basin, among the curdlike blood clots, I see an elfin thorax, attenuated, its pencilline ribs all in parallel rows with tiny knobs of spine rounding upwards. A translucent arm and hand swim beside." Like the baby of Sam's dream, the tissue is "slip[ped] into a bag and place[d] in the freezer, to be burned at another time."[7] Of course, Sam's dream foreshadows both the abortion that she suggests to Dawn and her failed coupling with Tom. However, it also leads to a series of dead- and deformed-baby images that Sam visualizes in her mind. Observing her baby sister sitting in an infant carrier, Sam wonders if the carrier will curve Heather's spine like the "tiny naked rubber dolls with crooked spines from the gum machine at the shopping center." Adding to this monstrous image, Sam tells her mother: "I've heard of babies born with teeth . . . and tails too. One in a hundred thousand babies is born with a tail. Does that baby have a tail?" Sam then links her sister, now hideously grotesque in her own mind, with Dawn's pregnancy, which she sees as equally disturbing: "Dawn was going to have a baby like that, and she'd have to take it everywhere with her. It was depressing. It was as though Dawn had been captured by body snatchers" (IC 155).

Mason skillfully furthers the dead-baby imagery to show the fear and ambivalence about motherhood that Dawn briefly experiences. When

6. Katherine Kinney, "'Humping the Boonies': Sex, Combat, and the Female in Bobbie Ann Mason's *In Country*," 43–44.

7. Sallie Tisdale, "We Do Abortions Here," 434, 438.

Dawn tells Sam about a chicken she bought at the grocery store, Mason brings together images of pregnancy, birth, abortion, and conflicted attitudes about motherhood. Dawn tells Sam: "And when I got home and pulled out those parts inside, all wrapped in paper, I had the sickening thought that the chicken was giving birth to a creature, but it was all in parts, so they had to be stuffed in a little bag. . . . When I pulled the package of parts out, I thought about you, and I knew what you'd think. Our minds must be that close" (IC 176). Indeed, Dawn's description of the chicken parts opens the door to Sam's directive to her to "Get an abortion—for your own good." Perversely, Mason completes the chicken/abortion image with a quirky play on words; Dawn rejects Sam's idea of an abortion, saying: "I could do a lot of crazy stuff, but not that. I'm just too chicken to do that" (IC 177). Or, as Kinney makes clear, Dawn is too conventional to challenge the social order, and, given that her own mother died soon after Dawn's birth, she "feels compelled to bear this child even at personal sacrifice."[8]

Mason also uses dead-baby imagery to link motherhood and war. Again, her baby sister Heather serves to fuel Sam's imagination and to further the imagery. When she hears her sister cry during the night, Sam likens the baby to "a growth that had come loose . . . like a scab or a wart—and Irene carried it around with her in fascination, unable to part with it." In quick sequence, Sam recalls how monkeys carry their dead babies around, that a friend of Emmett's knew a lot of dead-baby jokes, and that "[i]n Vietnam, mothers had carried their babies around with them until they began to rot" (IC 164). Like Leroy in "Shiloh," who associates his dead son with "Dr. Strangelove" and the fallen men at Shiloh, Sam connects dead babies to popular culture and war. While trying to envision the Vietnamese mothers with their dead children, Sam recalls the final television episode of M*A*S*H, in which Hawkeye falls apart after seeing a Korean woman smother her baby to keep it from crying and revealing their presence to the enemy. Sam's associations here reflect the terrible reality that, as Kinney says, "mothers have no supernatural power to sustain the lives of their children," and in war this is devastatingly true.[9]

When Sam goes to Cawood's Pond in an attempt to "face the wild"

8. Kinney, "Humping the Boonies," 44.
9. Ibid., 46.

and come to terms with her father's experience in Vietnam, the distinctions between male and female roles become less clear and the associations between war and motherhood even more entrenched (IC 208). She makes camp at the pond, a desolate area famous for snakes and other wildlife, in an attempt to go "in country" herself. At first Sam ruminates over men's ease with war and how they are "nostalgic about killing" (IC 209). She sees killing as something instinctive in men and notes that Emmett sets off a flea bomb and fires an Atari game button with perhaps the same casualness that he launched mortar rockets in Vietnam. Initially, Sam contrasts men's penchant for killing with women's avoidance of it, telling herself such things as "If it were up to women, there wouldn't be any war" and "Women didn't kill" (IC 208, 210). However, as the night closes around her and her "in country" experience at the pond intensifies, Sam realizes that men's experiences of war and women's experiences of motherhood are not so unlike. After envisioning her father's and uncle's experiences in the rice paddies and jungles of Vietnam, Sam's thoughts turn to Dawn's pregnancy and her mother's experience with Heather. This shift in Sam's thinking effectively links the paternal with the maternal and reveals that both can be powerful, destructive forces. The dead-baby images that Mason uses throughout the novel to demonstrate Sam's ambivalence about pregnancy, war, and the paralyzing restrictions of conventional gender roles coalesce here into Sam's grim realization that "[s]oldiers murdered babies. But women did too. They ripped their own unborn babies out of themselves and flushed them away, squirming and bloody" (IC 215). Throughout the novel, the maternal and paternal have been juxtaposed with each other, but here they are chillingly unified through these soldiers, mothers, and "murdered" babies.

The blending of mother and soldier, maternal and paternal into one image can also be found in Emmett's response to Sam's angry prodding about Vietnam after he finds her at Cawood's Pond. Here in the wilderness, a distraught and sobbing Emmett "gives birth to his sorrow," according to Kinney, a pain which she attributes to "not only the horror of smelling and tasting death and being too afraid to move, but the guilt of having failed to protect those who continued to protect him even in death."[10] Recalling the grotesque baby images of earlier passages, Em-

10. Ibid., 47.

mett's sorrow over Vietnam is "fullblown, as though it had grown over the years into something monstrous and fantastic" (IC 224). When Sam questions him about his plans for marriage and family, Emmett laments that he wants "to be a father. But I can't. The closest I can come is with you" (IC 225). In one sense, Emmett represents the failed paternal, but by giving maternal underpinnings to his identity, Mason allows him to transcend the limitations of traditional gender roles. The male/female, mother/soldier fusion is maintained when a broken but perhaps ready-to-heal Emmett leaves the pond. The maternal image he assumes of a "peasant woman hugging a baby" is a healing, transcendent one that melds the American soldier with the Vietnamese mother so that both now know each other's pain.

The final image of Emmett in the novel further suggests a transcendence over the restrictions of gender, the damnation of war, and the confines of history and culture. When Emmett visits the Vietnam Memorial with Sam and Mamaw, he carefully searches the wall for names of friends who died in the war, while at the same time checking to see if others made it out alive. Sitting cross-legged in front of the memorial, studying the finely etched names, Emmett appears Buddha-like: "[S]lowly his face burst into a smile like flames" (IC 245). The serenity and peace conveyed by this image indicates that Emmett's healing has at last begun.

The trip to the Vietnam Memorial also completes Sam's quest and yields perhaps the most profound and satisfying rendering of the maternal-body-and-birth metaphor in the novel. The Wall itself represents the maternal body and is described in terms that suggest female sexual anatomy: "It is massive, a black gash in a hillside, like a vein of coal exposed and then polished with polyurethane," and "The memorial cuts a V in the ground" (IC 239). The black gash and V of the Wall suggest the vulvo-vaginal region of the female body leading to the womb. Indeed, the Wall is a massive womb, symbolically containing the more than 58,000 soldiers killed or missing in the Vietnam War. The granite walls of the memorial gently and gradually emerge out of the earth and span nearly 250 feet, rising to a height of about 10 feet at the vertex. The walls are supported on pilings anchored to the bedrock; this gives the memorial an intimate relationship with "mother earth" and her rhythmical cycles of life, death, and rebirth. The shiny black surface of the walls contains the names of the dead and eerily reflects the living, momentarily fusing the two. Moreover, the rubbings of names taken by loved ones and the thousands of mementos and tokens left at the memorial represent a raw mix of guilt, grief, love, and remembrance, and perhaps a renewal of sorts for the living. When Sam stands "in the center of the V, deep in the pit," she is fully immersed within the maternal. Here, she stands at the epicenter of life and death, the Wall serving as both womb and tomb. For Sam, it is a moving but confusing experience. She realizes that the knowledge she has been seeking is not yet hers to possess and realistically concludes that she "will never really know what happened to all these men in the war" (IC 240).

When Sam sees the Washington Monument and the American flag, both powerful symbols of the national patriarchy, reflected in the Wall, she interprets them as "arrogant gestures, like the country giving the finger to the dead boys, flung in this hole in the ground." Unable to fully understand her feelings, Sam is overwhelmed by them. Her emotions are powerfully linked with the maternal, for they create sensations that mirror the wrenching contractions of the final stages of childbirth. She is much like an uninitiated mother about to give birth for the first time: "Sam doesn't understand what she is feeling, but it is something so strong, it is like a tornado moving in her, something massive and overpowering. It feels like giving birth to this wall" (IC 240). The full power of the maternal is made manifest in this image. When Sam finds her father's name on the Wall, the image has even more significance, for it suggests, says Kinney, that "the daughter gives birth to the father, the future to the past, the living to the dead."[11]

Sam's assessment of Dwayne's etched name links it with the Logos, with the paternal, but it is still somewhat incomprehensible to her. She sees it as "[a] scratching on a rock. Writing. Something for future archeologists to puzzle over, clues to a language" (IC 244). When Sam locates her own name, actually the name of a dead private from Texas, her recognition of the inscription's significance is intense. With a pounding heart, she rushes to the panel that contains her name and touches it, noting, "How odd it feels, as though all the names in America have been used to decorate this wall" (IC 245). Quite symbolically, she has found herself, and, given her earlier identification with the maternal, the fusion of male and female, mother and soldier is complete.

11. Ibid., 48.

In this final scene, Sam effectively reconciles the paternal and maternal aspects of her being, thus accomplishing a critical step in maturation and in the achievement of personal identity. More important, Sam's realization that the Wall contains many names besides her own moves her from individual consciousness to a more expansive view. She begins to understand the complex relationships that exist between a nation, its people, and the making of history. Or, as Sandra Bonilla Durham asserts about the scene: "[A]ll Americans are war casualties and are, in that way, united."[12] Thus, in delineating Sam's quest for knowledge about her father and the Vietnam War, Mason dissolves boundaries between past and present, public and private, and male and female. She demonstrates that history and war are shared experiences affecting families, communities, and entire nations. However, in the process Mason also effectively recenters the individual, whether it is a young father killed in Vietnam, a marginalized war veteran, or a teenaged girl who struggles to comprehend experiences that are foreign to her gender and generation. For Sam Hughes, this recentering leads to a greater understanding of self, family, and her own place in history.

12. Sandra Bonilla Durham, "Women and War: Bobbie Ann Mason's *In Country*," 52.

6

~

Spence + Lila

MEMORY, LANDSCAPE, AND THE MOTHER'S BODY

While Bobbie Ann Mason continues to juxtapose the maternal and paternal in her 1988 novel *Spence + Lila*, the experiences of the mother, rather than the father, are more central to this work. *Spence + Lila* is a love story about a rural Kentucky farm couple who, after forty years of marriage, must confront the realities of old age, illness, and mortality together. Lila Culpepper's diagnosis of breast cancer and the two surgeries that follow provide the pivotal crisis in the novel and place the female body center stage. Mason links Lila's body, particularly her breasts, to the passage of time, memory, and the landscape. These elements are bound cohesively in metaphor and imagery, thus giving maternal experience deep roots in time and place.

As in most of her works, Mason does not create a grand sense of the historical past in *Spence + Lila*, but rather a quiet personal past that emerges from the rural Kentucky landscape. The novel, too, is grounded in time and place—the bustling boom times of the 1980s when new housing developments and shopping centers transfigured the land and the lives of its people. Or, as Spence Culpepper reflects: "These days with all the new money, everyone has gone wild. . . . people either get drunk or go crazy" (SL 57–58). Paradoxically, Mason also creates an enduring sense of timelessness and continuity that surrounds her principal characters and that buffers them from the changes and crises visited upon their lives. Against this backdrop, Lila's body and maternal experiences are cast. They form the focal point of concern for Spence and Lila in their individual contemplations of their life together, Lila's illness, and the overwhelming sense of change and mortality thrust upon them.

The novel was largely constructed by alternating the points of view of husband and wife. Using Spence's and Lila's individual perceptions, each chapter provides glimpses into their marital and familial past as their present situation unfolds. As the novel progresses, the dual points of view create a gentle tension between the maternal and the paternal but also produce a fairly balanced perspective. This strategy yields a more complete portrait of the couple's satisfying union and demonstrates the importance of time and memory in human relationships. There is a far greater sense of marital wholeness in *Spence + Lila* than in *In Country* or in any of Mason's short stories. Even the title of the novel, which reads "Spence plus Lila," reaffirms this unity. Mason sees the novel as "a love story, with the title written in a notebook or carved in a school desk, with the words enclosed in a heart."[1]

Unlike the marriages in her stories, which dissipate or crumble under various strains, Mason creates a relationship in *Spence + Lila* that has lovingly endured for decades. This perhaps can be attributed to the real-life models that she used for her characters: Mason has admitted that Spence and Lila Culpepper are "very much based" on her parents, Wilburn and Christianna Mason. In her 1999 memoir, *Clear Springs*, Mason states that her parents' marriage lasted fifty-four years until Wilburn died in 1990, two years after the publication of *Spence + Lila* (CS 202). Mason draws heavily from her mother's life in her creation of Lila Culpepper, whose orphaned past is nearly identical to Christianna Mason's. Both lost their mothers and newborn siblings after difficult childbirths and were consequently raised by other family members. As older women, both suffer the same threats to life and wholeness: breast cancer and blocked carotid arteries, a condition that often leads to strokes. Mason's novel had its genesis in her mother's experience with breast cancer. She kept a notebook while her mother was in the hospital having a mastectomy and later realized that her notes provided the substance for a novel. As Mason explains, "I had all this material and I could see the whole book." She speaks with high and knowledgeable regard for her two main characters and, we might assume, her parents: "I would say they both face death with courage, they're both successful at having a good, long-standing relationship to their world and to each

---

1. Quoted in Bonnie Lyons and Bill Oliver, "An Interview with Bobbie Ann Mason," 468.

other, they're welded to each other, they have strong purpose, and they know what their work is. They're capable of great love and sacrifice. They know where they are and what needs to be done. Therefore they're strong models of moral integrity."[2]

Even the family farm finds itself in the text. Mason bases the Culpepper farm on the fifty-three-acre farm where she grew up and that now lies within the city limits of Mayfield, Kentucky. In *Clear Springs*, she discusses at length the role of the farm in her parent's lives and in her own. The farm sits at the center of a tapestry of memory woven through time and multiple generations of family members. Mason describes how its six fields are "laid out behind the woods like quilt blocks, with the shaggy fencerows stitching them together" (CS 278). She points out that, while many of her father's family "were rooted on the land like gnarled old trees," she and her two sisters were quick to leave Kentucky for such meccas as New York, Florida, and California (CS 18). She explains, "We've been free to roam, because we've always known where home is" (CS 13). Mason eventually returned to Kentucky, settling within driving distance of her parents' farm. Her father's death and her mother's subsequent move to a new house did not diminish her deep connection to the farm and the sense of the past it evoked. Mason describes visiting the farm with her mother to pick beans from the garden and berries from beside the creek, where "a jumble of memories rushes out, memories of a period in my own lifetime which links straight back to a century ago, and even further" (CS 11). She reaffirms the importance of her family's home and the fields that surround it, stating, "This land around me has a hold on my heart" (CS 278).

Like Mason's parents, Spence and Lila are inextricably bound together and their marriage functions in gentle harmony and balance. However, Lila's character, her maternal identity, and her life experiences take precedence, providing the central concerns and defining metaphors of the novel. Moreover, by foregrounding the mother's body, Mason attempts to reverse the mind-body split that has traditionally plagued women in Western culture. By focusing so attentively on Lila's sense of her body and her memories of it, Mason allows her character to accomplish what Adrienne Rich and Jane Gallop describe as "thinking through the body." In *Of Woman Born*, Rich calls for women to

2. Ibid.

question traditional definitions of womanhood and to reconceptualize the female self, linking mind, body, and senses in the process. She states: "In arguing that we have by no means yet explored or understood our biological grounding, the miracle and paradox of the female body and its spiritual and political meanings, I am really asking whether women cannot begin at last, to *think through the body*, to connect what has been so cruelly disorganized." Gallop, who incorporates Rich's directives into her own essays on women, literature, and culture in *Thinking through the Body*, views the female body as "a site of knowledge, a medium for thought" that must be given serious attention, both philosophically and politically.[3] While Mason does not give her character a propensity for such intellectualization, she does enable Lila to integrate mind, body, and senses as she struggles to cope with her breast cancer. Immured in the rhythms of farm life, Lila works to maintain the simple but innate sense of wholeness that has defined her life. Although her voice and language are plainspoken, Lila's thoughts are evocative and demonstrate the fluid interconnections that exist between her body and memories of her experiences as a woman, wife, and mother. Moreover, her thoughts, as they unfold during the course of her illness, show that Lila is indeed thinking through the body, but in her own way. As Lila deals with the cancer and the loss of her breast, her body serves as "a medium for thought," prompting memories that link her to the past and sustain her in the present. Her memories reflect a rich maternal subjectivity and result in a meditative, almost mythic reunification of the female body and psyche.

Lila's maternal identity is well established from the beginning of the novel. Although her children are grown and her maternal role has changed with time, it is clear that motherhood has shaped and defined her entire adult life. Rather than worrying about the breast cancer that threatens her life, Lila focuses her concern on her children, who have lives and problems of their own. She particularly worries over her divorced daughter Cat, whose affairs set "a bad example" for her two young children and whose chances for remarrying seem slim (SL 17). Discord between Cat and her brother Lee gives Lila worry as well. As she checks into the hospital, Lila's concern extends to her vegetable garden at home. The garden, which Lila is reluctant to give up, is symbol-

---

3. Rich, *Of Woman Born*, 236; Jane Gallop, *Thinking through the Body*, 3.

ic of the maternal domain. Here she plants and nurtures living things in much the same way she has cared for her family. This associates her with the earth and evokes an image of fertility and procreation. Worried about the corn and beans that need harvesting, Lila asks Spence to "supervise" the garden while she is in the hospital. When he suggests that he might "mow it down" instead, her reaction is swift and intense. Grabbing his arm, she forbids him from doing so and tells him: "The beans is about to begin a second round of blooming. . . . I want to let most of them make into shellies and save some for seed" (SL 17). Lila's response indicates that, despite the possibility of disfigurement and death that her breast cancer brings, she retains a sense of hope for the future. She looks forward to the renewal of the garden and her own life.

Lila's practical, farmwife sensibilities thinly disguise the mythic, earth-mother qualities with which Mason imbues her character. Virginia Smith sees Lila as "a female figure of suffering and regeneration" and associates her with "healing and growing, continuity and creativity." Smith also links Lila's garden to the maternal and points out that Lila herself thinks of childbearing and child-rearing "organically." When she looks at her grown children by her hospital bed, Lila wistfully thinks: "This is what life comes down to . . . replacing your own life with new ones. It's just like raising a crop" (SL 29). Lila, whose own mother died in childbirth, keeps the cycle of life and regeneration intact not only through her children but also through the dried peas that had been her mother's. Smith asserts that Lila "has kept her mother alive through the perennial cycles of sun and soil" and that her wish to have her daughter Nancy save the seeds continues this regenerative cycle "to grow and to eat the embodied lives of the mothers."[4]

These matrilinear connections, along with Lila's alignment with the natural world and its repetitive cycles of life, death, and rebirth, place her within the sphere of women's time. As feminist theorists such as Julia Kristeva, Hélène Cixous, and Luce Irigaray have made clear, the cyclical nature of a woman's body establishes dimensions of time and existence that stand in contrast with the linearity and traditions of patriarchal time. Besides repetition, the female body is also associated with eternity. In her essay "Women's Time," Kristeva describes maternal time, or "monumental temporality," that moves beyond the cyclical

4. Virginia Smith, "Between the Lines," 190–91.

into the timeless. Invoking resurrection myths and religious beliefs that perpetuate maternal cults, particularly Christianity, Kristeva explains how "the body of the Virgin Mother does not die but moves from one spatiality to another within the same time."[5] Both Lila's body and her garden represent maternal space and time. Both are given to time modalities that are cyclical and eternal. Despite her age and illness, Lila as eternal earth mother will not die, but will live through her children, just as the seeds from one season's crop regenerate into another.

Lila's powerful associations with the earth recall Barbara Christian's description of the African view of mothers as "a symbol of the marvelous creativity of the earth." She functions much like the goddess figure and the physical mother that Karla F. C. Holloway sees as central in works by black women writers. Given Lila's connections with Mason's own mother and family farm, she serves as a vehicle for preserving myth and memory. Through her character, Mason embraces Holloway's definition of myth as "a dynamic entity that (re)members community, connects it to the voices from which it has been severed, and forces it out of the silence prescribed by a scriptocentric historicism." In the remembering that takes place in Spence + Lila, Mason gives focus to family and home and provides voice for Lila's experiences and Christianna Mason's as well. She creates a bridge between past and present, with the mother/ goddess at the center, and eradicates the silences surrounding the maternal. The autobiographical underpinnings of Lila's character, the linking of her body and garden, and the seeds that link generations of mothers and daughters extend the mythic dimensions of the text. Through myth and metaphor, then, Mason undertakes, to echo Alice Walker, a search of her mother's garden.[6]

While Lila's garden provides an enduring symbol of her maternity, her breasts are also a powerful, living symbol of motherhood, sexuality, and memory. Indeed, like Sethe's breasts in Beloved, Lila's have meaning and importance that extend far beyond their physical appearance and function. They are an integral part of her female identity and personal histo-

5. Julia Kristeva, "Women's Time," 191.
6. Mason more fully undertakes this search in Clear Springs. Her mother serves as the work's defining center and provides Mason, and the reader, with insight into the importance of family and heritage. One richly evocative chapter near the end of the work is set in her mother's garden. The garden here symbolizes the tangle of memories and the depth of meaning that home, family, and her mother hold for Mason.

ry. This is not to say that the physical aspects are not important, since Lila's breast cancer thrusts the entire family into crisis and worry. Although she has never routinely examined her breasts, Lila is much aware of their physicality. They are "enormous" and so full of lumps from repeated bouts of mastitis that she is surprised she can find the "little knot" that is her cancer (SL 19). Lila calls her breasts "[m]y big jugs" and recognizes the practical function they have served: "I raised three younguns on these. I guess they're give out now." Her breasts have been her strength, an essential part of her being, and her diagnosis of cancer leaves her feeling shaken and vulnerable. To sort out her feelings, Lila uses imagery that links her body to the natural world she knows so well. She attempts to comprehend what has happened to her: "She can't say what she feels—that the last thing she would have expected was to be attacked by disease in the very place she felt strongest. It seemed to suggest some basic failing, like the rotten core of a dying tree" (SL 30). As she contemplates the upcoming surgery and the loss of her breast, Lila remains both protective and pragmatic. She cradles her breasts "like babies," but admits to her daughters that "they ain't worth more than living" (SL 31).

For both Lila and Spence, Lila's breasts are profoundly connected to time, memory, and the rhythms of farm life. In working through their worry and grief about the mastectomy, they progress through a series of memories associated with her breasts. Spence recalls how images of Lila nursing the baby and milking the cows helped him survive violent storms, enemy fire, and dark, cramped ship quarters during his stint in the Pacific in World War II. When he swabbed the decks of the ship, he invoked calming pastoral visions of his life with Lila. He imagined carrying buckets of milk from the barn to the house and remembered Lila's breasts "swinging like fruit on a branch in a strong breeze" (SL 79). Later in the novel, Spence thinks of Lila when he flies over his land in a crop duster and realizes that the topographical layout resembles a woman's body. From his vantage point in the plane, he sees that "[t]he woods are like hair, the two creeks like the parting of a woman's legs, the house and barn her nipples" (SL 164). In each of these instances, Spence connects Lila and her breasts with the farm, with sustenance, with the continued flow of life. The reverence with which he regards Lila's body and breasts contrasts sharply with the sexual brutalization that Sethe endures in *Beloved* when Schoolteacher's nephews steal her breast milk at the Sweet Home plantation, also in Kentucky.

Like Sethe, Lila recognizes the importance that her breasts have assumed in feeding and nurturing her offspring. She connects her breasts
to memories that seem to flow further backward through time as the
novel progresses. She first recalls events that are more recent, such as
nursing her youngest child, Lee. In the hospital before her surgery, she
teases him: "You sucked me dry and I had to put you on a bottle after
two months. I couldn't make enough milk to feed you." Still teasing,
and knowing that her breast will soon be gone, she asks him, "You want
one last tug?" (SL 20, 22). After her mastectomy, Lila likens the loss of
her breast to giving birth. Thinking back to her earlier experiences of
childbirth, she realizes that the mastectomy produces similar feelings.
She notes that "[p]art of her that used to bulge out is now vacant, the
familiar growth gone. It's an empty sensation, but not exceptionally
painful" (SL 82). This triggers more memories of her breasts, of her pregnancy with Lee, of her daughters, and of the hard work she endured as
a young wife and mother. She remembers in detail the nursing habits of
each child, how one was always hungry, another not weaning until two-
and-a-half years of age. Such memories are particularly physical and also
produce a "sudden swell of emotion" for Lila; memory and feelings in-
tertwine as she notes that "[t]he tugging sensation of nursing them as
babies is as clear as yesterday" (SL 86). Lila's recollections demonstrate
how the body stores memory and emotion and how the physical aspects
of the maternal body are intricately connected to a woman's experience
not only of motherhood but of life itself. They also suggest an integration of mind, body, and senses and indicate that Lila, in a way that has
meaning and relevance for her, is "thinking through the body."

Indeed, Lila associates her breasts with different events and stages of
her life. In each case, the memories connect her to other people. As she
travels backward in time and memory, Lila recalls her elopement with
Spence and how he persuaded her "to have the honeymoon first and
then look for the justice of the peace later" after they got lost on a back
road between woods and a cornfield. Spence argued and Lila conceded
that they would "never find this perfect, peaceful place again" (SL 111).
Later that night, after they were married, Spence sneaked her into his
parents' house before daybreak, and at milking time he brought her out
to meet them. Lila remembers the event and herself in terms of her
breasts. She recalls that "[s]he was tall and thin, but even then her
breasts were large, and they jutted forward into the surprised line of sight

of her new mother-in-law" (SL 112). In this brief and humorous memory sequence, Mason deftly connects Lila with the land, the rhythms of farm life, lactation, family continuity, and the maternity of another woman, her surprised mother-in-law.

The last in the series of Lila's memories has to do with her first experience of her breasts. Just as she is about to be discharged from the hospital, Lila recalls herself as a young girl playing ball and fighting with neighbor boys on Sunday afternoons. Again, evoking fertile images of the land and cyclical rhythms of growth and regeneration, Lila remembers: "Her breasts had gone through a short growing season, like something shooting out fast after a long, wet spring. 'Been eating sassafras buds, Lila?' they would say, and she would fly into them. She could beat those boys to pieces. She loved that" (SL 170). Lila's feisty, indomitable spirit matches her quickly growing breasts. Both parallel the burgeoning changes taking place in the springtime landscape. Lila's memory indicates how deeply she has connected her body with the land. In *Landscape and Memory*, Simon Schama examines the rich complexities of the landscape tradition in Western culture and its powerful connections with the human imagination. He notes that the landscape tradition is "built from a rich deposit of myths, memories, and obsessions." In an attempt to "recover the veins of myth and memory that lie beneath the surface," Schama asserts that "strength is often hidden beneath layers of the commonplace."[7] Such is the case with Mason's character: The ordinary world of family, home, and farm serves as a source of strength for Lila. Her entrenched alignment of body, memory, and the land reaffirms her sense of self and proves sustaining as she copes with breast cancer and surgery.

While Mason uses the pastoral to undergird Lila's identity, she incorporates technology and contemporary culture as powerful forces within her characters' lives as well. Television and pop music have long been staples in the lives of both Spence and Lila. Lila admits that their first television set brought "an unexpected harmony" into the house (SL 83). Spence, in particular, easily integrates the elements of contemporary culture into his life. He watches a variety of television programs, likes to listen to Fleetwood Mac, and has strong opinions on Phil Collins and Mick Jagger. As Spence attempts to deal with Lila's illness, tele-

7. Simon Schama, *Landscape and Memory*, 14.

vision and rock music provide him with a stabilizing sense of normalcy in the midst of crisis and change. Karen Gainey believes that popular culture provides Spence with "the structures to reflect his thoughts and feelings."[8] Unlike the breast cancer that mysteriously and savagely threatens Lila, television and rock music are familiar elements that Spence can comprehend. As such, they create a filter that diminishes the terror and impact of Lila's cancer.

In contrast with the ease with which pop culture is accommodated into their rural lives, however, medical technology and the hospital environment present a new and disturbing realm for Spence and Lila. Lila's cancer brings them into a new cultural milieu and the hospital represents the obverse of the procreative, rhythmical life of the farm. Tess Cosslett, in her study of childbirth and the discourses of motherhood, notes that medical discourse and medical institutions are often represented in women's writing as "both repressive and masculine, in opposition to the ideal of the primitive woman."[9] Mason also sets up these oppositions, showing how for Lila the hospital is an intimidating, patriarchal institution. It is also a place of confinement and dehumanization, where life and death are artificially manipulated. Although Lila's surgery and chemotherapy treatments are designed to preserve life, they are disfiguring and debilitating procedures. In the process of destroying cancer cells, the body and the spirit must undergo suffering as well.

As Mason presents it, the language of the hospital culture also serves to diminish the individual. In contrast with the rich personal memories Lila associates with her breasts, her doctor speaks impersonally of tumor size and types, second opinions, surgical techniques, and follow-up treatments. He dispenses such terms as "biopsy," "malignancy," "lymph nodes," "aggressive tumor," "lumpectomy," and "modified radical mastectomy" (SL 40–41). Later, in reference to the second surgery Lila needs, the doctor talks of "obstructions" and "plaque" in the arteries, a "carotid endarterectomy," and "transischemic attacks" (SL 42–43). Altogether, the medical terms pathologize the body and threaten to disrupt Lila's physical and psychological integrity as much as the surgery

8. Karen Gainey, "Subverting the Symbolic: The Semiotic Fictions of Anne Tyler, Jayne Anne Phillips, Bobbie Ann Mason, and Grace Paley," 158.
9. Cosslett, *Women Writing Childbirth*, 7.

itself, in effect reinforcing the mind-body split that patriarchal institutions and culture demand of women.

The doctor's casual patronization also serves to diminish Lila. When he asks: "What do you think, Mrs. Culpepper? You look like a pretty smart lady," an exasperated Lila retorts: "Why, you're just a little whippersnapper. . . . All the big words make me bumfuzzled." The conversation leaves Lila feeling disconnected, as if she were "floating around the room, dipping in and out of the situation" (SL 41, 42). This not only illustrates Lila's confusion, but also demonstrates Alice Adams's position that "women's experiences of their bodies are always *mediated* by their interactions with institutions and discourses" and that such mediation leaves a woman "mystified."[10] Lila's encounter with the paternalistic doctor and his "big words" in a sense mystifies her. However, unlike Pauline Breedlove in *The Bluest Eye,* whose treatment by the medical establishment leaves her without language or personhood during childbirth, Lila is not totally silenced; she is still able to voice her frustration and indignation, even if it is without erudite expression.

While the "official" language of medical discourse attempts to divest Lila of power, the hospital environment does the same. Lila's hospitalization represents an entombment of the maternal. She is depicted in places of enclosure—the lounge, corridors, her hospital room, the intensive care unit. In the hospital, there is no sense of the pastoral world except in Lila's memories and in the jigsaw puzzle of a barn and pasture she finds in the lounge. Furthermore, Lila is relegated to positions of passivity and powerlessness: She is often confined to bed, buckled in a wheelchair, or tranquilized with medication. Although the care she receives is deemed medically necessary, it is dehumanizing and creates a sense of imprisonment for Lila, making her feel not unlike the prisoner she sees trudging through the hospital corridors accompanied by a uniformed guard. With his gaping gown exposing "his hairy rear end," the prisoner-patient produces "a sudden foreboding of death" in Lila. He appears at other times in the text and symbolizes the sense of entrapment, powerlessness, and nakedness associated with Lila's hospitalization. However, she resists identifying with him and becomes more determined than ever to survive. After seeing the "bare-butt criminal" go by,

10. Adams, *Reproducing the Womb,* 5.

Lila swings out of bed and orders her half-sister Glenda, "Walk me down the hall. . . . I ain't ready to die yet" (SL 92).

As Lila attempts to understand the treatment and procedures she endures, she interprets them in terms of life on the farm. However, the images she calls up are far from pastoral and stand in stark contrast with her earlier associations with mythic, more idealized maternal images. The technology of the hospital creates depersonalized associations for Lila. The tubes and hoses to which she is connected after surgery remind her of the "electric milkers" she and Spence once had for their cows (SL 55). In a startling image of helplessness and death, Lila feels "as though she has been left out in a field for the buzzards" whenever the nurses come to change her bandages, check drainage bags, take her temperature or blood pressure, or give her an injection (SL 61). This metaphor links Lila's body with a bleak and terrifying landscape that symbolizes the overwhelming vulnerability she feels.

Lila makes similarly harsh connections to farm life as she wonders about the disposal of her breast following the mastectomy: "Did it all come out in one hunk, or did they hack it out? She thought about dressing a chicken, the way she cut out the extra fat and pulled out the entrails. She thought of how it was so easy to rip raw chicken breasts" (SL 112). Lila's thoughts about her body and amputated breast demonstrate her mental toughness and her willingness to contemplate the appalling realities of her surgery. However, the brutal images associated with her thoughts also suggest the torture and mutilation endured by Saint Agatha, an early Christian martyr who became the patron saint of breasts. In the third century, according to medical journalist Rose Kushner, Agatha spurned the sexual advances of the pagan governor of Sicily and refused to renounce her Christian beliefs. Consequently, the governor ordered that Agatha "be bound to a pillar and her breasts be torn off with iron shears." Some accounts say she was stretched on a rack and burned with hot iron plates before her breasts were ripped off. Agatha's story spread throughout Europe and she received sainthood for her faithfulness. In the Book of Common Prayer, February 5 is designated as Saint Agatha's Day, a day upon which, according to Kushner, "[h]undreds of thousands of women pray to her if their breasts are too small, too large, or too pendulous, do not produce milk or develop disease."[11]

11. Rose Kushner, *Breast Cancer: A Personal History and an Investigative Report*, 273–74.

By associating Lila's mastectomy with the ripping of raw chicken breasts, Mason not only conjures up images of Saint Agatha's torture, but also suggests that mastectomies are sometimes performed with dispassionate ease and with a relative insensitivity about the surgery's physical and psychological impact on women.

Acknowledging the brutalities of Lila's cancer and surgery, Mason does not leave her stranded in the unfamiliar techno-terrain of the hospital without resources. In addition to endowing her with inherent strengths, Mason has Lila use humor as an effective countermeasure against the dehumanizing aspects of her illness and hospitalization. After a volunteer from a mastectomy support group brings Lila a breast prosthesis, Lila and Spence discuss its expense and necessity. With humorous practicality, Spence tells her, "We can rig you up something." Lila concurs: "Why, shoot, yes. . . . I ain't spending a hundred and fifty dollars for a falsie." Her daughters proceed to tell funny, bizarre stories about women who filled their bras with buckshot or wore inflatable bras following their mastectomies. Finally, the entire family plays a game of catch in Lila's hospital room with the prosthesis. After Lila catches the last toss, she concludes, "Well, it'll make a good pincushion," in reference to her habit of keeping stray pins in her bra and more than once jabbing her breast with them (SL 105, 106). The humor, the storytelling, and the total irreverence toward the prosthesis serve to demystify the medical technology involved in Lila's cancer treatment and rehabilitation. In one sense, the prosthesis functions much like the ripped chicken breasts as a grim reminder of the amputated maternal breast. However, Mason's blending of humor and horror gives Lila and her family a means of coping with the confusion, pain, and mutilation associated with the mastectomy. The interjection of humor humanizes Lila's situation and gives her a modicum of control over her illness and the depersonalization she has experienced in the hospital.

Mason also has Lila use sex as an important resource following her surgery. Sex functions as a vital force that reaffirms life. Like humor, it empowers the maternal. Even in the face of illness and aging, the importance of sex is not diminished; for both Spence and Lila, it holds death at bay. Following Lila's mastectomy, an anxious Spence worries about the second surgery she has to face and considers the possibility of her death that might follow. His thoughts, however, turn toward sex with a loving pragmatism: "If this is going to be her time, then what he and Lila should do is have a last fling together." Although he realizes the impossibility of making love to Lila while she lies in "that white-cold bed with the nurses bumbling around the room like doodlebugs working on a cowpile," he embraces the impulse towards life that sex represents (SL 97).

Lila also thinks of sex in life-affirming ways. As she and a friend flip through a magazine together, they ogle a young man in an underwear ad. Lila exclaims, "Look at all that going to waste," and although the model is young enough to be her grandson, she feels "a twinge of desire." More significantly, she thinks of Spence and wishes "she could go home right now and get in bed" with him (SL 109). Not only does Mason imbue the maternal with sexual desire, she does so with an aged mother at that. She therefore defies conventional attitudes about motherhood and sexuality in two ways. According to psychologist Shari Thurer, a mother's sexuality is threatening to her family and to society. Thurer states, "Presumably a good mother extinguishes her libido with conception or else expels it along with her placenta in childbirth."[12] Moreover, given the desexualization of the elderly in today's society, sexual desire in an older mother is unfathomable by many people. In her rendering of Lila's sexuality, Mason also subverts prevailing cultural attitudes that link a woman's sexual attractiveness and worth with her breasts. For Lila, the loss of a breast does not diminish her sexual feelings or self-image. Still strong, they enable her to recover from the ordeal of cancer and mutilating surgery.

Lila demonstrates that sexual feelings are important throughout life, regardless of age, health, or proximity of death. She is much like octogenarian Granny Younger in Lee Smith's *Oral History*, who clearly thinks sexual passion is not just for the young. After recounting how she watched a local farmer and his lover having sex in an open field, Granny explains: "Now a person mought get old, and their body mought go on them, but that thing does not wear out. No it don't" (OH 43). The final passage in Mason's novel superbly reinforces this idea. It reveals the hopeful possibilities that sex engenders and underscores the sexuality of the maternal. After Lila returns home from the hospital, the novel is brought back full circle to her concern for her garden. Despite her weakness, she is determined to check on her garden almost as soon as she ar-

12. Thurer, *Myths of Motherhood*, xx.

rives home. She disregards her doctor's admonitions about handling dirt and the infection it might cause and plunges her arms into the okra, peppers, tomatoes, and cucumbers. In true maternal fashion, she "cradles" the vegetables in her arms. Like a doting mother, she revels with pride and laughter in what she has raised: "Look at that punkin, would you. . . . That's going to be the biggest one we ever had!"

In the same scene, when Lila announces that the cucumbers are ready for pickling, Spence responds with love and longing. He tells her: "You sure were gone an awful long time. . . . I thought to my soul you never *was* going to come home." Then, with a double entendre, he informs Lila, "I've got a cucumber that needs pickling" (SL 175). Her reaction to his sexual innuendo is one of joyful, affirming laughter. It provides evidence of female *jouissance*, the sexual pleasure that Kristeva sees contained within the mother's body. Moreover, the final image, of Lila's face "dancing like pond water in the rain, all unsettled and stirring with aroused possibility," makes the novel open-ended and suggests the continuance of life, love, and regeneration that the maternal embodies (SL 176). It also demonstrates that Lila and the landscape remain firmly bound together. Both are the substance of memory and renewal. Both are timeless elements in a changing culture. Lila is, as Virginia Smith contends, "the earthy and enduring goddess in every woman."[13] Despite disease, disfigurement, and the depersonalization she has experienced, Lila retains an inspiring wholeness. Mind, body, and spirit remain unified within her character. To echo the words of Adrienne Rich, Mason thus affirms "the miracle and paradox of the female body" and successfully restores that which "has been so cruelly disorganized."

13. Virginia Smith, "Between the Lines," 198.

7

~

Feather Crowns

COMMODIFYING SOUTHERN MOTHERHOOD

When Christianna Wheeler of Hopewell, Kentucky, gives birth in 1900 to the first known set of quintuplets in the United States, her life is forever altered. The young farmwife in Bobbie Ann Mason's 1993 novel *Feather Crowns* is thrust into the limelight and propelled along a bizarre and turbulent course of fame and self-discovery. The whole nation responds to the birth of the quintuplets with letters, tokens, congratulations, and, above all, curiosity. Trains are rerouted through Hopewell so that people can disembark at the Wheeler farmhouse to see the five tiny wonders. Born at the dawn of a new age of miracles, the quintuplets embody the hopes and dreams of the future and the sorrows and losses of the past for those who come to visit. Strangers throng into the house to marvel at the babies, Christie's fecundity, and her husband's virility. Family and friends pitch in to help the Wheelers manage the visitors, the farm, and the five newborns, but despite everyone's best efforts, the quintuplets die one by one.

Surprisingly, the deaths of the infants do not bring an end to the demands of the public. Preserved by new embalming techniques, the quintuplets are put on display at the funeral home, where they garner further attention. Christie and her husband, James, who are financially strapped by this time, take the dead babies on a "scientific" lecture tour in order to save their farm. Their journey takes them far from home, exposing them to a world on the verge of modernity. Eventually, they become disillusioned by the tour and take the quintuplets to Washington, D.C., where they donate them to the Institute of Man. Here the babies are to be kept and studied, but not displayed to the public. Satisfied that their children are at last in good hands, the Wheelers return home to Kentucky to live out the remainder of their lives.

Feather Crowns, which details Christie Wheeler's unusual maternal experience, is nearly twice as long as Mason's previous works and spans almost seventy-five years, from 1890 to Christie's ninetieth birthday in 1963. According to Jill McCorkle, Mason manages to present "the microscopic detail of everyday life." Her examination of human drama, however, is more far-reaching. As Judith Hatchett observes, this novel is not "Mason's usual minimalist text." Instead of grounding her characters in the realm of the ordinary, Mason takes them into a more extraordinary dimension, where they experience "the remarkable, the distinguishing, the fame-making."[1] Throughout *Feather Crowns*, Mason depicts people and places caught in a great cultural transition, with superstition and folkways colliding with science and rational thinking. The feather crowns of the title symbolize the conflict between these two disparate modes of interpreting the world. After the quintuplets die, tightly swirled, nestlike feathers are discovered in Christie's mattress. Shaken, she struggles to give them meaning, as she sorts through all the superstitions she has heard about such "crowns." They are considered to be a harbinger of death or an indicator that a deceased person has gone to heaven. However, in Christie's mind, "[a]n angel had left the crowns . . . the way a fairy would leave a nickel for a child's tooth" (FC 271). Though questions linger, Christie senses that the crowns are somehow connected to the deaths of her infants. In any event, the feather crowns are tangible signs that can be deciphered, whereas the microorganisms responsible for the quintuplets' deaths are still incomprehensible elements. Mason shows how, in a world on the brink of modernity, the individual is forced to grapple with personal, historical, and technological change. For the maternal, this has serious implications.

Throughout *Feather Crowns*, Mason examines the impact of a new age of scientific advancement, medical achievement, popular culture, and consumerism on southern motherhood at the turn of the century. She demonstrates how the forces of change and progress link motherhood with the larger public realm. These forces subvert and commodi-

1. Jill McCorkle, "Her Sensational Babies," review of *Feather Crowns*, by Bobbie Ann Mason, *New York Times Book Review*, September 26, 1993, 7; Judith Hatchett, "Making Life Mean: Bobbie Ann Mason's *Feather Crowns*," 12.

fy all aspects of maternal experience and usher motherhood into the twentieth century. Like Toni Morrison, Mason is concerned with the impact of history and culture on the mother's body. These powerfully shape Christie's experiences of pregnancy, childbirth, breast-feeding, and motherhood. Like Sethe in *Beloved*, Christie finds that her control of her own body is severely limited. As a result of the cultural changes at work around her, Christie and her dead babies become objects of exploitation by business, technology, and entertainment. Harriet Pollack observes that in *Feather Crowns* "the quartet of medicine, science, money, and male authority are pictured intersecting women's separate sphere of authority and relationship."[2] At each stage of her maternal experience, Christie must contend with the intrusion of these forces. They are unlike anything she has encountered in her constrained rural life. In one way or another, men of medicine, science, or money appropriate the babies and alter Christie's experiences as a woman and a mother.

Feather Crowns opens with Christie, "big as a washtub," in labor with the quintuplets, contractions clenching her belly (FC 3). Thus, Mason foregrounds female experience and the mother's body right from the beginning of the novel. However, like Morrison and her treatment of maternity in *Beloved*, Mason does not render the events of pregnancy, childbirth, and breast-feeding in sequential time order. Christie's labor is punctuated by flashbacks of her pregnancy, and after her delivery, she is taken further back in time. Her memories as a young wife and mother of three coalesce with the present, making the quintuplets and Christie's entire experience of motherhood an intricate weave of time, events, memories, and sensations. Mason's strategy here in rendering Christie's experience mirrors the shifting rhythms of the female body and the nonlinear aspects of time associated with the maternal. This stands in stark contrast with the forward march of history and progress that form the backdrop of the novel.

Mason also establishes a compelling maternal subjectivity in the novel to counterbalance the patriarchal forces of medicine, science, money, and male authority that objectify the mother. As in many of Mason's works, female voice is muted in *Feather Crowns*. She replaces it with a rich interiority that reveals the mother's experience nonetheless. In

2. Pollack, "From *Shiloh* to *In Country* to *Feather Crowns*," 102.

rendering Christie's maternal experiences, an interweave of thoughts, feelings, and bodily sensations override language. Indeed, maternal subjectivity is manifested through Christie's sexuality and through dreams and memories about her body that surface in conjunction with her pregnancy. These elements undergird and sustain her in much the same way that Lila Culpepper's experiences and memories of her body lessen the depersonalization created by her hospitalization and surgery in Mason's earlier novel *Spence + Lila*.

Christie, like Lila, represents the sexual, procreative earth mother, and, as such, stands in contrast with the rationality of science, business, and technology that intrudes upon her world. Christie is highly aware of her sexual feelings and the centrality of sex in her life. Mason aptly entitles the second section of the novel "Desire"; this section explores the sexual dimensions of Christie's pregnancy and her relationship with husband James. Her attitudes about sex seem markedly different from more conservative ones of her era. Christie views sex as something exciting that she and James had engaged in "shamelessly" and often throughout their marriage. While her own mother referred to sex as "the wifely duty," Christie takes great pleasure in it. As she did with Lila Culpepper, Mason links Christie's body and sexuality with the earth and the rhythms of farm life. Christie and James refer to sexual intercourse as "plowing," while their exploration into new areas of "surprising sensations" is called "plowing new-ground" (FC 41).

Christie's pregnancy is laden with earthy eroticism, almost in proportion to the number of babies she is carrying. At a camp meeting that she attends early in her pregnancy, the sight of Brother Cornett, a charismatic, black-haired preacher, sets Christie on fire. The sensations she feels suggest a comingling of the erotic and the maternal: "She felt her blood tingling, as it rushed nourishment to her baby" (FC 67). Later that night, she experiences a sexual and irreverent dream about the preacher. In the dream, as Christie churns butter, Brother Cornett comes to her, speaking softly and seductively: "[H]is voice, plush as velvet, caressed her—first her hair, then her breasts, then her legs. She could feel him in her, his long, hot tool churning in her, to the rhythm of 'Bringing in the Sheaves'" (FC 82). Even in the later stages of her pregnancy with the quintuplets, Christie possesses strong sexual feelings. In another image that unifies the maternal and erotic, Christie recalls how "[a]t night, James stroked her belly so sensuously she feared the baby might be born with unwholesome thoughts" (FC 11). After the quintuplets are born, Christie sees them as delicious and shocking proof that she and James "had gotten carried away with their secret pleasures" (FC 41).

The physicality of Christie's pregnancy is also magnified and depicted with intense subjectivity. Not unexpectedly, the sensations associated with the quintuplets are considerably different from those of Christie's previous pregnancies. Carrying so many babies, she feels the physical changes of her pregnancy most acutely. The twinges, bloating, distended veins, and difficult movement cause her to feel like "her body [was] turning into someone else's." She feels "like a cow," and when she walks, her legs are "heavy like fence posts." At night, her bulk heats up the bed so much that she feels "as if she were carrying a bucket of hot coals inside her" (FC 11). In figurative language that associates the maternal body with the earth, Christie links her pregnancy with the cataclysmic earthquake prophesized for the turn of the century. For the duration of her pregnancy with the quintuplets, Christie remembers, her womb "had rumbled and roared like the earth about to split open" (FC 57). This image is a complex and portentous one: It functions as a metaphor for the change and upheavals the new century will bring, and it also foreshadows how Christie's body will become a field of contention for a struggle between male authority and women's ways. It hints at the changes to come involving women's experience of their bodies: how maternal subjectivity will ultimately give way to scientific objectivity in such distinctly female areas as pregnancy, childbirth, and breast-feeding.

In portraying the impact of patriarchal forces upon the maternal, Mason, like Morrison, vigorously grounds her protagonist's experience in historical reality. In *Beloved*, Morrison examines the horrific realities of motherhood under slavery and demonstrates that institution's devastating effects on the body and psyche of the mother. Mason infuses Christie's experience with similar elements in order to convincingly render the realities of nineteenth-century pregnancy and childbirth. She constructs Christie's labor scene to demonstrate the growing tension between woman-centered childbirth and the new physician-controlled birth experience emerging at the turn of the century and to show the shift from female subjectivity to male objectivity in this arena. Christie is caught between the two forces, and as a woman in labor she is vulnerable both physically and psychologically. Unaware of the multiple births that await her, she worries because "the thing" inside her seems twice as large as her other children had been and thinks it "couldn't be a baby—it was too wild and violent" (FC 5).

Christie fears dying in childbirth, but takes solace in the fact that her previous births went well. In effect, she gives birth under what Judith Leavitt refers to as the "shadow of maternity." Although the impending birth of her quintuplets is exceptional, Christie resembles countless other women of nineteenth-century America who awaited childbirth with terror. This fear was not unfounded, as childbirth brought with it the great possibility of dying or surviving with permanent, debilitating injuries. As late as 1910, one out of every 154 live births in the United States resulted in maternal death.[3] The loss of children was much more frequent; the infant mortality rate in 1900 was one death per five live births.[4] Marriage and motherhood were not always welcome events in a young woman's life. On Christie's wedding day, her Aunt Sophie bluntly explains the facts of maternal mortality: "It's nine months from the marriage bed to the death bed" (FC 7). Given the statistics, Christie's fears for herself and her infants are understandable.

To assuage her anxiety, Christie is attended by a circle of women during labor, including her Aunt Alma; Mrs. Willy; her best friend, Amanda; and midwife Hattie Hurt. The women in attendance represent a common practice in the nineteenth century, when, Leavitt says, trained midwives or experienced friends and relatives came to help a mother in labor and to stay with her through the "days or weeks afterward, participating in the transition to motherhood." These women "suffered through the agonies and dangers of birth together, sought each other's support, and shared the relief of successful deliveries and the grief of unsuccessful ones."[5]

3. Leavitt, *Brought to Bed*, 14, 27. By contrast, the maternal death rate in the United States from 1987 to 1996 was 7.5 deaths per 100,000 live births, according to the Centers for Disease Control (CDC), "Maternal Mortality—United States, 1982–1996," http://www.cdc.gov/epo/mmwr/preview/mmwrhtml/00054602.htm. Other accounts, citing inaccuracies in the reporting of maternal deaths, suggest that the rate may be closer to 23 per 100,000; see Warren Leary, "Study: Maternal Death Rate Higher," *Charlotte (N.C.) Observer*, July 31, 1996, 6A.

4. Dorothy Marlow, *Textbook of Pediatric Nursing*, 42. The infant mortality rate in 1998 was 7.2 deaths per 1,000 live births, according to the CDC, "Infant Mortality," http://www.cdc.gov/nchs/fastats/infmort.htm.

5. Leavitt, *Brought to Bed*, 37.

Sally McMillen points out that southern mothers often created "a large network of attendants" to help them through childbirth. They preferred their own mothers and sisters to attend them, but also relied upon other relatives, friends, and neighbors. According to McMillen, women in isolated, rural areas were greatly distressed about giving birth alone or without sufficient female support. Jane Woodruff, a nineteenth-century southern mother, wrote in her diary about the loneliness and despair she experienced when she had to give birth unassisted except for the help of an unfamiliar "old negro woman out of the field." At the time of her confinement, Woodruff's husband was away, trying to find a doctor. Her poignant description of her baby's death reveals the devastating isolation she experienced during her parturition: "I was the only one awake to listen to the dying moans of my child which were becoming more and more faint; at last they ceased altogether."[6]

Although her own mother lives too far away to help, Christie is fortunate to face childbirth with the assistance of experienced women. Her choice of a midwife rather than a doctor not only reflects a common birthing tradition but is influenced by monetary considerations as well. Dr. Foote charges more money to attend a birth than the midwife does, and Christie had delivered her previous children successfully without him. She plans to pay Hattie with a ham and jars of green beans, whereas Dr. Foote's services would force her husband to sell a hog.

Christie's decision to use a midwife stems from other concerns as well. Like other women of her time, she retains much modesty about her body and possesses a fear of modern medicine. The physical examination that Dr. Foote gives Christie early in her pregnancy only reinforces her wariness and increases her reluctance to have him attend her during childbirth. Before he examines her, Dr. Foote gives Christie a towel to cover her face and pins her dress onto poles to create a barrier between their faces. Despite these measures, Christie suffers gross indignities during the course of the examination. She endures the doctor's "thick hands travel[ing] the mound of her stomach, with her drawers still in place" (FC 19). However, "the worst" occurs when he removes her drawers and thrusts his hand between her legs to conduct a pelvic examination. In her mortification, she is much like Pauline Breedlove in *The Bluest Eye*, who suffers the loss of language and is reduced to a moaning animal

6. McMillen, *Motherhood in the Old South*, 64; Jane Woodruff quoted, ibid., 66.

when she receives an impersonal pelvic examination during labor. Christie has a similarly dehumanizing experience. With chilling realism, Mason depicts the mind-body split that occurs because of the violating nature of her examination. Christie reacts to Dr. Foote's manual thrust with a sudden mental detachment, focusing her thoughts externally beyond her body. She notes: "The table was hard. Outside, a driver was running mules through town and there were loud shouts." The indecent penetration intensifies: "Slowly, the doctor worked his cold, thick finger up into her, while his other hand crawled over her belly" (FC 20). Mason reveals the imprecise science that modern obstetrics initially was, as Dr. Foote misdiagnoses Christie's multiple pregnancy as fibroid tumors and sends her home with a prescription to shrink them.

Christie's reluctance to use the services of Dr. Foote during childbirth extends beyond her concern for modesty and personal dignity. She also fears the instruments Dr. Foote might use. She has heard of a baby pulled out "by its head with metal tools" who died because it was so "squashed and bruised" (FC 19). Indeed, according to Leavitt, forceps were physicians' favorite instrument of intervention and "women both feared and respected the 'hands of iron.'" Forceps could be a salvation for women, but they often resulted in gross traumas to infants and mothers alike. In 1910, Dr. W. P. Manton of Detroit estimated that "not one in ten of those who are now employing [forceps] do so intelligently. . . . In the hands of a bungler, they become weapons of danger, leaving destruction and sometimes death in their wake."[7]

Christie's worry about forceps, her modesty, and her concern about money are not enough to keep her husband from fetching Dr. Foote when she goes into labor. Although James acts out of concern for Christie and their unborn offspring, his actions intensify the battle between woman-centered childbirth and male control of the event. Unwittingly, he helps pit women's ways against male authority. Pollack points out that when James brings in the doctor to attend Christie, "the imperfect authority" of Dr. Foote replaces "the traditional woman-craft" that Hattie Hurt represents. His presence and involvement at the birth of the quintuplets represent the growing movement in nineteenth-century America to physician obstetrics and male control of birth. With

---

7. Leavitt, *Brought to Bed*, 44; Dr. W. P. Manton quoted, ibid., 51.

not-so-subtle irony, Dr. Foote's name reflects this change, for it aptly corresponds to Mason's "revelation of gynecological history presented from a woman's most unofficial angle."[8]

Though well intended, Dr. Foote's actions during Christie's childbirth experience are the first in a series of events that ultimately contribute to the quintuplets' deaths. When he arrives at the Wheeler household, he promptly takes over from Hattie, who has successfully delivered the first baby. She has already discerned that "there's more'n one baby in there," but Dr. Foote looks contemptuously at her midwifery supplies and proceeds to take over the next delivery (FC 26). Although Christie is comfortably propped up in bed with her knees bent, ready to give birth to the next baby, she is told by Dr. Foote to lie flat instead. Hattie, recognizing that giving birth in such a position is difficult for the mother but convenient for the doctor, quickly retorts, "She needs to set up" (FC 27). Dr. Foote insists on his way and brusquely dismisses Hattie. He then places Christie in an uncomfortable and awkward position. When this increases her pain, he offers to give her "some powders," most likely laudanum (tincture of opium), which, according to Leavitt, was commonly used to accelerate labor and ease suffering.[9] Aunt Alma tries to intervene, telling Dr. Foote, "You better get her up and bend her over. . . . She can't get nothing out a-laying down." The doctor remains adamant, his reply echoing legions of obstetricians since: "No, I can work better with her in this position" (FC 28). He succeeds in wresting control from the women in attendance, sedating Christie and forcing her to deliver in a position that she finds horribly painful but "too embarrassing" to die in (FC 29).

Some historians, Leavitt notes, claim that when male physicians began attending normal births, particularly in the nineteenth century, "the presence of this male authority figure changed the power structure in the room." Certainly, Dr. Foote's actions would indicate this. However, other researchers contend that as long as birth remained a home-based event, women actively participated in the determination of childbirth practices.[10] Women such as Hattie and Alma, who remain by Christie's side throughout her ordeal, offered support and practical help to laboring mothers and kept birth a female-centered experience,

8. Pollack, "From *Shiloh* to *In Country* to *Feather Crowns*," 104.
9. Leavitt, *Brought to Bed*, 44.
10. Ibid., 86.

whether a male physician was present or not. At any rate, Dr. Foote, Hattie, and Alma are symbolic of larger issues involving women's lives, the cooperative experience of childbirth, and the increasingly powerful medical establishment in the late nineteenth century.

The conflicts present in Christie's home birth foreshadow the movement of childbirth to the hospital in the early twentieth century. With developments in anesthesia, antisepsis, and delivery techniques, hospitals were praised as "the newest and best place for delivery." By the 1920s and 1930s, modern obstetrics was entrenched as a scientific, systematized specialty that eliminated the social and woman-centered childbirths of the past. The folk wisdom and advice that abounds in *Feather Crowns*, such as Amanda's suggestion of placing an ax under Christie's bed to cut the pain and Mrs. Willy's pain remedy of gunpowder, stand in sharp contrast with the modern techniques that were arising in the "new" field of obstetrics. Leavitt observes that obstetrical medicine and the movement of birth to the hospital did not initially reduce maternal and infant deaths, which, ironically, many physicians blamed on the new techniques and their interference in normal births.[11]

Christie gives birth to the quintuplets, but the wrestle for control of maternal experience does not end. The quintuplets themselves become objects of contention between public and private domains. The train that brings visitors north from the Memphis exposition facilitates the intrusion of commercial and public interests into private spheres of experience. Symbolizing progress and change, the train serves as a link between north and south, urban and rural, future and present, science and folkways. The hordes of tourists, reporters, government officials, and medical specialists who arrive at the Wheeler farmhouse demonstrate the crushing impact that technology, government, and the media can have on the individual and, in Christie's case, the maternal. A hungry, demanding public regards the babies as products for consumption. Lined up in a row on Christie's bed, the babies are each wrapped snugly, like "a store package without the string" (FC 33). The visitors who descend on the farmhouse seem to feast on the babies. They tromp into Christie's bedroom to marvel and gawk at them. One visitor even comes through the window. Women (but not men) are allowed to hold the ba-

11. Ibid., 177, 182.

bies, and their enthusiasm is so great that Alma orders them to "[t]ake turns" (FC 168). To take advantage of the frenzy, Alma's husband proposes charging twenty-five cents for admission and sets out a collection box.

The feeding of the babies further commercializes the maternal experience and diminishes female control of motherhood. Breast-feeding becomes a source of conflict between the women and Dr. Foote, who suggests that Christie keep two infants and find someone else with milk to take the rest. Christie refuses to give away any of the babies, so Dr. Foote sends for Mittens Dowdy, a black cook with a nursing baby of her own. Christie worries about how to pay her, but Dr. Foote assures her "a few scraps" will suffice (FC 99). His words devalue both Mittens and the maternal. When James questions having a "colored woman" serve as a wet nurse, Christie responds: "Rich people do it. I guess it's all right" (FC 101).

Christie's words reflect the reality, described by McMillen, that many nineteenth-century southern families relied on wet nurses, both black and white, to feed the infants of mothers who were ill or had died. Both doctors and mothers viewed breast milk as far healthier for babies than any substitute. However, ass's milk was often recommended, as was a mixture of cow's milk, water, and brown sugar. "Pap," which consisted of cow's milk mixed with bread, was also used. But lack of refrigeration and hygiene created enormous problems. Bottles made of glass, metal, or bone and covered with a cow's teat or a piece of linen could not be easily sanitized. Hand-feeding practices increased infant deaths significantly, particularly in summer months. Thus, women who were successfully breast-feeding or had lost their own babies were much in demand in nineteenth-century America. Breast milk was an important commodity and advertisements for its sale or purchase were common. While advertisements often specified white or black wet nurses, it was the health of a wet nurse that was of greatest concern. Or, as Dr. Foote tells Christie, it was "hard to find a woman that's clean and ain't sick" (FC 121). According to McMillen, "Milk supply, not race, was the main worry."[12]

Although Mittens and Christie have the already difficult job of breast-feeding five newborns, much is done to hinder their efforts. Dr. Foote insists that Christie supplement her milk with cow's milk, but

12. McMillen, *Motherhood in the Old South*, 115, 123, 125.

Mittens questions the wisdom of this, reminding Christie, "Cow milk [is] for cows" (FC 121). Ironically, much truth can be found in her words, since today it is well known that baby formula derived from cow's milk can precipitate necrotizing enterocolitis, an often fatal diarrhea in premature infants. Breast milk, which contains important immunologic properties, protects against this disease, encouraging the colonization of helpful bacteria in the intestines and promoting the healthy development of the intestinal mucosal barrier in newborn infants.[13] Dr. Foote's suggestion to feed the quintuplets cow's milk is a risky one given their low birth weights and the problems associated with multiple gestation.

When Howell's Drugs and Sundries delivers glass nursing bottles and rubber nipples to the Wheeler household, Christie's efforts at breast-feeding are further sabotaged. A powerful symbol of progress, Howell's drugstore represents the growing influence of business, advertising, and consumer products on American life at the turn of the century. Stocked with baby bottles, cloth diapers, safety pins, worm medications, teething powder, baby ointments, and other tonics and salves, Howell's provides products that set the standard for modern infant care. However, the drugstore's goodwill gesture hastens the chain of events leading to the quintuplets' deaths. After receiving the baby bottles, Christie begins to doubt her own maternal judgment. She concedes that it must be all right to use cow's milk, since the drugstore sells the requisite feeding equipment. Tragically, she defers to the supposed expertise of others and begins giving the quintuplets cow's milk in the new bottles. The babies soon develop colic. Dr. Foote then prescribes an opium-based syrup that, not surprisingly, is sold by the drugstore to treat the colic. The sedated babies sleep soundly, but when they awake they are too weak to nurse at the breast. This increases Christie's reliance on bottles of cow's milk and eventually "sucky rags"—cloth soaked in cow's milk—to feed the babies (FC 236). With diminished amounts of breast milk, the babies' immature immune systems are further compromised, and they succumb one by one a few weeks later to respiratory infections. Although the infections likely stem from germs brought by the throngs

13. See M. B. Yellis, "Human Breast Milk and Facilitation of Gastrointestinal Development and Maturation," *Gastroenterology Nursing* 18:5 (1995), 11–15, for more about the physiological benefits of breast milk and gastrointestinal development in newborns.

of visitors to the Wheeler farmhouse, Christie blames the babies' deaths on her breast milk: "It's all my fault. . . . My milk wasn't good" (FC 237).

Perhaps the most bizarre intrusion of technology and commercialism upon the maternal comes after the death of the quintuplets. As in *In Country*, the dead-baby motif in *Feather Crowns* links the maternal to conflicts within the larger culture. More graphically than in the earlier book, the five dead babies in *Feather Crowns* are emblematic of larger issues involving clashes between private and public realms, folkways and science, and the maternal and the "official" culture of male authority. These conflicts quickly become apparent following the death of the first baby. When Minnie Sophia dies, Mittens washes her little body, ties her feet together, and bundles her up in fresh outing material. James then stores the baby's body in a canning pot in the springhouse until they can decide when to bury her. He sets a large rock on the lid of the pot to deter raccoons. The other babies are sickly too, and James pragmatically realizes it will be less trouble to handle the burials together. In contrast with the simple, familial care provided by Mittens and James, Mr. Mullins, who owns a "newfangled" funeral parlor, proposes to preserve "little Mindy" indefinitely (FC 223, 226).

After all the babies die, Mullins embalms them using the latest technology and displays them in a glass case in the Slumber Room of his funeral home. Seeing the babies there for the first time is shocking for Christie, and her thoughts indicate how completely business and technology divest the maternal of its offspring and sever bonds that were once intimate and natural. To Christie, the babies "no longer seemed to be her flesh and blood" (FC 259). She thinks they look like "objects," "tight and contorted," with "their little features frozen like knots on fence posts." However, Mullins proudly shows off his handiwork, bragging that the babies will stay "that way till the end of time, or till the air hits them" (FC 259–60).

This artificial preservation resembles the not uncommon practice in the nineteenth century of photographing dead children as mementos or "souvenirs" for the bereaved family. Since childhood deaths were so frequent, a photograph of a dead child, artfully posed as if sleeping, became a treasured reminder for parents of their child's brief life. These pictures were often displayed on a mantel or table in the sitting room.[14] How-

---

14. Lillian Schlissel, *Women's Diaries of the Westward Journey*, 133.

ever, Mullins's approach is far more impersonal and crass. He cannot get Minnie Sophia's name right; he makes the babies into artificial, unnatural "objects"; and then, like a carnival huckster, he shows off what he has accomplished with an offensive, self-congratulatory air. Mullins leaves the babies bonnetless to further display his undertaking skills, but the results are anything but natural: "The babies' heads were like carved wood. Their sleeves were pulled up to show their wrists, like peeled sticks. They still wore their bracelets. Their little fingers curved like bug legs" (FC 260). The new technology Mullins uses stands in bizarre contrast with the humble love and care that Mittens gives Minnie Sophia and with the practical folk wisdom that James employs when he places the baby's body in the springhouse. Mason shows how the rituals and practices of death, like those of childbirth, have moved beyond the sphere of private, familial control into a depersonalized commercial realm.

The scientific lecture tour upon which James and Christie embark with the quintuplets marks a further perversion of death and exploitation of the maternal. With enormous farm debts, the couple agrees to travel with the dead babies as part of the Fair Day Exhibition Series, "an educational series of lectures and diversions" (FC 303). The tour starts respectably enough, but quickly deteriorates into a carnival sideshow. People tromp through the "Amazing Five Babies" exhibit on their way to see such oddities as the Snake Woman from Borneo and the half-man, half-woman. The promoter for the quintuplets contracts with a St. Louis company to manufacture miniature baby beds with five tiny dolls strapped inside to sell as twenty-five-cent souvenirs. The tiny dolls and their real-life counterparts, the embalmed quintuplets displayed under glass, are perhaps the most shocking of the dead-baby images in Mason's fiction. The quintuplets represent the most vulnerable of victims, their tiny bodies having been poked, prodded, handled, fed, medicated, embalmed, and commodified by relentless forces within a rapidly changing culture.

Only when their parents donate the quintuplets to the Institute of Man in Washington, D.C., is their humanity even marginally restored. The institute's Dr. Johnson reassures Christie that only students and medical specialists will study the collection to which the quintuplets will belong for "the good of mankind" (FC 411). His concern seems genuine. Having lost his wife in childbirth, Dr. Johnson understands the complex dimensions of grief. As Christie prepares to hand over the quintuplets, she is flooded with memories of each baby. Even more intensely, she remembers giving birth to the quintuplets, "each birth distinct in her memory. . . . She could assign each birth pang to a particular baby" (FC 414). The scene suggests a merging of the maternal and the scientific, a union of the subjective and the rationally objective. Christie's memories and her divestment of the quintuplets at the institute poignantly reveal the intersections between private and public realms of experience. Moreover, the scene suggests the potential for transforming deep personal grief into public enlightenment.

More regrettably, perhaps, Christie's relinquishing of her babies—tiny wonders born at the dawn of a new age of miracles—suggests the capitulation of folk culture to science, a sign of old ways yielding to new ones. The feather crowns found in Christie's mattress earlier in the novel are not so much a prognostication of the quintuplets' deaths as they are a cautionary warning about things to come in the twentieth century. The rural culture of Christie's world will be overwhelmed by technology, business, modern transportation, and mass communication through a process that will be repeated over and over in a changing South. Maternity will be equally altered in the twentieth century as woman's intimate knowledge of the rhythms of life and death is lost in the name of progress. Mothers will give birth in hospitals where modern analgesia and anesthesia will eliminate the pain of childbirth, and perhaps the memory of it. Some women will try to reclaim the experience for themselves by enrolling in childbirth classes and delivering their babies in maternity centers that operate in competition with each other for insurance dollars. Young mothers will feed their babies Enfamil and Similac or opt to breast-feed their babies with the help of lactation consultants, who will teach them what their own mothers once would have taught them. Howell's Drugs and Sundries will be replaced by Wal-Mart and Babies R Us, with infant products becoming a billion-dollar business. All of these developments suggest a continuing commodification of motherhood, and some suggest a perversion of it.

Christie's eventful journey through motherhood and the twentieth century ends on her ninetieth birthday in 1963, months before a cataclysmic event rocks the nation. During her long life, Christie has witnessed remarkable historical and scientific developments, visited the Dionne quintuplets, and experienced the cultural phenomenon of Elvis.

She has lost a child to war and her husband in a farm-machinery accident. However, she has two surviving children, eight grandchildren, twenty great-grandchildren, and five great-great-grandchildren. Most important, by the novel's end, Christie finally achieves voice. While the rest of *Feather Crowns* is written in the third person, the final chapter, only ten pages long, is rendered in the first person as Christie tells her story into a tape recorder for a granddaughter. Christie remarks that she has tried not to live on just memories; she is too acutely aware of the nature of memory. She tells her granddaughter: "I'll tell you something about memory. It's like if you took anxiousness and dread and put it up in front of a mirror. What you'd see would be memory, like it's coming out the other side of an event. An event is always worse before it happens or after it happens. But not at the time it happens. You can get through that, because it carries you along. It's afterward that gets you." Christie is nonetheless willing to search through memory, if not for herself, then for her descendants. She has much to tell her granddaughter, promising her more about "the old-timey days" (FC 454). Pollack calls Christie's narration a "private communication sent in a public utterance." As Christie tells her story, Pollack explains, she does so in "a country voice less fully revealing than the one we have known in her head, but it is an informing historian's voice" nonetheless. It is also the maternal voice finally spoken aloud. The novel opens with scenes of labor and birth and closes with voice. The connection between the maternal body and the achievement of voice cannot be denied. Southern writer Nanci Kincaid believes that as women and mothers, "we are reluctant to claim our own stories."[15] As Christie speaks into the tape recorder, though her voice is aged and "country," we realize that she is at last claiming hers.

---

15. Pollack, "From *Shiloh* to *In Country* to *Feather Crowns*," 111; Nanci Kincaid's remark was made at a reading and discussion at the Little Professor Book Center in Charlotte, N.C., on October 1, 1997.

Lee Smith

The worlds and voices that Lee Smith creates in her fiction often function as metaphors for the Other. Her Appalachian women characters, by virtue of their gender and culture, stand in opposition to Eurocentric patriarchal traditions. Defined by forces outside themselves, many of Smith's female characters fall into the realm of the silent Other. Other female characters, however, are empowered with voice and language to counteract the silencing of women that frequently occurs in literature and society. According to psychiatrist and libertarian Thomas Szasz, definitions, "especially the power to construct definitions and to impose them on others," assume great importance in human interaction.[1] The law of survival in the modern world is quite simply: define or be defined. The individual who can speak, write, and articulate within a given society achieves greater control not only of his or her destiny, but that of others as well. Throughout her fiction, Smith demonstrates an awareness of these dynamics and of the serious implications that diminished voice and lack of language have for women, especially mothers.

In her rendering of maternal experience, Smith blends the hardscrabble realities of Appalachian life with the rich oral traditions, myths, and folklore of the mountains. Her portrayals of women and the life stages they pass through—from childhood and adolescence to marriage and motherhood and finally into middle and old age—are exacting and insightful. Like Toni Morrison and Bobbie Ann Mason, Smith is concerned with the complex realities of female experience, the mythic elements suffusing such experience, and the enormous impact of culture upon women's lives. Rooted in time and place, her characters struggle with issues of identity, roles, and relationships and possess much am-

1. Thomas Szasz, "Mental Therapy Is a Myth," 105.

bivalence about their circumscribed mountain lives. Anne Goodwyn Jones notes that women in Smith's fiction are "usually married, caught in a cycle of guilt, self-deprecation, entrapment, rebellion, and again guilt that screens them from themselves." Similarly, William Teems contends that a major theme in Smith's Appalachian works is that of women in conflict with "some version of culture." He states: "In a culture that places oppressive restrictions on all its members, an oppression which seems to grow out of the harsh mountain landscape itself, women often find themselves brutally repressed." Smith's female characters, Teems observes, respond in one of three ways: They "stoically accept" their situation, are destroyed by it, or "find a way to overcome cultural repression."[2]

Such responses are clearly evident in *Black Mountain Breakdown* (1980), *Oral History* (1983), *Fair and Tender Ladies* (1988), *The Devil's Dream* (1992), and *Saving Grace* (1995), works set in Appalachia. In these novels, as in most of Smith's fiction, voice functions as a vital, determining element in female survival. Women who achieve voice in some way—whether through storytelling, personal narrative, songs, letters, or just plain talk—seem to survive the oppressiveness of their culture. Granny Younger and Sally Wade, powerful storytellers of different generations in *Oral History*, are well integrated into their mountain communities and are unbent by any cultural repression. Country singer Katie Cocker in *The Devil's Dream* uses music to escape the confines of patriarchal culture. Ivy Rowe in the epistolary *Fair and Tender Ladies* uses letter writing to record her thoughts, feelings, and experiences throughout her life in the mountains and also as a means of psychic survival and even self-actualization. Grace Shepherd's lively first-person narration in *Saving Grace* provides testimony not only about her life but that of her mother, sisters, and countless other mountain women. More passive female characters who fail to achieve any substantial voice—such as Pricey Jane and Dory Cantrell in *Oral History*, the catatonic Crystal Spangler in *Black Mountain Breakdown*, and Ivy Rowe's strange sister Silvaney, to whom she writes her most intimate and compelling letters in *Fair and Tender Ladies*—retreat into silence, madness, or death. Unable to speak for themselves, their sto-

2. Anne Goodwyn Jones, "The World of Lee Smith," 253; William Teems, "Let Us Now Praise the Other: Women in Lee Smith's Short Fiction," 64.

ries must be narrated by others, usually their stronger, more verbal sisters.[3]

Indeed, voice and language are central features in Smith's works and lie at the heart of her attempts to render individual consciousness. In her essay "The Voice behind the Story," Smith claims that writers today are not as concerned with "the grand design, with the whole of society" and are instead more focused on the "individual consciousness." She explains: "This is partly because our real world has become so fragmented and diffuse and confusing that we feel we can't attempt to see it whole and partly because we have moved, it seems to me, farther away from our old beliefs and closer to the contemplation of our own psyches as the ultimate reality." Moreover, Smith believes that contemporary southern writers, who must write in the shadow of such literary giants as William Faulkner, Eudora Welty, and Flannery O'Connor, risk triteness and becoming "a bad imitation of those writers we most admire . . . those people who have 'done' Southern so well." Given these conditions, Smith insists that southern writers today must "make it new *through language*—through point of view, through tone, through style."[4]

Smith herself masterfully uses language, point of view, and voice. Or, as Jones points out, all of Smith's novels are "about language." Jones suggests that Smith's female characters, who are frequently caught between acts of assertion and passivity, struggle to achieve the voice and language that would articulate their experiences. Jones explains the challenge they face: "Finding a true voice is connected with locating a self within that can hate as well as love, can do bodily harm as well as feel bodily pleasure, can experience spirituality as well as sensuality." This struggle to unify body and voice is a recurrent theme in Smith's novels. She gives the body as much importance as voice in the development of individual female characters. "No one escapes the body," Jones asserts. In noting how Smith's women characters find "a kind of health in assertion centered in the self, in the body," Jones observes that those who disregard the body and "prefer intellectualizing to feeling, moralizing to sensuality, religiosity to spirituality, inevitably reveal in their diction and their taletelling their own unacknowledged rages and desires."[5]

3. See Buchanan, "Storyteller's Voice," for a discussion of a strong woman speaking for a passive woman in *Oral History*.
4. Lee Smith, "The Voice behind the Story," 95, 99.
5. Anne Goodwyn Jones, "World of Lee Smith," 253–55.

Smith's attention to body and voice in her rendering of female experience is apparent throughout her oeuvre. However, in *Oral History*, *Fair and Tender Ladies*, and *Saving Grace*, Smith subjects the body and voice of the mother to extensive development. She depicts them in complex relation with each other, as well as with their patriarchal counterparts. In these novels, as in the works of Morrison and Mason explored earlier, the maternal body becomes the substance of myth and metaphor. At the same time, Smith grounds female experience in physical reality, showing how the biological stages of sexual maturation, pregnancy, childbirth, lactation, menopause, and aging are critical underpinnings of a woman's sense of self. Smith's attention to the cycles of the female body and to female voice and language reveals her deep concern for sexual and symbolic difference as these function within the framework of Appalachian culture.

Smith belongs to the cadre of twentieth-century American women writers that Elaine Orr sees as writing "negotiating feminist fictions." Such fictions acknowledge the reality of limits in women's lives and feature protagonists "who are systematically positioned on more than one side of the fiction's sexual/textual politics." They also involve authors and characters who can think, act, and move across contested lines of authority, making "use of conflicting and imperfect cultural fields through simultaneous acts of discrimination and new conjunction." In her study *Subject to Negotiation: Reading Feminist Criticism and American Women's Fiction*, Orr examines texts—by authors including Morrison, Zora Neale Hurston, Edith Wharton, Eudora Welty, and Marge Piercy— that she describes as being "positioned between competing and unequal worlds." She cites, for example, how Hurston negotiates the frameworks of gender and race in *Their Eyes Were Watching God*.[6] Smith similarly traverses gender and cultural fields as a strategy for bridging the dichotomy of body and voice. In so doing, she enables many of her characters to lead authentic, discerning lives within the "competing and unequal worlds" depicted in her texts.

With her focus on the maternal, language, and culture, Smith also fits quite well in the newer generation of feminists described by Julia Kristeva in her essay "Women's Time." In this essay, according to Toril

6. Elaine Orr, *Subject to Negotiation: Reading Feminist Criticism and American Women's Fiction*, 4, 13, 23.

Moi, Kristeva discusses "the *multiplicity* of female expressions" and how different generations of feminists have addressed the concerns of time, language, and sexual difference. In particular, she examines the original "egalitarian" feminists, who demanded equal rights with men and a right to a place in linear time; the post-1968 feminists, who "emphasized women's radical difference from men and demanded women's right to remain *outside* the linear time of history and politics"; and more recent feminists, who have assumed the task of reconciling maternal time, which is both cyclical and eternal, with linear time. Kristeva raises important questions about women's reconciliation of the sexual and the symbolic, asking explicitly: "*What can be our place in the symbolic contract . . . how can we reveal our place, first as it is bequeathed to us by tradition, and then as we want to transform it?*"[7]

In *Oral History, Fair and Tender Ladies,* and *Saving Grace,* Smith seems to be addressing the very questions that Kristeva posits. In each novel and with each female character, Smith examines women's "symbolic contract" with the culture, the traditions within the culture, and the dichotomies that result because of sexual difference. Like Morrison and Mason, Smith is concerned with history, culture, and women's experience of these forces. Like them, she confronts the task of reconciling maternal time with linear or historical time. Through her intensive examination of female experience, language, and time, Smith strives to reconcile women's symbolic and biological existence. In the process, she accomplishes both a mediation of tradition and a transformation of it. Ultimately, she secures a place for women within the culture that incorporates a multiplicity of expression, allows for movement inside and outside of linear time, and permits free play of the corporeal and the mental, of body and voice.

7. Moi, ed., *Kristeva Reader,* 187; Kristeva, "Women's Time," 199.

8

~

Oral History

TELLING THE MOTHER'S STORY

Upon first assessment, Lee Smith appears to dichotomize body and voice to a significant extent in her rendering of maternal experience in *Oral History* (1983). The principal mothers in this multigenerational saga of the Cantrell family—Pricey Jane, Dory, and Pearl Cantrell—are essentially voiceless. Their stories, which constitute the mythic core at the heart of the novel, are narrated by others. There is little maternal speech in the novel. Like the maternal triad formed by Eva, Hannah, and Sula Peace in Toni Morrison's *Sula*, the grandmother-mother-daughter triad formed by the Cantrell women is associated with silence and death. All three die young and tragically, each death creating a palpable absence. Since these mothers are unable to speak for themselves, Smith uses nine narrators, including male and female voices and what appears to be a community voice, to tell their stories. Through the recitation of stories, folklore, and legends, the multiple narrators convey the rich Appalachian heritage and colorful history of the Cantrell family and foreground the maternal experiences of its women. Sadly, the maternal in *Oral History* also functions as a metaphor for the fragile culture of the mountains, soon to be overwhelmed, displaced, and silenced by larger social forces from the outside world. The family homeplace eventually will be developed into a theme park, a neighboring mountain converted into a ski run.

Oral History opens and closes in present time when Pearl Cantrell's daughter, Jennifer Bingham, comes to Hoot Owl Holler to record her family's oral history for a college class. She unwittingly unleashes the novel's narrative voices and sets the storytelling in motion when she leaves her tape recorder running in the haunted Cantrell cabin one night in order to record the strange noises and laughter that have forced her grandparents to move out. The tape recorder captures primal, ghostly sounds: "banging and crashing and wild laughter" (OH 291). The voices of Granny Younger, Richard Burlage, Jink Cantrell, Sally Wade, and others seem to be released into the air and then carried by the wind. Their stories are not recorded by the machine but are present nevertheless. Smith uses the tape recorder and the wind, which "has voices in it," as devices to help set up the structure of the novel and to allow the voices of the past to emerge (OH 13). Jennifer cannot hear these voices, but they come together to form the body of the novel, with each character given his or her own section. Reaching back into the late nineteenth century and returning full circle to the present, their narratives cover almost one hundred years in historical time.

Multiple voices relate the life story of family patriarch Almarine Cantrell, including his dangerous longing for the "witch" Red Emmy, his marriage to Pricey Jane, and the births of their children Eli and Dory. The Cantrell saga unfolds tragically and under a shroud of mystery. The deaths of Pricey Jane and Eli appear as the first manifestation of Red Emmy's vengeful curse upon the Cantrell family. Maddened by Almarine's abandonment of her, she vents her witch-anger upon several generations of Cantrell women: Pricey Jane's female descendants are similarly plagued by misfortune and heartache. Dory and Pearl inherit her gold earrings, a maternal token from Pricey Jane's own mother. Symbolic of the past, the gold hoops "cast an aura of enchantment" but seem to carry Red Emmy's curse as well.[1] A young, pregnant Dory, seduced and abandoned by her teacher, the gentried flatlander Richard Burlage, lives out a hard, restless mountain life, only to commit suicide years later on the railroad tracks near her home. Her daughter Pearl, possessed by the same disquieting restlessness, succeeds in leaving the mountains to become a teacher. She, however, deserts her husband and daughter to run off with one of her high school students. Pearl returns home to Hoot Owl Holler and dies soon after giving birth to a premature baby. In a rage fueled by grief and jealousy, Pearl's young lover, Donnie Osborne, comes to the cabin and murders her stepbrother Billy, who has

---

1. Rosalind Reilly, "*Oral History:* The Enchanted Circle of Narrative and Dream," 84.

been similarly devastated by Pearl's death. Only when Ora Mae, Pearl's stepmother, flings the gold earrings into the gorge does Red Emmy's curse seem to be broken.

As with Almarine Cantrell's story, Smith uses multiple narrators to relate Pricey Jane's, Dory's, and Pearl's tragic "herstories." Holding keys to the past, the various narrators move the novel forward to the present, where, paradoxically, the storytelling began with Jennifer's tape recorder. The multiple perspectives Smith uses in telling the maternal stories of Pricey Jane, Dory, and Pearl Cantrell present an exquisite and symbolic rendering of Julia Kristeva's "multiplicity of female expressions." While these women are given little voice themselves, the voices Smith creates to tell their stories reflect the plural realities and multiple modes of expression associated with female subjectivity. They provide separate yet interlocking pieces of knowledge essential to understanding the maternal mysteries at the core of the novel. Additionally, Smith's narrative strategy, along with her manipulation of time, creates a living, dynamic tension between the past and present. Her blending of linear time with other modes of time, most notably circular time and suspended time, demonstrate a desire to reconcile maternal time with patriarchal, historical time.

Although Smith dichotomizes body and voice in her rendering of the principal maternal figures in *Oral History*, the structure of the novel and her attention to female experience, language, and multiple modes of expression and time reverse the split between body and voice that has traditionally defined maternal experience. All of these elements create a textual complexity that recognizes the orality of Appalachian culture and the centrality of both physical mothers and ancestral mothers. Smith creates a maternal mythology to convey the stories surrounding the Cantrell women and to recover memory and meaning about their lives. In this regard, her novel fits well with the dynamics found in black women's texts and described by Karla F. C. Holloway in *Moorings and Metaphors*. Like the writers Holloway discusses—Morrison, Ntozake Shange, Alice Walker, and Flora Nwapa, among others—Smith recognizes the function of myth and its important connections to "a linguistic/cultural community as the source of the imaginative text of recovered meaning." Smith draws fervently on the language and oral traditions of Appalachian culture in conveying maternal mythology in *Oral History*. The multiple narrators, with their embrace of storytelling, song, and the supernatural, provide the means for unearthing the maternal stories within the text. They personify the essential function of myth, which Holloway sees as being a "vehicle for aligning real and imaginative events in both the present and the past and for dissolving the temporal and spatial bridges between them." While Holloway applies this definition to the texts of black women writers, her model also provides insight into the narrative construction and the culturally bound female experiences in Smith's novel. Like the writers that Holloway includes in her discussion, Smith is concerned with remembering community, uncovering voices that have been silenced, and challenging "scriptocentric historicism."[2]

These concerns are evident from the outset of the novel when Jennifer Bingham comes to Hoot Owl Holler to tape her family's oral history. Her efforts initiate an examination of both patriarchal and matriarchal history. Almarine Cantrell and Richard Burlage are important paternal figures in Jennifer's past, and their stories unfold as the novel progresses. Burlage's written accounts, in particular, represent Smith's challenge of "scriptocentric historicism," further entrenching the conflict between the maternal and paternal elements that undergird the family mythology. As the novel opens, Smith directs Jennifer's focus toward her maternal heritage. Jennifer is romantically drawn to her mother's home, the maternal source of her being. In seeking out her family's and her mother's stories, she is, in some regards, like Denver in *Beloved*, who also elicits the stories of her mother and foremothers. Both are daughters seeking connection with the maternal through language and narrative. Both search through family history and attempt to find meaning in the past. However, Jennifer's outsider status, her naïveté, and her inability to comprehend the rich, complex heritage of her family set her apart from Morrison's character. Unlike the memorably birthed Denver, who grows up immersed in female culture and narrative, Jennifer remains in the outer framing sections of the novel in which she appears. Her tape recorder represents a false orality; it is a modern, artificial device that stands in contrast with the lively, resonant voices that emerge in the text. Paradoxically, Jennifer succeeds in finding her roots and in locating the maternal histories of her mother, grandmother, and great-grandmother, but all is beyond her hearing and comprehension.

2. Holloway, *Moorings and Metaphors*, 25.

To a significant degree, Jennifer resembles her grandfather, Richard Burlage, who also fails miserably in his understanding of the mountain culture into which he ventures. Like Jennifer, he represents the powerful intrusion of the present and of the outside world. Burlage and his journal, which comprises the largest narrative section in the novel, reflect "the tension between oral and written culture."[3] Through his journal, Burlage makes pretensions to understanding the mountain community, but, as an outsider, he cannot achieve any real knowledge of the place or its people. His writings represent a split between the rational world and a culture that is still in touch with mysterious ways of knowing. Burlage's journal also aligns him with patriarchal speech and linear time, in much the same way that Dwayne's Vietnam diary in Mason's *In Country* aligns that character with patriarchal history. This puts Burlage even more at odds with the mountain community and its cyclical and enduring elements of maternal time.

Like Dwayne's daughter, Sam, who confronts the realities of war contained within her father's diary, Jennifer is thrust into contact with patriarchal history and language. As a university student, Jennifer has been indoctrinated with the same "academic father speech" that defines her grandfather, Burlage.[4] Her "speech" in the novel is limited to written journal entries not unlike those of her grandfather. She possesses the same narrow, romanticized vision of the mountains and the past as Burlage. The oral traditions of her mother's family remain foreign and any real connections with them elude her. In the end, Jennifer decides her mountain relatives are really "primitive people" and not the quaint, pastoral people she had imagined them to be (OH 290). Disillusioned and frightened by their coarseness, she flees the mountains and her maternal heritage for safer landscape, never to return.

Despite Jennifer's limited presence in the text and her close identification with the paternal, she nonetheless plays a pivotal role in the unearthing and articulation of maternal history. Not only does she unleash the novel's narrative voices with her tape recorder, she focuses her attention and the reader's on the maternal source of the stories. The haunted Cantrell cabin, whose ghostly noises Jennifer records, is not unlike Sethe's haunted house/womb in *Beloved*. The source of narrative

3. Anne Goodwyn Jones, "World of Lee Smith," 270.
4. Corinne Dale, "The Power of Language," 22.

in the novel, the Cantrell cabin is also a womb of sorts, containing the lives and stories of the past. Jennifer's initial impressions recorded in her journal imbue the house with a maternal identity. Poised high upon a hill, "[t]he picturesque old homeplace" looks out over the entire valley in a watchful maternal fashion. Jennifer likens the valley itself to female domestic arts: With its "varied terrain" of pastures and gardens, the valley appears "stitched together by split-oak fences resembling nothing so much as a green-hued quilt" (OH 6). The cabin is similarly associated with female identity and activities. Vines of ivy climb "sensuously up through the floorboards" of the sagging porch. Jennifer searches through the rooms of the house, noting the primitive kitchen, the handmade rocker, and dust covering the floor "like an even lacey carpet" (OH 7). She tries to visualize her mother playing as a child in its rooms. The cabin, symbolic of maternal space, represents the past and serves as a surrogate for Jennifer's dead mother.

Jennifer's nostalgic, pastoral observations about the physical body of the house are misleading, however, and stand in startling contrast with the house's "voice." The wild sounds associated with the cabin that are caught on the tape recorder suggest a more primitive, prelanguage state. The eerie, ghostly noises represent the nonspeech of the semiotic chora, as do the strange pulsions of light and the noisy baby ghost in Sethe's house in *Beloved*. Like the chora, the Cantrell cabin—the site of much tragedy and loss—represents negation and death. While the chora threatens the speaking subject, the cabin proves to be especially destructive to the maternal. It serves as both womb and tomb. Generations of Cantrells are born here, but, for the mothers particularly, the cabin is closely linked with death and the silencing of the maternal. Pricey Jane and her young son Eli are found dead in the cabin after drinking the "dew pizen" milk from a sick cow (OH 71); a searching, restless Dory continually flees the cabin before finally killing herself under a train; and Jennifer's own mother, Pearl, dies giving birth in the cabin after her scandalous affair.

The mountains where the cabin sits are another important and paradoxical symbol of the maternal. Similar to the way that Mason makes associations between Lila Culpepper's body and the Kentucky farmland in *Spence + Lila*, Smith links the female body with landscape in *Oral History*, but with more ambivalence. Carole Ganim sees an "identification of body and mind, of nature and spirit" with the mountains embedded within Appalachian literature written by women. In analyzing the connections between the mountains and the female self, Ganim asserts: "A woman born in the closely-clustered hills of the Appalachians is surrounded, if not almost suffocated, by symbols of herself from birth."[5] While Mason's treatment of the maternal body and the landscape yields timeless symbols of fertility and renewal, Smith's rendering is less life-affirming and regenerative. She depicts the mountains as a dangerous and mysterious realm, not unlike the foreboding terrain of the female body and the chora. Indeed, the present-day Cantrells flee Hoot Owl Holler and the haunted cabin, driven away by "terrible banging noises and rushing winds and ghostly laughter" (OH 8). Escaping the complexity of the past and its ghosts, Ora Mae and Little Luther, Dory's widower, move in with their son Al, whose house by Grassy Creek is devoid of history and myth. In contrast with the tragic but rich familial past associated with the cabin and Hoot Owl Holler, the lives of the younger generation of Cantrells are defined by television, Amway, and Mediterranean-style furniture—superficial, impermanent symbols of the present.

While the maternal body is metaphorically rendered through the mountain landscape and family home, the spirit and voice of the maternal finds its fullest expression in Granny Younger. As the first narrator after the initial, modern-day framing section, she sets the stage for the rich orality that infuses the novel. Her spirited, colorful narration stands in stark contrast with the flat, banal prose of Richard Burlage that follows. Granny Younger evokes the past in the richest sense possible. As midwife and healer, she is perhaps the last wise woman of the tribe. By virtue of age and attendance at most of the births and deaths in the community, she knows everyone's personal history. She has knowledge of the root culture of the mountains, the female mysteries of life, and the legends of the past. Through Granny Younger, such stories as Red Emmy's bewitching of Almarine Cantrell and Pricey Jane's mysterious origins and tragic death are integrated into the folklore heritage of the community. Like Baby Suggs in *Beloved*, she is the repository of memory, spirit, and the collective history of the community.

In many regards, Granny Younger represents time in all its dimensions and symbolizes Smith's efforts to reconcile maternal time with pa-

5. Carole Ganim, "Herself: Woman and Place in Appalachian Literature," 258.

triarchal time. Granny is associated not only with community history and the linear passage of time, but with cyclical time, suspended time, and "monumental temporality," the maternal time that Kristeva associates with eternity. Besides serving as a link to the past, she acts as a nurturing force in the present, significantly affecting the daily life, health, and well-being of the entire community. With her clairvoyance, Granny Younger is also the community's envoy to the future. As she explains: "Sometimes I know the future in my breast. Sometimes I see the future coming out like a picture show, acrost the trail ahead." She is able to interpret the natural signals around her; for example, a thick fog in August means heavy snow in the coming winter, and "blood on the moon" bears tragic portents and is associated with "graves and dying" (OH 27). Because she is so in tune with the rhythms of life and death in the mountains, her intuitive powers appear to be an inevitable extension of those connections.

Granny Younger's storytelling gifts have similar origins, which makes her a natural voice for the community. Unselfishly, she incorporates the viewpoints of other community members into her narrative, an action that mirrors Smith's overall narrative strategy in Oral History. In recounting "froze-time" in Hoot Owl Holler—the unnatural period when Red Emmy and Almarine Cantrell lived together in his mountain cabin and time seemed to stand still—Granny includes the observations of Rhoda Hibbitts, Harve Justice, and others to relate the strange goings-on (OH 40). When she concludes, "Well, they is stories and stories," she is in essence acknowledging the layering of stories and experiences that determines the collective memory of the community (OH 41). Symbolic of the maternal, Granny Younger is the vessel into which individual stories are poured, and she gives them final shape and meaning.

While Granny Younger represents the procreative, healing spirit of the maternal, she also speaks for the mother. She functions as the principal narrator for Pricey Jane Cantrell, whose maternal experience reflects a powerful dichotomizing of body and voice. The first of Jennifer's foremothers and an orphan herself, Pricey Jane is associated with mystery and silence. With her dark hair, large golden earrings, and uncertain lineage, Pricey Jane appears foreign and is referred to as Almarine Cantrell's "gypsy-gal wife" (OH 56). Like her own mother, daughter, and granddaughter, she possesses little voice in the novel. Smith limits

Pricey Jane's speech to such brief directives as "Come on and sleep here," "Let's get us some water," "Come on here," and "Git on" (OH 60, 64, 65). In narrating Pricey Jane's story, Granny Younger tells how Almarine traded a mule to get her for his wife and how easily she settled into domestic life and into the community. The perfect embodiment of wife and mother, Pricey Jane is nonetheless patriarchal property. Dorothy Combs Hill remarks that Pricey Jane's name "indicates her status as a valuable possession," and the mule trade marks her as disposable property.[6] Although her circumstances are exceedingly different, Pricey Jane is not unlike Sethe in *Beloved*. In varying degrees, both women are economic possessions belonging to their respective "owners."

Pricey Jane's domesticity stands in contrast with the wild sexuality of the witch Red Emmy, Almarine's previous consort and Granny Younger's nemesis. With her rampant sexual desire, Red Emmy bewitches Almarine and nearly destroys him with her insatiability. She acts openly, without restraint upon her sexuality. When Red Emmy makes love with Almarine in a freshly plowed field during a thunderstorm, she does so knowing that Granny Younger is watching. Corinne Dale sees Red Emmy as "powerful," both sexually and linguistically: "She cannot be silenced, not even by death itself." Dale believes that the wild sounds and laughter picked up by Jennifer's tape recorder in the Cantrell cabin are actually the threatening, primal voice of Red Emmy. Her discourse is "the secret language of witches, a powerful and disruptive voice that has been feared and muffled through the ages."[7]

In contrast with Red Emmy's sexuality, Pricey Jane's is far less overt, her voice more diminished. Her wifely passion is revealed through subtle imagery that only hints at the sexual desire she possesses. Smith gives her character's sexuality delicate but sensual expression. As in Pauline Breedlove's experience of the smashed berries and her "rainbow" orgasms in *The Bluest Eye*, the sensuality of the natural world provides sexual metaphors for Pricey Jane as well: "Two dragonflies mate in the shimmering air above the springhouse, blue in the sun. They fly together, a single enormous glittering dragonfly, and Pricey Jane smiles. '*Hit's a woman's duty and her burden*,' Rhoda said. Pricey Jane smiles and fills her

6. Dorothy Combs Hill, *Lee Smith*, 69.
7. Dale, "Power of Language," 31.

buckets at the spring" (OH 64). The passage indicates that Pricey Jane, like Christie Wheeler in *Feather Crowns*, finds her marital duty to be pleasing and satisfying. It also provides evidence of Kristeva's *jouissance*, the sexual pleasure experienced by the maternal body. However, the veiled eroticism of Smith's depiction confirms Kristeva's assertion that patriarchal society demands that such female pleasure be repressed "at all costs." Pricey Jane's status as patriarchal property and her identification with the maternal do not allow for overt expression of sexual feelings. Unlike the witch Red Emmy, who exists beyond the bounds of the patriarchy and whose desire for Almarine is given public expression, Pricey Jane's sexuality necessitates metaphoric and subtle rendering.

Given their differences, Pricey Jane and Red Emmy together embody the dualities of the total female principle: maternity and sexuality, procreation and destruction, passivity and power. When both become pregnant by Almarine, their experiences of maternity mirror their differences. Red Emmy is much like the sexually consuming Beloved in Morrison's novel, who seduces Paul D, takes the form of a pregnant woman, and disappears into the woods. Similarly, a pregnant Red Emmy disappears, returning to her home on the wild side of Snowman Mountain when Almarine, not wanting any "witch-children" in his holler, turns her out (OH 47). Like Joe Trace's mother, Wild, in Morrison's *Jazz*, Red Emmy gives birth alone in the wilderness. She nurses her baby for three days, but then dashes it into the fire. Like Beloved, Wild, and the tragic Pecola Breedlove, Red Emmy remains outside civilized society, "a-running through the woods talking all to herself and laughing" (OH 57).

In contrast with Red Emmy's solitary and fierce experience of maternity, Pricey Jane experiences the births of Eli and Dory with greater dependency and reliance on others. Unlike the powerful Red Emmy, the physically frail Pricey Jane suffers through childbirth with difficulty, attended by Granny Younger and other women. Indeed, Pricey Jane is supported by the same kind of female community that surrounds Christie Wheeler when she gives birth to quintuplets in *Feather Crowns*. Childbirth in Mason's and Smith's works is an active, woman-centered event. Like the women in attendance at the quintuplets' births, Granny, Rhoda Hibbitts, and Mrs. Crouse comfort and assist Pricey Jane not only through childbirth but also in the rituals that follow. As in *Feather Crowns*, a curious mix of folk wisdom and common sense abounds in Smith's novel. Rhoda and Mrs. Crouse prepare the birthing bed with an old quilt, place an ax under the bed to cut the pain, and pin back Pricey Jane's hair to make her comfortable through the more rigorous stages of childbirth. While Granny delivers the baby, they stand on either side of Pricey Jane "for her to hold onto" (OH 58). Afterwards, the women sprinkle the baby with dust "from between the chimley-rocks for luck," bury "the borning quilt," and take the ax from under the bed and "chop up the man's hat iffen they can find it" (OH 60).

Pricey Jane's maternal experience, which is powerfully aligned with the body, resembles Pauline Breedlove's in *The Bluest Eye*. Like Pauline's, Pricey Jane's experience of birth is wordless and intensely physical. She labors in silence, never complaining or giving voice to her pain. During Dory's birth, Granny Younger fears for Pricey Jane's safety and physical well-being, noting her narrow hips, her thrashing about, the "unnatural sweat," and the purple shadows under her eyes "like bruises." However, Dory is born easily enough, with Pricey Jane's only utterance "a little scream" (OH 59). Following Dory's birth, Pricey Jane is given her own narrative section, but like Pauline's reveries in *The Bluest Eye* it consists of female interiority rather than speech. The thoughts and images that emerge reflect Pricey Jane's continuing alignment with the maternal body. The maternal voice is muffled, the language nonexistent.

Pricey Jane's narrative section opens one July evening with Pricey Jane nursing Dory on the front porch of the cabin and "mooning" over Almarine, who has gone off trading in Black Rock (OH 61). As in Christie Wheeler's experience of nursing her babies in *Feather Crowns*, breast-feeding induces dreams and reveries for Pricey Jane. Through complex associations, Smith links breast-feeding with memory, with the mountain landscape, and with the maternal body and voice. Milk serves as a unifying symbol in the chapter and establishes generational connections between women as it does in *Beloved*. When Pricey Jane nurses Dory, the act triggers a rush of memories about her own dead mother, particularly her mother's silence about love and her bequeathal of the gold earrings. Just as milk is "let down" during lactation, breast-feeding unleashes "[q]uestions upon questions, like the mountains close by and the mountains beyond them," for Pricey Jane about love, her family, and indeed her very existence (OH 62). More compellingly, it resurrects a restless and unfulfilled longing to know and hear the mother's voice.

While she is breast-feeding Dory, Pricey Jane recalls a dream of her mother singing and dancing. She struggles to remember her mother's song, but, unable to understand the words, she is enveloped by the physical presence of the mother instead: "Her mother's hair was loose and dark and drifting as she whirled, she was dancing, singing a song for Pricey Jane. Her mother had leaned over and kissed her and Pricey Jane had been caught fast in the tent of her mother's long dark hair. What was the song she sang?" (OH 62–63). The maternal voice is thus manifested through wordless song rather than speech. Like the maternal song of Mrs. MacTeer in *The Bluest Eye*, it represents the primeval source of female voice that, as we have seen, Hélène Cixous calls the "first music from the first voice of love which is alive in every woman." Like the gold earrings given to Pricey Jane, the wordless song becomes a troubling legacy passed from mother to daughter. Dream and reality blur as Pricey Jane adopts the "voice" of her mother and "sings a song without words" as she nurses Dory. Smith, however, undercuts the idyllic, dreamlike scene by revealing the bondage inherent in motherhood. Dory's "steady pull" on her mother's nipple is a reminder of this reality; with some ambivalence, Pricey Jane realizes her irrevocable connection to husband, home, and the baby she is nursing: It is "like a chain that closes her in and holds her here, a chain of her own choosing or dreaming" (OH 63).

The deaths of Pricey Jane and Eli from drinking the milk of a sick cow shortly thereafter are ironic. The poisoned milk contrasts with the overwhelming sweetness of Pricey Jane's own milk, which she playfully tastes after nursing Dory. Whereas breast-feeding forges a chain that binds Pricey Jane to family and home, drinking the poisoned cow's milk breaks that bond. In a seasonal inversion similar to the one Morrison employs in *The Bluest Eye*, the deaths of mother and child occur in summer. Pricey Jane's death further emphasizes the voicelessness of the maternal. Like Morrison's Sula, the dying Pricey Jane is unable to speak: "[H]er mouth drops open and slack" and "[h]er breath smells like something dead" (OH 70).

Dory Cantrell, Pricey Jane's daughter, is also powerfully aligned with the female body. When the young Dory first visits Richard Burlage's schoolhouse, he is overwhelmed by her physical beauty. With her full red lips, violet eyes, alabaster face, and "finespun golden curls," she appears goddesslike to him. Her plain, homespun clothes accentuate her delicate beauty. Burlage likens her to a Botticelli painting; indeed, his description of her calls to mind *The Birth of Venus*, arguably Botticelli's most famous work, depicting the celestial Venus born of the sea. Burlage describes Dory's ethereal beauty in his journal: "The sun streamed in the schoolhouse door behind her, turning her curls into a flaming gold halo around her head" (OH 116). Ironically, given these impressions, Burlage soon learns that Dory possesses a forthright, earthy sexuality. She initiates their first sexual encounter, bluntly commanding Burlage to suck her breasts and guiding his hand inside her panties. On later visits, Dory is equally assertive; Burlage notes: "[S]he answered my passion with her own, taking me beyond all boundaries of physical sensation" (OH 154). Physically, Dory is Burlage's female counterpart—equal in passion, equal in size. Lying naked with her, Burlage observes: "A strange phenomenon: we are almost exactly the same size, toe to toe. I felt as if she completed me, and I completed her, as if we were truly one" (OH 155).

For the time being, Dory's speech, as rendered indirectly through Burlage's journal, seems as easy and open as her sexuality. Burlage imagines that she complements him linguistically as well as physically: "We spoke so easily . . . even our vastly different manners of speech seemed to meet and blend together into some single tongue we share" (OH 127). However, as Dale points out, Dory's powerful sensuality so overwhelms Burlage that he loses control of verbal expression and is given to "ejaculating both sexually and verbally."[8] At a loss for words, he records "!!!!!!!!" in his journal (OH 146).

After Burlage returns to Richmond without her, Dory seems to diminish both physically and verbally over time. Pregnant with Burlage's twin daughters Pearl and Maggie, Dory marries Little Luther Wade, and later bears his children as well. Marriage, motherhood, and the hard times of the Depression extract an enormous price. When Burlage returns to the mountains after a ten-year absence, he spies a greatly aged Dory through his camera lens: "She was reduced to an indistinct, stooped shape, the posture of an older woman" (OH 234). Dory's di-

8. Ibid., 24.

minishment is emblematic of larger changes around her. The pictures that Burlage takes of a tubercular young mother sitting on a street curb, a stooped old man leaning against a new World War I monument, and fighting boys whose muddy shoes are patched with cardboard reflect both the desperate times that have come to the mountains and the diminishment of an entire people.

Although Dory stands at the pivotal center of her family, she is silent and detached. Her daughter Sally Wade confirms her diminished voice and the restless unease that plagues her: "[S]he never raised her voice. . . . A lot of times, it was like she was listening to something couldn't none of the rest of us hear" (OH 243). Trapped between two worlds, Dory is drawn to the outside world introduced to her by Burlage and, at the same time, firmly rooted in the landscape of the mountains. Dory's apparent suicide on the spur line that leads down the mountain reflects this ambivalence. Her decapitation on the railroad tracks where she has frequently wandered is symbolic of her psychological struggle and her failure to be wholly integrated into either world. Suggestive of both a literal and metaphorical split between mind and body, the decapitation represents an irrevocable silencing of the maternal. Dory's daughter Pearl, who inherits her mother's cursed gold earrings and her restlessness, is similarly silenced. Pearl's death in childbirth following a ruinous affair with her high school student completes the tragic maternal trinity formed with Pricey Jane and Dory Cantrell. Pearl's story is largely told by her half-sister, Sally Wade, the novel's final and most positive narrator.

Unlike the other Cantrell women, who show a powerful dichotomizing of body and voice, Sally possesses both a strong, confident voice and a sure sense of her physical self. Smith fully integrates body and voice within this character. Relating her own maternal experience firsthand, Sally recounts her desperate pregnancy with daughter Rosy after running off to Florida with a disc jockey. She speaks candidly of the fatigue, colic, and "bleeding" that followed the birth of her son Davy (OH 267). At ease with her body, Sally says that she found breast-feeding both maternal and erotic: "There is something about a baby's pull on your nipple that puts you in mind of a man, but it is entirely different from that— it's different from everything else. And there's a lot of things, like that . . . you can't explain" (OH 271). Sally's words indicate that breast-feeding provokes memory of sorts, not unlike the maternal memory that

Pricey Jane experiences while nursing Dory. Although it seems to emanate from the same mysterious, nebulous realm as Pricey Jane's, Sally's memory has a decidedly more sexual component. It also confirms her ability to unify the sexual and maternal aspects of her being. Body and voice are given similar unity within Sally's character. As a twice-married mother and grandmother, Sally admits that talk and sex are the "two things I like to do better than anything else in this world, even at my age" (OH 237). She enjoys both, often at the same time, with her second husband: "Roy can fuck your eyes out, Roy can, and talking all the time. 'Talk to me,' he says. Well I like that" (OH 238). As Dale points out, the pleasure that Sally takes in both talking and sex indicates that she "has reconciled the language of the body with the language of the mind." More than any other character, she is able to accommodate "the sexual and the intellectual, the primal and the cultural."[9]

A natural storyteller and realist, Sally Wade is Granny Younger's modern-day counterpart; indeed, the two women serve as bookends for the novel. Bringing the Cantrell saga full circle, Sally's narrative of forty-four pages is equal in length to Granny's chapter, the first narrative in the novel. The most verbal of the Cantrell women, Sally completes the stories of Dory and Pearl, recounting their experiences for them. Smith professes to like this character and says she thinks Sally presents a strong, positive female image. However, she also believes that Sally's narration depicts how her language, like the mountain landscape, has changed. Compared to the lively mountain voices heard earlier in the novel, it "has become diluted toward the end through TV and everything else."[10] Fully aware that she talks like a "mountain girl," Sally seems to understand her linguistic limitations (OH 270). Nevertheless, she is sharply attuned to the variances of vocal expression in those around her. She recalls her father's singing voice, "so pure and true . . . it was like it was something he called up out of the dark green summer air and out of the mountains themselves" (OH 242). In addition to her mother's silences and diminished voice, Sally describes the sheriff's "rough way of speaking" and the "mumbling" of his men in the aftermath of Dory's suicide (OH 254). More humorously, she recounts how stepmother Ora Mae snores "like a mule" (OH 258). When Pearl re-

9. Ibid., 32.
10. Quoted in Edwin Arnold, "An Interview with Lee Smith," 246.

turns home from college, Sally observes the "breathy" affectations of her speech and notes that when Pearl gets upset, her language slips "from the fancy way she'd come to talk" (OH 267, 270). Without question, Sally's awareness of voice and language surpasses that of any other narrator in the novel.

Sally's narrative also possesses a multilayered complexity with metafictional dimensions. Essentially a story about storytelling, her narrative unfolds as a retelling of a story that she has already told her husband Roy during his recuperation from a broken leg. Not only does Sally recount various incidents and conversations contained within the primary story about her family, she also tells the reader about her husband's engagement with the storytelling, including his reactions, questions, and favorite parts. Dale asserts that Sally subverts traditional linguistic patterns by rejecting beginning-middle-end narrative structures and by her refusal "to find meanings or to make the tale coherent." Dale also notes that "Sally subverts her own formulations by starting her tale several times, observing that it is hard, even impossible to find the beginning." Sally nonetheless exerts an intuitive control over the direction and pacing of her storytelling. She pauses occasionally to inform the reader of shifts in her narrative. At one point, she announces, "I'm going to speed this story up now" (OH 263). At another point, when she seems to digress from Pearl's story to her own, Sally acknowledges the shift in direction, but promises to return to her original subject: "[T]his part is Pearl's story, not mine, from here on out, and I'll get to her in a minute" (OH 264). However, before concluding her half-sister's tragic story, she pauses again to comment, "I wish I could have stopped the telling there" (OH 280). She then explains that she has to rush through the "bad" parts, just as she had to rush the story to completion for Roy: "[W]e were pushing suppertime" (OH 280). Dale concludes that Sally's alternative narrative strategies, which are "responsive and responsible to her own experience," mirror Smith's own construction of *Oral History*. Both Sally's tale-within-the-tale and Smith's novel are devoid of conventional structures, consisting instead of "overlapping and sometimes conflicting testimonies."[11] As a result, both character and author conspire in their creation of the text.

Sally's significance in *Oral History* far exceeds the metafictional role

11. Dale, "Power of Language," 33–34.

she assumes. Her ability to transform traditional narrative places her in the company of feminists who are concerned with reconciling maternal time with linear time, the sexual with the symbolic. This, along with her understanding of language, family, and culture, demonstrates that Sally has found her place within the "symbolic contract" that Kristeva describes. Her rich, complex narrative serves as a satisfying response to Kristeva's question "[H]ow can we reveal our place, first as it is bequeathed to us by tradition, and then as we want to transform it?" Sally achieves not only a unification of body and voice but also a reconciliation of maternal time with linear time. She understands the intricate connections between the past and present, and her narrative adds circularity to the text. Sally does not view her family's troubled past as a crippling, tragic burden; rather, she transforms it into stories that ultimately link generations together. Moreover, through her narrative gifts, Sally resolves the dichotomies that characterize mountain life and overcomes the cultural repression that destroyed her mother and sister. Thus she is able to relate the stories of the past with a vitality and consciousness that, according to Ganim, demonstrate that she "understands the polarities of feeling and thought, passivity and action, female and male, and unifies them in her life."[12]

Sally is much like the "go-between characters" that Elaine Orr identifies in her study of negotiating feminist fictions. According to Orr, such characters "choose to remain connected to both dominant and subordinate worlds, knowing these designations are themselves slippery and changing."[13] Even with the intrusion of the outside world into the once-isolated mountain world, Sally successfully adapts to change. She remains connected to the competing worlds that surround her and can negotiate the sexual and cultural politics they ensconce. Furthermore, she realizes that in order to survive the suffocating hold of the past and the destabilizing forces of the present, she must adapt, accommodate, or leave the mountains. At the same time, she shrewdly knows that "there's no new life" (OH 270). Of all the Cantrells, Sally is the one most able to accept the rich but harsh heritage of her mountain past, establish her place in a rapidly changing culture, and give voice to her full experience.

12. Ganim, "Herself," 273.
13. Orr, *Subject to Negotiation*, 24.

9

~

Fair and Tender Ladies

LETTERS, LANGUAGE,
AND MATERNAL SUBJECTIVITY

Unlike *Oral History,* which employs multiple voices to tell the mother's story, *Fair and Tender Ladies* (1988) relies on the singular voice of protagonist Ivy Rowe to articulate her own experiences. In giving Ivy voice and language, Lee Smith challenges the notion of woman as the silent Other and elevates the subjectivity of female experience. Using multiple modes of language, she empowers Ivy to convey her own "herstory," to articulate directly her experiences of sexuality, pregnancy, childbirth, and motherhood. Like Sally Wade in *Oral History,* Ivy possesses a unity of body and voice. However, while Sally's voice and experiences are limited to one section of *Oral History,* Ivy's are given full and satisfying development and resonate throughout the entire text of *Fair and Tender Ladies.* Written entirely in epistolary form, the novel follows Ivy from her childhood on a mountain on Sugar Fork Creek to her death several decades later in the same cabin where she was born. Although she longs to see the world beyond, Ivy never ventures out of the Virginia mountains; she moves only to the nearby towns of Majestic and Diamond before returning home to Sugar Fork. Throughout these moves, Ivy writes to family and friends, documenting the events of her life.

Ivy's letters work on multiple levels: They function as a means of communication with loved ones as she moves from place to place; they serve as a repository of mountain culture and folkways; and they provide a rendering of female experience deeply rooted in social, sexual, and psychological concerns. Grouped into five sections that correspond to different geographic locales and time periods in Ivy's life, the letters

155

provide the narrative structure of the novel. In one sense, they establish a linear sense of time. However, given that the letters foreground
the female body and life experiences, they are associated with the fluidic, nonlinear dimensions of women's time as well. Throughout all of
her letters, Ivy speaks candidly about sexuality, pregnancy, childbirth,
breast-feeding, menopause, and aging, providing a rare degree of subjectivity. She also discusses the multiple and often overlapping roles she
assumes during her lifetime as daughter, granddaughter, sister, niece,
aunt, friend, lover, wife, mother, and grandmother. Ivy's narrative travels full circle: Her first and last letters originate from her familial home
of Sugar Fork, where past and present, child and woman, merge together. Altogether, the interweave of letters, language, and life roles
provides an authentic rendering of female experience and illuminates
the dynamic interplay between body and voice in the novel.

Given the rich oral traditions that she draws upon from her Appalachian culture, Ivy's letters also represent a mediation of spoken and
written discourse. In her study of Smith's earlier fiction, Anne Goodwyn Jones notes Smith's preference for the "traditionally female immanent art" and the spoken word over the "traditionally male transcendent art" and the written word. Jones claims that the art associated with
women's culture in Smith's fiction not only shapes life, but "is useful as
well, like cakes or quilts or hairstyles." Oral discourse has a similar func-
tionality and possesses "a human context more concrete than that of
written prose." Jones delineates Smith's multiple uses of the spoken
word: "She reveals character, distinguishes social class, creates irony,
and laughs affectionately at her people as they speak out and in speaking become themselves."[1] Ivy's letters, prima facie evidence of written
discourse, contain innumerable references to storytelling, songs, and
legends, thus revealing a concomitant emphasis on the spoken word. In
Smith's earlier *Oral History*, such duality creates a polarizing tension.
The Latinate prose of Richard Burlage's journal stands in sharp and jar-
ring contrast with the oral accounts of others in that novel. However,
in *Fair and Tender Ladies*, Smith attempts to unify oral and written
modes. The epistolary nature of the novel, along with Ivy's oral heritage, serves as a testament to this.

Traditionally speaking, women's letters have not constituted belles

1. Anne Goodwyn Jones, "World of Lee Smith," 252.

lettres. In having Ivy write letters, Smith not only embraces written discourse, but elevates a marginalized form of writing as well. Ivy's letters from childhood, though they contain nonstandard spelling and grammar, reveal a unique sensibility and acute awareness of the world around her. Ivy's later letters, like those of southern women of the nineteenth century, reveal how women's daily lives, so intensely focused on family, friends, and the care of others, can be truly extraordinary. Such letters depict lives full of devotion and responsibility and reveal only occasionally the private fears, longings, and regrets that punctuate daily existence. Not only does Smith give us Ivy's life and words, she privileges women's lives and women's writings in a greater sense as well. Through Ivy's letters, Smith redefines the language of writing so that it retains the elements of female culture and articulates with authority the experiences of women within the culture.

Besides the oral and written modes, Smith broadens her scope to incorporate other modes of language within the novel. The orality of Ivy's culture implies, as Jones contends about Smith's other works, that there is a speaker and a listener.[2] Indeed, Ivy grows up a keen listener, absorbing the sounds and stories of the mountains. She listens with rapt attention as the elderly, pipe-smoking Cline sisters relate the Appalachian folktales of Old Dry Fry, Mutsmag, and Bloody Bones. Through the Cline sisters, who trade stories for food, Ivy realizes the powerful connection between narrative and human existence. Stories are as sustaining to life as is food, for both teller and listener. Reading functions as a vital language activity for Ivy during childhood as well. A voracious reader of fairy tales, poetry, and romance classics, she integrates stories and poetry into the common realities of her everyday life. While growing up, Ivy likens herself to Charlotte Brontë's Jane Eyre, Alfred Noyes's Highwayman, and the Ice Queen (an apparent reference to Hans Christian Andersen's Snow Queen). Their fictional plights help her to understand her own.

Altogether, the four modes of language with which Smith infuses Ivy's life—speaking, listening, reading, and writing—provide a meaningful substructure for Ivy's articulation of her experiences. By empowering Ivy with these multiple modes of language, Smith ensures the development of her character's voice, her sense of self, and her place

2. Ibid.

within the world. Julia Kristeva observes that women traditionally "have been left out of the socio-symbolic contract, of language as the fundamental social bond." She notes that women have had to work "to break the code, to shatter the language, to find a specific discourse closer to the body and emotions, to the unnameable repressed by the social contract."[3] Smith's abiding concern for language and her emphasis on female experience demonstrates her participation in these efforts to integrate the female body and language within society. In *Fair and Tender Ladies*, Smith not only accomplishes a mediation of oral and written discourse, but also enables her protagonist to define her place within the symbolic order, *and* on her own terms. Thus, Ivy's full engagement with language and with life leads to the development of a wholly integrated self within a culture that silences and destroys other women.

Throughout *Fair and Tender Ladies*, Smith links Ivy's use of language with the landscape, another critical element that shapes female growth and experience. Each mountain locale from which Ivy writes her letters corresponds to a different developmental stage in her life. Part I, "Letters from Sugar Fork," tells of Ivy's childhood on Blue Star Mountain at the end of Sugar Fork Creek, where she lives with her parents and eight siblings in a double-wide cabin. They eke out a difficult life until her father's death scatters the family across the mountains. Part II, "Letters from Majestic," focuses on Ivy's adolescence and her early sexual experiences after she and her mother move into a boardinghouse in Majestic, Virginia. Here Ivy becomes pregnant out of wedlock by a town boy, Lonnie Rash, who is later killed in World War I. When her mother dies, Ivy moves to the mining town of Diamond to live with her married sister. Part III, "Letters from Diamond," documents Ivy's initiation into motherhood and adult sexuality, including the birth of her daughter Joli; her reckless affair with the mine owner's son, Franklin Ransom; and her courtship by childhood friend Oakley Fox. After Oakley survives a deadly mine explosion, the two marry and leave Diamond to return home to Sugar Fork. Parts IV and V, both entitled "Letters from Sugar Fork," bring Ivy's life full circle. Ivy and Oakley move back into the old Rowe cabin, where they build a life and a family together. Ivy's letters in these sections powerfully document her experiences of marriage and motherhood, as well as her transitions into middle and old age. Ivy ex-

3. Kristeva, "Women's Time," 199–200.

periences the births of several children; the difficult, demanding life of a farmwife; and another heedless affair, this time taking off with itinerant bee-man Honey Breeding, who comes to set up Oakley's hives. She not only endures the death of a child during the affair and the subsequent wrath of the community, but also must cope eventually with Oakley's death and the departure of other children as they grow up and leave the mountains. Ivy remains at Sugar Fork for the rest of her life, dying in the cabin where she was born many decades earlier.

By creating an alignment between Ivy's female experiences and these various mountain locales, Smith demonstrates how a woman's life is often inextricably bound to place and reveals the profound identification that Appalachian women share with their mountain surroundings. As Carole Ganim points out in her study of women and place in Appalachian literature, this is an "identification of body and mind, of nature and spirit." She further insists that women in Appalachian literature are either "at one" with their place or at odds with it. In any event, the mountains create an "inescapable presence" that leads to "the union of the female, both symbolically and physically, with her place."[4] The Appalachian Mountains themselves are symbolic of the female body. Among the most ancient of mountain ranges, they possess a timelessness and a seasonal changeability that aligns them with maternal time, which is both eternal and cyclical. Moreover, the rounded curvatures and gentle peaks of the Appalachians reflect the maternal body. As Smith's fiction so clearly demonstrates, the female body and the female psyche share intimate, although often ambivalent, connections with the mountains.

Ivy's childhood letters in part I, "Letters from Sugar Fork," reveal an intuitive awareness of the difficulties that marriage and motherhood hold for women. She witnesses how her own mother's beauty and vivacity have been destroyed by mountain life. Like Pauline Breedlove in *The Bluest Eye*, Maude Castle Rowe represents the silent maternal, closing her heart to her children. To Ivy, her mother "looks awful, like her face is hanted." Although Ivy is enchanted by the story of her parents' youthful courtship and longs to be in love herself one day, she is acutely aware of the realities of women's lives in the mountains. Seeing the price that motherhood extracts from her own mother, Ivy declares that

4. Ganim, "Herself," 258–59, 273–74.

she does not want to have babies or "get tittys as big as the moon" but will be a writer instead. Ivy senses an inherent incompatibility between maternity and the writer's life; certainly, her own mother discourages her engagement with language. Ivy notes that if she reads too much, Maude becomes angry: "Momma says it will do me no good in the end" (FTL 15). Moreover, Ivy's mother literally denies her any voice: "[H]ush yor mouth, shut up shut up Ivy. Hush, just shut up for gods sake" (FTL 65). Despite these maternal attempts to silence the daughter, Ivy's engagement with language and her quest for self-expression cannot be suppressed.

As Ivy documents her growth from childhood to adulthood, her letters reflect an intense identification with the mountain landscape. Her childhood letters in part I contain an abundance of mountain and family lore. Moreover, they are exquisitely sensate, filled with the sights, sounds, tastes, and smells of the mountains. Ivy tells how Sugar Fork sparkles "in the sun like a ladys dimond necklace" and how the guinea hens by the house say "pot-rack, pot-rack" (FTL 13, 16). She describes the fragrant smell of apple blossoms in the spring and the taste of birch sap "so sweet and tart on yor tonge" (FTL 82). She recalls her father's patient instructions to "[s]low down, slow down now, Ivy. This is the taste of Spring" (FTL 82). These descriptions reflect the sensory experiences that are important in the development of a young child and, in Ivy's case, a young writer. For Ivy, these experiences forge intimate, lasting connections with the mountain landscape that are both physical and psychological in nature and that fuel her engagement with language.

Ivy recognizes the presence of these same connections in her strange and beautiful sister, Silvaney. Stricken by brain fever at age five, Silvaney grows into a wild wood sprite. Ivy describes Silvaney as "so pretty . . . all silverhaired like she was fotched up on the moon" (FTL 17). As her name and appearance suggest, Silvaney is deeply connected to the sylvan woods and mountain moonlight. An elusive creature, she disappears repeatedly into the woods, an occasional footprint or broken leaf the only signs she leaves behind. Silvaney shares a strong bond with her brawling, womanizing twin brother, Babe. She is also Ivy's shadowy double, her mad sister without coherent language. With her wild laughter, crying, and nonsensical talk, Silvaney represents Kristeva's semiotic chora, the prelinguistic realm of the maternal that underlies symbolic language. In this regard, she is much like Toni Morrison's Beloved and Smith's own Red Emmy in *Oral History*, other mysterious women who haunt the woods and whose language borders on the primal and nonrational.

Ivy senses the powerful bond she shares with Silvaney: "[I]t is like we are the same sometimes it is like we are one" (FTL 17). The fusion of sentences in this passage mirrors the fused identities of the sisters. Lucinda MacKethan points out that both sisters suffer as their family slowly disintegrates from desperation, violence, and death. Their responses reveal not only their intense bond but also their obverse relationships to language. According to MacKethan: "Silvaney responds by running wildly, silently, through the hills; Ivy responds with words, in long, wild letters combining mountain legends with her own fantasies and experiences. In her letters, Ivy makes order out of the chaos that drives Silvaney deeper into wordless madness." To a great extent, Silvaney resembles the many "maddened doubles" in nineteenth-century women's fiction who, according to Sandra Gilbert and Susan Gubar in their study *The Madwoman in the Attic*, function "as asocial surrogates for docile selves." MacKethan describes Silvaney as such a surrogate, representing "the self that Ivy buries in order to fit into the patterns of woman's work in her home on Sugar Fork."[5] Ivy, though, understands her sister's strangeness and her need for the natural world. When Silvaney becomes violent after Babe's murder by an irate husband and is committed to an institution, Ivy laments her sister's displacement: "[S]he needs to wander the woods, and she needs some woods to wander" (FTL 73).

In another sense, Silvaney functions as the kind of subordinate character often found in feminist negotiating texts who, according to Elaine Orr, helps to "make a place for 'other' women to speak." Such a character gives "the subject a tool with which she can make narrative and critical progress."[6] Throughout the novel, Silvaney provides the means for Ivy to narrate her story and to complete her own life journey. She serves as Ivy's inner, spiritual double and enables her to explore woods of a different sort, the more concealed realms of female experience about which Ivy later writes with compelling intimacy. Ivy pens letters

5. Lucinda MacKethan, *Daughters of Time: Creating Women's Voice in Southern Story*, 107; Sandra Gilbert and Susan Gubar, *The Madwoman in the Attic: The Woman Writer and the Nineteenth-Century Literary Imagination*, xi.
6. Elaine Orr, *Subject to Negotiation*, 24.

to Silvaney, whom she calls "my other side, my other half, my heart," for the rest of her life, even after learning of her sister's death (FTL 312). Her letters to Silvaney constitute a dialogue with herself and provide an effective vehicle for expressing female subjectivity.

After her father's death and her subsequent move to Majestic, Ivy begins to establish connections beyond her family and to discern her place in the larger world. In part II, "Letters from Majestic," Ivy describes the people of Majestic, the bustle of town life, and the goings-on at the boardinghouse with adolescent exuberance. She also engages in contemplative introspection, employing a variety of literary touchstones that reflect aspects of her own being. At the same time, Smith weaves in allusions to several female writers who deal with women, writing, and madness in their works. Asserting an androgynous identity, Ivy wishes to be more like Charlotte Brontë's small, plain orphan, Jane Eyre. She detests her growing bosom and the lascivious stares of the boardinghouse men. Although she realizes that many girls her age are married, she dismisses any idea of marriage. Instead, in an echo of Virginia Woolf, she expresses extraordinary pleasure in having "a room of my own," a third-floor room tucked under the roof and symbolic of Ivy's interiority (FTL 87). She takes delight in her room's gray, peeling wallpaper, which, in a reference to Charlotte Perkins Gilman's "The Yellow Wallpaper," contains a picture of a woman in each of its pattern's squares. This symbol of entrapment, of course, is lost on Ivy, who loves the old-fashioned ladies with silver wigs. Bound together by pink ribbons running from square to square, the women wear pink dresses with "a skirt that resembles a bell," a veiled allusion to Sylvia Plath's *The Bell Jar*. Ivy embraces all of this: the women, the wallpaper, and the attic room where, like Emily Dickinson, she can retreat to the window and "push back my gauzy curtin and look out over all the town" (FTL 88).

The young, exuberant Ivy is the antithesis of the "madwoman in the attic" so frequently used by the very writers to whom Smith alludes. According to Gilbert and Gubar, mad or monstrous female characters often serve as doubles for more submissive heroines and for their authors themselves, dramatizing "their desire both to accept the strictures of patriarchal society and to reject them." Ivy clearly demonstrates Smith's intent to reconceptualize women's relationships to writing, the self, and society. When she declares, "This town is mine, Majestic Virginia, U.S.A.," Ivy not only asserts her connection with place but symbolically links her body and her own "majestic" virginity with the physical world as well (FTL 88). Ivy's words, along with her delight in the attic room, demonstrate a comfortable integration of inner and outer states of being. Gilbert and Gubar contend that virginity, as possessed by such archetypal figures as the Greek goddess Artemis and the snow maidens/angelic virgins of folklore with whom Ivy has earlier identified, represents power and "a kind of self-enclosing armor." Thus, virginity is not a "gift" a young woman gives her groom, but rather "a boon she grants to herself: the boon of androgynous wholeness, autonomy, self-sufficiency."[7] In Ivy's case, this seems to be true. Her embrace of the room and the town, so symbolic of the mind and body, suggests a comparable acceptance of self and projects a sense of virginal wholeness. Moreover, Ivy's desire to write and to get an education further advances the likelihood of autonomy and self-sufficiency. For the time being, the physical, psychological, and social aspects of the female self function in satisfying congruence.

Not unexpectedly, adolescence brings monumental changes for Ivy and a loss of the androgynous self. It particularly brings an awakening of new senses. Ivy becomes powerfully attracted to Lonnie Rash, whose strong hands, muscled arms, and deep kisses make her realize that "the firey hand grabbed me then for good" (FTL 103). Her sexual initiation with him, however, leaves her feeling displaced and sad. With a double entendre, she writes: "I have lost it now, Majestic Virginia which used to be mine" (FTL 112). Her words, which could easily refer to her lost virginity, again connect the female body with place and reveal a poignant uncentering of self. With the loss of innocence and the lost opportunities that follow Ivy's sexual initiation, Majestic, Virginia, and indeed life itself no longer hold the promise they once did. In short order, Ivy passes from youthful androgyne to sexual novitiate. With her subsequent pregnancy, she quickly enters the maternal realm and loses all possibility of reclaiming her former self.

Ivy reacts with disbelief when she discovers she is pregnant, her flat stomach giving no hint of the baby within. However, in a richly subjective and troubling reverie detailed in a letter to Silvaney, she imagines the baby "tiny and pink and all curled up . . . beating with its little fists against my stomach, trying to escape." Ivy's identification with her un-

7. Gilbert and Gubar, *Madwoman in the Attic*, 78, 616–17.

born infant is profound: "I <u>was</u> that little baby caught inside of my own self and dying to escape. But I could not. I could never ever get out, I was caught for ever and ever inside myself" (FTL 122). Her language evokes images of entrapment and death not unlike those found in the works of Gilman, Dickinson, Woolf, Plath, and the Brontë sisters, writers that Ivy has read or to whom Smith otherwise alludes. As Gilbert and Gubar point out, such writers portray the confinement of women in such do-mestic enclosures as parlors, kitchens, attics, haunted chambers, and even the grave. Their dramatization of imprisonment and escape reflects their discomfort and sense of powerlessness within patriarchal structures. To express their "claustrophobic rage" and to break from their entrap-ment, these writers enact their own rebellious escapes by creating char-acters who attempt to escape, "if only into nothingness."

While Gilman, Plath, Dickinson, and others, according to Gilbert and Gubar, use architectural space and domestic furnishings to depict confinement, Smith portrays the maternal body as both a physical and psychic enclosure.[8] Ironically, in medical discourse, the word "confine-ment" has long referred to the time period immediately following child-birth, conveying a sense of maternal imprisonment. With the realiza-tion of her pregnancy, Ivy's words reflect a similar and terrifying sense of imprisonment. Moreover, they project the fear that maternity and self-expression are incompatible. Unlike the child to whom she will in-evitably give birth, Ivy perceives that she, and by extension her words, will remain trapped and unexpressed "for ever and ever inside myself." Ivy's fears recall the fate of Pecola Breedlove, who, in *The Bluest Eye*, becomes locked in wordless madness because of her rape by her father and the blighted pregnancy that ensues. Ivy, however, uses her letters to Silvaney as a way to write out of the body, out of the entrapment she feels.

Although of a different generation, Ivy resembles Sam Hughes in Bobbie Ann Mason's *In Country*. While her view of love and marriage is more romanticized than Sam's, Ivy also spurns marriage because of the restrictions it imposes. Like Sam, Ivy associates pregnancy with the death of possibility and with the loss of self. Sam recommends an abor-tion to her pregnant friend, Dawn, and Ivy does not seem resistant to the abortion arranged for her by her landlady. Maude Rowe, however,

8. Ibid., 84–86.

intervenes and prevents Ivy from aborting her baby. While Sam's mother provides the basics necessary for her daughter's emancipation—that is, birth control, a car, and the encouragement to go to college—Ivy's mother thwarts any possibility for continued growth, education, and self-sufficiency. Maude's one act of assertion before her death sets her daughter on a path where independence and autonomy are severely limited. By prohibiting the abortion, Maude condemns Ivy to the same harsh female existence that she has endured, a life of domestic hardship and sorrow lived out in the inescapable presence of the mountains. Ironically, the child that Maude keeps Ivy from aborting is Joli, who grows up to leave the mountains and become the writer that Ivy longs to be— but only after she, with Ivy's help, becomes unshackled from the responsibilities of marriage and motherhood.

Following Maude's death, Ivy moves to Diamond to live with her married sister, Beulah, in hopes of starting life anew. In part III, "Letters from Diamond," Ivy more fully documents her maternal experiences, as well as her sister's difficult delivery of her second child. Their experiences of childbirth sharply contrast, revealing a tension between science and folkways, between physician-controlled and woman-centered childbearing. Like Christie Wheeler, who delivers her quintuplets with the help of Dr. Foote in *Feather Crowns*, Beulah gives birth in "a real medical way," attended by the mining company's doctor. Although he accomplishes the breech delivery satisfactorily, Dr. Gray refuses to "fix" Beulah so that she will not have any more children, leaving her angry, distraught, and vulnerable to the possibility of repeated childbearing (FTL 133). In Beulah's case, as in Christie's, modern medicine helps and yet ultimately fails the mother. In each instance, it diminishes the mother's active participation in childbearing and lessens her control over her body and the welfare of her offspring.

Beulah's emotional distress following childbirth delays the arrival of her milk, and the family has to consider hiring a wet nurse. The pregnant Ivy volunteers to nurse the baby, but folk wisdom prevails. Her offer is refused since "it is bad luck before you have had your own baby." With candid subjectivity, Ivy describes physical sensations that are both maternal and erotic: "I have got milk in my titties Silvaney right now, I can feel it when Curtis Junior is sucking, they want to be sucked too." Ivy suggests calling in Granny Rowe to help with her sister's recovery. However, Beulah, disdainful of the past and anything connected with

Sugar Fork, rejects Granny's assistance and her "crazy old ideas" (FTL 134). The birth of her second child resurrects painful memories of the first. Angrily, Beulah recounts the birth of her first child, which she delivered alone in the family cabin on a cornhusk mattress, cutting the cord with a hatchet.

Ivy's childbirth experience is far more cooperative and woman-centered than either of Beulah's. When Ivy gives birth to Joli, she is attended by neighbors and by Granny Rowe, who mysteriously appears just before Ivy goes into labor. Like Granny Younger in *Oral History*, Granny Rowe is an experienced midwife and is fully in tune with the rhythms of the female body and the natural world as well. She points to the full moon as a sign of Ivy's impending labor and shortly thereafter, Ivy's water breaks and labor commences. Granny's arrival with the full moon evokes the image of Artemis, Greek goddess of the hunt and childbirth. Associated with the moon, Artemis embodies women's time, the cyclical rhythms and eternal elements of the maternal body. Although childless herself, Artemis, as Adrienne Rich tells us, has come to represent "woman's mysteries." Indeed, the female menstrual cycle corresponds to the lunar cycle, while the full moon is often associated with an increase in births. According to Shari Thurer, Artemis was often invoked by women in labor and functioned as an overseer of childbirth, a sort of metaphysical midwife.[9] Granny Rowe is linked to Artemis through her own role as midwife. With deeply etched wrinkles and twinkling blue eyes that belie her age, Granny is both ancient and timeless. To Ivy, she smells like tobacco and woodsmoke, "like something old and tough I couldnt name you" (FTL 148).

In a letter to Silvaney, Ivy describes her experience of childbirth with painful honesty. Unlike most fictional accounts of childbirth—which, as we have seen, have long been given from the perspective of the father, the attending doctor, or an observer—Ivy's account provides rare subjectivity. Ivy admits to some difficulty remembering Joli's birth. Her words acknowledge the natural amnesia that often occurs with childbirth: "[I]t is awfully hard to remember having a baby because your body wants to forget it right away, it hurts too bad, and if you remembered it all, you would never have another, Granny says. So you forget. You have to" (FTL 147).

9. Rich, *Of Woman Born*, 77; Thurer, *Myths of Motherhood*, 63.

Granny's words to Ivy reflect an awareness of the complex interconnections that exist between the mind and body. However, what Ivy remembers demonstrates that childbirth nonetheless forges memories
that emanate from deep within the body. Ivy recalls not only her water
breaking and splashing onto her feet, but also the pressure and pain in
her thighs and "the great pushing opening tearing feeling" as she gives
birth to Joli (FTL 147). Unlike Pricey Jane in *Oral History* and Pauline
Breedlove in *The Bluest Eye,* who give birth in suffering silence, Ivy
screams loudly and, according to Beulah, "embarrass[es] them all." Besides this loud vocalization, Smith imbues the maternal body with a
voice of its own. Ivy writes: "I could hear my bones parting and hear
myself opening up with a huge horrible screeching noise." The sounds
of her body and voice become fused: "[M]ay be what I heard was me
screaming, but I don't think so. I think it was my screeching bones."
Ironically, Granny later tells Ivy that she has had "an easy time" (FTL
148). Ivy's description graphically demonstrates the merging of body
and voice. It also depicts the overwhelming physical and psychological
totality of the childbirth experience and the mother's intense involvement in the process. Ivy's experience accurately reflects Niles Newton's
assessment that the female biological role, unlike most cultural models
of femininity, is "far from passive."[10]

Ivy's account of the hours following childbirth reflects a gentler subjectivity, a mythic one that further entrenches her associations of body
and memory. While Granny Rowe tends to the newly born Joli, Ivy
watches as moonlight creeps "star by star" across her Heavenly Star bed
quilt. The moonlight invokes the presence not only of Artemis, divine
overseer of childbirth, but also of Silvaney, Ivy's spiritual double to
whom she writes. In addition, Ivy notes the sweet blood smell that "was
not like anything else in the world" as Granny removes the rag packing
from between her legs. Her unfamiliarity with this smell suggests
women's traditional unfamiliarity with their mother's bodies and with
their own. For Ivy, the blood symbolizes an anointment of sorts and
serves as a primal connection between mother and daughter. In her letter, Ivy says that the smell of her blood "will always be mixed up in my
mind somehow with the moonlight and my baby" (FTL 148). Ivy remains awake following Joli's birth, her senses and sensibilities at their

10. Newton, *Maternal Emotions,* 12.

sharpest. Initiated into a new maternal consciousness, she is intensely aware of the significance of the event: "This is important, I want to remember this, it is all so important, this is happening to me" (FTL 149).

The quilt, the blood, and the baby represent various aspects of female labor. Brought together in the moonlight, each are powerfully tied to memory. As in *Beloved*, blood solidifies memory and binds generations of women together. Sethe, Denver, and Beloved are united by blood, language, and the past in Morrison's novel. Similarly, Ivy, Joli, and Silvaney, whose presence is suggested by the moonlight, form a female trinity that reveals equally complex relationships between women. By forging such connections, Smith asserts a genealogy of women, the "female family tree" that Luce Irigaray sees as critical to female identity.

In *Sexes and Genealogies*, Irigaray calls for a language that speaks to women's experiences of the body and their relationships with each other: "We . . . need to find, rediscover, invent the words, the sentences that speak of the most ancient and most current relationship we know—the relationship to the mother's body, to our body—sentences that translate the bond between our body, her body, the body of our daughter. We need to discover a language . . . which accompanies that bodily experience, clothing it in words that do not erase the body but speak the body." Ivy's subjective exploration in her letters of the physical and psychological dimensions of childbirth, as well as the novel's foregrounding of female relationships, suggest that Smith is using the very language that Irigaray espouses. Ivy's recollections of gushing water, the tearing sensations that rip through her body, and the sweet smell of blood that follows indeed "speak the body." In rendering Ivy's childbirth, Smith invokes a primal female power and establishes a maternal voice that echoes the body's experience, producing a kind of language that is radically dissimilar from symbolic paternal language. To a significant degree, Smith appears to be heeding Irigaray's admonition to restore the mother's right "to speak, or even to shriek and rage aloud." As wrenching as Ivy's screams and the screeching of her bones are for both character and reader, they nonetheless represent maternal nonpassivity and mark an utter refusal to be silenced—or, as Irigaray describes, "to be swallowed up in the law of the father."[11]

While Ivy's first experience of childbirth marks an enhancement of

11. Irigaray, *Sexes and Genealogies*, 18–19.

voice and self, marriage and repeated childbearing impose silence and a loss of language. In part IV, Ivy, now married to Oakley Fox, returns to Sugar Fork to work the family farm. Her endless toil as wife and mother leaves little time for reading and writing. She sends books back to the library unread. She writes few letters to family and friends, only six or so over a span of ten years. With the birth of each baby, her letters become briefer. One letter is left incomplete, ending in midsentence as if Ivy had to rush off to attend to a child or some household calamity. Ivy's letters to Silvaney cease during this period, indicating a deeper disconnection and loss of self. Her disassociation from reading and writing illustrates Tillie Olsen's observation that motherhood means "distraction," "interruption," and "deferred, relinquished" work. Ivy, like so many mothers, must give urgent priority to the physical and emotional needs of her family. As Olsen declares: "The very fact that these are real needs, that one feels them as one's own (love, not duty); *that there is no one else responsible for these needs*, gives them primacy."[12] The end result for Ivy is that her own creative and intellectual needs, her very soul, are submerged.

With time, change comes to the mountains and eventually to Ivy. People, houses, and electricity spread throughout the mountains. Ivy watches in wonderment as the Appalachian Power Company switches on lights in the valley. The sight inspires her to write, and for the first time in years, she pens a letter to Silvaney. Once again, Ivy writes with startling subjectivity. She weaves associations among the mountains, the lights, the cries of her infant daughter, and the sudden letdown of breast milk, all of which culminate in a release of language in her letter. Ivy confesses to Silvaney how tired and lost she has felt, "caught up for so long in a great soft darkness, a blackness so deep and so soft that you can fall in there and get comfortable and never know you are falling in at all, and never land, just keep falling." Worn down by multiple pregnancies and continuous breast-feeding, Ivy, at thirty-seven, feels that her youngest baby is "sucking my life right out of me." She also imagines that "bits and pieces" of herself have "rolled off down this mountain someplace" (FTL 194–95). Ivy's words, which poignantly link her body with the mountain landscape, mourn the loss of self she has experienced as a result of motherhood.

12. Olsen, *Silences*, 18–19.

In another sense, Ivy is held captive by the mountains. Except for an occasional visit to town, she remains isolated and burdened by maternal responsibilities. Without family or neighbors nearby to help, Ivy laments that "[a] woman just can't go off and leave so many children" (FTL 195). To escape, she retreats into the comfort of rest, falling straight down into the "blackness" that she has described. Though Ivy's words link her body to the mountain landscape, her plunge into darkness suggests a retreat into the semiotic chora, the maternal space that underlies symbolic language and that represents, in Alice Adams's words, a place of "generation and negation" for the self. During the years spent in darkness, Ivy experiences a loss of symbolic language and suppression of self. On the other hand, the darkness also symbolically serves as a womb, a place to renurture her exhausted self and to renourish her linguistic underpinnings.

When Ivy begins to write again, it is with a vengeance. Her letters to Silvaney in part IV are the longest of any in the novel; each one comprises twelve to fourteen pages of text. Again, Ivy uses her letters to Silvaney as a way to write out of the body, out of the darkness and fatigue in which she has been immersed. The letters also constitute a search through memory and the past. Through them, Ivy recollects games from her childhood, stories told by the Cline sisters, and Granny Rowe's herbal remedies, all of which she passes on to her daughter Joli. Writing unleashes not only a flood of memories but also enables Ivy to explore the surge of energy that confounds and terrifies her. Unlike the soft, anesthetizing darkness she previously experienced, this surge now makes Ivy feel acutely alive, "tingling," and "on fire" (FTL 210). At first, she attributes these strange, new feelings to early menopause. But later she confesses to Silvaney that the restless, wild power within her body stems from a different source: Honey Breeding, a kind of Wandering Aengus who possesses a mythic, charismatic charm that works on women and bees.

Smith concocts the character of Honey Breeding from folktales, fairy tales, classical mythology, and southern literary tradition. The subject of local mythmaking, he can supposedly cut down a bee tree, catch swarms of bees, and never get stung. Moreover, he "roams these hills like a coonhound" and reputedly, as his name implies, "has daddied him some babies here and there" (FTL 212). With hair like "spun gold" covering him from head to toe, Breeding makes Ivy think of Rapunzel (FTL

214). His golden appearance, his gift for song and story, and his healing effects upon Ivy also suggest Phoebus Apollo, the Greek god of light and healing. In a more contemporary allusion, Honey Breeding resembles Eudora Welty's King MacLain in *The Golden Apples,* another golden, amorous wanderer who, according to Ruth Vande Kieft, bedazzles women and "irresponsibly populat[es] the countryside." Just as MacLain offers women a "glimmering vision" of love and adventure and the realization of "individual fulfillment," Honey Breeding gives Ivy a new vision of herself.[13]

When Breeding takes Ivy far up the mountain, supposedly in search of bees, she experiences a psychic and sexual rebirth. They take refuge together in a cave, a place symbolic of maternal space. Here, outside the boundaries of patriarchal society, time loses all meaning for Ivy as she reconnects with language and with her body. The days take on a dreamlike nature as Breeding showers Ivy with songs and stories, makes her laugh, and revives her sexual self. Most important, he helps Ivy retrieve long-buried stories and poems, essential parts of her former being. Like Silvaney, Honey Breeding represents a vital aspect of Ivy's self and functions as a potent source of language, creativity, and erotic energy. While Silvaney is suggestive of the goddess or anima, Breeding represents the animus, the male element that Annis Pratt calls "one's own internal Adonis." He functions as the archetypal green-world lover—the idealized, nonpatriarchal lover—who often appears to the "female hero" in women's fiction of rebirth and who leads her "away from society and towards her own unconscious depths." By taking Ivy up the mountain and into the cave, Breeding serves as such an initiatory guide, helping her plumb the depths of memory and self. As Rebecca Godwin Smith points out, "Their union signifies Ivy's recovery of self, in both sexual and linguistic terms."[14] Her reengagement with sex and with language, particularly her reclamation of forgotten stories and poems, represents a reunification of body and voice. Despite the terrible price she ultimately pays for her liaison with Breeding—the death of her daughter LuIda and the condemnation of the community—Ivy claims, "Honey had given me back my very soul" (FTL 232).

Part V documents the last years of Ivy's life. This section confirms

13. Ruth Vande Kieft, *Eudora Welty,* 91, 89.
14. Annis Pratt, *Archetypal Patterns in Women's Fiction,* 140, 142; Rebecca Godwin Smith, "Gender Dynamics in the Fiction of Lee Smith," 157.

that her experience with Honey Breeding enables her to face the remainder of her life with vigor, confidence, and a renewed spirit. Ivy's relationship with her husband, Oakley, becomes stronger and remains remarkably satisfying until his death. As Ivy's children grow up and leave home, her letters demonstrate that aging in women does not result in a diminishment of self but in a renewal of creative energy and social involvement. No longer housebound, she goes to church, helps her sister Ethel run her ailing husband's store, and assists a friend in starting a settlement school for rural children. Ivy also reestablishes ties with the literature and the stories that once undergirded her life. The library in town keeps her well supplied with books, and her numerous letters to children and grandchildren are filled with folktales and family lore of the past. At the same time, her letters provide commentary on the present, particularly on the rapid growth and changes of the post–World War II years. Like Christie Wheeler in *Feather Crowns*, Ivy sees her once rural, isolated part of the world brought into contact with the scientific advances and politics of the twentieth century. She particularly welcomes the development of birth control pills and enthusiastically recommends them to her daughter Joli. Ivy exclaims: "*They are the greatest thing since drip dry*. You ought to get yourself some . . . I would, if I was still young" (FTL 292–93).

In part V, Ivy's letters continue to speak the body. They reveal that sexuality remains an essential part of one's being, regardless of age. When her widowed brother-in-law comes to court her, Ivy admits to feeling "a stirring that I had not felt since Oakley's death." She asserts that "we are alive until we die" (FTL 288). Ivy's words acknowledge the link between the body and the spirit and the importance of sexuality as a vital life force that nourishes both. As Ivy grows older, her letters reflect the changes in the body that come with illness and aging. She writes about stomach trouble and losing weight: "I have fallen off some." She remarks, "My breasts look like those bean bags I used to make for the kids" (FTL 302). Not surprisingly, her last letter in the novel "speaks the body," blending memory, voice, and bodily experience. On her deathbed, Ivy writes one last letter to Silvaney in which she recalls the sensate experiences of her mountain childhood, making snow angels with Silvaney, dancing with lover Franklin Ransom, and giving birth to Joli in the moonlight. Even in dying, her senses, memory, and body remain intensely alive.

From first to last, Ivy's letters in *Fair and Tender Ladies* foreground female experience and contradict the notion of woman as the silent Other. Ivy's lively voice resonates throughout the novel, always speaking with honesty and compelling subjectivity. Her letters ebb and flow in frequency, depending on the domestic demands of her life. However, while the strength of her engagement with language may fluctuate, Ivy's full participation in life never diminishes. By creating variations in Ivy's life—in time, language, and experience—Smith effectively parallels the natural, fluidic rhythms that are inherent in the maternal and that do not conform to the linearity and rigid structures of patriarchal discourse. This preference is clearly evident in Ivy's last letter, written while she is dying. Employing a stream-of-consciousness style, irregular spacing, and sporadic punctuation, the letter moves randomly back and forth through time in a nonlinear fashion. The unfinished letter and its lack of final punctuation suggest a pause between the cyclical processes of life and death. The incomplete last sentence suggests that death is a temporary distraction, that Ivy's writing has been interrupted again, but only momentarily. Thus, with the life and letters of Ivy Rowe, Smith answers Irigaray's call to find a discourse that is close to the maternal body, one that replicates the natural cadences of life, language, and female bodily experience. Ivy's final letter confirms this fact. With body and voice still richly unified, Ivy's last words—"I walked in my body like a Queen"—celebrate and honor the female body she has long possessed (FTL 316).

10

~

Saving Grace

MEDIATING THE
MATRIARCHAL–PATRIARCHAL DICHOTOMY

The eleventh child of the charismatic Reverend Virgil Shepherd, Florida Grace Shepherd describes herself as "contentious and ornery, full of fear and doubt in a family of believers" (SG 3). Named for the state of Florida and the grace of God, Grace is often admonished as a child to "trust more in Jesus" (SG 4). However, Grace does not love Jesus; she hates Him. In her mind, Jesus is responsible for her father taking up traveling in His name and forcing her family to live like vagabonds. In Lee Smith's 1995 novel, *Saving Grace*, Virgil Shepherd drags his family across the South before settling down in the mountain community of Scrabble Creek, North Carolina. Here he saves souls in brush arbor revivals, where speaking in tongues, healing the sick, and handling copperheads and rattlesnakes are commonplace. At night, Grace and her sister Billie Jean fall asleep to the sound of serpents rattling in boxes under their bed. Despite her family's immersion in holiness ways, Grace resists salvation and becoming a "special servant of the Lord" (SG 30). She rages against Jesus in her heart, worried that others might think she is possessed by the Devil and try to cast him out if she voices her anger and hatred. Rather than have the truth known, Grace remains silent about her "awful secret" (SG 4).

Saving Grace opens with a thirty-eight-year-old Grace returning home to Scrabble Creek after two broken marriages to break her silence and tell her life story. She states, "I mean to tell the truth. . . . even the terrible things," including her sexual initiation with her half brother Lamar, her mother's suicide, her failed marriages to the saintly Travis Word and bad boy Randy Newhouse, and the abandonment of her own

174

children (SG 4). Her narration comprises the entire text, with her adult perspective framing the novel as she moves back in time to recollect experiences from childhood, adolescence, and young womanhood. In the process of recounting her own life story and maternal experiences, Grace also gives voice to the experiences of her sisters, her daughters, and other mountain women. In some regards, she models the kind of storytelling and testimony that Sheila Collins advocates in her essay "Theology in the Politics of Appalachian Women." Collins asserts that women must resist the silent, feminized roles traditionally expected of them in religious and political spheres and calls for Appalachian women to testify about the realities of their lives. "If theology is to be meaningful for us," Collins states, "it must not start with abstractions, but with *our stories*."[1] Grace Shepherd's narration in *Saving Grace* provides such testimony, foregrounding the distinctly female experiences of women's harsh, restricted mountain lives.

Grace also delves into an examination of certain dichotomies that undergird female existence. Throughout the novel, elements of sin and salvation, power and powerlessness, silence and voice are sharply juxtaposed. The death of her mother intensifies Grace's conflict with these elements and propels her on a journey of self-reckoning, which she recounts in her narrative. Her journey evolves into a spiritual quest, a search for belief that involves a questioning of the fundamental forces that shape her being. In particular, she examines the maternal and paternal elements undergirding her life. The voice and body of the mother are repeatedly posited against the father's; similarly, maternal spirituality is contrasted with paternal religiosity. This highlights the most entrenched dichotomy of all: the matriarchal-patriarchal dichotomy that pervades every aspect of the novel, manifesting itself through characters, events, themes, language, and imagery.

Throughout much of her life, Grace is attuned to the differences between the two parental realms, but is never fully reconciled with either. Theologian Carol Ochs, in *Behind the Sex of God*, examines how the dichotomy of matriarchy and patriarchy has affected religious thought. She notes that matriarchal religions are centered around a female deity, base their ethical systems on blood ties and parental responsibility, and find reality and value in the material world. Patriarchal religions, on the

1. Sheila Collins, "Theology in the Politics of Appalachian Women," 151.

other hand, see God as male, base their ethics on abstract principles, and see the spiritual world as the source of meaning and reality. Ochs calls for a mediation of sorts between the two modes, stating, "[P]atriarchal religions need a feminine component, and matriarchal faiths need a more abstract standard."[2] In many of her novels, most notably *Oral History*, *Fair and Tender Ladies*, and *The Devil's Dream*, Smith contrasts male-dominated Christianity and Western thinking with more mythic, immanent, female ways of knowing. She often depicts the male-female, matriarchal-patriarchal split as an unbridgeable chasm. In *Saving Grace*, however, Smith seeks a mediation between the two realms. In so doing, she allows her female protagonist to ultimately achieve spiritual wholeness, a stronger sense of self, and the voice she uses to tell her story.

To some extent, Grace's spiritual quest mirrors the author's own. Growing up in the Virginia mountains, Lee Smith attended what she has called the "straight-laced" Grundy Methodist Church, but was drawn to the more fervent revivalist churches in the area. She had a friend whose mother spoke in tongues, and, whenever she attended church with them, Smith loved the "letting go" that occurred. In addition, she has described how, as a teenager, she was constantly being saved at a boyfriend's "wild" church: "So religion and sex—you know, excitement, passion—were all together. I couldn't differentiate between sexual passion and religious passion. This was what we all did on dates, was go to the revival. It was a turn on."[3] Smith also visited several serpent-handling congregations while growing up in Grundy. Consequently, she developed a deep interest in expressions of religious ecstasy, which she describes as "those moments when we are most truly 'out of ourselves' and experience the Spirit directly." Smith feels that her writing constitutes "a lifelong search for belief." Thus it should be no surprise that one of her characters would undertake such a journey as well.

According to Smith, the character of Grace Shepherd was inspired by the real-life Anna Prince, whose autobiographical narrative she encountered in Thomas Burton's *Serpent-Handling Believers*, a 1993 study of snake-handling religious practices in eastern Tennessee.[4] Like Grace, Prince admits to having "suffered much over snake handling" during her

2. Carol Ochs, *Behind the Sex of God*, 86, 30.
3. Quoted in Susan Ketchin, *The Christ-Haunted Landscape: Faith and Doubt in Southern Fiction*, 45–46.
4. Lee Smith, "Notes" to *Saving Grace*, 275.

lifetime. As a child, she watched as her father—an itinerant Baptist preacher who traveled the back roads of Tennessee, Georgia, and North Carolina—handled dangerous snakes, drank Red Devil Lye, and picked up burning coals in God's name. She, too, was uprooted countless times as her father moved throughout the Southeast to preach in tents, brush arbor revivals, home prayer meetings, and on radio programs, as well as on street corners and at "a few churches that would let us in." Religion permeated the lives of Anna and her six siblings. As she recollects in Fred Brown's essay about her famous brother Charles: "God was the number-one conversation in our family. As children we just played and prayed. It was a way of life."[5]

Snakes were a constant presence in the daily lives of the Prince children. Like Grace Shepherd, Anna slept with serpents in boxes under her bed. She recalls, "It was as common to hear the snakes rattle as to hear my baby brother cry." One brother, Charles, went on to become a celebrated snake-handler himself—a "Billy Graham of the Holiness preachers," who, in 1985, at the height of his ministry, died after being bitten by a rattlesnake during a Tennessee church service. Refusing any medical treatment, he suffered internal bleeding and hemorrhaged to death thirty-six hours later. Anna helplessly watched as "blood gushed out like an open water valve" when her brother vomited into a bucket on his deathbed: "I wept for the life that was slipping away and for myself. We were both victims of snake handling and poison drinking!"[6]

Grace Shepherd experiences a similar ambivalence towards her family's religious practices. She is particularly pulled between her father's fervent holiness passion and her mother's quieter spirituality. The resulting tension between the paternal and maternal forces that shape Grace's life pervades all aspects of the novel. The magnitude of the male-female dichotomy created by this tension can be seen in the nearly 120 characters who are named in the novel and who are evenly divided by gender. The result is a complex tapestry of human relationships within family and community that affects Grace at different stages of her life. However, the male-female, paternal-maternal dichotomy is most profoundly evident within the characters of Grace's parents.

Novelist Sheila Bosworth has observed that southern women are

5. Anna Prince, "A Snake-Handler's Daughter: An Autobiographical Sketch," 109, 118, 112; quoted in Fred Brown, "Charles Prince: God's Hero," 99.
6. Prince, "Snake-Handler's Daughter," 124; Brown, "Charles Prince," 104.

taught to "have faith that God, or our fathers, or our husbands, 'Daddy' in one form or another, will protect us."[7] Certainly, Virgil Shepherd assumes these roles within his family and for Grace. As a child, Grace focuses an almost religious devotion on her father. Representing the paternal in more than one sense, Virgil is Grace's biological father and, as a minister of God, serves as a direct link to the divine Father. Indeed, Grace observes that Virgil often speaks to God as if he were "sitting right across from Him, like they were old friends." Her father's deep, resonant voice symbolizes the linguistic power of the paternal. When Virgil speaks, every word "registered, and seemed to settle directly on the soul." Moreover, Grace notes that, unlike preachers who yell and espouse shame and self-loathing, Virgil's voice makes "you feel good, like you were strong in the Lord, and proud to do his will" (SG 17). As a minister of God and the "master" of his own house, Virgil's voice and words come together in an almost holy cause to reinforce patriarchal structures, both earthly and divine (SG 28).

In addition to his voice, Virgil's commanding physical presence renders him godlike. With his deeply lined face, searing blue eyes, and long white hair, Virgil resembles the popular image of God that feminist philosopher Mary Daly describes as the "great patriarch in heaven, rewarding and punishing according to his mysterious and seemingly arbitrary will."[8] Virgil, who wields similar power, reminds Grace of "the God of the Old Testament who parted the Red Sea and sent boils to people and burned Sodom and Gomorrah and smote His enemies dead" (SG 28). He takes up deadly serpents with unbridled zeal during his brush arbor revivals, oblivious to the danger they pose. With his badly bruised arms and missing fingers—injuries that are not uncommon among serpent-handling believers—Virgil resembles an ancient holy warrior.

The serpent-handling practices that define Virgil's religiosity and his patriarchal power are part of a larger, more complex set of rituals and beliefs associated with the American Holiness and Pentecostal movements that arose in the late nineteenth and early twentieth centuries. Modern-day serpent handlers base their worship on a passage of Scripture, Mark 16:17–18, that records the words spoken by Jesus to his disciples immediately prior to his ascension: "And these signs shall follow them that be-

7. Quoted in Ketchin, *Christ-Haunted Landscape*, 141.
8. Mary Daly, *Beyond God the Father*, 13.

lieve; In my name shall they cast out devils; they shall speak with new tongues; They shall take up serpents; and if they drink any deadly thing, it shall not hurt them; they shall lay hands on the sick, and they shall recover" (King James Version). For the most part, serpent-handling believers consider themselves to be "simply Christians who are following the will of God," in Burton's words. Similarly, the serpents that Virgil Shepherd takes up, the strychnine he drinks, and his preaching and healing practices stem from a desire to "follow the signs" and to obey God.[9]

While serpent handling during religious worship ostensibly arises from biblical directives, various psychological and social interpretations have been given to the practice as well. At the psychoanalytic level, Weston La Barre suggests that the serpents represent "evil incarnate," the Devil himself, as well as "projected, hysterically unacknowledged, and unadmissable desires" and the "evil, phallic part of oneself." The handling of serpents can be viewed, he says, as "an *un*-mastery of sexuality on the phallic level" and a rebellion against the primordial father.[10]

Serpent-handling religious practices have also been viewed as a response to the environment, most specifically in remote, economically depressed areas of Appalachia where, Burton says, many people "live hard, often dangerous, demanding existences with little to give them hope, recognition, power, or self-esteem." According to Nathan Gerrard, who undertook a seven-year study of West Virginia serpent handlers in the 1960s, the practice provides "a safety valve" for many of the problems and frustrations of life. He learned that for the elderly, serpent handling "helps soften the inevitability of poor health, illness, and death," while for younger generations, "its promise of holiness is one of the few meaningful goals in a future dominated by the apparent inevitability of lifelong poverty and idleness." Kenneth Moore argues that serpent-handling believers are thus "sending a defiant socio-economic message in their sermons, testimonials, and songs." He concludes that while they "may not be economically powerful, they are spiritually powerful."[11] Whether serpent handling is a response to environmental

9. Thomas Burton, *Serpent-Handling Believers*, 6.

10. Weston La Barre, *They Shall Take Up Serpents: Psychology of the Southern Snake-Handling Cult*, 169–70.

11. Burton, *Serpent-Handling Believers*, 130; Nathan Gerrard, "The Serpent-Handling Religions of West Virginia," 71; Kenneth Moore quoted in Burton, *Serpent-Handling Believers*, 130.

forces, the result of psychosexual impulses, or God's will, a significant degree of personal and spiritual power is associated with the practice, particularly in the case of Virgil Shepherd. The serpents that he takes up become an extension of his body and his soul and render him god-like. Symbolizing both good and evil, the serpents reinforce the enormous power that Virgil holds within his family and mountain community.

Besides the powerful God of the Old Testament, Virgil also resembles a mythological deity who encompasses such contrasting elements as fire and water, light and dark, and night and day. A veritable sun or fire god, he illuminates whatever space he is in. Grace observes that when Virgil stands against the sun, his white hair and shirt appear "to be shooting off rays of light behind his dark form" (SG 10). At camp meetings, "a crown of flames" appears to rest on his head and "a dancing green light" to shine in the trees by the river where he is baptizing (SG 137). When drunken men disrupt a revival service by emptying sacks of snakes, Virgil scoops up the unleashed serpents and stuffs his shirt with copperheads and rattlers, praising God in "the wild light of the flaming lanterns" and giving off "light like the sun" (SG 21). Virgil's association with light, fire, and divine power is particularly evident when his fervent prayers and nightlong vigil bring a ten-year-old girl back from the dead following an asthma attack. At dawn, as the sun rises "in a fiery burst over Coleman's ridge," the child begins to breathe again, fully restored to life (SG 33–34).

In an image that unites fire and water, night and day, and the mythological and Christian at once, Grace describes seeing her father standing on the front porch at daybreak, "bare-chested in the pearly light, serpents running like water over his arms and hands" (SG 69), and realizing that he is preparing to walk across the French Broad River. Virgil's contemplated walk may be considered a demonstration of Christian faith, of following the will of God. It also brings the sun god to the river and powerfully blends the elements of fire and water. The paternal is invested with power from all sources, giving Virgil the power for good and evil, for creation and destruction. The comingling of light and darkness in this image hints at the troubling duality that lies within Virgil's nature. Grace explains that her father is "so busy following the plan of God" that he ignores his wife and children, except to deliver an occasional beating (SG 12). His daughters learn that he has a "hoor" in town and, worse yet, a trail of discarded women and abandoned off-spring throughout the South (SG 51). Given these circumstances, Virgil represents the paternal in the most basic, biological sense possible: as a contributor of seed without any attendant moral or parental responsibility for the life he generates. He is indifferent to the plight of his children and his blood ties to them.

Grace's mother, Fannie, stands in direct opposition to Virgil. The embodiment of the feminine, she serves as a maternal counterpoint to Virgil's godlike paternalism, her body and voice largely overshadowed by his. While Virgil is stern, authoritative, and physically commanding, Fannie is soft-spoken, gentle, and quietly abiding in her religious faith. A former "dancing girl" who met Virgil as a young widow, Fannie devotes her life to her second husband and his holiness ways (SG 23). However, she also plays with her children and entertains them with folktales, stories, and songs from her traveling-show days. Although often referred to as childlike, Fannie is a powerful representation of the maternal. As her name, Fannie Flowers, suggests, she is associated with the Eleusinian realm of nature and matriarchal religion. The mother of five children, Fannie first appears in the novel nursing a baby while butterflies flit around her. She exalts in the peonies, gladiolas, and roses that surround the Scrabble Creek cabin. Despite her association with nature and maternity, Fannie is pulled between matriarchal and patriarchal religious modes. Not only does she focus her attention on the godlike Virgil, she also gives herself to Jesus. Grace, like a jealous sibling, resents Jesus' presence in her mother's life, and when Fannie plunges her hands into the burning coals of the stove in a moment of religious fervor, Grace's hatred is reaffirmed. To Grace, Jesus is "burning [her] mother." To Fannie, the moment is "a perfect pleasure in the Lord" (SG 26).

Despite her singing and storytelling, Fannie is never given full voice in the novel. In contrast with Virgil's deep, ringing voice, Fannie's voice is "wavery" and "seem[s] to hang in the hot still air like the butterflies over the flowers" (SG 28). Even at the height of religious ecstasy, words do not come. Instead, she cries, shrieks, and makes "sharp animal noises" (SG 25). Such sounds associate Fannie with the semiotic chora, the nebulous maternal space underlying patriarchal language and where prelinguistic, presymbolic forces reside. Fannie's limited use of language and her delicate voice cause her to be "reduced to the role of the silent Other of the symbolic order" that Kristeva posits. Indeed, for the most part, great silences surround Fannie. Her life story is never fully known, her death a greater mystery.

When Grace discovers Fannie's thin body swinging from a rafter in the barn with its "mouth open, tongue out, eyelids drooping" and "awful sightless eyes," she surmises that Lamar Shepherd, Virgil's son by another woman, has driven her mother to suicide (SG 112). Lamar has seduced not only Grace and her sister Billie Jean, who becomes pregnant and is committed to a "home," but also a lonely and desperate Fannie, who finds it all too much to bear. Lamar, whom Grace likens to Satan, denies his role in her death and accuses Virgil instead, saying: "It was him, all along. . . . Him. That son of a bitch" (SG 113–14). Grace, taking on Eve's original sin of the flesh, which brought death into the world, blames herself because she slept with Lamar: "For I did it first. I started it all. Mama would still be alive today if it wasn't for me" (SG 115). In any case, sexual desire and the maternal are seen as irreconcilable, and Fannie's love for the father and desire for the son inevitably lead to her death. Her suicide can be seen as a symbolic, self-silencing gesture made in response to patriarchal sexual forces. It also suggests the tragic result of love displaced from God and Jesus onto a more corrupt father and son. Whatever the reason behind Fannie's suicide, the mother's voice is irrevocably silenced, her body transformed into a grotesque rag doll.

Fannie's death results in a severing of the mother-daughter bond that leaves the fourteen-year-old Grace emotionally orphaned and rootless. Daly claims that patriarchal religions "have stolen daughters from their mothers and mothers from their daughters." Similarly, theologian Carol Christ points out that "Christianity celebrates the father's relation to the son and the mother's relation to the son, but the story of mother and daughter is missing."[12] Like Sethe's loss of her mother in *Beloved,* the death of Grace's mother represents such a theft and negation of the mother-daughter relationship. The recurring Madonna-child imagery and doll imagery that permeate *Saving Grace* seem to mourn this loss. Smith, however, restores the primacy of matriarchal bonds through the depiction of numerous triadic female relationships. Similar to Toni Mor-

---

12. Mary Daly, *Behind God the Father,* 149; Carol Christ, "Why Women Need the Goddess: Phenomenological, Psychological, and Political Reflections," 285.

rison's rendering of female connections in *Beloved* and *Sula*, Smith's trinities of women involve mothers, daughters, and sisters. Grace is one of three sisters; she gains three sisters-in-law with her marriage to Travis Word; her sister Evelyn has three daughters; and her friend Dee Dee has two daughters. Grace herself eventually has two daughters whom she describes as "my whole life" (SG 195). Other threesomes of mothers, daughters, and sisters appear among the sixty or so female characters named in the novel.

The female trinities that Smith creates stand in direct opposition to the patriarchal trinity of the Father, Son, and Holy Spirit, and suggest a womanist theology that is far more relevant in the development of the female self. The female trinities in Grace's life do not represent idealized or divine perfection. Rooted instead in the realities of female experience, they profoundly shape Grace's growth. The many women she encounters after leaving home are particularly influential. They serve in absentia for her dead mother, their lives providing fundamental instruction about such female experiences as menstruation, pregnancy, childbirth, breast-feeding, and sexual pleasure. Most important, they counterbalance patriarchal influences and move Grace toward the development of a fully sexualized self.

After marrying Travis Word at the age of seventeen, Grace achieves a sense of completeness, albeit temporary, through maternity. She becomes pregnant during her first of year of marriage and, while pregnancy and childbirth prove somewhat difficult, adjusts to motherhood with ease. She proudly declares, "[I]t all came natural" (SG 193). The years following the birth of her two daughters are mostly happy ones. Motherhood assuages the pain and disruption caused by the death of her mother, but Grace's marriage to Travis undermines her achievements. As pastor of the Hi-Way Tabernacle Church and some twenty years Grace's senior, Travis serves as a paternal substitute for Virgil Shepherd. Indeed, marriage to Travis Word replicates the patriarchal strictures of Grace's earlier life. As his name suggests, his word is law. He forbids Grace to cut her hair, wear slacks, watch television, or work outside the home. When Grace becomes pregnant for the third time, the maternal appears to retaliate against the patriarchy: The baby, a boy, dies during the eighth month of pregnancy, and Grace suspects that her womb "had turned poison and killed it" (SG 199). The infant's death resurrects the pain, confusion, and anger Grace experienced over her mother's senseless death.

Consequently, she hardens her heart against God even more. Unlike her husband, who believes everything happens according to God's purpose, Grace begins to think "there [is] *no purpose at all*" (SG 202).

In utter rebellion against both mortal and divine patriarchs, Grace falls into an exhilarating but ruinous affair with the aptly named Randy Newhouse. Like Travis, Randy represents an aspect of Grace's father: He is the embodiment of Virgil Shepherd's carnality. Sex with Randy at the Per-Flo Motel makes Grace feel like they are in a "porno flick" (SG 223). Sexually and spiritually rejuvenated, she sings hymns all the way home and declares, "I thought I had been born again" (SG 225). At first glance, Grace seems to represent the sexualized maternal. However, given her own mother's experience, she senses that sexual desire and maternity within the patriarchy are incompatible. Rather than commit suicide as her mother had, Grace divests herself of husband and children and moves with Randy to Knoxville, where she "hole[s] up in the Creekside Green Apartments, fucking my brains out" (SG 234).

While much in *Saving Grace* renders it a novel of development, the latter parts of Grace's narrative confirm the work as one of rebirth and transformation. Grace's rebirth closely parallels the five phases of a woman's spiritual quest into the unconscious that Annis Pratt delineates in *Archetypal Patterns in Women's Fiction*. Drawing on Carl Jung's theory of personal transformation or "individuation," Pratt distinguishes between the social quest of the bildungsroman, in which a young hero seeks integration into the human community, and the spiritual quest found in women's novels that feature middle-aged female heroes. In these latter works, the "older woman hero" seeks "to integrate her self with herself and not with a society she has found inimical to her desires." She does this through a journey of rebirth involving a quest into the unconscious. Jung's *Wiedergeburt*—a German word meaning "rebirth," "revival," or "renaissance"—leads to a "renovation or transformation of an individual so that all of his or her faculties are brought into conscious play." The individual may experience a renewal in which parts of the personality, according to Jung, "are subjected to healing, strengthening, or improvement" or even a total transformation in which one's essential being undergoes change or "transmutation."[13]

13. Pratt, *Archetypal Patterns*, 136; C. J. Jung, *The Archetypes and the Collective Unconscious*, 114.

Pratt defines the first phase of the female rebirth journey as a splitting off from family, husbands, and lovers. Such an act stems from the protagonist's "acute consciousness of the world of the ego and her consequent turning away from societal norms" and patriarchal experience.[14] In *Saving Grace*, Grace's marital rebellion and her desertion of husband and children signal the first phase of the rebirth journey. (She eventually becomes disillusioned with Randy Newhouse's hard-drinking, womanizing behavior and breaks with him as well.)

The second phase of the rebirth journey occurs when Grace tracks an unfaithful Randy to the parking lot of Uncle Slidell's Diner and Christian Fun Golf. Pratt says that in this phase of the quest the ordinary suddenly takes on extraordinary significance and the woman hero is helped across the threshold of reality by a green-world guide or token. In Grace's case, she is lured by the faint and pitiful cry of a baby to the number ten hole of the miniature golf course. Here she discovers a bizarre nativity scene complete with ceramic chickens and ducks, plywood wise men, and angels dangling from a clothesline. A crying baby Jesus, His chubby arms outstretched, dirty snow dripping into His face, lies in Mary's lap beneath a wooden sign that says "TO:YOU FROM:GOD" (SG 248). Considerable ambiguity exists in the text about this baby, evidence perhaps of Smith's penchant for magic realism. While the infant is likely part of the plywood nativity scene, its crying seems to be real and its outstretched arms strike at the core of Grace's maternal guilt. The scene represents Smith's manipulation and inversion of the second phase of the spiritual quest. In one sense, she imbues the ordinary with extraordinary portent, but she also transforms the extraordinary into the mundane. Uncle Slidell's Christian Fun Golf represents the commercialization of mountain culture, while the grotesque nativity scene suggests a corruption of the most extraordinary and sacred of Christian mysteries. Both reflect a postmodern devaluation of culture and religion. Moreover, the perverse Madonna and child serve as a sad representation of Grace's failed maternity and of her own dead son lying in a snow-covered graveyard.

The crying baby Jesus of the nativity scene also symbolizes Smith's inversion of the third phase of the rebirth journey. Normally, in this phase an idealized, nonpatriarchal lover appears to guide the female

14. Pratt, *Archetypal Patterns*, 139.

hero through difficult parts of the quest. Pratt contends that this green-world lover (as distinct from the green-world guide) may be an actual person, an idealized figure found in reverie, or even an animal. In modern novels by women, she observes, this figure is often "a combination of the Native American animal guide, or spirit, and an incorporation into the personality of one's sexual and natural forces, one's Pan . . . one's own internal Adonis." Pratt points to the white heron in Sarah Orne Jewett's story of that name and to the corn god of Alexandra Bergson's reveries in Willa Cather's *O Pioneers!* as evidence of this green-world spirit/lover in women's fiction. As we have seen, Honey Breeding fulfills this role for Ivy Rowe in *Fair and Tender Ladies*. However, as fiction writer Nanci Kincaid has pointed out, in southern culture Jesus often fulfills this role in the lives of women; the embodiment of the perfect man, Jesus serves as a substitute for husbands who stay out too late, drink too much, and otherwise abuse and neglect their wives.[15] In *Saving Grace*, Smith inverts this image of Jesus as the idealized lover into a pitiful crying infant who guides a shaken Grace towards home and, ultimately, to salvation.

Grace's return to Scrabble Creek initiates the fourth phase of her quest: confrontation with parental figures. Pratt asserts that the female hero who has turned away from society because of disenchantment with her past must still come to terms with parental figures that reside in the subconscious, the "repository of personal memories."[16] Maternal and paternal symbology suffuses Grace's homecoming and represents Smith's efforts to mediate the matriarchal-patriarchal dichotomy in the novel. In an attempt to nurture and restore herself, Grace stocks up on groceries at the Food Lion located where her father's church once stood. She also seeks out Ruth and Carlton Duty, constant and enduring figures of parental love who once cared for Grace and her siblings. Grace moves back into her parents' deserted cabin and sleeps in their old bed. By doing so, she symbolically reunites with the mother and the father, the primal sources of her being. The cabin, like the haunted Cantrell cabin in *Oral History*, serves as a maternal womb and as a nourishing source for Grace's narrative. Only after returning to her childhood home is Grace able to articulate her life story, an act that allows her to

15. Ibid., 140; Kincaid's remarks were made in a guest lecture and interview at the University of North Carolina at Charlotte on May 26, 1993.
16. Pratt, *Archetypal Patterns*, 140.

come to terms with both parents, their relationship with each other, and their powerful influences on her life.

As Grace brings her story full circle, her narrative shifts into present time and present tense in preparation for the fifth and final phase of the rebirth journey, the plunge into the unconscious. With the past and the "truth" now disclosed, Grace is suspended in the present, much like an infant waiting to be born. She has no watch and the only marker of time in the cabin, a china clock, is broken. One Sunday morning while Grace lies in her parents' bed, her mother appears to her in a dream similar to Pricey Jane's reverie about her mother in *Oral History*. Like Pricey Jane, Grace is enveloped by her mother's hair and physical presence. Whereas Pricey Jane cannot make out the words of her mother's song, Fannie's whispered words to Grace are distinct and clear: "*Come to me, Gracie. . . . Oh come to Jesus honey. It is time now, it is never too late*" (SG 269).

Fannie's soft voice and the absence of linear time in the passage suggest the fluid, timeless realm of the maternal womb. We have seen that, according to the linguistic theories of Hélène Cixous and Luce Irigaray, the mother's body and voice serve as primeval sources of the female voice. Certainly, Grace's and Pricey Jane's attentiveness to their mothers' voices validates this. However, Fannie's articulation of distinct speech rather than wordless song marks an evolution from *Oral History* to *Saving Grace* in Smith's treatment of the maternal voice. Pricey Jane, unable to discern her mother's language, which is really a primeval song, eventually succumbs to silence and death. Grace, on the other hand, is called to action by her mother's words. In both cases, Smith uses the maternal body and voice to elicit the daughter's attention, but by giving Fannie distinct language, the maternal voice emerges out of the nebulous, prelinguistic realm into greater parity with patriarchal language. In *Saving Grace*, Smith does not seek to replace paternal language with the maternal, but rather to merge the two. Indeed, Fannie's words, "Come to me, . . . come to Jesus," suggest Smith's attempt to find a mediation between matriarchal and patriarchal spiritual realms. The use of womb imagery continues as Grace, minding her mother's words, rises from her parents' bed to dress for church. When Grace sheds her jeans and walks unclothed to her mother's wardrobe, her nakedness suggests the infant's original state; when she dons her mother's blue dress, she symbolically reenters the mother's body.

As she does in the earlier phases, Smith inverts the final phase of the rebirth journey as well. Rather than plunging into the unconscious, Grace experiences a leap into consciousness and into a new dimension of time and being. Dozing by the stove before church, she completes her confrontation with parental figures. As she drifts through memories of her mother, father, and siblings, she is suddenly jolted "terribly terribly awake." Her faculties are brought into conscious play in a manner consistent with Jung's *Wiedergeburt*: "The Spirit comes down on me hard like a blow to the top of my head and runs all over my body like lightning. My fingers and toes are on fire. Oh Lord it is hard to breathe and I am scared Lord, I am so scared but I will let my hands do what they are drawing now to do and it does not hurt, it is a joy in the Lord as she said. It is a joy which spreads all through my body, all through this sinful old body of mine." Similar to Morrison's Sula, who in dying comes to know her mother's fiery pain, Grace experiences an identification with the mother, but hers is a life-renewing one. Like her mother before her, she thrusts her hands into the burning coals of the stove and finds not pain but the same joy and perfect pleasure Fannie had felt. Grace describes her experience in terms that are almost sexual. Her spiritual ecstasy is perceived physically: "[M]y fingers and toes are on fire"; "it is a joy which spreads all through my body" (SG 271). Grace's words "I am coming now, I am really coming Jesus" are an orgasmic reference that blends the spiritual and sexual into one (SG 272).

Pratt sees the plunge into the unconscious in women's fiction as giving rise to extreme self-loathing, as "[w]omen heroes often blame themselves for their own normal human desires, warping their quests for Eros, for example, by internalizing patriarchal norms about feminine sexuality." Pratt notes that, unlike men whose successful rebirth journeys serve "as a boon" to society, female questers are likely to suffer punishment for succeeding in their "revolutionary" journeys. She further warns that, given its inherent risk and psychological danger, the rebirth journey can "as likely lead to madness as to renewal."[17] Grace's experience indicates Smith's departure from this pattern. As her words suggest, Grace successfully integrates Eros with the spiritual dimensions of her being. She does not resort to self-loathing, but to a celebration of her newly born

17. Ibid., 141–42.

state. Rather than succumbing to madness, Grace achieves a full mediation of the maternal-paternal dichotomy.

Brought to the Father through the maternal, Grace is restored to a
purer self. Reborn, she observes how the snow lies in a blinding divine
light "like a field of diamonds" (SG 271). In a fusion of sounds, the crying of a baby mixes with church bells ringing out over the snow, signal-
ing the completion of Grace's quest. The sounds prompt Grace to remember her "gray angel baby Travis [who] sleeps in peace beneath a lacy
blanket of snow" and the crying baby Jesus whom she has also abandoned but is coming for now as well. The two male infants, one mortal,
the other divine, are miniaturized representations of the patriarchy.
Grace's thoughts suggest an embrace of the paternal in its purest, most
uncorrupted state. Similarly, she recalls her own earlier, more innocent
self: "I know myself as the girl I was, who used to love stories so much.
Well this is the story of light Mama, this is the story of snow." When
she declares the Spirit to be a "joyful thing," she links her happiness
with both the maternal and paternal, exclaiming, "I *am* happy Mama, I
am" (SG 272).

Smith does not bring closure to Grace's life; the novel ends somewhat ambiguously immediately following her "anointment" by the
Spirit. Grace is simply shown driving off in her car, her destination and
future unstated.[18] However, the language and imagery of the final scene
reveal an affirmation of life consistent with spiritual rebirth. Echoing
the opening lines of the novel, Grace reestablishes her identity and
connection to God: "[M]y name is Florida Grace, Florida for the state
I was born in, Grace for the grace of God." Before she drives away, she
casts a final look at her parents' cabin and gazes at the "long white
sweep of snowy ground where me and Billie Jean made angels in the
snow" (SG 273). Grace's parting glance at the cabin, a repository of
personal history and memory, along with the tabula rasa implied by the
snow, depicts an embrace of the past and hope for the future. Moreover, the image confirms not only Smith's successful mediation of the

18. Whenever I teach *Saving Grace*, my students heatedly debate the conclusion of
the novel and its implications for the rest of Grace Shepherd's life. Some believe that
Grace has been reborn spiritually and will now, for better or worse, follow her parents'
religious practices. Others fear she is preparing to commit suicide like her mother. Not
long ago, one of my students contacted Lee Smith to ask her what actually happens at
the end of the novel. Smith replied in a letter that she believes that Grace is going to
church to take up snakes.

matriarchal-patriarchal dichotomy but also Grace's final reconciliation with the parental elements undergirding her being. Without question, the body and voice of the mother and the religion of the father have brought the daughter to salvation, wholeness, and a full acceptance of self.

11

~

Conclusion

"LISTENING TO THE STORIES THAT MOTHERS HAVE TO TELL"

> Unless feminism can begin to demystify and politicize
> motherhood, and by extension female power more general-
> ly, fears and projections will continue. Feminism might be-
> gin by listening to the stories that mothers have to tell, and
> by creating the space in which mothers might articulate
> those stories.
>
> —Marianne Hirsch, *The Mother/Daughter Plot:*
> *Narrative, Psychoanalysis, Feminism*

I opened this book with a discussion of my personal and professional experiences, my mother's childbearing experiences, and my grandmothers' voices as a way to lead into my discussion of maternal experience in
the novels of Toni Morrison, Bobbie Ann Mason, and Lee Smith. As I
bring my book to its conclusion, I find that I am once again immersed
in issues of maternity, but in quite new ways. For one, I am awaiting the
birth of my granddaughter, my first grandchild and a happy addition to
two families containing many men. I have three sons; my daughter-in-
law has four brothers. Thus, we are both jubilant about balancing the
gender scales a bit more (though we would welcome any new baby with
unmitigated joy). My sons are remarkable human beings, and I am con-
vinced that they are my best and most important lifework. However,
while they were growing up, I found it hard to find aspects of myself in
their faces, bodies, interests, or intellects. Their very maleness obscured

whatever characteristics we might have shared, and it thwarted the emotional bonds I strived to forge. From the moment of their births, my sons were driven—preprogrammed, it seemed—to separate from me. I often felt like an outsider in my own family and had to learn a new language in order to belong.

Now that my sons are grown, I realize that we indeed have similar values and concerns and that we possess the same strong will and sense of responsibility, especially in regard to work and human relationships. I must admit, however, that I am savoring the prospect of having a granddaughter, a delicious reward for reaching this stage of life. It renews me and completes my connection with the female lineage that I have had with my sisters, mother, aunts, and grandmothers. It provides a new and special bond with my adored daughter-in-law, Whitney, whose entry into our family enriched and civilized our lives. I am eager to have more daughters-in-law and grandchildren to love and cherish. Meanwhile, I feel positioned on a generational bridge, one that spans the past and reaches into the future. I look ahead and see my granddaughter making her journey into this life; I look behind me and sense my grandmothers guiding me into the new role I am about to assume.

Recently, my sister Candice returned home from a trip to Canada with another surprise for me. She had attended the funeral of one of our few remaining aunts and brought back with her a small, musty box containing forty years of diaries kept by our maternal grandmother, Hulda Humbke. My sister gave me the diaries when we met for supper. At the restaurant table, I opened the box and picked out one of the diaries. As I read aloud from the fragile book, our grandmother's voice floated up from the pages, her words enveloping us and transporting us back through time into her life, our mother's younger life, and even our own childhoods. By sheer chance, I had picked the diary that covered the years of my mother's wedding and my own birth. It was truly like finding lost parts of myself, my own "herstory." I scanned other entries, other diaries, and found equally compelling moments of recorded time. My favorite was an inscription my grandmother had made inside the cover of one diary: "The railroad came north from Calgary in the spring of 1891 I came May 6 1894." I noticed that the sentences were devoid of punctuation, fused together like the railroad tracks that carried my grandmother to her new home in Alberta when she was a child, five years after her birth in Ostersund, Sweden. Now, over a hundred years

later, I look forward to introducing my granddaughter to her female relations and especially to her great-great-pioneer-grandmother, who cultivated a new, raw land when she was a young wife and mother and
whose diaries we will read together.

In the past few months, I have also had the opportunity to witness
my daughter-in-law's forging of her own "herstory." Whitney's much de-
sired and happy pregnancy has been punctuated by worry, discomfort,
and complications. She has endured three hospitalizations for pre-term
labor. I have admired her strength, determination, and assertiveness in
obtaining quality care for herself and her baby. She is a proactive, knowledgeable young woman who makes wise choices. I especially admire
Whitney's decision to attend an obstetrical practice consisting of three
black female physicians, dynamic women who undoubtedly have altered the racial and sexual politics of medicine and rescripted the birth
room scene for the better. They listen carefully, pay attention to every
detail and concern, and deliver impeccable care. They possess humor,
energy, and empathy for their patients. One, I know, is a mother herself. I saw her making hospital rounds with her five-year-old son one
Sunday after church.

While I applaud the changes that make for healthier mothers and babies, I also realize that some factors have not been altered by time or
technology. Certain elements still impact a woman's experience of maternity with serious enormity. A mother's age, race, social class, level of
education, whether or not she has adequate insurance or convenient
access to quality medical care—all these have a strong bearing on the
outcome of her pregnancy and the well-being of her offspring. Such factors breed disparities that will prevent maternity from ever becoming a
genuinely universal experience. These differences were starkly laid out
for me during Whitney's most recent hospitalization. While she was being settled into a labor room and tethered to an intravenous line and fetal monitor, another mother was arriving in the room next door to have
her pre-term labor halted as well. The nurse on duty confirmed to us that
she would have another patient to attend, saying, "Yes, she's my prisoner." I looked at her quizzically, not understanding what she meant. The
nurse continued, "She's an inmate from the state maximum-security
prison. She'll be shackled to the bed and will have an armed guard with
her the whole time. I wouldn't go in there otherwise."

I was stunned by the disparate situations of the two mothers and by the nurse's comments. In the past I had looked after patients, male and female, with criminal records, ones that stemmed mostly from drug use or from getting into fights with knives or guns. For some reason, I never thought of them as criminals; they were simply patients who needed my care. None were maximum-security inmates as far as I knew. In any event, I did not fear them, and I actually found myself drawn to them just so I could hear their stories. Despite my experience with these patients, I was caught off guard by the nurse's words and shaken by the reality of the prisoner-mother's situation. In the latter's case, I realized that the most human of acts—the act of giving birth—would likely take place in dehumanizing circumstances. The prisoner-mother would get competent professional care, I felt certain. But I was not sure how much dignity or humanity she would be able to retain during her labor and delivery, given her maximum-security-criminal status. Clearly, she was a feared and despised moral outcast, perhaps a violent and murderous one, and she would be handled accordingly. Protective measures were necessary to ensure the safety of other patients, the staff, and, I guess, the mother herself. But shackling her to the bed seemed vilely inhumane. She was still a woman, a mother-to-be, a human being. I imagined her giving birth chained to the bed like an animal, handcuffs cutting deeper into her flesh with each contraction. I could sense her panic at being so restrained, unable to obey the dictates of her own body. Her baby, I was told, would be given to a family member or to social services after it was born and the woman would return to prison. My brain struggled to comprehend the paradox of the situation and to reconcile the divergent realities I was witnessing.

I will never know what happened to the mother from the state prison. I will never know her age, race, or crime. But I would like to think that her childbirth experience evolved quite differently from my first imaginings. I hope she labored with confidence and dignity. That she was attended by caring nurses and a compassionate doctor. That she trusted her body and the people around her. That she gave birth without a gun-brandishing guard standing over her bed, threatening to punish or subdue her if she misbehaved. Most of all, I like to think that she was able to hold and kiss her child before it was taken away from her, perhaps for years, perhaps forever. I imagine the mother breathing in, for memory's sake, her baby's warm, newborn musk—a sweet, earthy fragrance as old as time but new to her, a perfume full of hope and promise.

As these experiences demonstrated to me and as the novels of Morrison, Mason, and Smith confirm, motherhood is a complex subject. It is one that still mystifies and disturbs me. I hope, however, that I have shed some new light on the rich and varied expression that three important writers of our time have given to maternal experience. To a significant degree, their presentation of motherhood reflects the racial and cultural differences that exist among them. Morrison grounds female experience in the cloistered African American communities of southern Ohio, while Mason centers women's lives on the farms and in the small towns of western Kentucky. Smith, on the other hand, ensconces her female characters in the Appalachian Mountains of Virginia, North Carolina, and Tennessee. My goal has been to show that such differences are not divisive, that maternity and female experience provide common ground that links these writers together.

In my introduction, I quoted Elaine Showalter's argument that women's culture forms a collective experience "that binds women writers to each other over time and space." Throughout the writing of this study, I have been reminded of these words. I believe the novels of Morrison, Mason, and Smith form this kind of collectivity. Although situations and characters vary greatly in their fiction, these writers reveal maternity to be not only a transforming experience that contains mythic and spiritual dimensions but also one in which biological, social, and economic realities collide. Their novels illustrate how women's experiences are powerfully defined by place and by the communities in which they live. Social norms, cultural proscriptions, family expectations, and even the geography of a particular locale exert influence on motherhood and female experience. In a larger sense, the novels of Morrison, Mason, and Smith demonstrate how the South, particularly its history and patriarchal culture, figures sharply in the lives of its mothers, regardless of race. This results in an objectification of the maternal that all three writers rail against. They are powerfully unified in their concern about the impact of history and culture on a woman's experience of her body and on her ability to articulate that experience. I believe this to be perhaps the strongest link binding the three writers together.

In their rendering of maternal experience, Morrison, Mason, and Smith juxtapose the body and voice of the mother through similar means in their novels. They employ related image patterns, metaphors, and symbols to convey both maternal objectification and maternal subjectivity. The mother's body is given complex and often paradoxical representation, and serves as the central metaphor in their depiction of maternal experience. With pregnancy and childbirth depicted as pivotal, defining events for many female characters in their novels, all three writers reveal the mother's body to be a source of power, creativity, and language. At the same time, they portray the maternal body as something that is often feared and reviled. This latter representation is disturbing but necessary, for it allows each writer to show how various patriarchal institutions attempt to exert power and control over the mother's body and how they commodify and denigrate the mother's body in the process. In one manner or another, the three writers depict the female body as a text inscribed by the patriarchy, as property to be bought and sold, as dehumanized flesh subjected to indignity and violation. Mutilation of the maternal body occurs frequently in their novels, providing explicit evidence of such oppression.

To some extent, the mutilations that Morrison, Mason, and Smith portray in their fiction represent age-old fears and hatred of the mother's body. Feminist psychoanalyst Dorothy Dinnerstein points out in *The Mermaid and the Minotaur* that "woman serves her species as carnal scapegoat-idol." She reminds us of Simone de Beauvoir's assertions in *The Second Sex* that human culture associates woman with death: "The Earth Mother engulfs the bones of her children"; woman is "night in the entrails of the earth." Dinnerstein goes on to explain that the female body inspires fear, awe, worship, and sometimes disgust: "Alien, dangerous nature, conveniently concentrated near at hand in woman's flesh, can be controlled through ritual segregation, confinement, and avoidance; it can be subdued through conventionalized humiliation and punishment; it can be honored and placated through ceremonial gifts and adornments, through formalized gestures of respect and protectiveness."[1]

This ambivalent regard for the mother's body finds violent expression in the novels under study here. Morrison is particularly graphic in her depiction of the "humiliation and punishment" inflicted upon the female body. The suffering endured by her maternal characters arises from both sexist and racist attitudes that objectify, denigrate, and subjugate

---

1. Dorothy Dinnerstein, *The Mermaid and the Minotaur: Sexual Arrangements and Human Malaise*, 117–18.

the mother. In *Beloved*, Sethe, Baby Suggs, and their respective off-spring are regarded as property within white southern patriarchal culture, human chattel to be sold or traded. Sethe's body emblematizes male control of the mother's body. The theft of her milk by the plantation manager's nephews degrades her maternity; the whipping she endures produces bloody inscriptions upon her body that provides a visual text bearing the seal of patriarchal ownership. The body of Sethe's mother, Ma'am, also serves as a text inscribed by the southern patriarchy. The circled cross branded under her breast marks her as property and provides the only means of identification after her violent death. This perverse signification of the maternal body has its counterpart in the story of Eva Peace in *Sula*. Commodification and mutilation go hand in hand in this novel as a desperate Eva sacrifices her leg to collect money to feed her children. Whereas Sethe and Ma'am endure pain and suffering inflicted by the institution of slavery, Eva willfully endures pain and suffering, bartering her body so that she can ensure the survival of her offspring. Morrison seems to suggest that the maternal sacrifice, suffering, and death that pervade her novels stem from the fear and loathing that the patriarchal culture often directs towards women and towards African American women in particular. As Morrison terrifyingly shows, the self-hatred and internalized negative attitudes that result can have devastating consequences.

Mutilation of the maternal body also occurs in Mason's *Spence + Lila*, though for quite different reasons. When breast cancer strikes, Lila Culpepper experiences a direct confrontation with the patriarchal forces of modern medicine. With her hospitalization and subsequent mastectomy, she is denied power and identity. The care she receives throughout her hospital stay is depersonalizing and relegates her to a position of passivity. Lila likens the mastectomy itself to the ripping of raw chicken breasts. Although the procedure is done to save Lila's life, the surgical scars that result are not unlike those borne by Sethe, Ma'am, and Eva. All four women bear the marks of pain and sacrifice on their bodies.

Mason further explores the commodifying of female experience in *Feather Crowns*. Like Morrison in *Beloved* and *Sula*, Mason uses a historical perspective in her treatment of Christie Wheeler's maternal experience at the turn of the last century. The birth of Christie's quintuplets, their feeding, and their deaths involve the usurpation of female experience by what Harriet Pollack calls "the quartet of medicine, science, money, and male authority." These patriarchal forces not only wield control over every aspect of Christie's maternal experience but also objectify and commodify it. Whereas Sethe and her children are regarded as patriarchal property in *Beloved*, Christie and her five "miraculous" babies become products to be consumed by a hungry, demanding public.

Like Morrison and Mason, Smith, in *Oral History*, portrays the commodification and mutilation of the maternal body. When Almarine Cantrell decides that he wants Pricey Jane for a wife, he trades a mule for her. This marks Pricey Jane as disposable property to be bartered between men. Her daughter Dory experiences a worse objectification. Dory's death is one of the more shocking examples of maternal mutilation in the novels studied. Like Morrison and Mason, Smith indicts patriarchal culture for a tragic deed. Impregnated and abandoned by Richard Burlage, Dory lives out the remainder of her harsh mountain life in restlessness and ambivalence. Her apparent suicide along the railroad tracks near her home symbolizes her conflicting desires to stay in the mountains and to pursue a life in the larger outside world that Burlage represents. Moreover, her decapitation symbolizes the mind-body split ascribed to women by patriarchal culture, a split that Smith seems to suggest can only result in silence and death.

Besides using maternal mutilation to depict objectification of the mother, Morrison, Mason, and Smith use dead-baby imagery to further project its horror. All of the novels studied here contain dead infants or dead children that suggest disturbing inversions of the maternal. In Morrison's novels, such imagery represents not maternal failure but the warping of African American female experience by white patriarchal culture and its institutions. In *The Bluest Eye*, Pecola Breedlove's fervent desire for beauty and love turns to madness after she is raped by her father and gives birth to a premature infant who dies. Pecola's dead baby mirrors her own failure to thrive in a culture that denigrates her blackness, prizing white standards of beauty above all. In *Beloved*, Sethe murders her baby daughter rather than see her returned to the cruel institution of slavery. The ghost of the dead child haunts the text and the lives of her entire family. In *Sula*, Eva Peace's son, Plum, is infantilized by his country's failure to assimilate him after he returns home from service in World War I and by the heroin addiction that follows. His fiery death in Eva's bed and the return-to-the-womb imagery that Morrison employs reflect this regression.

Mason incorporates dead-baby imagery in her novel *In Country* and, like Morrison, links that imagery to the larger culture. The *Newsweek* cover photograph of a Vietnamese mother carrying her dead infant provides a riveting image of war and loss that Sam Hughes must confront in her quest for her father. In addition, her dreams contain deformed and frozen babies that show her ambivalence about conventional gender roles. In *Feather Crowns*, however, nightmare becomes reality when Christie Wheeler experiences the deaths of her quintuplets. Embalmed with the latest scientific techniques, the infants are grotesquely preserved under glass like dolls. The bizarre lecture tour upon which Christie embarks with the quintuplets further objectifies mother and children. The dead babies cease to be maternal creations, becoming instead public oddities shaped and molded by the forces of science, technology, and business. In *Spence + Lila*, the dead-baby imagery is given less grotesque treatment than in Mason's other works. We learn that Lila, at the age of four, experienced the deaths of her mother and infant sister following childbirth. This loss creates the central metaphor of life, death, and regeneration that manifests itself in the peas Lila inherits from her mother, her concern for her daughters, and the hopes and fears she has about her own future. The dried peas give positive meaning to the dead mother–dead baby imagery in *Spence + Lila*, as they provide generational links among mothers, daughters, and sisters that transcend death and time.

In her novels, Smith connects dead infants and dead children to female defiance of the patriarchy and, in some instances, to the punishment that results from this defiance. Maternal death also occurs frequently, creating heavy psychic burdens for surviving offspring, particularly daughters. In *Oral History*, the witch Red Emmy kills her newborn infant after Almarine Cantrell throws her out of his cabin and, presumably, his life. Later, his wife and young son die from drinking tainted milk, their deaths suspiciously linked to Red Emmy's curse upon the Cantrell family. Two generations later, Pearl Cantrell and her baby die in childbirth. Like her mother, Dory, an apparent suicide, and grandmother, Pricey Jane, Pearl provides an image of the sacrificed maternal. In *Fair and Tender Ladies*, Ivy Rowe endures the death of her mother and the loss of a daughter. Blamed for her child's death, Ivy must contend with the community's wrath over her affair with Honey Breeding and the subsequent neglect of her family. In *Saving Grace*, Grace Shepherd gives birth to a stillborn son, his death symbolic of her spiritual impoverishment and failed marriage. Moreover, it illustrates the continuing conflicts between maternal and patriarchal forces in the novel, which originated with the hanging of Grace's mother years earlier.

By creating images of horror and loss—burned flesh, ripped breasts, amputated legs, decapitations, dead babies, and dead mothers—Morrison, Mason, and Smith provide extreme examples of the objectification of the mother and the devaluation given to her body. Such radical gestures are necessary to call attention to the negation of female experience and the silencing of the female voice that take place within a patriarchal culture. To a significant degree, these disturbing images illustrate the deeply ingrained fears and negative attitudes associated with the female body. They reflect beliefs long held and perpetuated by religious, educational, medical, political, and economic institutions in Western society. The devastating objectification of the mother's body depicted in the novels of all three writers serves as an indictment of patriarchal culture and its construction of women. Each writer challenges the duality that has been ascribed to women and their bodies: that women are vessels of fertility, regeneration, and continuance, while at the same time representing the abyss that threatens to swallow up and annihilate man. The mutilated maternal bodies and dead babies in these writers' books stand in antithesis to the life-giving aspect of female nature.

While these images reflect the fear and discomfort associated with the maternal body, such horrific objectification also serves another purpose. It suggests both female suffering and an equally insidious cultural malaise. Whereas male malaise is often depicted in literature through war, impotence, addiction, and violent behavior, Morrison, Mason, and Smith show that women's suffering is evidenced through the body in more intimate ways that span the gamut of female sexual and biological experience. These writers do not depict simply a loss of fertility and sexual potency, but rather a loss of voice and an astounding devastation of the body and self. The mutilated mothers and dead babies provide a distinct female wasteland imagery that symbolizes the destruction of hope and renewal. These subversive images mirror the dominant culture's failure to nourish and support its members, manipulating, maiming, and, in some cases, killing. Given that Morrison, Mason, and Smith all write about marginalized cultures, such violent assaults are directed not only towards individuals but also towards entire communities whose fragile existences are threatened by the forces of change and modernity. Thus the maternal mutilation and dead babies in their works stand as a metaphor for the loss of culture suffered by African American, Appalachian, and rural communities that have been oppressed, silenced, or consumed by the larger culture. As the images of dead mothers and babies suggest, the texts mourn this loss.

Despite the extent of this oppressive imagery and the objectification of the mother that it suggests, Morrison, Mason, and Smith are able to provide varying degrees of maternal subjectivity as a counterbalance. The dichotomizing of body and voice that occurs in their texts is not absolute. In many instances, these writers imbue their female characters with a rich consciousness, if not actual speech and language, that lessens maternal objectification and reverses the mind-body split that traditionally has defined female experience in patriarchal culture. Maternal subjectivity, particularly as revealed through the mother's voice and consciousness, proves to be an important, sustaining force undergirding the texts and the characters' lives.

For daughters especially, the maternal voice is critical to healthy growth and development. This is clearly evident in Morrison's *The Bluest Eye*. Mrs. MacTeer's expressive, insistent voice provides daughter Claudia with a growth medium for her own voice and identity. While growing up, she rejects the idealized white standards of beauty thrust at her by society and thus manages to escape the crippling denigration that Pecola Breedlove endures. Possessing a strong sense of self and her mother's facility with language, Claudia constructs the narrative of the text, giving voice to Pecola's tragic maternal story in turn. Denver in *Beloved* is equally attuned to her mother's voice, though it is not as strongly rendered as Mrs. MacTeer's. Since much of what she has to tell is "unspeakable," Sethe's voice seems hesitant and muted. Rarely given direct treatment, it largely exists outside the reader's range of hearing or is fused with the voices of Sethe's daughters. However, this does not prevent Denver from hearing her mother's stories. She fervently listens to them and is particularly enthralled by her own birth story, which she enthusiastically recounts to Beloved. Moreover, given her grandmother Baby Suggs's alignment with voice, Denver grows up nourished by language and storytelling. So nurtured, she provides critical strength to her family when the past threatens to disrupt their lives.

The maternal voice similarly empowers daughters in Mason's and Smith's novels. Although Irene is not given full voice in *In Country*, she serves as a major influence in her daughter's quest for self. Irene links Sam with the past and her dead soldier father but also pushes her towards the future. She encourages Sam to leave Hopewell, to go to college, and to define herself outside the twin enclosures of marriage and motherhood. Sam, like Claudia and Denver, develops the healthy identity necessary for survival in a patriarchal culture. She successfully completes her quest, coming to a realistic understanding of war, gender roles, and her own place in history. For the wayward Grace Shepherd in *Saving Grace*, the maternal voice is muted but holds much importance nonetheless. Although her father's booming, patriarchal voice dominates Grace's life and the text itself, her mother's quiet directive from beyond the grave ultimately leads to Grace's salvation and the renewal of self that she experiences at the end of the novel.

Besides showing the importance of the maternal voice in shaping the lives and psyches of female offspring, Morrison, Mason, and Smith create space within their texts for those maternal stories that exist beyond the realm of direct speech. Despite the differences in culture and individual circumstances that surround female experience in their novels, all three writers succeed in making audible what Naomi Schor, as we have seen, calls the "muffled or silenced maternal voice." They overcome the reticence that, according to Marianne Hirsch, many female writers have about rendering maternal consciousness and experience, so much of which lies beyond rational understanding. One must look no further than the horrific maternal experiences in *Beloved*, the grotesque events in *Feather Crowns*, or the tragic saga of *Oral History* to know that Morrison, Mason, and Smith have no reluctance about rendering unspeakable, irrational, or devastating maternal experiences. They convey maternal consciousness in multiple ways: through dreams, reveries, interior monologues, threnodies, schizophrenic dialogues, and letters written to a dead sister. These strategies create places within their texts for even the most muffled or silenced of maternal voices to have presence and meaning. Here, female characters "speak the body," giving the most intimate details of their sexual and maternal selves.

Through interior monologues, Pauline Breedlove in *The Bluest Eye* likens sexual desire to smashed berries and describes the "rainbow" orgasms she experiences. She also speaks of her couplings with Cholly and the birth of her daughter. She reminisces about breast-feeding Pecola, the only positive interaction that mother and daughter share in the novel. Although Pecola's sexual and maternal experiences are recounted through Claudia's narration, Morrison creates space for Pecola's consciousness as well. Pecola's desire for love, acceptance, and blue eyes finds expression in the interior dialogue that she holds with her divided self at the end of the novel following her rape and blighted pregnancy. An even more complex rendering of female consciousness is manifested in what Morrison has called the "unspoken . . . unuttered" threnody that unfolds as a three-way conversation in *Beloved*. The poetic rememory passage involving the fused voices of Sethe and her daughters is full of love, longing, and lament that speak to the unseverable bonds that the worst horrors of slavery cannot destroy. As Morrison depicts it, maternal consciousness transcends time, death, and patriarchal history to foster the reclamation of memory and identity.

Like Morrison, Mason renders maternal subjectivity through interior, psychological means. In *Feather Crowns*, Christie Wheeler's pregnancy, labor, and postpartum experiences are punctuated by dreams and reveries that illuminate the sensual and sexual dimensions of the maternal. Christie links these feelings, particularly the tumultuous rumblings caused by the quintuplets in her womb, to the cataclysmic earthquake predicted for the turn of the century. The rich subjectivity of Christie's intensely sexual dreams about Brother Cornett and her recollections of sex with her husband, as well as the deeply felt psychological and physical sensations that accompany her unusual pregnancy, indicate a complex inner life that belies her farmwife persona and her limited speech within the novel. Mason creates similar contrasts between Lila Culpepper's exterior and interior selves in *Spence + Lila*, giving her evocative memories of the body that infuse her maternity with timeless, mythic qualities. As Lila copes with breast cancer and surgery, the sexual-maternal memories connected with her breasts sustain her. Time, memory, and the body thus become integral components of maternal consciousness, all of which fuel the psychological and physical regeneration required for her survival. Like her mother's dried peas and the seasonal cycles that define farm life, Lila's maternity and consciousness contribute not only to a reintegration of self—a fusing of mind and body—but also to the continuity leading from one generation of women to another.

Pricey Jane's reveries in *Oral History* are much like those of Pauline Breedlove, Christie Wheeler, and Lila Culpepper in that they link female interiority and sexual desire with the natural world. The dragonflies that mate in "the shimmering air" provide the same evidence of sexual *jouissance* as Pauline's smashed berries and rainbow orgasms (OH 64). Like Christie and Lila, Pricey Jane's speech is limited within the text, but the experience of her body is rich and full. Through dreams and reveries, she is linked with her mother, whose voice she struggles to hear. In *Fair and Tender Ladies* and *Saving Grace*, Smith depicts the muffled voices of other mothers. However, the daughter-narrators of these texts ensure that the stories of their silenced mothers are not neglected or lost. Ivy Rowe, in her letters, and Grace Shepherd, in her first-person narrative, include their mothers' experiences, acts that in turn enable them to write and speak about their own experiences. Maternal subjectivity finds its most complete expression as Ivy and Grace "speak the body" directly, telling about their experiences of sexuality, pregnancy, childbirth, and lactation firsthand. They give voice to the most essential of female experiences, which, throughout much of human history and literature, have been ignored, reviled, or narrated by others when they are considered at all.

As these examples suggest, the maternal consciousness that evolves within each novel is the most important accomplishment that Morrison, Mason, and Smith achieve in their rendering of motherhood and maternal experience. This consciousness, formed through the juxtaposition of body and voice and the interweave of biological, psychological, and cultural factors, is a multifaceted creation that conveys the richness of maternal experience. Morrison, Mason, and Smith show that southern history, patriarchal culture, and the definitions imposed by family and community profoundly shape female experience and consciousness. However, each writer also demonstrates that maternal experience, although deeply rooted in time, place, and culture, can transcend these boundaries and bind women together. While their individual experiences vary greatly, the African American mothers of Morrison's fiction have much in common with Mason's and Smith's rural southern women, who struggle to maintain a presence, an identity, and a voice within their respective cultures. The consciousness that results from these efforts is really a collective one that has significant implications for the larger culture. It suggests that to silence the mother, to denigrate her body, and to disavow her experience diminishes all of humanity.

Clearly, as the novels studied here reveal, the maternal is a force that can play a vital role in the development and sustenance of not only individuals but also entire communities. However, it must be respected, valued, and nurtured in return. In rendering the maternal in their fiction, Morrison, Mason, and Smith call for the reintegration of the body, mind, voice, and senses of the mother. They insist that women reconceptualize the self and, in Adrienne Rich's words, "connect what has been so cruelly disorganized." Lastly, they remind us that to hear the mother's voice and stories helps us to make our own. They help us to honor each other's voices and stories. This, perhaps, is the most pro-creative element born of the maternal experiences presented in their fiction.

BIBLIOGRAPHY

Adams, Alice. *Reproducing the Womb: Images of Childbirth in Science, Feminist Theory, and Literature*. Ithaca: Cornell University Press, 1994.

Arnold, Edwin. "Falling Apart and Staying Together: Bobbie Ann Mason and Leon Driskell Explore the State of the Modern Family." *Appalachian Journal* 12 (1985): 135–41.

———. "An Interview with Lee Smith." *Appalachian Journal* 11 (1984): 246–54.

Baker, Houston. *Blues, Ideology, and Afro-American Literature: A Vernacular Theory*. Chicago: University of Chicago Press, 1984.

Bizzell, Patricia, and Bruce Herzberg, eds. *The Rhetorical Tradition*. Boston: Bedford-St. Martin's, 1990.

Blais, Ellen. "Gender Issues in Bobbie Ann Mason's *In Country*." *South Atlantic Review* 56:2 (1991): 107–18.

Brinkmeyer, Robert. "Finding One's History: Bobbie Ann Mason and Contemporary Southern Literature." *Southern Literary Journal* 19:2 (1987): 20–33.

Brown, Fred. "Charles Prince: God's Hero." In *Serpent-Handling Believers*, by Thomas Burton, 97–108. Knoxville: University of Tennessee Press, 1993.

Buchanan, Harriet. "Lee Smith: The Storyteller's Voice." In *Southern Women Writers: The New Generation*, ed. Tonette Bond Inge, 324–45. Tuscaloosa: University of Alabama Press, 1990.

Burton, Thomas. *Serpent-Handling Believers*. Knoxville: University of Tennessee Press, 1993.

Busia, Abena. "Words Whispered over Voids: A Context for Black Women's Rebellious Voices in the Novel of the African Diaspora." In *Black Feminist Criticism and Critical Theory*, vol. 3 of *Studies in Black American Literature*, ed. Joe Weixlmann and Houston A. Baker Jr., 1–41. Greenwood, Fla.: Penkevill Publishing, 1988.

Byerman, Keith. "Beyond Realism." In *Toni Morrison: Critical Perspectives Past and Present*, ed. Henry Louis Gates Jr. and K. A. Appiah, 100–23. New York: Amistad Press, 1993. Originally published as "Beyond Realism: The Fictions of Gayl Jones and Toni Morrison" in Keith Byerman, *Fingering the Jagged Grain: Tradition and Form in Recent Black Fiction* (Athens: University of Georgia Press, 1985).

Campbell, Joseph. *The Masks of God: Primitive Mythology*. New York: Viking, 1972.

Caputi, Mary. "The Abject Maternal: Kristeva's Theoretical Consistency." *Women and Language* 16:2 (1993): 32–37.

Chesler, Phyllis. *Women and Madness*. New York: Avon, 1973.

Chesnut, Mary Boykin. *Mary Chesnut's Civil War*. Ed. C. Vann Woodward. New Haven: Yale University Press, 1981.

Christ, Carol. "Why Women Need the Goddess: Phenomenological, Psychological, and Political Reflections." In *Woman Spirit Rising: A Feminist Reader in Religion*, ed. Carol Christ and Judith Plaskow, 273–87. San Francisco: Harper and Row, 1979.

Christian, Barbara. *Black Feminist Criticism: Perspectives on Black Women Writers*. New York: Pergamon Press, 1985.

———. "The Contemporary Fables of Toni Morrison." In *Toni Morrison: Critical Perspectives Past and Present*, ed. Henry Louis Gates Jr. and K. A. Appiah, 59–99. New York: Amistad Press, 1993. Originally published in Barbara Christian, *Black Women Novelists: The Development of Tradition, 1892–1976* (Westport, Conn.: Greenwood Press, 1980).

Cixous, Hélène. "The Laugh of the Medusa." Trans. Keith Cohen and Paula Cohen. In *The Rhetorical Tradition*, ed. Patricia Bizzell and Bruce Herzberg, 1232–45. Boston: Bedford-St. Martin's, 1990. Revised version of an essay originally published as "Le Rire de la Méduse" in *L'Arc* (1975): 39–54.

Cixous, Hélène, and Catherine Clément. *The Newly Born Woman*. Trans. Betsy Wing. Minneapolis: University of Minnesota Press, 1986. Originally published as *La Jeune Née* (Paris: Union Générale d'Éditions, 1975).

Collins, Sheila. "Theology in the Politics of Appalachian Women." In *Woman Spirit Rising: A Feminist Reader in Religion*, ed. Carol Christ and Judith Plaskow, 149–58. San Francisco: Harper and Row, 1979.

Cosslett, Tess. *Women Writing Childbirth: Modern Discourses of Mother-hood*. Manchester: Manchester University Press, 1994.

Dale, Corinne. "The Power of Language." *Southern Quarterly* 28:2 (1990): 21–34.

Daly, Brenda, and Maureen Reddy, eds. *Narrating Mothers: Theorizing Maternal Subjectivities*. Knoxville: University of Tennessee Press, 1991.

Daly, Mary. *Beyond God the Father*. Boston: Beacon Press, 1973.

Darling, Marsha. "In the Realm of Responsibility: A Conversation with Toni Morrison." In *Conversations with Toni Morrison*, ed. Danille Taylor-Guthrie, 246–54. Jackson: University Press of Mississippi, 1994. Originally published in *Women's Review of Books* 5 (1988): 5–6.

Davis, Angela. "Reflections on the Black Woman's Role in the Community of Slaves." *Black Scholar* 3:4 (1971): 2–15.

Davis, Cynthia. "Self, Society, and Myth in Toni Morrison's Fiction." In *Toni Morrison*, ed. Harold Bloom, 7–25. New York: Chelsea House, 1990. Originally published in *Contemporary Literature* 23:3 (1982): 323–40.

Denard, Carolyn. "The Convergence of Feminism and Ethnicity in the Fiction of Toni Morrison." In *Critical Essays on Toni Morrison*, ed. Nellie McKay, 171–78. Boston: G. K. Hall, 1988.

Dinnerstein, Dorothy. *The Mermaid and the Minotaur: Sexual Arrangements and Human Malaise*. New York: Harper and Row, 1976.

Durham, Sandra Bonilla. "Women and War: Bobbie Ann Mason's *In Country*." *Southern Literary Journal* 22:2 (1990): 45–52.

Dwyer, June. "New Roles, New History, and New Patriotism: Bobbie Ann Mason's *In Country*." *Modern Language Studies* 22:2 (1992): 72–78.

Fox-Genovese, Elizabeth. *Within the Plantation Household: Black and White Women of the Old South*. Chapel Hill: University of North Carolina Press, 1988.

Friedan, Betty. *The Feminine Mystique*. 1963. Reprint, New York: W. W. Norton, 2001.

Gainey, Karen. "Subverting the Symbolic: The Semiotic Fictions of Anne Tyler, Jayne Anne Phillips, Bobbie Ann Mason, and Grace Paley." Ph.D. diss., University of Tulsa, 1990.

Gallop, Jane. *Thinking through the Body*. New York: Columbia University Press, 1988.

Ganim, Carole. "Herself: Woman and Place in Appalachian Literature." *Appalachian Journal* 13 (1986): 258–74.

Garner, Shirley Nelson, Claire Kahane, and Madelon Sprengnether. *The (M)other Tongue: Essays in Feminist Psychoanalytic Interpretation*. Ithaca: Cornell University Press, 1985.

Gauthier, Lorraine. "Desire for Origin/Original Desire: Luce Irigaray on Maternity, Sexuality, and Language." *Canadian Fiction Magazine* 57 (1986): 41–46.

Gerrard, Nathan. "The Serpent-Handling Religions of West Virginia." In *Poor Americans: How the White Poor Live*, ed. Marc Pilisuk and Phyllis Pilisuk, 61–71. N.p.: Transaction Books, 1971.

Gilbert, Sandra, and Susan Gubar. *The Madwoman in the Attic: The Woman Writer and the Nineteenth-Century Literary Imagination*. 1979. Reprint, New Haven: Yale University Press, 1984.

Grewal, Gurleen. "Memory and the Matrix of History: The Poetics of Loss and Recovery in Joy Kogawa's *Obasan* and Toni Morrison's *Beloved*." In *Memory and Cultural Politics: New Approaches to American Ethnic Literatures*, ed. Amritjit Singh, Joseph T. Skerrett Jr., and Robert E. Hogan, 140–73. Boston: Northeastern University Press, 1996.

Gwin, Minrose. *Black and White Women of the Old South: The Peculiar Sisterhood in American Literature*. Knoxville: University of Tennessee Press, 1985.

Hatchett, Judith. "Making Life Mean: Bobbie Ann Mason's *Feather Crowns*." *Kentucky Philological Review* 9 (1994): 12–15.

Hill, Dorothy Combs. "An Interview with Bobbie Ann Mason." *Southern Quarterly* 31:1 (1992): 85–118.

———. *Lee Smith*. New York: Twayne Publishers, 1992.

Hirsch, Marianne. *The Mother/Daughter Plot: Narrative, Psychoanalysis, Feminism*. Bloomington: Indiana University Press, 1989.

Holloway, Karla F. C. *Moorings and Metaphors: Figures of Culture and Gender in Black Women's Literature*. New Brunswick, N.J.: Rutgers University Press, 1992.

Hurston, Zora Neale. *Their Eyes Were Watching God*. 1937. Reprint, Urbana: University of Illinois Press, 1978.

Hymowitz, Carol, and Michaele Weissman. *A History of Women in America*. New York: Bantam, 1978.

Irigaray, Luce. *Sexes and Genealogies*. Trans. Gillian C. Gill. New York: Columbia University Press, 1993.

Jacobs, Harriet. *Incidents in the Life of a Slave Girl*. Ed. Jean Fagan Yellin. Cambridge: Harvard University Press, 1987.

James, Joy, and T. Denean Sharpley-Whiting, eds. *The Black Feminist Reader*. Malden, Mass.: Blackwell Publishers, 2000.

Johnson, Michael. "Smothered Slave Infants: Were Slave Mothers at Fault?" *Journal of Southern History* 47 (1981): 493–520.

Jones, Anne Goodwyn. "The World of Lee Smith." In *Women Writers of the Contemporary South*, ed. Peggy Prenshaw, 249–72. Jackson: University Press of Mississippi, 1984.

Jones, Jacqueline. *Labor of Love, Labor of Sorrow: Black Women, Work, and the Family from Slavery to the Present*. New York: Vintage–Random House, 1985.

Jones, Suzanne. "City Folks in Hoot Owl Holler: Narrative Strategy in Lee Smith's *Oral History*." *Southern Literary Journal* 20:1 (1987): 101–12.

Jung, C. J. *The Archetypes and the Collective Unconscious*, 2d ed. Trans. R. F. C. Hull. Vol. 9, part 1, of *The Collected Works*. N.p.: Bollingen Series 20, 1968. Reprint, New York: Bollingen/Princeton University Press, 1990.

Kahane, Claire. "Questioning the Maternal Voice." *Genders* 3 (1988): 82–91.

Ketchin, Susan. *The Christ-Haunted Landscape: Faith and Doubt in Southern Fiction*. Jackson: University Press of Mississippi, 1994.

Kinney, Katherine. "'Humping the Boonies': Sex, Combat, and the Female in Bobbie Ann Mason's *In Country*." In *Fourteen Landing Zones: Approaches to Vietnam War Literature*, ed. Philip Jason, 38–48. Iowa City: University of Iowa Press, 1991.

Kristeva, Julia. *About Chinese Women*. Excerpted in *The Kristeva Reader*, ed. Toril Moi, 139–59. New York: Columbia University Press, 1986.

———. "Stabat Mater." In *The Kristeva Reader*, ed. Toril Moi, 161–86. New York: Columbia University Press, 1986.

———. "Women's Time." In *The Kristeva Reader*, ed. Toril Moi, 187–213. New York: Columbia University Press, 1986.

Kushner, Rose. *Breast Cancer: A Personal History and an Investigative Report*. New York: Harcourt Brace Jovanovich, 1975.

La Barre, Weston. *They Shall Take Up Serpents: Psychology of the Southern Snake-Handling Cult.* Minneapolis: University of Minnesota Press, 1962.

Leavitt, Judith. *Brought to Bed: Childbearing in America 1750–1950.* New York: Oxford University Press, 1986.

Lerner, Gerda, ed. *Black Women in White America: A Documentary History.* 1972. New York: Vintage–Random House, 1973.

Lyons, Bonnie, and Bill Oliver. "An Interview with Bobbie Ann Mason." *Contemporary Literature* 32:4 (1991): 449–70.

MacKethan, Lucinda. *Daughters of Time: Creating Women's Voice in Southern Story.* Athens: University of Georgia Press, 1990.

Marlow, Dorothy. *Textbook of Pediatric Nursing.* Philadelphia: W. B. Saunders, 1969.

Mason, Bobbie Ann. *Clear Springs.* New York: Random House, 1999.

———. *Feather Crowns.* New York: Harper Collins, 1993.

———. *In Country.* 1985. Reprint, New York: Perennial–Harper and Row, 1993.

———. *Shiloh and Other Stories.* 1982. Reprint, New York: Perennial–Harper and Row, 1985.

———. *Spence + Lila.* 1988. Reprint, New York: Perennial–Harper and Row, 1989.

McCorkle, Jill. "Her Sensational Babies." Review of *Feather Crowns*, by Bobbie Ann Mason. *New York Times Book Review*, September 26, 1993, 7.

McDowell, Deborah. "'The Self and the Other': Reading Toni Morrison's *Sula* and the Black Female Text." In *Critical Essays on Toni Morrison*, ed. Nellie McKay, 77–89. Boston: G. K. Hall, 1988.

McMillen, Sally. *Motherhood in the Old South: Pregnancy, Childbirth, and Infant Rearing.* Baton Rouge: Louisiana State University Press, 1990.

Miner, Madonne M. "Lady No Longer Sings the Blues: Rape, Madness, and Silence in *The Bluest Eye*." In *Toni Morrison*, ed. Harold Bloom, 85–99. New York: Chelsea House, 1990.

Moi, Toril. *Feminist Literary Theory.* 1985. Reprint, London: Routledge, 1991.

Moi, Toril, ed. *The Kristeva Reader.* New York: Columbia University Press: 1986.

Morrison, Toni. *Beloved*. 1987. Reprint, New York: Plume-Penguin, 1988.

———. *The Bluest Eye*. 1970. Reprint, New York: Washington Square Press, 1972.

———. *Jazz*. New York: Knopf, 1992.

———. *Song of Solomon*. 1977. Reprint, New York: Signet-New American, 1978.

———. *Sula*. 1973. Reprint, New York: Plume-Penguin, 1982.

Naylor, Gloria. "A Conversation: Gloria Naylor and Toni Morrison." In *Conversations with Toni Morrison*, ed. Danille Taylor-Guthrie, 188–217. Jackson: University Press of Mississippi, 1994. Originally published in *Southern Review* 21 (1985): 567–93.

Neumann, Erich. "Transformation Mysteries of the Woman." In *Birth: An Anthology of Ancient Texts, Songs, Prayers, and Stories*, ed. David Meltzer, 83–84. San Francisco: North Point, 1981.

Newton, Niles. *Maternal Emotions*. New York: Hoeber-Harper, 1955.

Nwapa, Flora. *Cassava Song and Rice Song*. Enugu, Nigeria: Tana Press, 1986.

Ochs, Carol. *Behind the Sex of God*. Boston: Beacon Press, 1977.

Oha, Obododimma. "Culture and Gender Semantics in Flora Nwapa's Poetry." In *Writing African Women: Gender, Popular Culture, and Literature in West Africa*, ed. Stephanie Newall, 105–16. London: Zed Books, 1997.

Olsen, Tillie. *Silences*. 1978. Reprint, New York: Delta-Dell, 1989.

Orr, Elaine. *Subject to Negotiation: Reading Feminist Criticism and American Women's Fiction*. Charlottesville: University of Virginia Press, 1997.

Page, Phillip. *Dangerous Freedom: Fusion and Fragmentation in Toni Morrison's Novels*. Jackson: University Press of Mississippi, 1995.

Pearlman, Mickey, and Abby H. P. Werlock. *Tillie Olsen*. Boston: Twayne Publishers, 1991.

Pollack, Harriet. "From *Shiloh* to *In Country* to *Feather Crowns*: Bobbie Ann Mason, Women's History, and Southern Fiction." *Southern Literary Journal* 28:2 (1996): 95–116.

Powell, Dannye Romine. *Parting the Curtains: Interviews with Southern Writers*. Winston-Salem: John F. Blair, Publisher, 1994.

Pratt, Annis. *Archetypal Patterns in Women's Fiction*. Bloomington: Indiana University Press, 1981.

Prince, Anna. "A Snake-Handler's Daughter: An Autobiographical Sketch." In *Serpent-Handling Believers*, by Thomas Burton, 108–25. Knoxville: University of Tennessee Press, 1993.

Reddy, Maureen. "Motherhood, Knowledge, and Power." *Journal of Gender Studies* 1:1 (1991): 81–85.

Reilly, Rosalind. "*Oral History:* The Enchanted Circle of Narrative and Dream." *Southern Literary Journal* 23:1 (1990): 79–92.

Rich, Adrienne. *Of Woman Born*. New York: W. W. Norton, 1976.

Ruas, Charles. "Toni Morrison." In *Conversations with Toni Morrison*, ed. Danille Taylor-Guthrie, 93–118. Jackson: University Press of Mississippi, 1994.

Rubenstein, Roberta. "Pariahs and Community." In *Toni Morrison: Critical Perspectives Past and Present*, ed. Henry Louis Gates Jr. and K. A. Appiah, 126–58. New York: Amistad Press, 1993. Originally published as "Pariahs and Community: Toni Morrison" in Roberta Rubenstein, *Boundaries of the Self: Gender, Culture, Fiction* (Urbana: University of Illinois Press, 1987).

Ruddick, Sara. "Maternal Thinking." In *Mothering*, ed. Joyce Treblicott, 213–30. Totowa, N.J.: Rowman and Allanheld, 1983.

Ryan, Barbara. "Decentered Authority in Bobbie Ann Mason's *In Country*." *Critique* 31:3 (1990): 199–212.

Schama, Simon. *Landscape and Memory*. New York: Knopf, 1995.

Schlissel, Lillian. *Women's Diaries of the Westward Journey*. New York: Schocken, 1992.

Schor, Naomi. "Feminist and Gender Studies." In *Introduction to Scholarship in Modern Languages and Literatures*, 2d ed., ed. Joseph Gibaldi, 262–87. New York: Modern Language Association, 1992.

Sellers, Susan, ed. *The Hélène Cixous Reader*. New York: Routledge, 1994.

Showalter, Elaine. "Feminist Criticism in the Wilderness." In *Writing and Sexual Difference*, ed. Elizabeth Abel, 9–35. Chicago: University of Chicago Press, 1982.

Smith, Lee. *Black Mountain Breakdown*. 1980. Reprint, New York: Ballantine, 1982.

———. *The Devil's Dream*. New York: Putnam, 1992.

———. *Fair and Tender Ladies*. New York: Putnam, 1988.

———. *Oral History*. 1983. Reprint, New York: Ballantine, 1984.

————. *Saving Grace*. Putnam: New York, 1995.

————. "The Voice behind the Story." In *Voicelust: Eight Contemporary Fiction Writers on Style*, ed. Allen Weir and Don Hendrie Jr., 93–100. Lincoln: University of Nebraska Press, 1985.

Smith, Rebecca Godwin. "Gender Dynamics in the Fiction of Lee Smith." Ph.D. diss., University of North Carolina, 1993. Ann Arbor, Mich.: UMI, 1993. Microfilm (9324103).

Smith, Valerie. "'Circling the Subject': History and Narrative in *Beloved*." In *Toni Morrison: Critical Perspectives Past and Present*, ed. Henry Louis Gates Jr. and K. A. Appiah, 342–55. New York: Amistad Press, 1993.

Smith, Virginia. "Between the Lines: Contemporary Southern Women Writers Gail Godwin, Bobbie Ann Mason, Lisa Alther, and Lee Smith." Ph.D. diss., University of Pennsylvania, 1989. Ann Arbor, Mich.: UMI, 1989. Microfilm (9018283).

Spillers, Hortense. "Interstices: A Small Drama of Words." In *Pleasure and Danger: Exploring Female Sexuality*, ed. Carole Vance, 73–100. London: Routledge and Kegan Paul, 1984.

Stepto, Robert. "Intimate Things in Place: A Conversation with Toni Morrison." In *Conversations with Toni Morrison*, ed. Danille Taylor-Guthrie, 10–29. Jackson: University Press of Mississippi, 1994. Originally published in *Massachusetts Review* 18 (1977): 473–89.

Suleiman, Susan Rubin. "Writing and Motherhood." In *The (M)other Tongue: Essays in Feminist Psychoanalytic Interpretation*, ed. Shirley Nelson Garner, Claire Kahane, and Madelon Sprengnether, 352–77. Ithaca: Cornell University Press, 1985.

Szasz, Thomas. "Mental Therapy Is a Myth." In *Thomas Szasz: Primary Values and Major Contentions*, ed. Richard Vatz and Lee Weinberg, 99–113. Buffalo: Prometheus, 1983.

Teems, William. "Let Us Now Praise the Other: Women in Lee Smith's Short Fiction." *Studies in the Literary Imagination* 27:2 (1994): 63–73.

Thurer, Shari. *The Myths of Motherhood: How Culture Reinvents the Good Mother*. Boston: Houghton Mifflin, 1994.

Tisdale, Sallie. "We Do Abortions Here." In *Life Studies*, 5th ed., ed. David Cavitch, 431–38. Boston: Bedford-St. Martin, 1995.

Vande Kieft, Ruth. *Eudora Welty*. Boston: Twayne Publishers, 1987.

Walker, Alice. *In Search of Our Mothers' Gardens*. San Diego: Harcourt Brace Jovanovich, 1983.

Ward, Geoffrey, Ric Burns, and Ken Burns. *The Civil War: An Illustrated History*. New York: Knopf, 1994.

White, Deborah. *Ar'n't I a Woman?* New York: W. W. Norton, 1985.

———. "Female Slaves: Sex Roles and Status in the Antebellum Plantation South." In *Half Sisters of History*, ed. Catherine Clinton, 56–75. Durham: Duke University Press, 1994.

Williams, Sherley Anne. "Some Implications of Womanist Theory." *Callaloo* 9 (1986): 304.

Wynter, Sylvia. "Beyond Miranda's Meanings: Un/silencing the 'Demonic Ground' of Caliban's 'Woman.'" In *The Black Feminist Reader*, ed. Joy James and T. Denean Sharpley-Whiting, 109–27. Oxford: Blackwell Publishers, 2000.

INDEX

Abortion: imagery of, in Mason, 93, 94, 95, 96, 97; in Morrison, 36; and slave women, 65; in Smith, 164–65
African American mothers. *See* Motherhood; Mothers, slave
Agatha, Saint: as patron saint of breasts, 112
Agent Orange, 84
Aging: in Mason, 81, 101, 113, 114; in Smith, 172
American Holiness Movement, 178
American Pentecostal Movement, 178
Amniotic fluid: in Morrison, 57, 68
Andersen, Hans Christian, 157
Animus, 171
Antimaternal: in Mason, 93; in Morrison, 57
Appalachian culture: in Smith, 133, 136, 138, 139, 140, 142, 185; and women, in Smith, 133. *See also* Mountains
Archetypal Patterns in Women's Fiction (Annis Pratt), 184–88 passim
Artemis, 163, 166, 167

Babies, dead. *See* Dead babies
Baker, Houston, 45
Baptism: imagery of, in Morrison, 57
Beauty, female: in Smith, 150; white standards of, in Morrison, 38, 44, 54–55
Behind the Sex of God (Carol Ochs), 175
Bell Jar, The (Sylvia Plath), 162
Biblical references: in Smith, 178
Birth control: in Mason 90, 91; in Smith, 172
Birth of Venus, The (Botticelli), 150
Black Mountain Breakdown (Lee Smith), 134
Black women writers, 7, 31

Blood: in Morrison, 48–49, 58, 66–72 passim; in Smith, 145, 167, 168; and transformation mysteries, 66
Blues matrix: in Morrison, 45
Body. *See* Body-voice; Mind-body
Body, female: associated with Appalachian Mountains, 159; blood transformation mysteries of, in Morrison, 66–71 passim; contradictions of, 11; as the "Dark Continent," 27; as impure and corrupt, 11; and language, 28; as linguistic source, 27; Old Testament injunctions against, 58; rhythms of, in Morrison, 66; as site of knowledge, 104; in Smith, 135, 136, 137; and southern patriarchy, 12
Body, maternal: and connections with history and the past in Morrison, 70; and connections with the landscape in Smith, 143, 144; and connections with voice in Mason, 131; and connections with voice in Smith, 167; contrasted with father's voice in Smith, 175; erasure of, in Morrison, 55; fear of, 9, 196; as haven in Morrison, 61; imagery of, in Mason, 92, 98–99; imagery of, in Smith, 143; impact on daughter of, in Smith, 190; impact of patriarchal culture on, 7; impact of slavery on, in Morrison, 67–68, 71; as inscribed text in Mason, 93–94; as inscribed text in Morrison, 67, 68, 197; inversions of, in Morrison, 57; Irigaray on, 28, 29; and language, 168; language of, in Mason, 81, 82, 89, 101, 103, 104, 115, 118, 119; language of, in Smith, 152; linked with creativity in Mason, 105; and memory in Mason,